PRAISE FOR
Michael Sinclair and the 1920s Mystery Series

"Michael Sinclair displays a mastery of pace and mystery in this suspenseful and satisfying historical thriller."

—Amazon.com

"*An Unfortunate Coincidence* is a delight to read, filled with complicated and duplicitous characters all of whom look guilty until the final surprising end of this mystery. The plot is perfect for the 1920s and the characters have so many secrets it takes till the end to figure out the truth. Well-written and worth the read. Enjoy!"

—Marcia Rosen, author of *Murder at the Zoo*,
The Senior Sleuths and Dying to Be Beautiful mysteries

"The author springs some very good surprises."

--Elizabeth Ferrars, veteran writer
of over fifty novels of mystery and suspense

"It's been a long time since I've enjoyed a mystery as much as this one. The historical background in 1927 was fascinating. The suspense was so effective that I wanted to keep reading and not put it down. The characters were cleverly drawn and believable. Highly recommended."

—Goodreads.com review of *Murder in Cucumber Alley*

RAISE YOUR GLASS TO MURDER

A 1920s Mystery

featuring Sloan Sheppard, private investigator

MICHAEL SINCLAIR

By Michael Sinclair in the 1920s historical mystery series:

An Unfortunate Coincidence
The Consequences of Murder
Murder in Cucumber Alley
Darker than the Night
Raise Your Glass to Murder

RAISE YOUR GLASS TO MURDER

ISBN: 978-1-78324-316-7 (paperback)
ISBN: 978-1-78324-317-4 (ebook)

First Edition
Published by Wordzworth Publishing, United Kingdom

Author's Note

Warren G. Harding, twenty-ninth president of the United States, died at 7:30 p.m. Pacific Standard time, on August 2, 1923, in San Francisco, California. His unexpected death shocked the nation and the world. As communication was primarily limited to radio and newspapers, the Albany, New York newspaper *Knickerbocker Press* published an extra evening edition after midnight on August 3rd with the headline *PRESIDENT HARDING IS DEAD.* Many residents learned of his death while reading the morning editions of the Albany newspapers and hearing it on the radio. His death was mourned for weeks while the new president, former Vice President Calvin Coolidge, reassured a stunned nation by a radio address that he would continue to follow in the footsteps of the late president.

During Prohibition, breweries and beverage companies switched to non-alcoholic and legal drinks, as close to liquor as possible. Albany had several beverage manufacturers but the Empire State Beverage Company is fictitious. The Empire Advertising Agency is also fictitious.

William Hackett was the mayor of Albany from 1922 until his death at age 57 in a car accident while on vacation in Cuba in 1926. An Albany native, he became a lawyer and was admitted to the bar in 1899. He ran for office in 1922 and was reelected in 1923 and 1925. While campaigning for the third term, it was speculated Mayor Hackett would become a contender for the Governor of New York State in 1928.

Readers of the previous novels in this series may notice a spelling change to the first name of the private investigator. While Sloane is a unisex spelling, the name *Sloan* was decided as the more correct spelling for the illustrious investigator. The author hopes it meets with his approval.

Michael Sinclair

Dedicated to the memory of my best and truest friends
my mother and father

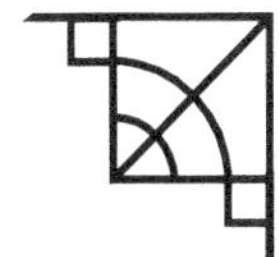

CHAPTER ONE

June 1923

Albany, New York

The bleak headlines and radio broadcasts of the horrific discovery sent shockwaves throughout the city, resulting in a crescendo of unparalleled fear and unease amongst residents. Afterward, Officer Millard Davis regretted his confusion as to precisely what happened. As he was the first on the scene, his usual definite pronouncement was lost to ambiguity. Perhaps because it was nearing the end of his shift and he was rather tired and eager to return home. His usual patrol was the daytime and early evenings, but recently he was assigned the overnight shift, much to his indignation.

The shocking discovery occurred at the Port of Albany on a humid, stifling morning. The Hudson River glowed majestically, the sun just poking through the clouds. Few people were about as the multitude had yet to awaken. A hotbed of vagrants and unscrupulous shenanigans, the waterfront of the Hudson River was notorious for bootleggers, rum-runners, loan sharks, hoodlums and clandestine gangster hideaways.

Officer Davis strolled along the river, carefully looking for drunkards and other unsavory characters. A muscular man in his fifties with a serious approach to work, he retained a youthful ebullience. He took out a handkerchief from his pocket and wiped his brow rather irritably. Already he was perspiring; another day of searing heat was in store for the capitol city. Albany had been baking in record high temperatures and there appeared no break to the extreme weather. The uncomfortable conditions only added to the seemingly rattled nerves and vulnerability of its citizens.

He observed nothing out of the ordinary, for which he was glad. He had already addressed two cases of drunkenness. His shift was soon over and he looked forward to breakfast with his wife at their apartment on Sheridan Avenue, within a short walking distance away.

He reached the landing almost directly across from Union Station. Even the railroads were asleep, he thought whimsically, but soon the lifeblood of movement in the city would awaken. He glanced toward Broadway and saw trollies just starting service. He noticed the Ritz Theater and the Charlie Chaplin film *The Pilgrim* proudly emblazoned on its marquee. Looking further toward North Pearl Street, he saw the towering Ten Eyck Hotel, a city landmark famous for its fine dining and luxury accommodations; although Officer Davis reflected that he could not afford such exuberance on a police officer's salary.

Officer Davis continued his patrol, the mist and the reflected light off the water causing him to squint, so at first he did not notice the obstruction almost in his path. Refocusing his vision, he blinked and saw it, a man lying on a bench.

Well, what do you know, a drunkard, sleeping it off on a park bench, too inebriated to go home, he thought somewhat disgustedly. Well-dressed, too, and not noticeably young either. His fedora hat partially shielded his face, his suit jacket and dress pants were impeccable, reeking of money. Moving the hat to see his face better, Officer Davis guessed his age at least seventy, possibly more. Certainly, he seemed someone distinguished though his appearance was disheveled. Odd for a discriminating man, in such a sordid condition and place. He knew he could not leave him there, so he decided to waken him. He shook him gently.

It did not take long for Officer Davis to realize the man was dead. His skin was a pale white and cold to the touch. He looked around but there was nobody in sight. A hot breeze blew off the river. At this point, he headed rapidly toward his patrol car on lower Broadway to radio headquarters for assistance.

Within minutes, another police car arrived while an ambulance pulled up near Union Station. Officer Davis led them to the body on the bench and while examining the man, the police officers discovered he had been stabbed. His suit jacket covered the gaping wound in his abdomen. The man was quickly identified as a Mr. Walter Lennon of Albany. His billfold was still in his pants pocket, easily establishing identity. It also eliminated robbery as a motive as it contained twenty-eight dollars in cash. The police officers conferred with Officer Davis, as to the exact nature of the discovery. Another police car soon arrived. It was the police photographer, who began to take photographs of the body and the location in which the victim was found. The police officers scoured the area looking for clues, a weapon and witnesses

A boy on a bicycle delivering the morning newspaper was questioned but as the police officers assumed, he knew nothing. He had just started his route and was unaware of any calamity. The police spoke to a milkman. He also could not provide any information.

It was a few hours later when a Mr. Nathan Turner called the police to report his brother-in-law, Mr. Walter Lennon, missing. The police soon contacted the Turners with devastating news; Mr. Lennon had been found lying on a park bench at the Port of Albany, dead from an apparent knife wound to the stomach. The police learned the details on Mr. Lennon.

Mr. Walter Lennon, a widower, lived with his sister, Mrs. Louise Turner and brother-in-law, Mr. Nathan Turner, a prosperous couple in their late sixties, in a mansion on prominent Englewood Place overlooking Washington Park, an address of much prestige.

Mr. Lennon was last seen at the Valencia, a popular restaurant on lower Broadway. He had accompanied his sister and brother-in-law there for dinner and afterward, decided to shop at Whitney's Department Store on North Pearl Street. He assured his sister he would catch the trolley home and then set off from the restaurant on foot around seven-forty last evening and had not been seen since. Arriving home after visiting friends, nearly two hours later, Mrs. Turner assumed her brother had gone to bed without waiting up for them.

While speaking to police at their home, the Turners vehemently denied Walter was involved in anything illegal. Mrs. Turner, overwrought as expected, could not help them in establishing the reason for her brother's presence at the Port of Albany.

The newspapers mentioned Mr. Lennon was a partner in the Empire State Beverage Company, of which the Turners were owners. Mr. Turner identified his brother-in-law at the city morgue and subsequently commented to the press that Walter was a kind and generous man. At seventy, he had no health concerns and no enemies. Newspapers turned from malicious speculation to appropriate sentiment, extolling the virtues of such a distinguished gentleman.

The murder of Walter Lennon and its repercussions reverberated throughout the city. Patrols increased, officers were on high alert and prohibition agents blanketed the Port of Albany.

City life continued apprehensively, in anticipation of another grievous attack.

Across from the State Capitol, the Empire Advertising Agency, located on the fifth floor of an impressive office building on upper State Street in downtown Albany, was thriving in business, prospering rapidly in all its endeavors. Numerous projects were in progress, so it came as little surprise that a request from a potential client would arrive on the desk of Mr. Caleb Dean.

It was a little after nine o'clock on Wednesday, July eighteenth and another hot morning in downtown Albany. The soaring humidity continued incessantly, relentless, creating excruciatingly vexatious conditions for city residents with no relief from the stifling heat. Although the window in his office overlooking busy State Street was open, it did not alleviate the room temperature and the fan on the floor was of little help.

Caleb's office was small yet smartly furnished. A rather large desk was in the center, a filing cabinet stood against the far wall and two chairs were evenly placed in front of his desk. An adding machine and a typewriter were on a small table next to the filing cabinet.

Resigning himself to another busy workday, he picked up his mail from Gabrielle, who worked in the main office. He shuffled through the envelopes. Several return addresses he recognized of former clients, most likely requesting further service. He noticed an envelope from the Empire State Beverage Company. He held it in his hands meditatively.

The Empire State Beverage Company was a major manufacturer and distributor of non-alcoholic beverages, but he knew nothing more about it. He put the envelopes aside and focused on current assignments. Soon the candlestick telephone on his desk rang almost continuously and numerous inquiries consumed him. Requests for outstanding promotions, in which the agency specialized, held Caleb's attention. As always, he prioritized the foremost details.

With negotiations for recent projects finalized, he found time to review the rest of the morning mail. He slit open the envelope from the Empire State Beverage Company, placed the letter flat on his desk and read it carefully.

Empire State Beverage Company
190 Baldwin Street
North Albany, New York

July 16, 1923

Mr. Caleb Dean
Empire Advertising Agency
150 State Street
Albany, New York

Dear Mr. Dean:

I am the president of the Empire State Beverage Company and am writing to inquire if the Empire Advertising Agency would be interested in working with us to promote a new beverage we have recently developed.

It is a champagne imitation, with just enough sparkle to entice people to try it. With the advent of prohibition, we recognize the need for imitation liquor and have been at the forefront of producing the best soft drinks for our customers. We have a state license to produce non-alcoholic beverages.

We believe our imitation champagne is headed for great success and we would be honored to have the Empire Advertising Agency assist us in this endeavor. My son-in-law, Mr. Jeffrey Nichols, who works at your agency, suggested I contact you to inquire about your availability and willingness to work with us.

We anticipate this new champagne imitation beverage, perfect for any occasion, will have a pronounced impact on expenditures, which have made the Empire State Beverage Company so profitable.

Please feel free to contact me at the above address or by telephone at AL 5768.

With kindest regards,

Nathan Turner
President, Empire State Beverage Company

Caleb put the letter aside and lit a cigarette. A strange feeling overcame him. Certainly, nothing wrong with the Empire State Beverage Company contacting him. It was simply an inquiry, after all. Nevertheless, something nagged at his mind. It was the unsolved murder from last month of an employee of the beverage company. Now what was his name? Mr. Lennon, of course, the brother-in-law of the owner. Reports on the radio and in the daily papers were consistent for weeks. Caleb wondered how the Stevensons, the agency owners, would relish getting involved with a company with murder in its midst. The newspapers reported just yesterday that the police were continuing investigations into the brutal homicide.

He doubted it would affect the agency, he thought wisely. Putting the letter aside, he decided to work on contracts with current clients. He took a final puff at his cigarette before extinguishing it in the ashtray. He put the Empire State Beverage Company in the back of his mind, at least for the moment.

Caleb Dean was in his third year at the Empire Advertising Agency. After graduation from West Point in 1914, he served as an Army Officer for five years, and while still a member of the army's reserve component, he returned to his hometown of Albany. He soon landed a sales position with a public relations firm. Although his career choice was that of a diplomat with the Foreign Service, he applied for an account executive opening with Empire Advertising. He learned the business quickly and within three years became a chief account executive.

At only thirty years old, he knew he was fortunate to hold such a lucrative position. Caleb worked diligently and intelligently, and his demeanor and rapport with clients fermented solid business relations. He was clear-headed, sensible and resourceful, certainly diligent in his endeavors and committed to his work. At six foot three inches tall, his soldierly presence was commanding, his curly blonde hair and green eyes pleasing. While in top physical form at West Point, he continued strength training after graduation. He was active in weight lifting and exercise. His attire, which always included a pristine shirt, tie and vest were impeccable, even during the humid summer months. Caleb thought wryly that he managed to stay cool despite the heat. For the most part, his relationships with colleagues were amiable and pleasant. A secretary who had been with the agency for only a year was interested in him. Gabrielle was a typist and clerk in the main office, so Caleb did not have much interaction with her. Mr. Stevenson did not approve of employees becoming involved. He considered it bad for business and a conflict of interest. He and Gabrielle saw each other a few evenings and on weekends. He found her company pleasant enough and Gabrielle was thrilled to have a handsome West Point graduate as her companion. While he spent time with Gabrielle, he also kept in touch with friends from West Point who visited him occasionally on weekends.

Patriarch Mr. Leonard Stevenson and his pleasant wife Celeste, long time owners of the agency, doted on Caleb, treating him like the son they never had. Caleb knew the Stevensons planned to retire soon. They had spent more than thirty years at the agency to much success. The imposing brownstone house they lived in on Dudley Row in the city was proof of their sharp business acumen. Caleb had proven his allegiance to the Stevensons and they in turn bestowed their confidence and approval on him, both monetarily and vocationally.

By contrast, Caleb had to endure a seemingly endless stream of vituperation from Wilbur and Minerva Hill, both down the hall from his office. He knew Wilbur was eager for the president position. He did not know much about Wilbur Hill or Minerva for that matter, but he thought they must be in their fifties. Money consumed them and they invested wisely, too. In Wilbur's own words, they prospered enormously, reaping in the benefits of a lucrative stock market.

Caleb picked up the telephone to call Mr. Turner, and then changed his mind, considering he should speak to Mr. Stevenson first. At that moment, he looked up and saw Roy Carter in the doorway. With a cigarette in hand and an overall exhausted appearance, he gave a tired smile. Without being asked, he entered the office and sat in a chair in front of Caleb's desk. He continued puffing at his cigarette, a far off expression on his face.

Roy Carter was twenty-five and good-looking in a reckless way, and to Caleb's standards he was a rather careless sort. He graduated from the State Teachers College but Caleb never knew what he studied. He did know he drank often and attended speakeasies as though they were his second home. He did not know much about his background. He lived in an apartment on Dove Street, not far from the action as he put it, which Caleb assumed, was how Roy obtained liquor. It occurred to Caleb that Roy purchased liquor from bootleggers, but he kept his discourse with him to business only and what he did outside of the agency wasn't his concern. Of medium height with a slim build, he looked rather insecure and forlorn, as though unsure of himself and his duties. Caleb did not know why the Stevensons kept him on. He must be doing something right, he mused. He sat in front of his desk smoking incessantly, silently, as though unable to formulate words. Caleb took the initiative and got to the point.

"Can I help with something, Roy?" he asked patiently. Shuffling a few papers, stalling, he expected him to reply. Although they worked in the same agency, Caleb did not handle the same accounts as Roy, so they had little contact on projects. He cleared his throat and looked him directly in the eyes. "I am busy, so if there isn't anything of importance…"

Roy Carter crushed his cigarette in the ashtray. "Actually there is, Caleb. The Empire State Beverage Company wants an advertising campaign. Jeff's father-in-law, Mr. Turner, called Mr. Stevenson this morning. The Big Boss mentioned Mr. Turner sent you a letter."

Caleb cringed inwardly. He hated when Roy referred to Mr. Stevenson as the Big Boss. It was a derogatory term, as he knew Roy was not too keen on the agency president. He waited for Roy to continue.

"The Big Boss wants us to plan it down to the wire," he said.

Caleb nodded, disregarding his platitudinous verbiage. Admittedly, he found it odd Mr. Stevenson would include the entire agency. It must indeed be a large account, one that would include a large profit for both parties. He assumed Mr. Stevenson would soon call a meeting on this new client. Certainly, a contract to be presented to Mr. Turner would be forthcoming. He waited for Roy to add more.

"What did Mr. Turner tell you in his letter?" Roy asked.

"Just what you mentioned. He'd like us to create an advertising campaign for a new champagne imitation drink his company produced."

"This'll draw a lot of publicity not only for them but for us, too. Moreover, it should pay pretty well. I bet the Turners have enough money to spend."

"We'll negotiate with them when the time comes," Caleb remarked patiently. "In the meantime, you should continue with your own projects while I speak to Mr. Stevenson first."

A voice spoke from the doorway. "You're talking about the Empire State Beverage Company campaign?"

Caleb looked up and saw Peter Cunningham, another account executive. Unlike Roy Carter, he asked Caleb if he wasn't too busy and Caleb beckoned him to the second chair in front of his desk, next to Roy.

"Like you said, Roy," Peter Cunningham said, sitting comfortably on the chair. "It'll be worthwhile financially and will help us to grow as an agency."

Caleb smiled, rather pleased at Peter's incisiveness. He did not know much about Peter Cunningham. He did know he was in his early forties and had worked in advertising for close to twenty years. He had numerous contacts throughout the city and his perceptive business sense was an asset. Caleb knew he was divorced with no children and was dating Polly, a typist and clerk in the main office, much to Mr. Stevenson's chagrin. He remembered Polly mentioning she was divorced and was not looking to jump into marriage again any time soon.

Peter Cunningham was smoking and as usual, the office was full of smoke. Caleb watched as it eddied and swirled around, finding its way out the window into the hot, stifling air. Peter added more to his foresight into the new contract with the Empire State Beverage Company.

Caleb thought he sounded intelligent and ingenious. He had only worked with him once in the last two years so he welcomed the opportunity to collaborate with him again. Observing his dark eyes, his rather firm yet pleasant way of speaking and his professional dress, he wondered why he was not promoted to chief account executive as he had been with the agency longer. He did not detect any hostility, unlike the Hills who resented his youth and his camaraderie with the Stevensons.

"I'm surprised Mr. Turner is so eager after his brother-in-law was murdered last month," Roy commented. "But then, I suppose, business is business."

Peter agreed. "With a large facility to upkeep and workers to pay, he'd have to find new ways to bring in more revenue."

"You're certainly right there, Pete," another male voice spoke from the doorway.

Caleb saw Jeff Nichols enter, casually as was his usual manner and stand in front of the window. Jeff was the son-in-law of Mr. Nathan Turner, the president of the Empire State Beverage Company. Caleb knew that had certain monetary advantages but then remembered that Jeff and his wife were separated and from all accounts were not on speaking terms. He did not know if Jeff was acquainted with the man who was murdered last month. He did not hear him speak of it. If he remembered correctly, he did not even seemed affected by it.

"I gave my father-in-law your name, Caleb," he said, loosening his tie in the hot office. "You've done a great job on previous campaigns so I thought you could spearhead this one."

Jeff Nichols was thirty-seven and the accountant at Empire Advertising. He had been with the agency for over ten years. His expertise in finance and assisting in publicity campaigns were an advantage, which Mr. Stevenson and his wife valued. Like Caleb, he knew the business and was rather shrewd and diligent in his endeavors. Making money was at the forefront for Jeff.

"What about your wife, Jeff?" Roy asked. "Doesn't she still work there? You would have contact with her, you know. You told me you weren't on speaking terms."

Jeff shrugged. "It won't affect business. My soon to be ex-wife won't stand in the way."

"Your father-in-law and mother-in-law are on speaking terms with you?" Roy asked.

Jeff nodded. "Of course. Why wouldn't they be? I haven't done anything wrong."

Caleb was sure his wife would think otherwise but kept his opinion to himself. He hoped his associates would take leave of his office so that he could approach Mr. Stevenson about the letter from Mr. Turner. He held up the letter from Mr. Turner and handed it first to Roy, who read it carefully. He handed it to Peter and then to Jeff.

"Did you know the man who was murdered last month, Jeff?" Roy asked him. "I read in the newspaper his name was Mr. Lennon. Didn't he work with your father-in-law?"

Jeff shrugged, indifferently. "I met him once at my in-laws for dinner." He paused. "I don't think the murder would affect my father-in-law's eagerness to make money. Besides, with the ridiculous prohibition we're forced to abide with, a champagne imitation drink is precisely what people want. I'm sure Mr. Stevenson will negotiate a lucrative contract for us."

His tone implied he did not really care about the murder and was more concerned with starting the advertising and reaping the momentary benefits. Peter commented that with the passing weeks, it seemed unlikely the police would find whoever was responsible for the murder.

Jeff mentioned he was in the process of buying stocks and enjoying the dividends. Roy and Peter agreed to its worthiness and they left Caleb's office discussing not the upcoming campaign for the Empire State Beverage Company but the profitable stock market.

Caleb glanced at the letter from Mr. Turner. It was another advertising campaign, what I specialize in, he thought sensibly. Certainly timely and paramount to promote a champagne imitation beverage during prohibition. He was sure people would buy it in droves, thinking it was as close to real champagne that they could possibly get.

Again, his mind flew to Mr. Lennon, an employee of the beverage company and Mr. Turner's brother-in-law. He remembered the newspaper articles detailing the savage murder last month but that had no bearing on this latest business venture, of course. He picked up the letter and briskly left his office, on the way down the long hallway to see Mr. Stevenson.

"Ask Polly to type these reports," Mr. Stevenson said to his wife, Celeste, as she stood in front of his massive desk in his office. He handed her a thick wade of papers. "And see if you can find another fan. The heat is too much in here."

"Yes, dear," Mrs. Stevenson said placating to her husband's tyrannical tone.

His executive suite overlooked State Street and was the largest room in the agency, his desk stood in front of two large windows and a conference table in the far corner took up most of the space. Two filing cabinets were on the opposite side and two chairs were placed in front of his desk. A large executive office, consistently hectic and at times cringed at by employees.

Mrs. Stevenson was about to leave when Caleb knocked on the door. Upon seeing him, she smiled brightly and welcomed him in.

"Hello, Caleb dear. Another hot day, isn't it?"

"Let the boy speak for himself, Celeste," Mr. Stevenson barked from behind his desk.

Caleb hated it when his boss referred to him as *the boy* but then he had heard him refer to Roy, Peter and even his son-in-law Jeff the same way. He wondered how Mr. Stevenson would feel if he knew Roy referred to him as *the Big Boss*. While Mr. Stevenson was not garrulous, he did make his point known, often demanding and at times rather harsh. Caleb did not know if the Stevensons got along or just depended on each other to maintain the business and keep it afloat.

Mrs. Celeste Stevenson looked fresh and pleasant, a light blue dress with a string of pearls highlighted her tastefully arranged gray hair. Little make-up, but a genuine smile and a natural disposition made her appealing. She was seventy and still working in the agency she had founded with her husband over thirty years ago. Caleb had worked with Mrs. Stevenson on numerous projects and while some found her style irritating, he respected her keen insight into publicity and working with diverse clients. Surreptitiously, she made her way to the door, leaving the men to their business. Before Caleb had the chance to speak, Mr. Stevenson ordered him to sit and got straight to the point.

"Mr. Turner from Empire State Beverage telephoned me late yesterday. A most distinguished and industrious man. He mentioned he wrote to you and I understand Jeff recommended you. A wise decision. Once we reach contractual agreements, I intend to appoint you in charge of that account. I know you will perform admirably, Caleb, as always." He noticed the paper in his hand. "Is that the letter from Mr. Turner? I'd like to see it."

Caleb handed him the letter he received this morning from Mr. Nathan Turner. As he read it. Caleb studied the imposing giant that was Mr. Stevenson on the other side of the desk.

Mr. Leonard Stevenson was seventy-five and had over forty years' experience in advertising and public relations. Considered an absolute genius in publicity campaigns, his business prospered and after the Great War, he saw his revenue quadruple. Along with his wife Celeste, Mr. Stevenson virtually increased profits for countless businesses and his ventures did not stop there. He was instrumental in promoting the New York State Museum, the Albany Institute of History and Art and the Hudson River Day Liner cruise fleet. Smaller organizations turned to the Empire Advertising Agency for guidance in promotion and Mr. Stevenson was at the forefront in providing the best service possible, for a stiff fee to his clients. Sweating almost profusely, and wiping his forehead in annoyance, Mr. Stevenson read the letter several times and continued staring at it as though trying to memorize it. He was a tall, heavy-set man with a thick head of gray hair, his face lined with wrinkles. He had a perpetual frown and was known to have bouts of anger and irritation while in his office. While many businesses contacted him for his expertise, others were disinterested after his rambunctious and rather overbearing façade.

Caleb had seen a gentler side to him. When his employees exceeded his expectations, as Caleb consistently performed, Mr. Stevenson was complimentary and gracious. He knew little more about the Stevensons and he did not consider it his business to pry. He knew they had no children and were originally from Albany. He knew Mrs. Stevenson had been a suffragette and was thrilled when the eighteenth amendment was passed three years ago, prompting her to vote for the first time in the 1920 election for President Harding. Caleb knew Mr. Stevenson liked the fact that he was a West Point graduate. He knew Mr. Stevenson served as a local nursing volunteer during the Civil War in 1865 while only seventeen. He and his wife volunteered during the Great War at the local hospitals, too. Certainly admirable and impressive.

"…I entrust this to you, Caleb. It will be your project and as always, I expect a full report. I want to include Jeff, Peter, Roy and the Hills."

"I'll look forward to working with Mr. Turner," he said positively, exuberance marking his enthusiasm. "Since you already spoke to him, I'm sure he is eager to get in touch with me."

Mr. Stevenson nodded. "Why don't you call him and introduce yourself? Then arrange a meeting at his facility. Meanwhile, I'll set up a meeting and you can fill us in on what you discussed with him." He paused, looking past Caleb. "Hello, Minerva. Good morning to you. And Wilbur."

Caleb turned and noticed the Hills. They greeted him perfunctorily and then turned their attention to Mr. Stevenson. Wilbur had a cigarette between his lips and carried a folder overflowing with papers. Minerva had a dictation pad in case her services were needed.

Caleb stayed focused on Mr. Stevenson and listened while he spoke to Wilbur and Minerva Hill. He noticed Minerva looked pristine, dressed to the nines, a well-fitting brown dress curved around her shapely figure, red lipstick heavily applied as usual. She was somewhere in her fifties and was quite attractive. Caleb found her demeanor spurious.

Next to her was Wilbur Hill. Tall, gaunt, a heavy smoker, rather rough looking, but quite wealthy in his own right. He and Minerva had not been with the agency for too long. He was close to sixty, exacting and mocking, certainly impatient with the younger workers, Caleb included. Wilbur Hill all but ignored Caleb as he continued sitting in the chair in front of the desk. After listening to the Hills drone on and on, Caleb stood to leave and mentioned to Mr. Stevenson that he would get back to him soon.

"New account, Caleb?" Wilbur asked a touch of sarcasm in his voice.

Caleb turned from the doorway. "Yes," he said simply and added nothing more. He almost collided with Polly Ormerod who was about to enter the office. She approached his desk and deposited several typed papers in front of him.

"Coffee and letters for you," Polly said pleasantly. "You just need to sign them."

"On a hot day like this you bring me coffee?" Mr. Stevenson said harshly. "What's the matter with you? I don't need to sweat any more than I already am!"

Caleb hid a smile as he watched Polly in front of his desk, next to Minerva and Wilbur. He found Polly Ormerod rather curious. She was about forty, certainly well dressed, a fashionable olive green dress with pearls made her charming and even alluring. Her makeup and lipstick were excessive. She dated Peter from time to time and while divorced, she had no children and admitted she enjoyed the nightlife; dance halls and speakeasies were her cup of tea. She assisted Gabrielle and Mrs. Stevenson in the main office as a typist and clerk, but was gossipy and rather nosy, too.

"Caleb, there are numerous files in the next office," Mr. Stevenson said. "Go through them and see if there are any we should consider for future contracts."

Caleb told Mr. Stevenson he would get right on it and as though eager to get away from Minerva and Wilbur, even Polly, he entered the next office which was used as a storage for files and office equipment. He opened a drawer of a file cabinet and grabbed a pile, then returned to his office and planted them on his desk.

Sitting at his swivel chair, he shuffled through them. He marveled at the expertise of the agency and the huge dollar amounts it accumulated. The innumerable and esteemed clients the agency served included the Clinton Street Hotel, dated 1915, proprietor Mr. Cyrus Newcomb, Mr. George Bennett of the Gateway Furnace Company from 1899, Mr. and Mrs. Ronald Smith, of the Hillcrest Lodge dated 1918. Contracts illustrated the success each enjoyed due to the agency's collaboration.

He looked again at the letter from Mr. Nathan Turner. With the fervency he exhibited in publicity campaigns, he picked up the handset on the telephone and asked the operator to connect him to the Empire State Beverage Company.

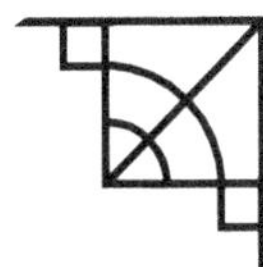

CHAPTER TWO

It was later in the afternoon when Caleb spoke to Mr. Nathan Turner. He had called the Empire State Beverage Company and spoke with his secretary, leaving a message for him to return his call at Empire Advertising. She regretted Mr. Turner was not available now but she promised he would return his call as soon as possible.

The workday consumed Caleb with more demanding clients, further meetings with Jeff, Roy and Peter and negotiating agreements. Memos typed, contracts drafted, telephone calls returned. A hectic morning that continued after lunch. It was not until close to three o'clock when Gabrielle entered his office, informing him that Mr. Nathan Turner of the Empire State Beverage Company was on the line and wished to speak with him. Caleb thanked Gabrielle and watched as she left his office, and then picked up the handset of his telephone and greeted Mr. Turner amicably.

"Hello, Mr. Turner, thank you for returning my call. This is Caleb Dean and I would like to speak to you about a publicity campaign. I received your letter and I understand you already spoke with Mr. Stevenson." On the other end of the line, Caleb could hear a rustle of papers and a dry cough, and then a rather deep voice spoke, bluntly but pleasantly enough.

"Yes that is correct, Mr. Dean. I wrote to you on the recommendation of my son-in-law who works at your agency. My goal is to promote the new imitation champagne beverage we have created here at Empire State Beverage. My wife and I anticipate it will be an enormous success and we would like your assistance."

"It'll be a pleasure, Mr. Turner," Caleb said sincerely, although he had never dealt with promoting beverages. He likened it to restaurant promotions he undertook in the past. He asked Mr. Turner what he hoped to achieve in the publicity campaign.

Caleb then heard a long and rather exacting narration of the nature of the new beverage; the brainchild of his wife, who suggested an imitation champagne to alleviate consumers thirst for liquor during prohibition and the method for creating it. He also mentioned their credibility as a beverage manufacturer, the state license which permitted them to produce such beverages and the many satisfactory reviews from delighted customers. Mr. Turner provided details on the company history, how it was handed down to him from his father, the numerous fruit juices, sodas, root beers and ginger ales they produced. The new beverage would be introduced within a month. He believed the imitation champagne beverage his company created would be a resounding achievement and he looked forward to collaborating with Caleb and his team.

There followed an awkward silence as Caleb expected him to continue but realized he was finally finished. It was then arranged that Caleb would visit the facility tomorrow morning at ten o'clock. Mr. Turner mentioned he would introduce him to his wife Louise and give him a tour of the plant, showing the manufacturing area, the business office and the shipping department. Caleb thanked him and told him he would look forward to meeting him and his wife tomorrow.

As he replaced the handset, Caleb leaned back, putting his feet up on the desk, ruminating on the conversation he just concluded with Mr. Nathan Turner. Certainly, a robust, business-like individual, although money-hungry might be more appropriate, as his son-in-law would be the first to concur. He did not sound in the least bothered by the recent murder of his brother-in-law. Of course, if he were still coping, Caleb did not think he would mention it in a publicity inquiry. As Roy said, business was business and Mr. Turner had a facility to maintain and workers to pay. He assumed the Turners were well off financially. He remembered Jeff mentioned his in-laws lived on affluent Englewood Place, an address of much prestige. Certainly, the mansions on Englewood Place were some of the best homes in the city.

Caleb stared out the window irritably as the afternoon sun warmed his office uncomfortably. He got up and approached the window, shutting it quickly and then closing the blinds. He turned the fan on the floor on high to try to relieve the heat.

Returning to his desk, he put his feet up and leaned back, frowning. Usually he felt exhilarated on beginning a contract for a new client. He shook his head. Something somewhere was not quite right.

At a little before four o'clock, the workday almost over, a gentle knock came on his office door. Caleb looked up and saw Gabrielle in the doorway.

"You looked relaxed," she said. She noticed his feet up on the desk and the cigarette in his hand. "I wouldn't let Mr. Stevenson see you lounging like that."

"I don't think he'd mind," Caleb said rather defensively. "I've seen him like this myself."

He swung his long legs off the desk, extinguished his cigarette and asked Gabrielle what she wanted. His tone was rather abrupt. Although he liked Gabrielle Woods, he was not in the mood for small talk. Gabrielle entered and sat in front of his desk. Perhaps she just wanted to see him, which was pleasant enough. She started to tell him about her work in the main office and Caleb listened, commenting as appropriate.

Gabrielle Woods was twenty-nine, petit, with a stunning smile that highlighted her pretty face and her naturally curly red hair. Her brown eyes were pensive and alluring, her persona charming and appealing. She wore a simple dress of olive green that fitted her svelte figure nicely, a lovely string of pearls, and bright red lipstick. Although they knew Mr. Stevenson did not approve of office romances, Caleb and Gabrielle enjoyed each other's company.

"I hear you're starting a new contract with the Empire State Beverage Company. From the way Mrs. Stevenson talks, it'll bring in a lot of money."

Caleb mentioned how he planned to visit the Empire State Beverage Company tomorrow and report on his findings, after interviewing Mr. Turner. He commented how Mr. Stevenson wanted not only his input but also contributions from nearly everyone in the agency.

"Including you," he added with a smile.

Gabrielle was rather taken aback. "I'm a clerk and typist, Caleb. I type reports and contracts but the publicity angle is out of my realm." She paused. "Although I have assisted in the past with suggestions that Mr. Stevenson took seriously. So perhaps I can contribute something."

Caleb nodded. "That includes the Hills as well as Jeff, Peter and Roy."

"Sounds like the entire office will be a part of it," Gabrielle said.

Caleb shuffled a few papers. "Mr. Turner didn't specify what he wanted, but after meeting with him tomorrow, I'll have a better idea."

"Too bad about the murder last month," Gabrielle said. "Didn't the man who was killed work there? I heard about it on the radio. It was in all the newspapers, too."

Caleb nodded. "Mr. Turner's brother-in-law. I don't know the details just that he was found stabbed at the Port a month ago. I haven't read the police found who was responsible."

Gabrielle shivered slightly, despite the hot office. "I heard on the radio that gangsters are arriving here from Chicago. I wish President Harding would do something about it."

"He has his hands full with enacting prohibition," Caleb remarked.

"But gangsters in Albany," Gabrielle said, dismayed.

"Most likely bootleggers," Caleb said dryly, He then opened a desk drawer. "I consult the newspapers to see how businesses are managing. These headlines speak for themselves." He held them out to Gabrielle, who took them and started to read.

Knickerbocker Press, Albany, N.Y.
Thursday, April 26, 1923
POLICE START NIGHT PATROLS
TO END ALBANY CRIME

Albany Evening Journal, Albany, N.Y.
Wednesday May 2, 1923
INCREASE IN PATROLS IN ALBANY
TO CURB CITY WIDE CRIME

Gabrielle read the articles, shaking her head. She returned the newspapers to Caleb.

"Are you taking the trolley home?" he asked her, trying to lighten the conversation.

Gabrielle nodded. "I thought of buying a new hat at Whitney's but this heat is too much."

Caleb lived in a one-bedroom apartment on Irving Street and Gabrielle lived one block away on Elm Street. The trolley brought them to the corner of Hamilton and Lark Streets, where their apartments were within walking distance.

"Caleb, do you know more about the man who was murdered at the Port of Albany last month? Suppose someone there murdered him and we get involved?"

"Not to worry, Gabrielle. I'm sure the police will find whoever is responsible. Besides, what does it have to do with the publicity campaign?"

"I suppose you're right," she said uneasily. "I've never been so close to murder before. The killer could be someone at the plant or even someone we know."

"How could that be?" Caleb asked her, rather daunted by her obvious precariousness. "Mr. Turner has no connection to this agency." He then realized his mistake. "Of course, Jeff, Mr. Turner's son-in-law works here."

Caleb and Gabrielle were silent a few moments. He told her he would meet her in the main office so they could take the trolley. Gabrielle nodded and left his office.

Caleb's mind flew to Mr. Turner, to Jeff Nichols who was just down the hall and the murdered man, Mr. Walter Lennon. His sister and brother-in-law were the company presidents and Jeff was Mr. Turner's son-in-law. Jeff mentioned his wife, Mr. Turner's daughter, also worked at the beverage company. He wondered if the family got along, working so closely and if there were issues no one suspected.

He then concentrated fully on finishing contracts before five o'clock rolled around, absorbed in his work.

The stubborn clock above the door finally moved to four thirty. Roy Carter had been looking up at it for the last half hour, anticipating the five o'clock time when he could leave. He continued working on proposals for contracts, always in long hand, before submitting them to either Polly or Gabrielle for typing. He was pleased he had reached the stage in his employment at the agency that he first did not need the approval of the Big Boss or Caleb, for that matter.

He was the newest assistant account executive the agency hired. He had some public relations experience but gained a foothold in the industry thanks to the Big Boss. While he respected Mr. Stevenson and his dainty wife, he stayed clear of them as much as possible and only had to tolerate Wilbur, Minerva and Caleb. Fortunately, that did not occur too often.

Roy came from Dunkirk, New York, in the western part of the state and after graduating from the State Teachers College, decided to remain in Albany. He studied marketing and decided to pursue advertising. Occasionally he took the train home to see his parents but it was a long ride, past Buffalo and not something he ever looked forward to.

Roy enjoyed downtown Albany and he frequently spent time at speakeasies and dance halls. He bumped into Peter and Polly more than once. On a few occasions, he saw Caleb and Gabrielle shopping at Whitney's. He did not remember ever seeing Jeff, but then he was in the process of divorcing his wife, so he most likely kept to himself.

Roy was of medium height and while not as tall as the other men in the agency, he displayed a certain flair, his brown hair and brown eyes were noticeable and attractive to women, his stylish shirt, tie and vest were pristine. He spoke intelligently and politely although at times his patience was tried when dealing with the rest of his colleagues in this wretched advertising agency. Now they were about to land an exclusive contract with that beverage company, where one of its employees was stabbed at the Port of Albany last month. In Roy's opinion, it was bad press for the agency. The company had a murder hanging over its head, but that did not appear to bother Mr. Stevenson. Obviously, he thought of the financial outcome and nothing else.

He glanced over at Peter, who also was busy writing, but exactly what Roy did not know. They had collaborated on numerous projects, but Roy found his manner evasive and not too friendly. He wished he had his own office, like Caleb and Jeff next door, but perhaps that would happen soon enough.

He saw Polly enter, carrying several folders. She smiled at him and handed them to Peter. They started a conversation in muted tones, as they usually did when together, and Roy kept his eyes focused on his own work.

"Almost time to go, Roy," Polly said, smiling, looking his way. She stood in front of Peter's desk, obviously counting down the minutes herself.

"Hopefully it'll be cooler when we leave," Roy said, although he rather doubted the humidity would decrease. Glancing out the window near his desk, he saw a mixture of hazy sun and clouds, with a hint of thunderstorms for the evening.

"Any plans for tonight, Roy?" Peter asked him.

Roy shook his head. "No, not this evening. This weekend for sure. I might go to see the new Charlie Chaplin film. It's still playing at the Ritz."

"Well, I don't like going out at night," Polly said, uneasily. "There's a killer loose somewhere in this city."

Peter was his usual good-natured self. He addressed Polly jovially, with a carefree tone.

"Polly, we've been through this before. Albany is completely safe."

Roy agreed. "I heard on the radio the police have increased patrols."

Peter smiled, convincingly. "So you see, Polly, there's absolutely nothing to worry about."

Polly was still uncertain. She mentioned she needed to return to the main office and would wait for Peter so they could take the trolley home. Jeff then submerged himself in whatever he was doing. Roy continued at his desk, feeling oddly alone and out of place.

The beverage company was the next highly anticipated moneymaker for the agency, certainly at the forefront, regulating other projects aside at least temporarily. Nevertheless, what about the unsolved murder, Roy thought uncomfortably. Business was business and not even murder could stand in the way of making a lot of money and reaping the benefits

For some reason, the beverage company contract annoyed him. It was the unsolved murder, of course, and the fact that everyone would get involved. He did not relish collaborating with the entire agency, which was a first in the time he had been working there.

The financial incentive was paramount to the Big Boss; otherwise, he would not include everyone's input. Most likely, it will be a large campaign, he thought gloomily, as though he anticipated the worst. He sighed and put the cap on his pen, staring ahead reflectively.

In the office next to Roy and Peter, Jeff Nichols was busy adding up figures. The new adding machine the agency recently purchased was the cat's meow and Jeff loved it. It made his work so much easier and

less time consuming. The old adding machine was a real clunker but this was a beauty and he marveled at its efficiency.

He rubbed his eyes and glanced at the wall clock; almost five o'clock. No matter how much he enjoyed his work, he was always glad when his workday was over.

Jeff had been with the agency for ten years, after several accounting positions with firms in downtown Albany. He liked being the only accountant on staff and while he collaborated with Caleb, Roy and Peter on publicity campaigns, his forte was mathematics and balancing the agency's financial records. He considered himself a pro in his endeavors and Mr. Stevenson never doubted his expertise. He could not complain. Mr. Stevenson paid him well and he had earned a reputation as a top-notch accountant. He prepared taxes on the side during tax season so with the added income, he did quite well financially.

Jeff was a tall, handsome man in a rather conventional way. He was thirty-seven, his brown hair worn tastefully, center parted, his blue eyes thoughtful and alert. He was in the process of divorcing his wife, Prudence, the daughter of Mr. Nathan Turner, the owner of the Empire State Beverage Company. He had tolerated her for over ten years but irreconcilable differences was the easiest way out, he told his lawyer. He kept an eye open for another female suitor but Jeff was in no rush, as the separation and the process of divorce embittered him. He and Prudence lived in an apartment on Washington Avenue, but after separating, Jeff moved out and found a one bedroom on Dove Street, near busy Lark Street, where shops, restaurants and speakeasies flourished.

He knew his soon to be ex-wife had given up the apartment and moved back in with her wealthy parents on Englewood Place. He had spent time at his in-law's, where he had met Mr. Walter Lennon, Prudence's uncle. He did not remember anything outstanding about him and he could not imagine what he was doing at the Port of Albany late at night last month.

Jeff sighed and looked around his rather bland but adequate office. One window overlooked State Street. The ceiling fan was of little help to break the excruciating heat and humidity but Jeff tolerated weather conditions as much as he tolerated Mr. Stevenson. He was grateful to have his own space rather than sharing, like Peter and Roy and the women in the main office.

Jeff recommended Caleb to his father-in-law about a publicity campaign. He assumed Mr. Turner held no ill feelings toward him, despite his initiating divorce proceedings against his daughter. He maintained cordial and business relations with Mr. Stevenson and his wife Celeste. He found Wilbur and Minerva at times intolerable. It was obvious Wilbur had his eye on the presidency position and he assumed Mr. Stevenson would retire shortly. Of course, Caleb was in line for that position too, and personally, he preferred him to Wilbur, the lesser of two evils.

Jeff lit a cigarette and laughed to himself. Caleb was not all that bad, he thought. He had had disagreements with him, but that sort of thing occurred in offices from time to time. Neither he nor Caleb held grudges but they kept to themselves, which is how he liked it and he was sure Caleb felt the same.

He sat back and thought of Polly Ormerod. He had considered asking Polly out to dinner, but then remembered she and Peter were an item, or supposedly so. Gabrielle was smitten with Caleb, the West Point graduate. He remembered Mr. Stevenson frowning upon office romances, but that apparently did not stop Caleb, Gabrielle, Peter, and Polly.

Life had taught Jeff Nichols to look out for himself, because no one else was around to give a damn. Dog devour dog, he thought bitterly and lived by that standard. His parents divorced, his father remarried and lived in Geneva, New York and his mother too remarried, settling in Mayville, New York. His older brother lived out west, in California. He was never particularly close to his parents, and his brother was like a stranger to him, even while growing up. He had not spoken to them in years and as there was no love lost between them, he rather preferred it that way.

He picked up the morning edition of the *Times Union,* noting several bleak articles. The murder of his wife's uncle, the rise in gangster activity and the overall crime rate in Albany, which had soared since prohibition, disturbed Jeff. He then turned to the stock market pages. He was pleased the stocks he invested in continued to grow. Another added source of revenue; he folded the paper and put it back on his desk with satisfaction.

From in the hallway, he heard Peter and Roy close their office door and make their way to the main office. He doubted they would poke their heads in the doorway to say goodbye. Occasionally, Roy would display a certain friendliness but Peter rarely did. Jeff never expected it so he was not disappointed.

Glancing at the wall clock, he realized it was just past five o'clock. He tidied his desk, stuffing files and assorted papers in a drawer. He put the cover on the new adding machine and was ready to leave for the day.

Mrs. Celeste Stevenson inserted a fresh sheet of paper into her typewriter and despite the late hour, began typing in earnest. An important letter to an existing client was paramount to continued success and after collaborating on publicity campaigns for them, she did not want to lose their business. During her forty years in public relations and advertising, Celeste never missed the opportunity to improve business relations and client satisfaction.

The only child of a prosperous Albany family, Celeste graduated from the State Teachers College in 1874 with a degree in English, anticipating a career in teaching; instead, she began working for public relations in the city until after her marriage to Leonard Stevenson. They soon opened their own advertising agency in 1893 and saw their business grow tremendously.

Mrs. Stevenson was of the theory that work did not end once the five o'clock hour arrived. When a publicity campaign was in process it was normal for staff to remain during the evening hours but that did not happen too often. She rested her fingers on the keyboard and noticed Polly and Gabrielle chatting, clearing their desks and getting ready to depart.

These younger girls, she mused, always concerned with their appearance, wearing excessive make-up, the latest perfumes, the most stylish hats. They should be more concerned with their professional duties and offer to stay, but then Celeste realized that was foolish. That was of the old school and those bygone days were history.

"Will you need anything else before I leave, Mrs. Stevenson?" Gabrielle asked as she approached her desk. Her tone was sincere and Celeste could not help smile.

"No, dear, I'm just typing a letter to a company in Schenectady we've worked with before."

Gabrielle hesitated a moment, looking toward the hallway. Celeste wondered if she expected Caleb to join her. After a few trivial words, Gabrielle left, rather flustered and headed for the door. Soon Polly approached, her pocketbook in her hands.

"I'm off, Mrs. Stevenson," she said. "Jeff mentioned he finished the last of the checks that need signing. I completed the report for the cleaning company which also needs your signature."

Like Gabrielle, she spoke pleasantly although Celeste did not quite warm up to her personality. She knew Polly smoked and drank liquor in speakeasies, which as a devout Catholic appalled Celeste. On the other hand, Gabrielle was more down to earth and was certainly a good girl for Caleb. She watched as Polly and then Jeff, Roy and Peter cut through the main office, wishing her a good evening.

Looking toward the hallway leading to her husband's office, she knew Wilbur was still here as well as Caleb. Minerva was taking dictation from her husband or at least she was a half hour ago. She thought about Wilbur, Minerva, and Jeff Nichols. Seemed like they always had something up their sleeve, cunning, untrustworthy, unscrupulous. Perhaps corrupt would be appropriate, too. She had approached her husband, hoping to find grounds for termination but her husband did not share her point of view. Mr. Stevenson reminded his wife that Jeff was a stellar accountant, Wilbur was acute in business affairs and Minerva was proficient in dictation and managing agency records. Celeste let it go but she would be immensely satisfied if they decided to seek employment elsewhere, although she knew that was highly unlikely.

Her thoughts raced to the Turners. She met them once at some function. Certainly, a pleasant couple. But their son-in-law, Jeff, was employed here and he was in the process of divorcing their daughter. He recommended his father-in-law contact Caleb. A conflict of interest, she wondered. Perhaps something worse, too.

Celeste crossed herself, saying a prayer silently, hoping there would be no trouble ahead.

Minerva finished typing the report Mr. Stevenson dictated to her earlier and was about to bring it into his office when Wilbur stopped her. He reminded her they needed to finish the accounts for two outstanding contracts. He held them in his hands, practically blocking her egress from their office. She told him she had indeed finished those reports, and then brushed past him into the hallway to Mr. Stevenson's office.

Wilbur shook his head then returned to his desk. A resolute executive, Wilbur Hill exhibited a meticulous approach to his endeavors, achieving great success and reaping the financial benefits. Wilbur Hill was fifty-eight and came from western New York. At an early age he knew how to succeed in business, from sales to lucrative advertising positions. He maintained good business relations with the Stevensons, although Mrs. Stevenson did get on his nerves with her lady of the manor attitude. Even Mr. Stevenson was haughty and condescending at times.

He worked for advertising agencies in Binghamton and Norwich before settling in Albany, where he found the market more advantageous and profitable. He had been in the capital city previously and upon returning was astonished by the growth in industry. He planned to make the most of his return to Albany,

Wilbur and Minerva lived in a traditional brownstone on Madison Avenue, within walking distance of downtown. While they shared the same office, Wilbur and Minerva had their difficulties over the years but managed to persevere. He knew Roy, Jeff and Peter drank furiously. He imagined Caleb was more intent on pleasing Mr. Stevenson, lauding himself of his accomplishments and demonstrating his ease and agility in client relations. Wilbur puffed at his cigarette. Well, good for him, he thought bitterly. He pictured Caleb teaching Sunday school at the local church.

As for liquor, he hardly thought prohibition stopped anyone from drinking. The police knew of speakeasies downtown, yet they did little to close them. Of course, there were bribes and some police officers even frequented the illegal establishments themselves. He admitted he and Minerva enjoyed speakeasies and drinking was certainly high on their list of favorable pastimes. He looked up and saw Minerva return. She looked flustered, her face rather red from the intense heat. She sat at her desk chair and put her head in her hands. She then looked up at Wilbur.

"How about a cold beer after work?" she suggested.

Wilbur smiled. "It's always whisky for me."

"No mention of murder," she said wryly.

"Murder?" Wilbur was surprised. "Whatever are you talking about?"

She turned off her banker's lamp. "You know perfectly well." She gathered her purse, intending to leave. "I could use a drink about now."

They looked forward to their evening out. As usual for Wilbur and Minerva, plenty of booze restored their vitality and kept them in fine spirits.

Caleb closed his notebook and put his pen aside, He had been drafting a contract for Mr. Turner, with suggestions on the publicity campaign. He stretched, and then glanced at his watch and realized it was almost five thirty. It was still warm and humid and the air in the office was oppressive. He decided it was time to leave for the day.

He took his cap from a desk drawer and turned off the light. He headed down the hall to say goodbye to Mr. Stevenson. He stopped in the doorway and noticed he was busy at his desk. He looked up and saw Caleb.

"I have an appointment with Mr. Turner at the beverage company tomorrow morning, so I thought I would go directly there first, then come here" He hesitated. "Is that all right with you?" Mr. Stevenson was at his desk, certainly a patriarch looking every bit his seventy-five years, but wise and prudent. He waited for his reply.

Leonard Stevenson nodded. "Of course you can go there first. You do not need my approval." He glanced out the windows overlooking State Street. "Celeste and I should get going too. Good evening, Caleb."

Caleb thanked him, then walked down the hallway and entered the main office. He chatted briefly with Mrs. Stevenson and then once outside, he crossed State Street to catch the uptown trolley to Hamilton Street.

The afternoon rush hour was in full swing; trollies, cars and taxis littered the streets. Caleb held up his hand to shield his face, as the afternoon sun was intense. He managed to board an already crowded trolley and jumped off at the corner of Hamilton and Dove. He walked briskly crossing Madison until he arrived at Irving Street. The brownstone house he lived in had been converted into apartments and his was on the top floor; a spacious one bedroom, with a view of Irving Street and the alley from the back.

Usually a meticulous housekeeper, Caleb allowed items to pile up around his living room; scattered clothes, books in different corners, chairs misplaced, a shirt here and another there. Not a welcome sight, he knew, depositing his keys on the kitchen counter. The chaos of a bachelor apartment, he thought wryly.

He wanted nothing more than a cool shower. He turned on the fans in the living room, bedroom and kitchen but as usual, they did not cool the air. Caleb remembered reading in *Popular Science* just recently that air conditioning was in its infancy and would be available in the future. And not soon enough, he thought, entering his bedroom and taking off his clothes.

A cool shower reawakened him and restored some vitality. He put on clean boxer shorts but decided not to wear anything else. It was too humid and the apartment was like a boiler room, a real scorcher of a night ahead. He turned on the radio in the living room to a station playing jazz. Count Basie, Duke Ellington and Bessie Smith were all the rage and Caleb loved them. The hit song by Bessie Smith, *Downhearted Blues*, soon came on and he turned up the volume. The evening news would be broadcast next, along with the weather report, which he hoped included a break in the stifling heat.

He remembered he must call Gabrielle. He was so engrossed with the Turner account that he totally forgot about taking the trolley home together. He reached for the telephone and upon lifting the handset gave the operator Gabrielle's number. It rang several times, allowing Caleb to put his feet up on the coffee table. After six rings, Gabrielle answered, rather out of breath.

"Hi, Caleb, I'm glad you called. I hoped we would take the trolley home. I thought of going to see you but you didn't come to the front office, so I figured you were busy." She paused, nervously. "There's a killer loose around here. I admit I'm scared. Poor Mr. Lennon."

He tried to sooth her. "Sorry, Gabrielle, I was so involved with the new contract I forgot about our taking the trolley together." He hesitated. "Mr. Lennon was murdered at the Port of Albany and we don't go there at night." Inwardly, he felt a certain fear, knowing that the murderer could be walking amongst the crowd in Albany. Or anywhere else for that matter. He reminded her they lived in one of the best neighborhoods in the city, her apartment on Elm Street just a block away from Irving Street.

"I don't trust Polly or Minerva," Gabrielle said unexpectedly. "I saw Polly looking through old files in the spare office and Minerva and Peter talking silently. Roy is sneaky, too. I saw Wilbur talking in hushed tones to Jeff."

Caleb did not know what to say. He also had seen Minerva and Peter conversing as well as Wilbur and Jeff but he had no idea about Polly snooping around or Roy being sneaky.

"I feel sorry for Prudence Nichols," Gabrielle commented, conversationally. "I don't know her, but she must be going through hell. Jeff's father-in-law must think well of him, even though he is in the process of divorcing Prudence. From his own accounts, he and his wife are not on speaking terms. It may create an uncomfortable situation."

Caleb changed the subject by mentioning the latest 78 record by Duke Ellington he recently purchased for his new phonograph player. He invited her over to listen to it. Gabrielle made appropriate comments but still expressed worry about the unsolved murder. Caleb told her not to worry so much and that he would see her at work tomorrow. He continued sitting on the sofa, ruminating over the conversation he just concluded with Gabrielle.

He slept fitfully that night, tossing and turning. He irritably kicked away the sheet, got up around two o'clock and upon entering the living room, switched on a lamp. He turned on the radio and found a local news station. Commercials for *Lucky Strike Cigarettes, Borden Ice Cream, Palmolive Soap* and *Listerine* were broadcast and then the news announcements began.

...It is advisable residents do not attempt to make their own alcohol. Real alcohol laced with flavorings such as malt is not real liquor and is not suitable for consumption…A robbery at gunpoint at a dry cleaner last night resulted in an uncertain amount of cash taken…The murder of Mr. Walter Lennon, a prominent executive and city resident, is still under investigation by police. Mr. Lennon, a seemingly innocent victim of the violence that has plagued our city. So far, no leads have been determined…

Caleb got up and turned off the radio. He went to the windows overlooking the darkness of Irving Street, quiet in the overnight hours. The murder of Mr. Lennon; was it a random act of violence or premeditated murder? Of course, he had no personal connection to Mr. Lennon or the Turners but an unsolved crime disturbed him, especially in his hometown.

Perhaps Mr. Lennon knew certain incriminating information that could destroy someone. If that were the case, then he must have known the perpetrator. Perhaps it was somebody who felt threatened and, quite possibly, would not hesitate to strike again.

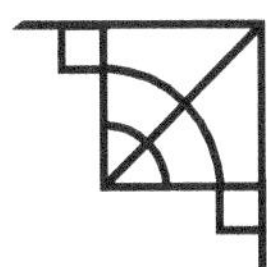

CHAPTER THREE

On Thursday morning, at Albany Police Headquarters, Inspector John Harris, chief of police, Lieutenant Frank Taylor, head of criminal investigations and Patrol Officer Millard Davis sat at a long table in the center of a conference room, reviewing documents and photographs. They were discussing the Walter Lennon murder, compiling data and attempting to undercover new leads on what had already become a cold case.

"I read your report, Officer Davis," Inspector Harris said, looking up from the official document. "I studied the photographs of the deceased, too. You were the first on the scene. What else can you tell us that you observed that early morning?"

Officer Davis squirmed uncomfortably in his chair. It was hot in the room, and police headquarters was not the most comfortable building. Plain, sterile, uninviting; certainly, the conference rooms were bland. He looked at his superiors and sized them up rather quickly. Lieutenant Taylor was a stout, middle-aged man with a firm, no-nonsense manner, who came directly to the point when speaking. Inspector Harris, also in his fifties, on the other hand, was more subtle, tall, with fierce, determined brown eyes.

Officer Davis tried to hide his displeasure. "I didn't see a weapon anywhere and there were no witnesses. At that hour in the morning there usually aren't many people around." He paused. "It must've been a long handled knife, judging by the look of the wound. I really cannot say anything else and neither could the other police officers at the scene." He added the last part to take the emphasis off of himself.

"We've spoken to them but as *you* discovered the body, your input is especially important."

Officer Davis continued. "There were no defense wounds."

Inspector Harris nodded. "From our conversations with Mr. and Mrs. Turner, they were at the Valencia on Broadway having dinner, and then Mr. Lennon told his sister he wanted to shop at Whitney's. From there, the Turners drove to visit friends and did not arrive home until two hours later. Mrs. Turner assumed her brother had already arrived, decided not to wait up for them and had gone to bed. When he didn't appear in the morning, Mr. Turner checked on him and discovering he was not in his bedroom, called the police." He paused. "We spoke to a few salesmen at Whitney's but none of them remembered seeing him in the store that evening. Certainly, Mr. Lennon was not the type to be wandering around the Port of Albany late at night. There must have been something that brought him there."

Lieutenant Taylor cleared his throat. "His sister, Mrs. Louise Turner, refuses to believe her brother was involved in anything underhanded. He might have witnessed something or maybe had knowledge that could ruin someone or something."

"He was part of the Empire State Beverage Company," Inspector Harris added. "He worked alongside his brother-in-law. Mrs. Turner claimed her brother was committed to his work and that he was quite a distinguished gentleman. He also volunteered at local charities. We asked Mrs. Turner for the names of the organizations and after speaking to people at the charities, nobody appeared to have a grudge against Mr. Lennon. In fact, they spoke very well of him."

"They live on Englewood Place, near the college," Officer Davis said.

"Obviously, the Turners are well-to-do," Lieutenant Taylor said. "We've already spoken to them and we've sent two additional officers to interview them. Only people with good incomes could afford a house on Englewood Place." He paused. "Mr. Turner's daughter is married to Mr. Jeffrey Nichols at Empire Advertising. We went there about three years ago when the president of the agency, Mr. Stevenson, thought the premises were being robbed. Turned out a false alarm."

"One of the officers learned that Mr. and Mrs. Nichols are separated and are in the process of a divorce," Inspector Harris said, making further notes. "The Turners did not mention that when we spoke to them. They may not see the relevance, but perhaps it does fit in somehow."

"The officers spoke to the niece," Lieutenant Taylor said, filling his superior in on the details. "They said she was evasive and hardly knew her uncle. According to the officers, in her own words, she is going through a nasty divorce."

"Then we have our work cut out for us, don't we?" Inspector Harris said sardonically.

The Empire State Beverage Company was located in North Albany, away from the city center. A large manufacturing establishment, its layout comprised an entire block. While the building contained just two floors, its sprawling design was paramount to its effective production. Upstairs contained the business offices, including the executive suites and conference rooms, the lower floor contained the manufacturing plant and a few additional workrooms.

An illustrious and extensive facility, with close to a hundred employees, the production of soft drinks entailed a thorough supply of chemicals, dyes, malt flavorings and other enhancements to produce these popular beverages. In nearly a quarter century of success, the Empire State Beverage Company was at the forefront of producing and supplying customers in upstate New York the best in non-alcoholic liquid refreshments.

The company's business was not in the least impacted by prohibition; to the contrary, it saw its production quadruple since 1920. Its endless demand for products was testament to its continued profitability and unprecedented growth. With the new champagne imitation drink they anticipated introducing, profits were projected to be insurmountable, further enhancing the company's reputation.

In a corner office on the upper floor, not far from the executive suites of her father and uncle, Mrs. Prudence Nichols finished typing a report. Her father took great pride in having his daughter as his chief secretary; she typed eighty words a minute and her shorthand and business acumen were impeccable. While her father was moody and difficult at times, she knew he considered her his most valued employee. She pulled the paper out of the machine carefully, looked at it approvingly and put it aside as it required her father's signature.

Prudence Turner Nichols was thirty-five and while not beautiful, she caught the eye of several men who admired her pristine dress, her bobbed hair and her flapper appeal. Just enough jewelry and lipstick, she gave a pleasant appearance.

At this stage in her life, Prudence was of the opinion that success in business mattered most and earning money was a top priority. With her father's guidance, she invested in the lucrative stock market and enjoyed the profitable dividends. Her separation from her husband was leading to a divorce. Through his multiple connections, her father recommended an excellent attorney who would fight for her best interests. Besides, her husband had no legal right to any part of the beverage company, even if he tried to claim it in the divorce proceeding. In the back of her mind, she knew it would turn nasty as her husband had a mean streak but she kept a positive outlook, even if they were no longer on speaking terms. She lit a cigarette, drew deeply and exhaled in some trepidation.

Her thoughts turned to her Uncle Walter, who was murdered last month. The office next door belonged to him and was now strangely empty. She was not especially close to him, but after moving back in with her parents earlier this year, she had gotten to know him better. She liked his keen insight on money matters and his sense of humor. She enjoyed conversations with him on the stock market and about President Harding and Mrs. Harding.

But her uncle was murdered, needlessly, his lifeless body found on a park bench overlooking the Hudson River at the Port of Albany. Now what in the world was he doing there so late at night? He and her parents had dinner reservations at the Valencia, and then her mother told her Uncle Walter planned to shop at Whitney's.

She knew none of this until the next morning. She had gone out to the theater with a few friends and was then invited to a house party, not far from her parents. She arrived home after midnight and since the house was silent, she assumed her parents and uncle had gone to bed. Her mother always left a light on in the kitchen, which she turned off before proceeding upstairs.

She explained that to the police when they questioned her, but she did not think it was of any help. She knew extraordinarily little about her uncle. They asked her about her husband, but she did not like speaking for him and recommended they speak to him themselves, which she had the distinct feeling they did not appreciate.

The ridiculous prohibition we are living under, she thought as she puffed at her cigarette. People were so desperate for booze, they made it at home, using real alcohol! It had been just three years since prohibition went into effect but it had seemed much longer. Perhaps the advertising agency will help in promoting the new beverage, she thought positively, inserting another sheet of paper into her typewriter. After all, there was no publicity department here and the most they advertised was in the newspapers. Obviously, her father anticipated great fortunes with the newly created drink, so she assumed he wanted a large publicity campaign. An imitation champagne was better than no champagne at all!

Her thoughts were clouded, distorted. The unsolved murder of her uncle, the pending divorce proceedings…too much happening in such a short time. She then noticed someone standing in the doorway. It was Miss Medford, a typist from down the hall.

"Excuse me, Mrs. Nichols," she said. "There is a gentleman here for his appointment with Mr. Turner. A Mr. Caleb Dean from Empire Advertising."

Prudence blinked several times. Momentarily she forgot about Caleb's visit this morning. Miss Medford, the most experienced clerk who had been with the company close to thirty years, repeated her announcement. She was not one to waste time when there was work to be completed.

"Thank you, Miss Medford," Prudence said, coming around from her desk and joining her in the hallway. "I will bring Mr. Dean to see my father. I believe my mother is also here today."

Miss Medford nodded. "Yes, I brought Mrs. Turner a cup of tea a little while ago."

Prudence followed her down the hall to the waiting room reserved for visitors. She thanked Miss Medford and then directed herself to the young man sitting in a chair and flipping the pages of the July issue of *The Saturday Evening Post.*

"Good morning, Mr. Dean," she said. "I'm Mrs. Nichols, the executive secretary. Welcome to the Empire State Beverage Company."

Caleb put down the magazine and stood, shaking hands with her. Prudence smiled at the young man in front of her. She looked up at his tall figure. About thirty, his blond curls and deep green eyes were certainly alluring, even seductive. She wondered if he were single. She did not remember Jeff ever mentioning a Mr. Dean, but then her husband rarely spoke about the agency. He held a notebook and appeared ready to start negotiations. Father's type of executive, she thought. She told Caleb her father was expecting him and led him down the hallway to his office.

The door to Mr. Turner's office was wide open and upon entering, Caleb noticed a woman sitting in front of his desk, looking through a folder stuffed with papers. A rather large man sat behind the desk, scribbling on a pad and looking every bit preoccupied. They looked up to see their daughter enter.

"Father, Mother, this is Mr. Dean from Empire Advertising," Prudence said, introducing Caleb. "He's here for his appointment with you."

"Yes, I know," Mr. Turner snapped. "That's all for now, Prudence."

Prudence nodded, as though used to the tantrums of her moody father and left the office. Mr. Turner motioned to Caleb to sit next to his wife. Mrs. Turner placed the folder on the desk, turning her attention to him. Mr. Turner did likewise and for a moment, Caleb was unprepared for the intense scrutiny, as though he was subjected to their approval. Of course, they were investing a large amount of money in Empire Advertising to promote their latest beverage. They seemed to expect him to speak first, so Caleb mentioned he was pleased to meet them.

"Thank you, Mr. Dean," Mrs. Turner said graciously.

Caleb looked to his left and saw a stylish, older woman dressed formally in a dark blue dress, a string of pearls hanging daintily around her neck. Quite possibly, in her late sixties, she had a pleasing disposition. Her gray hair, although not in the bob style, suited her pretty face. She mentioned she had spoken to Mr. and Mrs. Turner and looked forward to working with them.

"The president of your agency, Mr. Stevenson is an industrious man," Mr. Turner said. "Very diligent and dependable. He is most eager to work with us."

Caleb looked across the desk at Mr. Nathan Turner and at once was reminded of Mr. Stevenson. Large, patriarch, firm, a no-nonsense approach to business, judicious in money matters, close to seventy, he appeared the typical experienced executive. After all, it was his company and he had worked there his entire life. He listened to Mr. Turner and knew it would be a long narration, much more detailed than the telephone conversation from before.

Mr. Turner expanded on the company history, the huge profits it made since prohibition and the newly created imitation champagne. He anticipated it would be their biggest seller.

Mr. Turner lit a cigarette and continued his speech. "Since 1920, drugstores have seen a rise in medicinal alcohol. Speakeasies and bootleg liquor continue to increase here in Albany."

Mrs. Turner coughed. "The point we are making, Mr. Dean, is that our new imitation champagne beverage will bring people to buy something close to alcohol that is legal."

"Black market liquor has a reputation for harshness and dubious ingredients," Mr. Turner said seriously. "Supposedly, those imitation liquors can be highly toxic. I've read that some have made people quite ill, even partially paralyzed."

Caleb was surprised. "I had no idea they were so poisonous."

"That's where we come in," Mr. Turner said and smiled. "Soda based cocktails, which were uncommon before prohibition, are the new style for flappers and sheiks in the speakeasies." He spoke as though he had first-hand knowledge of what happened in those illegal establishments. "Certainly, a young man like yourself has frequented speakeasies here in Albany."

Caleb meekly admitted he had gone to a few speakeasies but was not one to drink. Mr. Turner nodded and opened a folder on his desk, looking at several documents.

"Our new beverage will be quite popular. We would like to market it as the new champagne drink for the 1920s. It can be drunk straight or used as a mixer."

"We plan to call it *Champagne Twist*, a New York style nightclub drink and sell it in miniature champagne type bottles," Mrs. Turner expanded. "This will appeal to speakeasies and since it is not an alcoholic beverage it will be available in markets, too."

Caleb looked up from his notes. "What are you looking for in a publicity campaign? I have several ideas that may interest you."

"By all means, Mr. Dean," Mr. Turner and smiled. "My son-in-law highly recommended your services so I am eager to hear your input."

Caleb suggested a marketing platform of intense radio advertising and displays at local markets. He added additional publicity in the local newspapers would generate interest. He suggested a taste testing event to introduce the beverage, inviting the public and covered by the media, too. Mr. Turner nodded approvingly and Mrs. Turner exhibited much enthusiasm for Caleb's ideas. She especially liked the taste testing event where the media would be welcomed.

Mr. Turner mentioned they plan to roll out the imitation champagne drink within two weeks. He then offered Caleb the opportunity to tour the facility and soon they left the office, down the hallway to the stairs bringing them to the first level.

Quite a busy and rather hectic place, Caleb thought impressively, looking around at the conveyor belts, the production areas, the cases of soft drinks ready for shipment, the secretaries typing, filing and answering telephones. Mr. Turner explained the production line; how each drink was developed, which included adding malt flavorings as well as fruit extracts such as oranges, lemons, limes, berries, citrus oils, sugar, salt, pepper, vanilla and cinnamon. Caleb watched as bottle after bottle was filled from a conveyor belt, while another conveyor belt pasted labels on each bottle as it made its way to the end, where they were placed in packing cases. He followed the Turners as they showed him the accounting offices, the receiving areas, the business offices and the back entrance, intended for employees.

"My brother's death has affected us terribly," Mrs. Turner said unexpectedly to Caleb. They stopped in front of the shipping area, where trucks were being loaded with cases of beverages.

Mr. Turner agreed. "We had no idea why he went to the Port of Albany that evening."

Caleb did not know what to say so he decided to remain quiet. It was a delicate subject, so he waited for Mr. Turner to continue with the tour. They soon made their way to the front entrance.

"I look forward to seeing your proposals, Mr. Dean," Mrs. Turner said brightly.

Caleb nodded, realizing his appointment had ended. He did not want to prolong it. He believed in maintaining respectful communication with clients and the beginning stages were crucial to the agency's success. He shook hands with the Turners and mentioned he would be in touch soon, with the ideas he created typed up along with a contract for Mr. Turner to sign.

As he walked along Broadway in the hot sunshine to catch the trolley, he removed his suit jacket, loosened his tie and undid buttons of his vest. His mind returned to the Turners. While encouraged by meeting them, touring the facility and anticipating the promotion and the revenue it would bring, Caleb felt an uneasy sense of catastrophe, as though despite the planning, the publicity was destined for an unforeseen disaster.

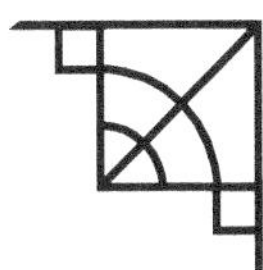

CHAPTER FOUR

Caleb arrived at the advertising agency close to noon. It was oddly quiet as he got off the elevator. He bid Harry the elevator attendant a good afternoon and after the gates closed and the car shot upward, he made his way down the hallway to the Empire Advertising Agency.

As he realized it was almost the lunch hour, he assumed people had left offices to enjoy a meal in Albany's fabulous downtown restaurants. Upon entering, he was greeted pleasantly by Mrs. Stevenson and Gabrielle, busy at their desks, typing and answering the telephone. Mrs. Stevenson asked Caleb about his visit with the Turners. Gabrielle also looked his way, although Caleb could not tell if she was interested in the Turners or had something else on her mind.

He was about to explain briefly about his visit with the Turners when Polly joined them, having just returned from the storage area, carrying an armful of folders. She set them on her desk and looked at Caleb curiously as though surprised he was there. Roy entered at that moment carrying a few reports. He was about to approach Gabrielle but stopped when he saw Caleb.

"Back from the Turners already?" Polly asked as though expecting him to have stayed longer. She was eager to hear about his visit to the beverage company and looked at him expectedly.

"How did it go this morning, Caleb?" Roy inquired. "I bet it's the cat's meow!"

Gabrielle agreed. "The bee's knees for sure. Tell us about it, Caleb."

Caleb felt rather overwhelmed but at the moment did not feel he wanted to explain anything to Polly, Gabrielle or Roy. "The Turners will be great to work with. They anticipate success with their new beverage," he told them and added nothing more.

"And we'll gladly help them achieve that success," a deep male voice boomed from the hallway entrance.

Caleb looked up and saw Mr. Stevenson. A large commanding figure, distinguished, at times menacing, and certainly demanding, it was unusual for Mr. Stevenson to come to the front office. Caleb smiled in spite of himself and repeated that he found his meeting with the Turners extremely rewarding.

"Do you need anything, dear?" Mrs. Stevenson asked him as though she too found it odd her husband would make an appearance in the front office. She waited for him to elaborate but as usual, Mr. Stevenson was never loquacious.

"I am eager to hear what Caleb learned this morning. I will call a staff meeting later."

He led Caleb down the hallway to his office. Sitting behind his desk, Mr. Stevenson lit a cigarette, as though ready for a long discourse from Caleb and offered him one. Caleb gladly took it, as though his energies were sapped from the extreme heat and humidity and his meeting with the Turners. He watched as Mr. Stevenson lit it for him and then they sat back as though they were old friends, just catching up with each other. Mr. Stevenson blew smoke, cleared his throat and asked Caleb to tell him what he learned from his visit with the Turners this morning.

Caleb opened his notebook. He explained to Mr. Stevenson all that he experienced while at the Empire State Beverage Company, his meeting with the Turners, the tour of the facility, the anticipated success of the champagne imitation drink and its appeal to the speakeasy crowd. He detailed what he planned for the publicity campaign, including intense advertising through all mediums and the taste testing event in which the public would be invited. He concluded that the media would also attend, adding to the publicity.

Mr. Stevenson blew smoke and nodded in approval. "Excellent, Caleb. Now we need to draw up a contract for Mr. Turner to sign and once that's completed, we can start on the campaign."

"Thank you, Mr. Stevenson," Caleb said humbly. "I haven't divided up the tasks yet but I want to be in charge of the taste testing event. I'll be in touch with the Turners to inquire what date is best for them"

"I imagine they would want it sometime this month, since the beverage is expected to be introduced soon. We have two weeks to make the arrangements, but the advertising should come first. You've handled the newspapers before, so you should work on that angle."

Caleb nodded. "I have contacts at the local papers and placing advertisements shouldn't be a problem. Full page ads would be beneficial."

"What more did you learn about the imitation champagne drink? Do they anticipate it will be a hit with speakeasies? I can't imagine that crowd warming up to an imitation champagne."

"Speakeasies will be interested in this beverage, as it will appeal to people desiring alcohol. The name of it is *Champagne Twist*. It'll be for sale in markets since it is not an alcoholic beverage."

"Perfect," Mr. Stevenson said. "The bigger the publicity the higher we can charge them. I'll tell Gabrielle to inform the staff of a meeting in my office at three o'clock."

Caleb thanked Mr. Stevenson. "I'll have everything completed by then." He left the suite, on the way to his office, where he would draft the assignments on the publicity campaign.

Mr. Stevenson called Gabrielle, telling her to let everyone know there was a meeting at three o'clock in his office. And that it was urgent.

Caleb completed the agenda on time and arrived at Mr. Stevenson's office exuberantly. Sitting at the conference table, he opened his pad and looked at the notes he had written. He noticed Mr. Stevenson was still busy at his desk, seemingly unaware that he had even entered.

Caleb saw Wilbur and Minerva arrive first. Minerva carried a steno pad. Wilbur fumbled in his shirt pocket for a cigarette. It looked as though they were unsure of what was happening. From the glances they threw him, Caleb could tell they did not relish listening to him talk. They sat the farthest from him, at the end of the long table. He wondered if they intended to discredit his suggestions as they have in the past, but he was ready for it. He had Mr. Stevenson on his side so that was all that mattered. Gabrielle and Polly followed, each with their own pads, looking rather forlorn and irritable as though agency meetings were the most dreaded part of the workday. Caleb greeted them but could sense a certain friction, perhaps because they were in Mr. Stevenson's executive suite and they, like Wilbur and Minerva, did not quite know what to expect. He assumed Gabrielle relayed the purpose of the meeting, so why the dubiousness from them he was not quite sure.

Caleb then saw Peter, Roy and Jeff saunter in together, as though they were doing everyone a favor by their presence, as if they had more important tasks to worry about than a meeting. Peter, while lighting a cigarette, practically said just that but not within earshot of Mr. Stevenson. He was careful to keep his voice low, while the others at the conference table talked amongst themselves. Caleb glanced over at Mr. Stevenson, noticed he was still absorbed in writing in a notebook, and apparently had not heard Jeff's inadequate remark.

Mrs. Stevenson entered, smiling cheerfully and appearing fresh as always. She sat next to Caleb and waited for her husband to join them. Caleb looked again toward the massive desk and watched Mr. Stevenson, his large figure groping as he walked, almost staggeringly, making his way heavily toward the conference table. Caleb wondered if he ever considered using a cane, his steps seemed an effort. He ensconced himself in a chair next to his wife, greeted everyone cordially and then turned his attention to Caleb. He mentioned Caleb would be presenting his findings on his recent visit to the Empire State Beverage Company, the purpose of today's meeting. All eyes turned to Caleb who cleared his throat and began.

"I met with the Turners this morning and they are eager to begin work with us. The imitation champagne beverage they have produced is destined to become a big seller. The product's name is *Champagne Twist,* a New York style nightclub drink. They plan to sell it in miniature champagne type bottles, which will appeal to the speakeasy crowd. It'll also be available in markets, as it's a non-alcoholic beverage. They plan to start distribution in two weeks, which gives us plenty of time to commence a publicity campaign."

Jeff whistled. "Sounds like my father-in-law knows what he's doing. Old money bags thinking only of himself and his vast fortune."

"None of that, Jeff," Mr. Stevenson said, rather firmly. "We must respect the Turners as they are our new clients. Whatever their wishes for the publicity campaign, we will abide with them. Is that understood?" He spoke to Jeff as though he were a child.

"I'm sure Jeff meant nothing by it, dear," Mrs. Stevenson spoke placatingly as usual.

Caleb looked again at his notes. "For print advertising, I plan to call the local newspapers where I have contacts. Full page ads promoting the new beverage are worthwhile."

A low murmur of assent was heard around the table.

"Minerva, I'd like you to contact the local radio stations, including WGY."

Minerva had been writing on her pad. She assured Caleb she would take charge of the radio publicity, something she had done in the past. Caleb then addressed Roy.

"Roy, I'd like you to create a brochure on the new champagne beverage. A written information piece would be beneficial. We can do a mass mailing, especially to previous clients."

"Another great idea, Caleb," Mr. Stevenson said approvingly.

Roy demurred, but his face held questions. "I should call Mr. Turner first."

"I suggest speaking with Mrs. Nichols, his executive secretary," Caleb told him.

"And my soon to be ex-wife," Jeff added.

"She would have more information on the particulars. I don't want to bombard Mr. Turner with too many inquiries at once." Caleb paused, wondering if he had lost his audience. "Peter, I'd like you to contact markets in Albany and Schenectady to see if we can have a sampling. We've done publicity for the markets before, so we have a good rapport with them."

Peter nodded. "I have contacts at Albany Public Market and some of the others."

"Wilbur, you can contact local theaters to inquire about actors willing to promote it. Actors at the Strand and the Ritz might be interested if we offer them payment for their services. I don't know what that would be yet, but let's see if you can find someone willing to do it."

Wilbur blew smoke from his cigarette and looked at Caleb irritably. Obviously, he did not like being told what to do. But he relented, as he did not want to cause friction in front of Mr. Stevenson. He told Caleb he would contact various theaters in Albany and Schenectady.

Caleb mentioned that after Roy finished with the rough draft of the brochure, he wanted Mr. Turner's approval first. Gabrielle and Polly would proofread it, offer additional suggestions as appropriate, and then type it up, before sending it to the printer.

"The biggest part of this particular publicity campaign is the taste testing event. I plan to contact people we have done business with in the past. I also want to contact the mayor's office and people at city hall. I think opening it to the public is a good idea and the Turners agreed. The date for the taste testing will appear in the print advertisements and on the radio commercials." He hesitated. "Jeff, I'd like your help in this endeavor. It means setting up the event at the facility, having the drink accessible where people attending can purchase it. And Mr. and Mrs. Stevenson, Polly and Gabrielle, I would also ask for your assistance. Peter and Polly, you can start reviewing some of the old files in the spare room. See what former clients we could contact. The local markets we've negotiated with in the past should have their files there. After Roy finishes the brochure and Mr. Turner approves it, we can have it available at the taste testing. As I mentioned, we will make enough copies for a mass mailing. I will coordinate with the Turners as to the date and time. We could offer light refreshments to go along with the drink that would entice people to attend. I know a local caterer who can help with providing food."

"We'll be glad to assist, Caleb," Mrs. Stevenson said pleasantly. "Mrs. Turner is a charming woman and it'll be nice seeing her again."

"Likewise for Mr. Turner," Mr. Stevenson said. "A fine man and a distinguished one, too."

"I don't relish seeing my wife," Jeff said bluntly, not caring if Mr. Stevenson disapproved.

Caleb paused, expecting Mr. Stevenson to retaliate but surprisingly he sat in silence, as though contemplating the enormous amount of time and effort they were about to invest in this new campaign.

"Why don't we call some of our former clients?" Polly suggested.

"Excellent idea," Caleb said, writing on his pad. "We'll do both; send out brochures to former clients and then call to invite them to the taste testing. Should bring a good crowd."

"The newspapers would be interested in covering it, too," Minerva suggested.

Mrs. Stevenson agreed. "Leonard and I can ask some of our friends to attend."

Mr. Stevenson cleared his throat. "Caleb, you have far exceeded my expectations for this publicity campaign. I will call Mr. Turner tomorrow to let him know we are ready to begin." He turned to Gabrielle. "I'd like you to type up the contract after I finish with it. I'm sure Mr. Turner will agree to the price for our services."

"Sounds worthwhile," Polly said brightly.

"It sounds like a lot of work," Jeff whined. "More than what we usually do for our clients. Why the big showdown for the beverage company in the first place?"

Mr. Stevenson glared at him and spoke rather harshly and to the point.

"Because they are paying a hefty price for our work. We cannot afford to do a shoddy job for the Turners. They are entrusting us to deliver a publicity campaign to boost their sales and we will not disappoint them." He looked at Caleb expecting him to continue.

Caleb mentioned he was finished with the agenda and asked his listeners if there were any questions. An uneasy silence reigned upon them, as though there were unspoken thoughts but nobody dared speak, at least not in front of Mr. Stevenson, who was obviously annoyed.

At that moment, Mr. Stevenson cleared his throat, irritably mentioned he wanted to continue with the new contract and then dismissed everyone, abruptly concluding the meeting.

It was close to four thirty and although the five o'clock hour was almost upon them, the employees of the Empire Advertising Agency were hard at work. With their tasks divvied up amongst them, their labors on the new publicity campaign were just beginning. The enthusiasm Caleb displayed during the meeting was certainly exemplary and appreciated by Mr. Stevenson although none of the others really shared his acute eagerness.

In the spare room, Peter and Polly were reviewing old files, deciding which clients to contact for the taste testing event. The others had retreated to their offices, giving Peter and Polly time to unwind and have the room to themselves. Most of the files had a musty smell and Polly was hard pressed to continue rummaging through the file cabinets.

"Some of these files must be as old as Mr. Stevenson," she complained, thumbing through the folders. "I'm sure most of these people are dead, so what's the point?"

Peter also looked through a file cabinet. He lit a cigarette and kept it between his lips. "I see what you mean. Some date to 1888 and 1890, with places that don't exist anymore." He paused. "So far, I don't see the markets we've done business with. I'll just call them to save time. This looking for old files is rather time consuming."

Polly agreed. "What did you think of the meeting earlier?"

Peter was reviewing a file. "Well, there isn't much to think, is there? Sir Caleb gave us our tasks and we have to adhere to them. Fortunately, what he gave me is not too bad. I know people at the local markets, so my work shouldn't be too difficult."

"He'll want us to get involved with that ridiculous taste testing," Polly said, closing one drawer and opening another. "A big waste of time if you ask me."

"Of all the asinine ideas for a publicity campaign," Peter said, smoking furiously, rather in annoyance. "Why would he think people would want to attend in the first place? Nobody would care about an imitation champagne drink, except speakeasy and restaurant owners."

"He says it'll be for sale in markets," Polly reminded him. "I guess that's where you come in. Although a sample at the local markets is a silly idea, too."

Peter paused, smoking incessantly, too agitated to concentrate on the files. "I don't think there's anything we can do about it. He didn't mention that I'd need to be present, so after markets acquire the beverage, they can do it themselves." He paused. "So you don't think the taste testing is a good idea either?"

Polly shook her head. "Not on your life, but I certainly wasn't about to say so with Mr. Stevenson in awe of it. What's wrong with him, anyway? Has he gone off his rocker?"

"Sometimes I wonder," Peter said. "He is getting up there in age, his wife too."

With the spare room door open, they evidently did not realize their voices could he heard in the hallway. They continued reviewing records of former clients they felt would have an interest in the taste testing event. They were silent for some time until Polly observed a record of interest.

"Peter, look, here's one on Mr. Cyrus Newcomb from the Clinton Street Hotel." She paused reflectively. She skimmed through the file. "We must've done publicity for them. These papers are dated 1915." She paused. "There's something else here, too."

Peter was not listening to her as he should have been. The files he sorted contained names and telephone numbers of clients from 1918 to 1922, more current customers who would be easy to contact. Polly kept talking but Peter suddenly noticed she stopped as though she were at a loss for words. He put down the folder he was reviewing and looked over at her questioningly. It was unusual for Polly to stop speaking once riled up. He asked her if something was wrong.

She glanced up from the folder she held in her hands, rather flustered. "Oh, no, just surprised at what's in these files. Chock full of information." She continued looking in the folder, as though memorizing its contents, and then she put it down and smiled. "Where are we going tonight? I am in the mood for dancing the night away. You promised you would take me dancing. My ex-husband hated the nightlife, but I love kicking up my heels!"

Peter nodded. "Are the dance halls open tonight? Besides, we have to work tomorrow."

Polly almost laughed. "Since when has that ever stopped you from a night on the town?" She sighed. "Well, I'm done with sorting through old records. I've had enough nostalgia for one afternoon. I'll leave these files here and pick up tomorrow." She glanced at her watch. "Almost time to leave, dear. Why don't you call me later and we'll make plans? And don't keep me waiting."

Peter watched as she abruptly left the room. He walked over to the doorway and saw her disappear into the main office. He looked along the hallway, which was quiet as a mouse. Suddenly, he had a strange feeling someone had been standing outside the spare room door, listening.

Minerva looked through the city directories for Albany and Schenectady, jotting down the names and telephone numbers of radio stations in both cities. She did not relish contacting them, requesting their presence at a taste testing of a new drink. What fools would be interested in it anyway? Of course, if it were a big seller, then the radio stations would want to advertise it. On the other hand, Mr. Stevenson would argue that promotion equaled large profits as he had said many times in the past and she admitted he was always proven correct.

She finished with her list of radio stations when Roy entered. He asked her what her thoughts were on the meeting. From his tone, morose and hardly enthusiastic, she could tell he was not too keen on the campaign. She tried to steer him in a more positive direction.

"You're an excellent writer, Roy. You've written copy for previous clients and it's always been outstanding, so I don't fear you won't produce another fine promotional piece." She paused. "Besides, Mr. Stevenson and his wife have always been pleased. You have nothing to worry about."

Roy had a cigarette in his hand and he crushed it in the ashtray on her desk. “It does seem like a lot of our hours will be spent on this particular campaign. As Jeff mentioned, we haven’t gone out of our way for a new client like this before. I’m just finishing work for the Cherry Spring Project and now I don’t have any time to organize my desk before diving into this new one.” He paused. “Caleb seems like he’s running the entire show. Of course, he is a chief account executive.” His tone hinged on envy and even resentment.

Minerva glanced at him. “Why don’t you talk to him and voice your concerns?”

Roy shook his head. “I don’t think that’s a good idea.”

“Well, we have to go along with him. The tasks are not too bad, but I’m not fond of this taste testing event. I assume it’ll be held in the evening or on a weekend. He didn’t mention that.”

“Which means we’ll have to give up our free time,” Roy lamented.

Minerva nodded. “Didn’t he think of that beforehand?”

“Sometimes it seems Caleb doesn’t think at all,” Roy said. “He is the Big Boss’s right hand man, you know. So he has to play his cards right.”

Minerva looked up and saw Wilbur enter. He had a list in his hand, which contained the names and telephone numbers of theaters in and around Albany. He mentioned he compiled them from a list Gabrielle kept on file in the main office.

“Saves me time,” he explained, crossing to his desk. He lit a cigarette and sat back on his chair, putting his feet up. “Almost five o’clock, Min. Time to leave soon.”

Roy turned to him. “Do you think the new campaign will be a good one, Wilbur?”

“Perhaps,” Wilbur answered laconically, as though his thoughts were elsewhere.

"It could be worthwhile," Minerva said, looking at the brighter side. "But honestly I don't see it as much of a success, unless the publicity pays off."

Wilbur looked at the young man standing before his desk, looking rather insecure despite his skills and success in previous assignments. He puffed casually on his cigarette and loosened his tie, attempting to cope with the heat.

"You've always written good copy for us, Roy," he told him encouragingly.

"Do you know the Turners?" Roy asked him.

Wilbur shrugged. "I may have met them," he said in an offhanded way. He then addressed Roy again, assuring him of his expertise. "From your end, I wouldn't worry. You're a natural in writing promotions. What could go wrong?"

Minerva agreed. "That's right, Roy. Your work is exceptional and the Turners will appreciate it. So will the Stevensons. We might really enjoy the taste testing. It's just a harmless event, after all."

Jeff finished adding up figures from the current expense report, jotted down the total and then turned the page. It was a lengthy document and it would take time to finish. He admitted he was enjoying the new adding machine, which made his work so much easier.

He noticed Wilbur, Minerva and Roy walk past his door, most likely leaving for the day. He sat back and lit a cigarette, taking a break from adding up figures. He glanced at his watch and saw it was almost five o'clock. Just a few more pages, he was pleased to notice.

His mind raced to the meeting Mr. Stevenson called and Caleb sitting at the head of the conference table, expostulating his ridiculous ideas for this hare brained publicity campaign. While Jeff had worked on previous campaigns, it was not his forte. He reminded Mr. Stevenson he was primarily an accountant, not a publicist and he was hired as such. Mr. Stevenson acknowledged this but reminded Jeff that at Empire Advertising, it was often a group effort and with the new contract, Caleb expected everyone's participation. Mr. Stevenson was annoyed at him, but he really did not care. He let his feelings be known whether the old man liked it or not.

And of course, dear Prudence again. He expected to earn part of the beverage company, as he was still in good relations with his father-in-law. Even his mother-in-law liked him, telling him he was the son she never had. So Prudence be damned, he thought jeeringly. We'll see who comes out victorious in the divorce case, he thought viciously. With all her parent's money, acquiring part of the beverage company earnings should not be too difficult. He had an excellent lawyer who knew how to finagle the system. He had contacts in the courts too, which was in Jeff's favor. A little bribery never hurt, he thought sensibly.

He drew heavily on his cigarette, his face contorted into tight creases. His marriage was a terrible mistake and he blamed his wife for ruining not only the marriage but also his life. Her selfishness, flimsy manner, flapper lifestyle, insensitivity and unwillingness to have children amongst many other issues caused Jeff to leave her. He would call his lawyer as soon as he arrived at his apartment to find out how long the divorce proceeding would last. He reminded him he wanted it to be over as soon as possible. His lawyer told him he had not heard yet from his wife's attorney. He also told him divorce cases take time and cannot be rushed, so patience was a virtue.

I'll bet, he thought bitterly, putting his feet up on his desk and leaning back on his swivel chair. Jeff could easily have another woman in his life if he wanted one but he was too embittered to socialize. He was content to live in his one bedroom apartment on Dove Street and enjoyed walking through Washington Park, attending performances at Harmanus Bleecker Hall and the Albany Institute of History and Art.

He swung his legs to the floor and crushed his cigarette in an already overflowing ashtray. He unbuttoned his shirt at the neck and took off his vest. It was extremely warm and the late afternoon heat was relentless.

He resented Caleb's taking the lead in the publicity campaign, but then, he had only himself to blame. He suggested his father-in-law contact him, but he did not think it would turn into such a big production. He assumed it would be a small campaign. He admitted Caleb did have a good business sense. The West Point graduate, living up to the mantra of duty, honor, and country. And old man Stevenson fell for it hook, line and sinker.

His thoughts turned to Polly Ormerod. He considered more than once of asking her out. But she was so fixated with Peter. She came across as sneaky, untrustworthy and unscrupulous. He had seen her snooping around, including the spare room. Peter, too, was divorced but he knew little about him. He silently thanked Mr. Stevenson for having his own office.

Jeff was surprised his father-in-law, Mr. Turner was back to business so soon after the murder of his brother-in-law. He was surprised, too, his mother-in-law would return to work so quickly as if the murder had not even taken place. Perhaps involvement with the company was solace for them. He wondered what Mr. Lennon was doing at the Port of Albany so late at night, when that area had a notorious reputation for criminal activity. From his brief encounters with him, he struck Jeff as an intelligent man, certainly not someone who would get involved with anything underhanded. He did not think Mr. Lennon ever worried where his next dollar came from.

His involvement with the taste testing event meant seeing his in-laws and his wife. He shook his head. Honestly, he could have cared less if they dropped dead tomorrow.

Jeff looked at the expense report and with just a few pages left, bent his head down and got back to work.

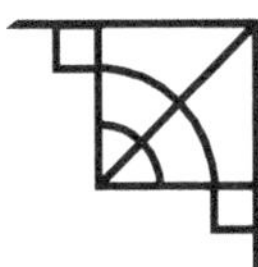

CHAPTER FIVE

Friday morning, July twentieth and the heat and humidity continued unabated. Caleb was busy in his office, anxiously waiting for the agenda for the publicity campaign as Gabrielle was in the process of typing it. As soon as she brought it to him, he planned to call Mr. Turner and review it with him again. He had spoken with Mrs. Turner only an hour ago and she told him she and her husband decided the taste testing would be held at their facility on Wednesday August fifteenth. She suggested the time for four o'clock. She mentioned they would like to open it to the public, which should appear in the advertisement. She also reiterated the name of the new drink was *Champagne Twist*, and that they wanted it promoted as a non-alcoholic drink.

Caleb entered Mr. Stevenson's office and repeated this information. Mr. Stevenson mentioned they had enough time to accomplish what he planned for them. Mrs. Stevenson thought the date was fine for her to invite friends to the event, too. She asked Caleb if he had contacted the local newspapers

"So far I have ads appearing in the *Times Union*, the *Albany Evening Journal* and the *Schenectady Gazette*," he told her. "With the date for the taste testing secure, I plan to contact the mayor's office, too."

"Wonderful, Caleb," Mrs. Stevenson approvingly. "I am so proud of West Point graduates. You certainly make a fine soldier, Caleb dear."

"Celeste, please," her husband implored. "Let the boy get on with his work."

Caleb thanked them, cringing inwardly as usual upon being referred to as a *boy* by Mr. Stevenson and then went to check on his associates, to see if they were implementing or at least beginning to implement their contributions to the new campaign.

He walked a short distance down the hall to see Roy. Which also meant, of course, he would have the opportunity see Peter. He was pleased to see both hard at work, quite diligently, putting their total effort into their assigned task. Roy looked up and acknowledged Caleb, then turned to Peter, whose desk did not face the doorway and mentioned Caleb was there.

"Hello, Caleb," Peter said, swinging around in his chair. "I've just gotten off the phone with *Albany Public Market*, *A & P* as well as other local markets. They are interested in the new champagne imitation and in a sample testing, too."

"I have a rough draft of the brochure written," Roy told him. "It needs a little polishing but so far I think it's a good copy." He handed it to Caleb, who read it several times and then handed it back to him.

"Good job, Roy. You may want to add more detail on the drink, so people know it is an imitation champagne. By the way, the taste testing is four o'clock on August fifteenth. You should include that in the brochure."

Roy got right back to work. Peter asked Caleb when the drink would be available.

"Mr. Turner told me in two weeks," Caleb said. "You should call the markets back and let them know to contact the beverage company themselves to place an order for it."

His next stop was the office of Wilbur and Minerva. Upon entering, he noticed Minerva smoking fiendishly, chatting on the telephone with someone from a local radio station. He heard part of the conversation about the publicity campaign, so he was pleased she was doing her part. Wilbur was also occupied at his desk, making a list of the theaters he had contacted. Caleb was always unsure about Wilbur; the resentment was transparent, although he wondered why with his apparent wealth. Certainly, he had more than enough money. Wilbur looked up as he saw Caleb.

"I have an actress interested in doing a radio spot for the new drink," he told him. "Her name is Miss Penelope Barker and she's been popular at local theaters. She is the only one who expressed interest so far. Eve Tanguay is busy at the moment."

Caleb thanked him, noted Minerva still busy on the phone and then left their office, intending to go directly to his own. Jeff, standing in the doorway of his office, stopped him.

"Hello, Caleb, another hot morning, isn't it? Look, I don't want to get too involved with the taste testing idea. I don't relish seeing my wife, as I'm sure you know we are in the process of divorcing. We aren't on speaking terms."

He told him of the date and time, and that it will be held at their facility in North Albany.

"Yes, I know it well," Jeff grumbled. He took a pack of cigarettes from his pocket, shook one out and lit it almost angrily. "As long as my contacts with my wife and in-laws are minor."

Caleb assured him again he did not anticipate that being a problem, then noticed Polly hovering near his entrance doorway. He scurried down the hallway and came up to her. He noticed she was holding a document, which he gathered, was the publicity campaign ready for his review.

"Gabrielle finished typing it and I proofread it," Polly said, handing it to him. "It really is an incredibly good publicity campaign, Caleb, one of the best I've ever seen. You have done a fine job. The Turners will be pleased."

Caleb glanced at the document, briefly skimming it. He thanked Polly for her help. He then returned to his desk, with the intention of calling Mr. Turner and reviewing the campaign once again. He looked forward to finalizing the details. Polly returned to the front office, humming a popular tune nonchalantly, as though she did not have a care in the world.

In a shadow down the hallway, unseen by Caleb or Polly, Jeff stood in the doorway to his office, smoking furiously, thinking of the ridiculous taste testing event and glaring at them with a hard-set look on his face.

"Well, go if you must," Mr. Stevenson said, blowing smoke from his cigarette and looking at his wife, rather impatiently. "I know how important it is to you."

Mrs. Stevenson nodded. She was seated in a chair before his large desk and looked at her husband, a large mountain of a man, looking older than his years, as though he owned the world. She did not feel she needed his permission to go to church, but she wanted to let him know before leaving. She had mentioned it to Gabrielle in the main office already

Celeste was a communicant of the Cathedral of the Immaculate Conception, Albany's cathedral on Madison Avenue. It was almost eleven thirty and Celeste planned to attend the twelve fifteen Mass. She mentioned she had missed services for several days although she knew that was wasted on her husband, who did not share her Catholic beliefs. Looking at him, sitting rather hunched over his desk, a steadfast expression on his face, he made it sound like she were going to some place unimportant. Well, to him, it most likely was, she thought. However, that did not stop her from attending services.

"I will be back after it's over. On a nice day like today I can walk to the cathedral."

"Despite the work we have to accomplishment for the Turner's publicity campaign, Celeste? And of course, the other contracts that need finishing before the end of the month."

Celeste was used to her parsimonious husband, who saw dollar signs in nearly everything he did but who did not spend an extra penny if he could save it. Of course, with the economic boom and the lucrative stock market, she never understood her husband's frugal thoughts on money. Sometimes she wondered how someone could live his life concerned only with money and making more of it. He invested in the stock market wisely, certainly playing his cards right.

"Polly and Gabrielle have been quite busy," she reminded him, changing the subject. "Roy and Peter also are making excellent progress. I don't know where Polly and Gabrielle get the speed to type so many words! These younger girls certainly have the most modern skills, don't they?"

Mr. Stevenson cracked a smile on his wrinkled face. "Indeed. We are fortunate to have them here."

"Do you anticipate any problems with the Turners?"

"Problems? What sort of problems? The Turners are most agreeable and pleasant people. I'm surprised you would even ask. You've met them before and enjoyed their company."

Celeste hesitated, looking past her husband at the window, overlooking State Street. She pushed back some gray hair from her forehead. "I just thought there could be trouble between Jeff and his wife. I understand they are not on speaking terms, which would make it rather difficult if they are together."

Mr. Stevenson brushed it off. "Never mind, dear. The Turners get along with their son-in-law even if he and their daughter are divorcing. I do not anticipate any trouble. In fact, I expect great revenues for them and for us. This is a large campaign, Celeste, one of the largest we have ever handled. The publicity is great for us, too."

Celeste agreed, although not as exuberantly as her husband. She sighed, causing her husband to look up and ask if something was troubling her.

"I feel so sorry for Mrs. Turner, poor dear. Her brother was murdered and the police still haven't found who killed him. How dreadful! I am sure it has affected Mr. Turner, too. After all, Mr. Lennon was employed there. I hope it does not cause difficulties for the publicity campaign."

Mr. Stevenson looked at her. "How could it, Celeste? People will be interested in the new beverage and the last thing they will think about is Mr. Lennon's murder. Besides, it has no bearing on this publicity campaign."

"Well, it has received a lot of bad press in the newspapers and on the radio. The city is still reeling from the shock of it. Just the other day, at the market, I heard a few ladies discussing it."

Mr. Stevenson nodded. "Of course, it's still recent news. That's to be expected."

"Quite honestly, Leonard, I am concerned about Polly. She is one of the flappers. I do not approve of that lifestyle. She's made light of Mr. Lennon's murder. I've seen her snooping around the office, looking in file cabinets in the spare room. I do not approve of that, either."

"Celeste, I would not worry about Polly. We would be lost without her expertise."

"Well, thank you, Mr. Stevenson."

Leonard looked up and Celeste turned in her chair. They saw Polly in the doorway. She entered the office breezily, with the Turner campaign typed. She mentioned she had given a copy to Caleb for his review and wanted to give one to him, too. She smiled, putting on the charm as usual. Her excessive make-up, black dress and pearls certainly made her svelte figure provocative.

Polly addressed them, rather sarcastically. "Maybe someone we know did poor Mr. Lennon in. Rather exciting, isn't it? Certainly thrilling to say the least. A real murder mystery!"

She left the office haughtily, leaving the Stevensons speechless. Celeste looked at her husband startled, wondering how long Polly had been outside the door, obviously eavesdropping.

She is up to something dishonest, Celeste thought. Her eyes met those of her husband and his expression alone communicated that he agreed with her.

Later that afternoon, an impromptu meeting was held in Caleb's office. In attendance were Minerva, Wilbur, Jeff, Peter and Roy. Caleb summoned them to his office, to answer questions or concerns regarding the publicity campaign for the Turners, as well as the status of outstanding projects for other clients. While the contract with the Turners was of the utmost importance, Caleb wanted to ensure their other clients were equally satisfied with the agency's output. Public relations, marketing and advertising never end, he thought wryly, looking at the assembled faces before him.

Judging from their expressions, he could tell they were not relishing another meeting. Peter knocked ash from his cigarette, while Minerva continued smoking incessantly. Roy and Jeff sat silently, drawing heavily on their cigarettes, while Wilbur kept his cigarette between his lips, eyeing Caleb with a mixture of annoyance and resentment.

Caleb reached for his own cigarettes, and upon lighting one and drawing deeply exhaled a trail of smoke, feeling the release of the frustration he always felt in dealing with his associates. If the deep-seated issues obviously inherent were made clear and resolved, perhaps assignments would go more smoothly, he thought. They sat in silence, until Caleb, knocking ash from his cigarette in an ashtray already filled with butts, addressed them positively.

"I am pleased with the work everyone has done so far on the campaign for the Turners. Roy, your copy is excellent. Minerva, your work with the radio stations is an asset. Peter, the local markets will be interested, especially as you've dealt with them previously. Wilbur, your task is a bit problematic but I commend you for contacting theaters and inquiring if an actor would want to promote the new beverage. We will offer to pay the actor for his services, of course."

"It may be an actress, Caleb," Wilbur interrupted. "I believe I told you Miss Penelope Barker was interested, so I may have already secured someone. I will let you know, of course." His tone hinged on arrogance and impatience, but Caleb ignored it and proceeded.

"Tomorrow ads will appear in the local newspapers on the new beverage. The Sunday editions will include a full page ad in the *Times Union* and *Albany Evening Journal*." He paused. "Are there any more questions on the campaign for the Turners? What about previous contracts?"

Roy mentioned he was completing work for the Cherry Spring project and Minerva discussed two contracts she had recently finished. The others also spoke on projects that were concluded. Caleb noticed Jeff remained aloof and distant, smoking furiously and not commenting. It seemed as though he were observing everyone as an outsider, not wishing to contribute to the meeting. Of course, he was the agency's accountant and did not often directly involve himself with publicity campaigns. Most likely Caleb could tell he would prefer not to become involved with the Turner's campaign as well.

Caleb got their attention. "The purpose of this meeting is to discuss the taste testing event scheduled for the fifteenth of August. It will be held at the Empire State Beverage Company in North Albany at four o'clock. I have already put in a call to the mayor's office. Mayor Hackett was out of town but will return my call by next week. I did speak with his secretary who asked for the brochure to be sent to city hall."

"I imagine the Turners are preoccupied with Mr. Lennon's murder," Roy commented. "The police haven't found who killed him. With the murder unsolved, it must be hanging over their heads pretty badly."

Caleb agreed. "Naturally, they are still distraught over what happened to Mr. Lennon. But they want to persevere with their business. They hired us and we cannot let them down. We need to meet and even exceed their expectations and have it profitable."

"I don't believe Mr. Lennon's murder would affect the event," Jeff remarked dryly.

Caleb directed his attention to him. "Jeff, you and I, along with the Stevensons, Polly and Gabrielle, will have the bottles ready, including setting up the glasses. I spoke to a caterer and they will supply appetizers for the event."

Jeff continued smoking. "Sounds like you've done your homework."

Caleb smiled wryly. "I know you are not on speaking terms with your wife, but she will be present, so you will need to maintain a sense of decorum while there."

Jeff smoked and nodded. "I admit, Caleb, I'm not really fond of this taste testing event. And not just because I will have contact with my soon to be ex-wife. Do you really think it will be well attended? Besides, what makes the Turners think people will want to buy the beverage?"

"With the publicity and the sampling, there should be people willing to buy it," Roy said, rather in Caleb's defense. "Especially since it's as close to champagne as possible."

"After we conclude the publicity," Minerva interjected, "there'll be plenty of advertising where it'll be well known by the public."

"And with prohibition as our lifestyle," Peter said grimly, "the public just may want to try this imitation champagne beverage. As Roy mentioned, it is the closest to real champagne that the public could purchase legally. At first, I admit I was not too keen on the event, but perhaps it will be worthwhile. The fancy name *Champagne Twist* is rather enticing itself."

Minerva agreed. "It may be bigger than what the Turners anticipated, especially since we're promoting it as a New York nightclub style beverage."

Caleb continued. "It will be open to the general public, which will appear in the newspaper advertisements and on the radio promotions. We will be there to assist, answer questions, hand out the brochure and encourage attendees to purchase it. I anticipate it won't go longer than two hours, so plan to be there till at least six o'clock."

"So we are sort of ambassadors of the product," Roy commented.

Caleb grinned. "Indeed, Roy. The employees of the facility will also be on hand, but we are the promotion experts. We need to emphasize the importance of the beverage, the impact it will have on consumers, and how great it tastes."

He decided he had held their attention long enough. The meeting concluded on a positive note, cigarettes were extinguished, smiles were apparent and appropriate comments were made as the office cleared out, leaving Caleb alone to organize not only his desk but also his thoughts.

He leaned back on his swivel chair and looked toward the window at the hot sunshine. The only problem he foresaw was Jeff and his wife. With the Stevensons present, he certainly would not create a scene in front of them over his wife. Suddenly he felt relieved as though he was assured the taste testing would go off without a hitch.

Had he known what would transpire and the tumultuous days to follow, he might have wished he had never heard of the Empire State Beverage Company.

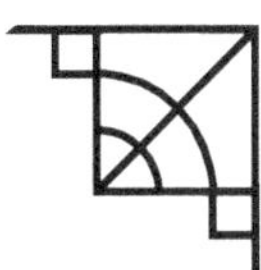

CHAPTER SIX

On Sunday, thunderstorms overspread the city, which alleviated residents of the oppressive heat, but it continued muggy. Many people resorted to using fans, which brought some relief, although most had been accustomed to it without much complaining.

On Monday morning, at the Empire State Beverage Company, Mrs. Prudence Nichols, having just arrived at the facility, turned on the floor fan as her office was like an oven. Opening the windows was futile, as it would only bring in the warm air. She dressed coolly in a white sleeveless dress. Not usually affected by the heat, she was feeling extremely irritable, although she did not think it was because of the weather.

She sat behind her desk, ready to begin the workday and unfolded the morning paper. She flipped through the local news section and looked with interest at the large full-page advertisement for the *Champagne Twist* beverage. She smiled, reading it several times, admiring the fine verbiage, the eye-catching picture of a large bottle with the words *Champagne Twist* boldly emblazoned on it and the projection that it will appeal to everyone's taste.

They certainly know what they are doing, she thought irritably. She should be satisfied, of course, but her mind flew to her husband, knowing he was somehow involved and would ultimately be present for the taste testing.

She sat back in her chair, wondering if her parents had seen the advertisement. As they were voracious newspaper readers, she was surprised they had yet to speak to her about it. But then her father was not one to display much excitement and her mother was rather reserved, although she could be emotional at times.

Prudence arrived to work after her parents, as her father was adamant about arriving before eight thirty. If it bothered her father that she walked in just before her shift began, he never mentioned it. She looked at the advertisement again, nodded her head in satisfaction and was about to type a letter when her parents appeared in the doorway. They asked if she had seen the advertisement in the morning paper.

"I think it's wonderful," she told them, not caring if they approved of it or not.

But here Prudence had a surprise indeed. She looked at her mother, smiling contentedly and could not remember when she had seen her so serene. She appeared young and carefree as though she had not a care in the world. A simple blue dress, a lovely string of pearls and just enough makeup highlighted her pretty face. Her father, too, looked robust and even jovial, smiling heartily. His suit was impeccable as always, his hair neat and his wrinkled faced did not appear as drawn as usual, as though he had come into a sizeable fortune. She waited for them to speak, not wanting to disturb their obvious serenity.

"We think it's wonderful, too, dear," Mrs. Turner exclaimed happily. "Your father and I are incredibly pleased. We called Mr. Dean to tell him how satisfied we are with the advertising."

"A first rate job," Mr. Turner added.

"The date for the taste testing is the fifteenth of August," Prudence said, as though to verify the date. "What do you want me to do for the event?"

Mr. Turner explained how Mr. Dean had divided certain tasks to associates of the Empire Advertising Agency, so there was extraordinarily little for them to do. He suggested she give tours of the facility, offer samples to attendees and answer questions on the product.

"Mr. Dean told me the contract is already in the mail, along with a draft of the promotional brochure," Mr. Turner continued.

"Mr. Dean mentioned radio stations will be promoting it, too," Mrs. Turner said. "They have found a local actress willing to do a radio commercial."

"And there will be sample testing at local markets," Mr. Turner added. "We have already received orders from retailers wishing to stock *Champagne Twist.* Two weeks from now, it will be released. I've already communicated that to Mr. Dean."

"I noticed the date for the taste testing is in the advertisement," Prudence commented. "Do you want it open to the public, Father?"

Mr. Turner nodded. "If we have the public attend, as well as more important people, it would be a rousing success. After all, we want consumers to buy it."

"How thrilling for people to come here,' Mrs. Turner added. "It'll be a rousing success!"

"I'm sure it will," Prudence said, not quite emulating her mother's enthusiasm.

"Think of the profits, Prudence," her father told her. "We're in business to make money and the *Champagne Twist* could be our biggest seller yet."

It all came down to dollars, Prudence thought looking at her money-hungry father and wondering what else he had in life to preoccupy his thoughts. Even her mother was becoming greedier and perceptive when it came to the almighty dollar. Had they forgotten about Uncle Walter's murder? It was as though it had slipped their minds, or at least they did not mention it.

"Have you heard from the police about Uncle Walter?" Prudence asked them boldly. At the moment, she felt as though they were strangers, almost zombie like, alien to anything else except the rolling out of the new beverage and the anticipated profits from it.

"No, dear, we have not heard from the police," her mother commented. She sighed as though her daughter mentioning her brother's premature death suddenly eliminated her good mood. "They will be in touch once they have more concrete information, of course."

"Of course," Prudence repeated awkwardly.

They mentioned work to be completed and left her office. Prudence felt as though anything else mentioned would destroy their optimism. She understood their zealousness but a tragedy had befallen them. They acted as though it was better not discussed. On the other hand, perhaps the new beverage was a diversion. She nodded, seeing it in that perspective.

She inserted a fresh sheet of paper into her typewriter. The morning wore on and more letters, memos, contracts and agreements were typed. Prudence was busy answering the telephone, directing inquiries and taking orders for beverages. But as the day progressed, she felt incredibly anxious and distressed for the remainder of the afternoon.

CHAMPAGNE TWIST – THE NEW CHAMPAGNE BEVERAGE FOR 1923 AND BEYOND!

THE EMPIRE STATE BEVERAGE COMPANY PROUDLY ANNOUNCES THE LATEST IN TANTALIZING REFRESHMENT! GUARANTEED TO QUENCH YOUR THIRST!

CHAMPAGNE TWIST – A NEW YORK STYLE NIGHTCLUB NON-ALCOHOLIC BEVERAGE! AVAILABLE IN CHAMPAGNE STYLE BOTTLES BEGINNING AUGUST FIRST. YOU WILL NOT WANT TO MISS THIS REFRESHING DRINK!

REQUEST YOUR LOCAL STORE CARRY IT AND YOU WILL ENJOY IT! PERFECT FOR ANY OCCASION – BY ITSELF OR AS A MIXER!

CHAMPGANE TWIST – MANUFACTURED BY THE EMPIRE STATE BEVERAGE COMPANY OF ALBANY, NEW YORK – ALWAYS PROVIDING THE VERY BEST IN LIQUID REFRESHMENTS.

THE PUBLIC IS CORDIALLY INVITED TO A TASTE TESTING AT THE EMPIRE STATE BEVERAGE COMPANY ON THE FIFTEENTH OF AUGUST AT FOUR P.M. AT ITS FACILITY IN NORTH ALBANY.

Caleb looked at the newspaper advertisement as it appeared in the *Times Union, Albany Evening Journal* and *Schenectady Gazette.* He smiled in satisfaction. He placed an excellent ad, convincing and to the point. To the left of the advertisement was a picture of a champagne style bottle, certainly enticing and alluring. It had appeared in yesterday's Sunday editions and will continue to run for the next two weeks. Mrs. Stevenson, who stood in the doorway, broke his reverie.

"Caleb, dear, these advertisements are just the best," she exclaimed. "I spoke with Mrs. Turner and she told me they are so pleased. A fine job. You are to be commended."

"Thank you, Mrs. Stevenson," Caleb said humbly. He mentioned time was of the essence and that they had much work to accomplish before the first of August and then the taste testing for the fifteenth. Celeste asked him if he had heard anything more about the other endeavors he proposed.

"Earlier this morning, Peter mentioned local markets are planning to stock the beverage and a few are interested in a sample testing. Minerva said radio stations would have commercials starting tomorrow. And Wilbur told me Miss Penelope Barker plans to promote it as well on the radio, perhaps including a jingle of sorts. According to Wilbur, Miss Barker has connections at WGY and a few other local radio stations, so that definitely is an asset."

"Wonderful," Celeste beamed. "We should have a decent turnout at the taste testing. I am sure most people have never seen how beverages are made. It should be quite an exciting event."

Celeste then began talking about the taste testing event, extolling the advantages of such a publicity stunt. She commented enthusiastically that she and Mr. Stevenson anticipated it would be a great accomplishment, worth the agency's time and effort. It could lead to future contracts, she added wisely.

Roy entered at that moment with what he hoped was the final copy of the brochure. Looking drawn and rather haggard as though the writing and research had drained him of any fortitude, he nodded at Celeste and handed the document to Caleb.

"I gave it to Peter for his opinion," he mentioned. "Of course, you have the final approval." He spoke as though he could not improve on it and had reached the maximum in his effort.

Caleb glanced at it, nodding in approval. "It really is a fine copy, Roy. I see no difference from the previous version. You've worked hard and you certainly have a way with words."

"A lot of time and effort, Caleb," Roy said, and then regretting it as he realized Celeste was still in the room. He mentioned Peter and Polly had compiled a list of former clients from the files in the spare room. Celeste mentioned she needed to assist Gabrielle and Polly while Roy returned to his office, reiterating to start the mass mailing.

Caleb was elated his associates were unwavering in their work. Despite his previous misgivings, he looked forward to the taste testing on the fifteenth. He was confident it would be an unequivocal success.

The next week and a half was of extreme deadlines and expectations. The mass mailing was carried out in time for *Champagne Twist* availability on the first of August. Many markets in Albany and Schenectady sold out of the beverage in less than a day and placed orders for another supply. Local actress Miss Penelope Barker was soon heard on radio stations, promoting the product with a jingle accompanied by a lively piano player. Other commercials just as valuable were heard on WGY and soon flooded the airwaves. Advertisements in local newspapers continued, further promoting the beverage, proclaiming it the new drink for 1923. Indeed, *Champagne Twist* had arrived to much anticipation and high praise.

Caleb was busy at his desk, fielding questions from former clients and state executives from city hall on the telephone about the new beverage. He also responded to numerous written inquiries about the product. He encouraged them to attend the taste testing event on the eighteenth. He also received calls from local newspapers and radio stations, interested in covering the event.

Minerva stopped by his office, telling him she also had received numerous calls from radio stations she had previously contacted. She commented the publicity was certainly paying off and it looked like *Champagne Twist* was headed for much acclaim. Wilbur saw Caleb in the hallway later, mentioning Miss Barker's radio commercial seemed destined to draw consumers to try the new beverage. He believed the commercial was enticing enough for people to buy it.

Caleb was surprised Minerva and Wilbur would display such enthusiasm in a campaign in which he spearheaded. He knew there was much antagonism with them, but he was pleasantly astounded by their professionalism and attitude toward *Champagne Twist* and even the taste testing event. Minerva told him she looked forward to it.

It was almost noontime, but Caleb did not feel much like eating lunch. He leaned back on his swivel chair, putting his long legs up on the desk. He looked up and saw Jeff in the doorway. He was puffing on a cigarette rather angrily. Caleb could tell he was not in a good humor and waited to hear what he would tell him.

"You look comfortable," he remarked. "But then as chief account executive, I suppose you can put your feet up and nobody would mind. Certainly, the Stevensons would not say anything. Fortunately, I have my own office too, so I do the same."

"Something bothering you, Jeff?" Caleb asked, now very annoyed. It took a great deal to anger the usually placid Caleb but every so often someone like Jeff got him rattled. It was obvious Jeff was not keen on the taste testing event, which Caleb assumed he planned to discuss with him again. He had made known his displeasure for over two weeks. Sure enough, he reiterated his feelings to Caleb as he stood in front of the desk.

"I'd prefer not to attend," he told him, rather harshly. "I don't relish seeing my wife or my in-laws. Besides, do you really need me there? I'd think there would be enough people to assist."

"Mr. Stevenson wants us to get involved. I know you don't like seeing your wife, but if you help with the samples and answering questions, it should go smoothly."

Jeff smirked. "Easy for you to say, Caleb. You've never had a wife. You don't know the first thing about marriage and the misery it causes. My wife is a true flapper, not the kind of girl you would want to bring home to your parents. I made a mistake marrying her. I get so angry on how she ruined my life, I could kill her with my bare hands."

Caleb looked at Jeff Nichols not quite knowing what to tell him. He did not feel he needed to console his irritabilities; after all, his concern was for the promotion and the taste testing event. He thought of speaking to Mr. Stevenson again about Jeff's involvement, but he knew he would insist he attend. From the last meeting, Jeff was already on Mr. Stevenson's bad side; he did not think he needed to increase it any further.

"We're set for the taste testing," he told Jeff. "The radio commercials are currently on the air, the mass mailing has produced an enormous response, the local markets including *Albany Public Market* and *A & P* will stock the beverage."

"So, what's the point?" Jeff aside irritably.

"The point is you have relatively little to do. If you noticed, I assigned you to help with the samples and answering questions. You'll be with Mrs. Stevenson, Gabrielle and Polly."

Jeff continued smoking. "Where will you be, Caleb?" His tone hinged on sarcasm.

"I'll be with the Turners, answering questions, encouraging people to buy it. Roy will answer questions and fill cups. It'll be an event to remember."

"What about Peter, Minerva and Wilbur? I find it hard to believe they would even want to get involved. They're going to answer questions about the product too?"

By now, Caleb had had enough. He swung his long legs onto the floor, crushed his cigarette almost angrily to the point where the ashtray wobbled on his desk, causing ash to topple over. He looked Jeff directly in the eyes and his voice was firm and to the point.

"Jeff, I am the organizer of this particular publicity campaign, under Mr. Stevenson's guidance and supervision. If you really have an issue with something, I suggest you speak to him. Otherwise, you will be there and will assist like the rest of us whether you like it or not. I am not here to hold anyone's hand, to sooth your insecurities or to pacify your feelings toward your wife or your in-laws. Do you understand me?"

Jeff continued smoking, his anger pent up, leaving him momentarily speechless. He blew smoke angrily and found his voice. He spoke hoarsely at first then regained his composure, the words coming quickly and forcefully.

"We'll see, Caleb," he told him, sneeringly. "We'll find out what happens at this ludicrous taste testing you're so hyped up about. I should have my head examined for giving your name to my father-in-law as a contact. Indeed, this ridiculous event will be one to remember, mark my word. And my wife will find out I mean business, too." He extinguished his cigarette in the ashtray, contributing to the spilled ashes on the desk, then turned abruptly and left the office.

Caleb looked after him, wondering what he meant by his insidious remarks. Nevertheless, he was confident the taste testing would proceed smoothly. Unless there were other unforeseen circumstances, hovering in the background he was unaware of.

As word spread rather quickly at Empire Advertising, Mr. Stevenson called a meeting in his office. Celeste sat next to her husband at the long table while the rest shuffled in, somewhat leery, not knowing what to expect. Their countenance seemed to imply not another meeting. Even Caleb was surprised at the announcement of a meeting as he assumed everything was progressing smoothly. Usually unexpected gatherings like this meant something of an unpleasant nature had occurred. Sitting next to Minerva, he wondered what Mr. Stevenson planned to tell them. He looked at him while he arranged a few papers. He recognized the publicity campaign for the Turners, so whatever he wanted to tell them obviously pertained to it.

"This meeting will be brief," Mr. Stevenson said. He cleared his throat and looked at the assembled faces before him. "I am pleased that the progress for the Turners has gone according to schedule. The commercials, radio promotions and advertisements in the newspapers have been magnificent."

Caleb cast a quick glance at his associates wondering, as they did, where this was headed. Mr. Stevenson certainly did not call them together to reap praise upon them. He did not think he was humble enough to do so. He listened as Mr. Stevenson continued addressing them.

"However, I am aware of Jeff's discontentment regarding the taste testing event." Mr. Stevenson looked at Jeff. "I understand your feelings about the event and your reluctance to attend as you do not wish to see your wife." He paused. "My wife and I have decided that you will participate along with the others. You will work alongside Polly, Gabrielle, Caleb and Mrs. Stevenson and I in setting up the bottles, pouring samples into cups and answering questions about the new drink."

"I would have preferred if you had spoken to me privately, Mr.

Stevenson," Jeff said.

Mr. Stevenson coughed. "I spoke with Mr. Turner earlier and he told me his daughter plans to give tours of the facility while helping the caterers set up the appetizers." He paused again, focusing his attention on Jeff. "There will be little chance of you speaking with your wife. Mrs. Stevenson and I have valued your accounting skills and your input on previous publicity campaigns. I entrust you will be an asset for the taste testing."

Rather taken aback, Jeff thanked him, continued smoking and lapsed into silence.

"I do not want anything to ruin this event for the Turners," Mr. Stevenson continued. "They have entrusted us with ensuring the best promotion possible for their latest beverage. It is my intention to make sure that occurs on the fifteenth."

Everyone seemed to concur with him on his agreeable attitude. Even Jeff nodded and appreciated what he told him. Caleb thought he felt relieved that his involvement with his wife would be minimal. With that obstacle cleared up, Caleb did not foresee any difficulties ahead. He looked as Celeste cleared her throat and addressed them.

"I invited Sister Catherine from St Peter's Hospital and my church to attend. She graciously accepted my invitation. The taste testing will be a success, I am sure of it."

A low murmur of agreement was heard and Celeste thanked them, and then turned it back to her husband for final thoughts. He reiterated his pleasure at the outstanding contributions they made on the latest publicity campaign. He hoped to continue business with the Turners, as this success might lead to additional publicity campaigns for them in the future. He was about to dismiss them when Gabrielle spoke, rather anxiously, causing everyone to look at her.

"Mr. Stevenson, I heard on the radio there are gangsters arriving in Albany. I read about it in the paper, too. They are coming from Chicago."

"I didn't think we had gangsters here in Albany," Polly commented.

"Has Mayor Hackett acknowledged the rise in crime?" Gabrielle asked, rather alarmed. "President Harding should do something to curb gangster activity! Al Capone is notorious. The train comes directly here from Chicago, you know."

"Don't worry yourself, dear," Celeste told her soothingly.

Mr. Stevenson smiled wryly. "Mayor Hackett has addressed the increase in crime in our city. As far as Al Capone is concerned, he is a long way from Albany."

"President Harding should address it," Gabrielle repeated, worriedly.

Mr. Stevenson shook his head. "I did not vote for Mr. Harding and from what I have seen in the last two years, I do not feel he has done anything substantial for this country. Most likely gangster activity and the increase in crime are not high on his agenda. Honestly, some politicians could drop dead tomorrow for all I care."

A few mumbles of astonishment were heard. Caleb knew Mr. Stevenson lamented the loss of Mr. James M. Cox, a Democrat whom he voted for in the 1920 election. He also remembered Mrs. Stevenson happily voting for the first time that year, for Mr. Cox, of course, as she also was a Democrat. They contributed to fundraisers for the Democrats, where they must have met Mayor Hackett, so he concluded Mr. Stevenson would hardly pay much attention to a Republican president. Certainly, he was entitled to his opinion. Caleb knew the Stevenson's political allegiance was much stronger than that of his own generation.

Mr. Stevenson asked for questions and to Caleb's relief there were none. He exchanged brief conversation with Peter, Roy and Polly on returning to his office. Settling at his desk, he emerged himself in his work. Mr. Stevenson's offhanded remark would come back to haunt him in a rather unsettling way.

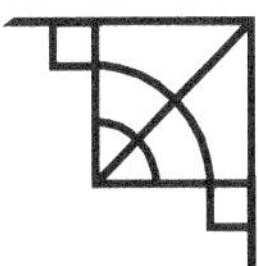

CHAPTER SEVEN

Caleb reached over and shut off the alarm clock on his bedside table. Another workday, he thought, lazily stretching in bed before rising. He lay still for another five minutes before he threw back the sheet and padded over to the bathroom. He filled the sink with water and proceeded to shave.

After work yesterday, he and Gabrielle stopped for iced tea at a coffee shop on State Street. Gabrielle continued her fears of gangsters in Albany, and then mentioned she was going to visit an aunt in Schenectady. Caleb was rather glad, as he did not feel like continuing with idle small talk and even pacifying her fears, which he understood but did not wholly agreed with

He then proceeded to his apartment, feeling buoyant as he enjoyed his evenings to himself. After a dinner of a cheese sandwich and milk, he dressed in gym shorts and a tee shirt and headed over to Washington Park. An elaborate jungle gym, one for children and the other for adults, was popular with city residents and Caleb performed a variety of strength building exercises. He counted over a hundred pull extensions on the monkey bars. He continued exercising until the sun was slowing descending and he realized it was getting late. He was rather fatigued by the time he returned to his apartment and did not even bother to listen to the radio. He thought he heard his telephone ring but he was too exhausted and headed straight to bed, falling asleep quickly.

After shaving, a warm shower replenished him. He let the soothing water douse his face and hair. He stayed in the shower longer than usual, until somewhere in his mind he heard an insistent banging. He realized someone was at his door. Now, whoever it was, thumped rather loudly and persistently.

Reluctantly, Caleb turned off the shower, and stepping out, grabbed a towel and wrapped it around his waist. The pounding continued. He entered the living room and made his way over to the door. Without even asking who it could be at this early hour, he opened it to see Roy and Gabrielle before him, fully dressed for work and clearly alarmed by their expressions.

Caleb thought they appeared drawn and even haggard, as though they had not slept. Gabrielle wore a flowered dress; little make up, her bobbed reddish hair fixed neatly. Roy too was dressed appropriately, his tie and vest neat and his hair combed evenly. However, Caleb knew something was apparently troubling them, which must be the cause of this unexpected visit. He moved aside for them to enter.

"Caleb, we have got to talk to you," Roy said.

Caleb was taken aback, but clearly annoyed. "Roy, I've just gotten out of the shower and I am dripping wet."

He felt foolish standing before them in just a towel around his waist, dripping water onto the living room floor. He brushed a hand over his still wet face, wondering what this early morning visit was about.

"Caleb, this is urgent," Gabrielle told him as she and Roy sat together on the sofa. "We wouldn't have come over if we didn't feel it was important."

"Have you been listening to the radio?" Roy asked him. Before he could answer, he spoke again, hurriedly and excitedly. "I called Gabrielle as soon as I heard late last night and then I called you but you didn't answer your telephone. It's in this morning's paper but not the evening edition from last night. I think the *Knickerbocker Press* published an extra edition after midnight but I haven't seen it. I called you just a little while ago too…"

"Roy, as you can see, I have just gotten out of the shower," Caleb repeated. "What are you talking about?" He reached for his cigarettes on an end table. After lighting it, he went to his bedroom and returned within a few minutes, wearing a shirt, tie, vest and dress slacks.

"Did you listen to the radio late last night and this morning?" Roy repeated.

Caleb sat in an armchair across from them and shook his head. "No, I was in the park exercising last night and went straight to bed afterward. I got up a little while ago. What is this about? Is there something I should know?"

Normally Caleb was patient with his associates but to arrive at his apartment unannounced, so early in the morning before work, clearly meant something was wrong. Roy cleared his throat and casting a quick look at Gabrielle took a deep breath.

"Caleb, it's the president," he said gravely.

"President Harding?" Caleb asked, surprised. "What about him?"

"He's dead," Roy continued bluntly. "He died last night in California and Vice President Calvin Coolidge is now the president."

Caleb looked at him then at Gabrielle. At first, he did not quite take in the words he just heard. He then got up and almost leaped for the radio against the far wall. Upon turning the dial to WGY, he stood transfixed in disbelief as he listened to the somber report.

...It is with great sadness we report the death of President Warren G. Harding. President Harding died last night in California while on his Voyage of Understanding speaking tour of the western United States. His successor, Vice President Calvin Coolidge, visiting family in Vermont, was unaware of the circumstances. He learned of the president's death by a messenger only a short time ago. He was sworn in as the new president just recently at the home in Vermont...

Caleb returned to the armchair, too shocked to speak. He looked at Roy and Gabrielle who, although already aware of the president's death, were clearly traumatized.

"Looks like Mr. Stevenson's prophecy came true," Roy remarked dryly. He paused. "What are we going to do? Should we report to work as usual?"

"It's good you came to see me," Caleb said, finding his strength. "We have to proceed with caution with Mr. Stevenson's today. I imagine he's either not caring or has a guilty conscious."

Roy agreed. "We thought you would want to know before arriving to work this morning."

Caleb puffed on his cigarette, thoughtfully. "I didn't think of listening to the news when I got back from the park. I went straight to bed. I don't even remember the telephone ringing."

"I hope this doesn't put a damper on the taste testing event," Gabrielle said, worriedly.

"How could it?" Roy said, turning to her. "We have already made the plans."

Caleb agreed. "The date for the taste testing has been finalized and the mass mailing was completed. Advertisements and commercials promoted it as the fifteenth of August." He paused. "Unless the Turners decide to postpone or cancel it. Ultimately, it is up to them."

"We'll be in mourning soon for the president," Gabrielle said sadly. "At least, I know I will be in mourning. I liked him, despite what Mr. Stevenson feels."

"You're entitled to your opinion," Roy said. "I liked him and Mrs. Harding, too."

Unspoken confusion and sadness prevailed. Roy started to speak but Caleb held up a hand for quiet as further news of the president's sudden demise came over the airwaves.

> *...President Harding's body will be placed in the East Room and will be viewed by Mrs. Harding, family and close friends. It is expected the coffin will be taken to the capitol for the funeral. At the conclusion of the service, the public will be admitted to the rotunda to view the coffin. While details are not concrete at this time, it is assumed the president's body will leave Washington for Marion, Ohio where the burial will take place. We will continue to update this headline as soon as more information is available. Repeating our top story, President Warren G. Harding has died suddenly while on a speaking tour in California...*

"It's almost eight o'clock," Roy said, still stunned at the news. He looked from Gabrielle to Caleb. "We should get going." He spoke nervously. "I imagine Mrs. Stevenson will be upset."

The death of the president was certainly the most grievous event that could occur to the American people, and in their young lives, Caleb, Roy and Gabrielle found it undoubtedly difficult and extremely unsettling. Caleb's mind flew to the Great War, the flu pandemic and oddly, the murder of Mr. Walter Lennon, still unsolved. However, he never imagined the death of a president would occur in his lifetime. He continued listening to the repeated announcement of the death of President Warren Harding. Roy and Gabrielle mentioned they would see him at the office. Caleb remained in the armchair and heard their footsteps down the stairs.

Too much happening, he thought, his mind overwhelmed. Bad news usually came in triplicate, often more. Uneasily he thought the death of President Harding was a forbearance of a future unfortunate incident, only occurring much closer to home.

PRESIDENT WARREN HARDING IS DEAD AND THE NATION MOURNS

San Francisco, August. 3, 1923 – President Warren Harding has died, mourned by an entire nation and world. Death came suddenly and with no warning, at 7:30 last night. The American people, shocked beyond words, mourn for him and his wife. After a private funeral service at the hotel, the president's body will be placed aboard a special train, which will leave San Francisco for Washington. He will be laid to rest in Ohio. The president's body will lie in state in Washington.

Mr. Stevenson looked at the front page of the *Times Union*. He scanned the details on the death of President Harding, and then put it aside. He picked up the late edition of the *Knickerbocker Press*, which came out after midnight. He knew it was urgent for the *Knickerbocker Press* to publish a second evening paper. He read the glaring headline.

PRESIDENT HARDING HAS DIED

San Francisco, August 3, 1923 – Our nation's leader, President Warren G. Harding has died. His death was marked by a shudder and collapse as Mrs. Harding read to him by his bedside.

Turning the page, he read the additional headline about its effect on Albany.

ALBANY MOURNS AS NEWS SPREADS IN CITY

Albany, August 3, 1923 – Stunned and grief stricken at the dramatic suddenness of the death of President Harding, Albany and the Capital District received the news from midnight on with profound mourning and shock.

He shook his head in deep contemplation and sadness, overcome by the devastating news. He continued sitting at his desk, brooding, clenching and unclenching his fists. He glanced at his watch and noticed it was almost nine thirty. He thought he heard most of his associates but was unsure if Caleb had yet to arrive. He picked up his phone and spoke to Gabrielle, telling her he wanted to speak to everyone in his office. In five minutes, all of the Empire Advertising employees, including Caleb, occupied the long table in his office suite. Mr. Stevenson acknowledged them and got right to the point.

"We are in a sad time for this country. Our president has passed away unexpectedly. While I did not endorse Mr. Harding, it is still quite a shock to me and my wife as well."

Celeste looked at her husband, and then murmured she planned to start a novena for the late president. She encouraged everyone to attend the requiem Mass at four o'clock today at the cathedral. She nodded to her husband to continue.

"I called Mr. Turner to inquire if he and his wife want to proceed with the taste testing for the fifteenth. I spoke with Mrs. Nichols, who told me her parents were too upset over the president's passing. She planned to ask her father to return my call as soon as possible."

Caleb looked at Jeff and thought he wanted to add something but then changed his mind. He did not realize how just hearing his wife's name was enough to cause him distress, even anger. He realized Mr. Stevenson stopped speaking and asked if there were any questions or concerns.

"There will be funeral services soon," Polly said, visibly shaken by the news. "How terribly sad, to lose our president while in office."

"Let's hope Mr. Coolidge is effective," Minerva added, clearly shocked.

"Effective or not he is our new president," Mr. Stevenson said firmly. "We can only hope Mr. Coolidge will lead the country in the right path."

"I still can't believe the president is dead," Gabrielle said, tearfully.

Caleb noticed her shedding a few tears and even Polly and Minerva choked up, holding their emotions inside. Roy, Wilbur and Peter were dumbstruck, as though the president's death rendered them speechless. Even Jeff was stoic, reserved, and just as stunned as the rest.

"We must pray for him," Celeste said solemnly. "God will have mercy on his soul. Mrs. Harding is also in my prayers. President Harding is in a much better place now."

Mr. Stevenson coughed. "I believe it is best we carry on with courage and plan on the taste testing for the fifteenth, unless we hear otherwise. The country will be in mourning for some time and we must respect and honor our fallen leader."

"Didn't you tell us you could care less if some politicians died tomorrow or something like that?" Roy asked inappropriately. "It was during the meeting on Wednesday. We all heard you say it."

Caleb wanted to kick him from under the table. Of all the audacity to bring that comment in the open, as though Mr. Stevenson did not recall saying it. Surprisingly, Caleb found his reaction almost melancholy. Mr. Stevenson smiled briefly and addressed Roy.

"Yes, I did make that comment at the time. I was rather taken by my emotions and certainly did not mean what I said. The grieving has only just begun. Our thoughts must also be with Mrs. Harding and her family. I will continue to support the Democrats, but I would never wish any calamity to a candidate from the opposing party."

A low murmur of assent went around the table. Caleb found Mr. Stevenson's demeanor genuine; shock, surprise, anticipatory and mournful.

"Soon the fifteenth will be here and we will have the utmost pleasure of assisting the Turners with the taste testing event. I assume many businesses will be closed Monday, although I plan to open as usual. If you feel the need to take Monday off or a few days to recuperate from this tragic loss, then please let Mrs. Stevenson or I know of your intention. I will close the agency early on the day of the funeral." He requested them to listen to the radio for further details, wished them all well, rather stonily and dismissed them.

They left his office in silence. A somber mood prevailed for the rest of the day at Empire Advertising. An early evening edition of the *Knickerbocker Press* was delivered to the office with the stark headline *PRESIDENT HARDING DEAD*. Gabrielle acquired several copies, bringing one to Caleb in his office. He read how the somberness extended throughout Albany, leaving people grief-stricken and practically crying in the streets. Soon places of worship were overflowing with mourners and as Mr. Stevenson predicted, the grieving period had only just begun. Caleb felt terribly uneasy. He could not believe President Harding had died. It was very unsettling.

But he knew it was not just President Harding's untimely demise that was troubling him. An uncomfortable dread overcame him again. He stared out the window, noticed dark clouds had rolled in, fitting for a city in bereavement, he thought.

He looked at several documents needing his attention and found momentary comfort in absorbing himself in his work.

It was close to four thirty. Mrs. Stevenson, along with Gabrielle, Peter and Roy attended Mass at the Cathedral of the Immaculate Conception in honor of President Harding. Minerva and Wilbur already left, saying they were too unnerved to continue working. Jeff worked through the afternoon but told Mr. Stevenson he needed a rest from the devastating news and left about three o'clock. It was strangely quiet at the agency for the remainder of the day.

Caleb finished several new contracts for established clients, documenting the possible publicity choices and putting his notes in folders for Gabrielle to type tomorrow. He rubbed his tired eyes and stretched his arms above his head, feeling disheveled from the devastating news of the president's death and the anticipation of the taste testing event for the Turners.

He picked up the *Knickerbocker Press* that Gabrielle handed him earlier. The entire front page was devoted to President Harding. He read how the White House confirmed the president's funeral services for

Friday, the tenth of August and that President Coolidge had declared a national period of mourning. Indeed, further articles stated schools holding summer classes would be closed, as well as state and federal offices. Postal services were suspended on Monday, the sixth and most restaurants, markets and shops were closed or had limited hours. Like the rest of the country, Albany was in mourning for its fallen president.

Articles further stated how Mrs. Harding was being attended by family members and was too grief stricken to speak to reporters. Radio stations planned to broadcast the funeral service as it took place in Washington. Caleb noticed the president would be buried in Ohio, his home state.

He tossed the paper onto a nearby chair and walked moodily over to the windows. As expected, it had started to rain, lightly at first, then steadier and heavier with rumbles of thunder. Caleb frowned, realizing he did not have an umbrella and only hoped the rain would soon diminish.

He saw by the wall clock that it was almost five o'clock and as he had completed work for the day, decided to leave. He straightened out his desk, turned off the banker's lamp, placed folders neatly in his top drawer. He grabbed his cap from the top desk drawer and straightened it comfortably on his head. He loosened his tie and unbuttoned a few buttons of his vest. It was still quite warm and the humidity had increased due to the rain.

He turned the ceiling light off and was about to enter the main office, when he noticed the spare room door closed. This was unusual, as Mr. Stevenson always wanted it open, since it was used quite frequently. Glancing further along the hallway, he saw lights coming from Mr. Stevenson's office, so he must not have left. Caleb did not think he would have left yet, despite the overwhelming grief felt during this national period of mourning.

Curiosity getting the best of him, he walked to the spare room, opened the door and saw someone standing in front of a file cabinet, ruffling through folders. Caleb realized it was Polly, thumbing through folders haphazardly, almost in a frenzy. She opened a folder, placed it on top of the file cabinet and started to review its contents. Caleb asked what she was looking for. Polly turned, surprised at seeing him. She returned the file to the drawer and fumbled for words.

"Oh, hello Caleb," she exclaimed, forcing a smile. "Mrs. Stevenson wanted me to review a few files. Thought I'd get a head start."

"What files were you looking at?" Caleb asked, taking a step into the spare room. Polly had a way to minimize her guilt, batting her eyelashes, speaking softly. Caleb knew Peter enjoyed her company. He was surprised she was not with him now. He also knew she infuriated both Mr. and Mrs. Stevenson from time to time, so he was on guard when addressing her.

Polly hesitated. "Just a few on a hotel and some others." She made light of it, as though it was nothing important. Caleb, however, was not put off by her attitude.

"That can wait for tomorrow," he told her. "It is five o'clock. Everything is closed out of respect for the president."

Polly closed the drawer of the file cabinet firmly. "Well, Caleb, you are not my boss and if I decide to stay late, I do not need your approval." She then changed her tone. "Besides, work is best for me right now. I am too overcome by the death of the president. I don't want to hear any more about it on the radio now. It's just too disturbing."

Caleb nodded, although looking at her carefully he did not think she seemed overcome by the president's death or anything else for that matter.

She gathered her purse she left on a table, walked past him through the main office and out the doors. Caleb looked after her, then turned his attention to the file cabinet.

Opening the drawer, he thumbed through the folders and recognized the file for the hotel Polly mentioned. He opened it and saw several documents from Mr. Stevenson dated 1915, a publicity campaign for the Clinton Street Hotel and many more papers, too many to look through. The hotel owner, Mr. Cyrus Newcomb must have been someone prominent in Albany. He considered speaking to Mr. Stevenson but decided to wait. With the taste testing fast approaching and the death of the president, his boss did not need any more anxiety. He returned the folder and closed the drawer thoughtfully. He tried to dispel the notion that something clandestine was happening. Maybe she really was completing an assignment for Mrs. Stevenson.

He glanced back at the file cabinet, and then walked through the main office, toward the entrance doors. He wondered if the name Newcomb was a possible harbinger of danger or possibly something much worse.

CHAPTER EIGHT

PRESIDENT HARDING LAID TO REST TODAY

WASHINGTON, D.C. August 10, 1923. – President Warren G. Harding, twenty ninth president of the United States, will be laid to rest today in Marion, Ohio. The funeral train will leave Washington and is expected to arrive sometime this afternoon. President Calvin Coolidge has declared today, the tenth of August another day of national mourning in honor of the late president.

It was a week later and another hot, sultry morning in Albany. Caleb sat in the living room of his apartment, reading the front page of the *Times Union*. He was in his boxers, sleep still in his eyes. He had gotten up a little while ago. He felt the stubble on his face and realized he needed to shave. A cup of coffee was on the end table next to him. He continued reading about the death of President Harding when his telephone rang. It was still early, not quite nine o'clock and the telephone ringing took him by surprise.

He did not feel like chatting with anyone. He had not even turned on his radio. Reluctantly he put the newspaper aside and reached over for the candlestick phone on the end table nearest the window. To his surprise, he heard Roy at the other end.

"Caleb, I'm glad I caught you! I have something to tell you."

His voice was excitable. What else could go wrong, Caleb thought, reaching for his cigarettes and lighting one while holding onto the handset of the phone. He expected to hear Roy utter something drastic but to his surprise, it was completely unexpected.

"Mrs. Stevenson spoke with the Turners about Mayor Hackett attending the taste testing."

"I know that, Roy. I contacted city hall myself. They told me he wasn't available to attend."

"Well, Mrs. Stevenson told me the Turners called him personally and he told them he would be delighted to attend! Isn't that the bee's knees for sure!"

Caleb was impressed. "That's terrific, Roy. Are the Stevensons at the office today?"

"Yes, the Stevensons are in the office today. I was there about a half hour ago and Mrs. Stevenson told me I didn't have to stay, that they planned to close earlier than usual."

Caleb agreed. "How are the Stevensons? When I left yesterday, Mr. Stevenson was still in his office." He didn't mention he found Polly snooping around the spare room file cabinets.

"Mrs. Stevenson sounded upset over the president's death. But she was elated over the mayor attending the taste testing! She told me Mr. Stevenson is rather withdrawn and not speaking to anyone now. The president's death has hit him rather hard."

Caleb was surprised. It showed Mr. Stevenson's vulnerability and his compassion, rather than the usual total consumption of his business. He listened as Roy continued talking.

"I'm going to St Mary's for a memorial service, and then I'll be back to my apartment to listen to the funeral. Too bad the funeral train doesn't pass through Albany so we could see it."

He broke off and Caleb could tell he was having a difficult time, like nearly everyone. Caleb assured the younger man of his excellent work at the agency, and that President Coolidge would be a fine successor. After a few more encouraging words, the conversation ended.

He got up and turned on the radio to WGY. The broadcast detailed the funeral service, the casket lying in state in the rotunda of the capitol in Washington. The service was to start this morning; afterward, a period of the public filing past the casket was permitted before it was placed on the funeral train for the trip to Marion, Ohio.

Like Roy, Caleb also wished it were passing through Albany. He considered traveling to Washington, but the commentator mentioned the line to enter the rotunda was long. Most likely many people would not have the chance to see it, despite waiting for hours. He read in the paper how several local residents took the train to Washington to see the casket. He preferred to listen to the broadcast from the comfort of his apartment. He felt a deep sadness descend upon him, as the nation continued to mourn.

He sipped his coffee and extinguished his cigarette. His mind was still reeling from the unexpected death of the president, the murder of Mr. Lennon, Polly snooping around the files in the spare office and this Newcomb character, whoever he was. He tried to shake the notion that a dark cloud loomed over them, as though a nightmare of malice was at the forefront of his thoughts. It was the president's untimely demise, of course.

He entered the bathroom, removed his boxers and turned on the shower. As the cool water flowed over him, hitting his face refreshingly, he was sure, he told himself repeatedly, that with the strenuous publicity, the taste testing event would be a resounding success.

The death of a president curtailed many events in Albany but it did not stop the workings of the law. Police activity proceeded as usual, with arrests, warrants issued and patrols in the various neighborhoods. City life continued, unabated.

At Albany Police Headquarters, Inspector Harris and Lieutenant Taylor reviewed notes on the Lennon murder. It had been almost two months and no breaks in the case. Interviews were conducted, patrols enforced, previous criminals questioned, speakeasies staked out but no new leads were apparent. Police were scrambling to find answers but none was forthcoming.

"Life goes on even after the death of a president," Inspector Harris commented dryly. "You'd think we wouldn't be so busy. Last night two arrests were made. One for drunk driving and the other for domestic assault."

Lieutenant Taylor nodded. "With the Lennon murder, robbery was not a motive. His wallet was still on him. The killer would have taken it. His watch also spoke of good quality." He sighed irritably. "This case is going nowhere."

At that moment, the door opened and Officer Davis entered. He sat next to the Inspector and opened a folder, which he placed on the table. He spoke about a few other cases he had been handling then brought their attention to something he felt was noteworthy.

"Do you remember the case of Mr. Newcomb? His name came up regarding businesses that no longer exist. His hotel burned down some years ago. I looked to see what we had on him and I found this report."

Lieutenant Taylor looked bewildered. "So what does that have to do with the murder of Mr. Walter Lennon?"

Officer Davis looked at the notes in the folder. "That's what I came to tell you. According to this document, Mr. Lennon knew Mr. Newcomb. The police report stated Mr. Lennon was present when a dispute erupted at Mr. Newcomb's hotel involving gangsters."

Inspector Harris read the report. "It states here that Mr. Lennon was at the Clinton Street Hotel when a fight broke out, but it doesn't mention he was involved. Mr. Lennon and Mr. Newcomb were acquainted. The hotel was used by gangsters." He paused. "Maybe there's more about Mr. Newcomb we don't know."

"Perhaps Mr. Lennon, too," Lieutenant Taylor added.

"I found out Mr. Newcomb died in 1920 in Corning, New York, just three years ago," Office Davis continued. "He must've moved there after he retired from the hotel. His wife died young and they had no children and no relatives."

Lieutenant Taylor had taken the police report from 1915 and read it carefully. "The police at the time questioned Mr. Newcomb extensively. Apparently, gangsters caused a ruckus and the police made several arrests at the hotel. I don't remember this case and this police officer who drafted this report has since retired."

"I still don't see a connection," Inspector Harris said.

"Maybe there isn't one," Officer Davis said, as he closed the folder. "But I find it strange that Mr. Lennon's name came up in this police report. I thought he was such a distinguished man. He also had no criminal record."

Inspector Harris grimaced. "Most people have a past, Officer. Gangsters were arrested that evening at the hotel. Certainly, Mr. Lennon would not have involved himself in a simple hotel robbery that led to a fight."

"As the owner of the hotel, I'd say Mr. Newcomb was well-off." Officer Davis reflected. "I remember the Clinton Street Hotel as a child. It was a popular place. My father told me hoodlums and gangsters would hang out there, so it became rather seedy as the years went on."

"Like other places around Albany," the Inspector remarked dryly.

Officer Davis left the file on Mr. Newcomb with them, mentioning he planned to work only half day, as he wanted to listen to the president's funeral on the radio this afternoon with his wife. He then got up and left the office. Inspector Harris lit a cigarette and looked at his colleague.

"Well, what do you think?"

Lieutenant Taylor had been studying the Newcomb file succinctly. He looked up and met the Inspector's eyes. "I think there is something here we are not seeing. There may be a connection between these men, but what it is exactly, I cannot say."

"Newcomb had moved away and died in 1920. He could not have murdered Mr. Lennon."

The Lieutenant nodded. "Let's see what else we can find out about Mr. Newcomb. Surely there's more information we can uncover."

Life slowly returned to its everyday routine beginning the week of August the thirteenth. Schools reopened and most businesses resumed operations, although many people still harbored a deep loss for the sudden demise of the president. In a radio speech, President Coolidge addressed the nation, ensuring a smooth transition, adhering to the policies and procedures of the late president. Although skepticism abounded, most people were forthright in their outlook for the new leader, anticipating the best for the new administration.

On Wednesday, the fifteenth, Caleb arrived early to the Empire State Beverage Company. He had worked half a day at the agency and told Mr. Stevenson he would head over to the beverage company. He spoke to Mr.

Turner earlier in the day, confirming arrangements had been finalized. He reminded his associates to arrive at the beverage company no later than three o'clock, to give them enough time to arrange the event.

Caleb felt satisfied as he sat on the trolley, heading to North Albany. He brought a folder containing copies of the brochures Roy had written. He had listened to President Coolidge's speech on WGY last evening and was confident the new leader would lead the country in the right direction. He also felt confident about himself, his work and even life in general. He had not felt this way in quite some time. He knew the taste testing would be phenomenally successful and he was full of pleasurable anticipation.

It was a humid, sultry day in Albany and light rain was falling, with thunderstorms possible later, but the bleak weather did not dampen his good mood. He disembarked from the trolley and walked the short distance to the Empire State Beverage Company. The receptionist welcomed him and mentioned the Turners were in a room in the back, close to the manufacturing area.

Caleb followed her directions and made his way to a large meeting room, amply furnished with chairs and several tables. Two big windows looked out onto the street. In the center was a long table, decorated with a lace tablecloth and several bottle of *Champagne Twist*. Stylish plastic glasses were placed neatly next to the bottles and further along the table was a rather large spread of different types of cheese, crackers and dainty appetizers. The caterers were finishing the arrangements; the light fare was meticulously adorned, encouraging participants to enjoy the food. Plates and napkins along with utensils were strategically placed, enabling people to form a line and easily choose what they wished from the delicious offerings.

Caleb looked at the display in satisfaction then noticed Mrs. Turner speaking to one of the caterers. She saw him and came over to him.

"Hello, Mr. Dean, so nice to see you. This is going to be an enormous success!"

Caleb smiled. "I think so too, Mrs. Turner. I thought I would arrive early to get everything in order." He held the folder containing the brochures. "In here are copies of the brochures."

"Wonderful," Mrs. Turner said beamingly. "Prudence will give tours of the facility. My husband thought once we had a sizeable crowd, he would introduce the drink from the podium over there and propose a toast."

Caleb saw a smaller table, with more bottles of *Champagne Twist* and next to it a podium, and a microphone, set on a platform, resembling a small stage. He then asked Mrs. Turner what he could do to help.

"You can assist in setting up chairs. And the copies of the brochure can be placed on the table here, so when people come in, they'll see it right away."

Caleb opened the folder, placing it flat on the table and the brochures on top. He stood back and looked at the display. It was truly a remarkable demonstration, he thought agreeably. He imagined *Champagne Twist* would interest many people, certainly enticing enough with the exhibit they would encounter upon entering.

He then assisted a few of the beverage workers in setting up more chairs and opening up more bottles of *Champagne Twist*. He noticed Mr. Turner had just entered, carrying a phonograph player and several 78 records. He set it on the table near the podium and carefully chose a Rudy Vallee record. After starting up the phonograph player, he placed the needle on the 78 record and the soothing voice of the jazz great filled the room. Mr. Turner noticed Caleb and smiled.

"Caleb, I'm so glad to see you," he said jovially, resorting to his first name. "This will be a remarkable day for the Empire State Beverage Company! And we have you to thank for its enormous success."

Caleb was extremely impressed. "Thank you, Mr. Turner. I'm glad the mayor will be here."

"My wife called Mayor Hackett personally and invited him," he told Caleb.

He then rushed off to assist a caterer with a tray of appetizers, while Mrs. Turner chatted amicably with Caleb. At that moment, the Stevensons arrived, along with Roy, Polly, Peter, Minerva, Wilbur and Gabrielle. Greetings to Mrs. Turner and much polite conversation ensued; hand shaking, and words of encouragement adored the group. Mrs. Turner thanked them on such a magnificent publicity campaign. She nodded to her husband, who was busy with the caterers, and how they appreciated their hard work and commitment to excellence. Polly commented on how terrific it all looked. Roy told them he wanted to try *Champagne Twist* after writing about it, which provoked much laughter among them. Peter, Minerva and Gabrielle complimented the fine display and wished them good luck with the new beverage.

Caleb was listening to Gabrielle and Peter as they were conversing with him, but his mind flew to Jeff, who had yet to arrive. He listened and smiled as Peter discussed the magnificent display, the great job they achieved in the publicity and how he anticipated good outcomes. He noticed Roy walking around the room, seemingly approving of everything. He made his way over to the Turners, complimenting their presentation and wished them success with *Champagne Twist*.

Members of the press soon arrived, including reporters from the *Times Union*, *Knickerbocker Press* and *Albany Evening Journal*. Radio station WGY had a reporter present and he spoke at length with the Turners on the newly created champagne imitation drink.

Gabrielle joined Caleb and stood next to him, listening to Peter and Polly talking almost endlessly about trivial matters. Caleb politely listened but wondered when Jeff would arrive. He looked up and saw

Prudence Nichols enter from a rear door, which led to the manufacturing area. She greeted her parents and the Stevensons amicably, then joined Caleb and introduced herself to Peter, Polly, Gabrielle and Roy.

"Quite a set-up, Mrs. Nichols," Roy said. "I'm really impressed."

"Thank you and please call me Prudence," she insisted, as though the name Nichols was too much for her to bear. "I am pleased to meet all of you and welcome to the Empire State Beverage Company. I plan to give tours of the facility. If you would help with the sampling and answering questions, that would be most appreciated."

It was close to five o'clock and Caleb noticed the room was filling up rather quickly. Many distinguished guests, most likely friends of the Turners entered. They hugged Mrs. Turner and spoke to her quite light-heartedly. He noticed friends of the Stevensons as well as many people he did not know. There was much laughter amid the conversations and the atmosphere was festive. Sister Catherine, Mrs. Stevenson's friend, entered at that moment, looking rather severe but wearing a smile, joining Mrs. Stevenson. Obviously, they were well acquainted as they spoke quite intimately. He was surprised Mrs. Stevenson would invite a nun to attend a champagne imitation taste testing but he kept his opinion to himself.

Prudence led more tours to visitors and Caleb helped Peter, Polly and Roy open the champagne style bottles and pour samples into the stylish plastic glasses. They handed them to guests who sipped at the delicious beverage, complimenting on its refreshing taste, rather fruity, and expressing a desire to purchase it. The music of Bessie Smith and Count Basie filled the room and several people began to dance, creating a scene of much merriment and frivolity.

Caleb marveled at how well the event turned out. He looked at Gabrielle and noticed she too was enjoying herself. He then saw Jeff enter the room.

Caleb noticed as Jeff looked around, a cigarette dangling from his mouth. He wondered if Jeff had been drinking, he appeared not too steady on his feet. He saw him sway slightly, entering the crowded room, obviously perturbed, wondering why he was there in the first place and what he was supposed to do. He then saw Caleb and went over to him.

"Well, here I am," he said, rather loudly. "What do you want me to do?"

Caleb tried to hide his anger. Of all times for Jeff to drink, it had to be this afternoon. He smelled the liquor on his breath. He knew he dreaded coming here and further dreaded seeing his wife. Before he could answer him, the Turners called him over and Jeff soon joined his in-laws, who, Caleb noticed, seemed glad to see him.

More visitors entered the large conference room, sampling *Champagne Twist*, enjoying the light fare and chatting with Caleb, Gabrielle, Peter, Polly, Wilbur, Minerva and Roy. They answered questions on the beverage and many people bought several bottles and a few bought entire cases. Caleb was glad the event was going smoothly. Even Jeff was remarkably calm. He was chatting up a few young women, who he seemed rather smitten with, regardless if his in-laws noticed his behavior.

Peter and Polly started to dance to a Count Basie record, while Roy handed out copies of the brochure, answering questions almost nonstop. Mrs. Stevenson introduced Caleb to Sister Catherine, who told him she was also a nurse at St. Peter's Hospital, adding she was happy to meet him as she had heard so much about him from Mrs. Stevenson.

Caleb blushed slightly. She was tall and rather matronly, close to seventy or even older. She looked as though she had weathered many storms in her life. "Thank you, Sister Catherine. The Stevensons are fine people and I enjoy my work."

Sister Catherine smiled, her rather wrinkled face creased into fine lines. "I'd say a West Point graduate is a fine character in any business. May God bless you, Caleb."

She then walked around the room with Mrs. Stevenson, while Mr. Stevenson was talking incessantly with Mr. Turner. Mrs. Turner was chatting with Gabrielle, while answering questions about the new drink to visitors eager to learn more.

More guests arrived, smiling and rather wet as they had nearly escaped a heavy downpour. Caleb looked toward the windows and noticed it was raining quite heavily now. Minerva approached and asked what more she could do to help.

"You can answer questions about the beverage," he told her "And perhaps just mingle with the crowd and encourage people to buy it."

Wilbur smiled. "The music is great, too." He notice Peter and Polly dancing. "Minerva and I may kick up our heels a bit!"

Caleb wondered if Wilbur had been drinking, too. He noticed how they started to chat with a few people and then joined others in what became the dance area, whirling around, obviously showing off, much to Caleb's chagrin.

He saw Mr. and Mrs. Turner head to the entrance and welcome Mayor William Hackett. It was obvious they were well acquainted. They chatted for some time, rather seriously, it seemed to Caleb. They then entered the room, introducing him to the Stevensons and the group embarked on a lively and rather animated conversation. Mrs. Turner handed him a sample of the beverage and he seemed to like it and asked for another.

Caleb looked up and noticed Prudence had returned from giving a tour. Her back was toward the room so she did not notice her husband was also there. She approached Caleb and thanked him profusely for his great work and his enthusiasm. Caleb smiled and hoped she would not turn around and notice Jeff, but he knew that was unavoidable.

Jeff found his way over to the table bearing the samples. Boldly he picked up a glass and finished it off, smacking his lips in satisfaction. He returned the cigarette to his lips, smoking furiously. He stood next to the table bearing the samples, seemingly deep in thought.

Caleb stood frozen at the head of the table. People were all around him, tasting the beverage, asking him questions about it. He worried Jeff was intoxicated and would cause a scene. He noticed Prudence approached the table, totally unaware her husband was also there. She chatted with visitors, then turned, and almost bumped directly into Jeff. Caleb held his breath as he witnessed an uncomfortable silence, while around them people continued talking, laughing, dancing and enjoying the festivities. Some turned and noticed as Jeff and Prudence interacted, but mostly they ignored them, too wrapped up in enjoying the event.

"Well, what brings you here, Jeff?" Prudence said mockingly. "I'm surprised you would lower yourself." She paused. "Drinking as usual? I can smell the liquor on you."

"Why don't you mind your business," he snapped. "If you have anything to say you can say it to my lawyer. I'll see you in court."

"Don't be so sure about that," she remarked. "You won't gain a foothold in this company."

"Don't threaten me, Prudence. I'll get even with you if it's the last thing I do."

Prudence laughed. "And what will you do? You don't stand a chance at this company. I'll make sure of it, Jeff dear. I've already talked to my father."

Suddenly, he grabbed her arm, roughly, causing her some discomfort. "You'd really do that, wouldn't you? Well, we'll see about that." In that moment he hated this woman he had called his wife and the cold bright look in her eyes told him the feeling was mutual. He roughly shook her off and went to another part of the room. Prudence, feeling rebuffed, sought out her parents as though for support.

Caleb was glad not many people witnessed the scene between Jeff and Prudence. The dancing continued and the light fare was practically finished. He noticed Polly, Peter, Minerva and Wilbur still dancing, laughing and obviously enjoying themselves, chatting with visitors on what he hoped was the beverage and its advantages as a champagne imitation. He noticed Roy chatting with a few young women. He wondered if he wanted their telephone numbers or if he talked to them about the beverage. More people entered and tried the samples of *Champagne Twist*. Questions asked and answered, more music, dancing and tours of the facility continued for another half hour. Mr. Turner then approached the podium, cleared his throat and requested everyone's attention. He looked at the assembled faces before him and started to speak into the microphone.

"Good afternoon, ladies and gentlemen. Thank you all very much for coming here today to the Empire State Beverage Company in North Albany. It is a privilege and an honor to have you all here today. I am especially proud to welcome Mayor Hackett and members of the press to this festive occasion." He paused and looked again at the people before him from his perch at the podium. "We are in deep mourning for the late President Harding. We have lost a great leader and a fine man. We extend our support to President Coolidge, our new leader." He paused. "It is our intention to continue our service in providing the best in liquid refreshments. At the Empire State Beverage Company, we take great pride in our products. It is fitting that during this time of prohibition we have created…"

Mr. Turner stopped abruptly, looking straight into the crowd, his face aghast, his eyes glassy. He put his hand to his chest and coughed slightly, as though gasping for breath. At first, Caleb did not know what was happening. He looked around and noticed Mrs. Turner hurriedly approached her husband, speaking to him softly, helping him to regain his composure.

Later Caleb was to realize Mr. Turner's behavior had a significant impact on the events that were to follow. He watched, transfixed, as Mr. Turner clung to the sides of the podium, as though trying to steady himself. Caleb noticed he appeared stunned and might even faint.

At that moment, a loud clap of thunder was heard, shaking the entire building. The lights dimmed and then completely went out, not only in the conference room but in the entire facility. The room was dark, and more thunder and pelting rain stormed the building. People moved about, bumping into each other, while a door closed somewhere and someone tried to open the window. People stood around in the darkness, wondering what had happened, asking when the lights would return. Exclamations of apologies, dismay, fear, horror and stepping on shoes were soon heard. Caleb tried to see in the dark but only heard Mrs. Turner gasp and ask someone to grab a flashlight. The darkness was unsettling and unexpected. Someone fumbled to the door and returned after what seemed an eternity with candles, matches and two flashlights.

Soon candles were lit and the flashlights were turned on, enabling shocked faces to return to some semblance of normalcy. Caleb noticed Polly, Roy and Gabrielle were indeed shocked, even frightened, while Peter, Wilbur and Jeff looked more annoyed. He did not see Minerva anywhere. Mr. Stevenson remained stoic, trying to make light of the situation while Mrs. Stevenson crossed herself, standing next to Sister Catherine and seemed deep in prayer. Mrs. Turner stood by her husband at the podium, providing support to him, as he apparently still appeared rather weak.

The lights came back on shortly and everyone seemed to heave a sigh of relief. After a moment, Mr. Turner cleared his throat and spoke into the microphone, addressing the group and chiding the unexpected delay.

"We cannot control the weather," he joked, causing several people to laugh. He appeared more collected and in control. "But we can enjoy our new beverage, *Champagne Twist*. So please, I ask you to raise your glasses to the new *Champagne Twist*!"

Caleb toasted Gabrielle and those near him, while everyone raised their glasses in an amicable toast to the new delicious fruity beverage. He noticed the raised glasses and felt extremely satisfied. He heard overwhelmingly positive comments on the drink.

It was not until a moment later, when something was obviously terribly wrong. Near the podium, where her parents stood, Prudence leaned over, holding onto her stomach, evidently in excruciating pain. She gasped for breath, convulsing and collapsing heavily onto the floor.

Mr. and Mrs. Turner quickly went to their daughter, while Mrs. Stevenson pleaded for someone to call an ambulance. They tried to rouse Prudence, not knowing what had happened. Caleb heard someone mention an ambulance was on the way. Sister Catherine came forward and reminded them she was a nurse.

Immediately she took control of the situation, feeling for Prudence's pulse, listening for a heartbeat and touching the pallor of her skin. She looked up into the startled faces of the Turners and then at Caleb. She glanced at Mrs. Stevenson, standing next to her husband, terribly upset. An eerie silence pervaded and the festive atmosphere of a few minutes ago soon became lugubrious.

"We need an ambulance at once," Sister Catherine spoke seriously, straightening up from the floor. "Her pulse is weak, her breathing shallow." She paused. "Her heartbeat is irregular." She looked into the shocked faces of Mr. and Mrs. Turner.

An ambulance soon arrived and Prudence was rushed to St. Peter's Hospital. In less than a half hour, she was pronounced dead in the emergency room.

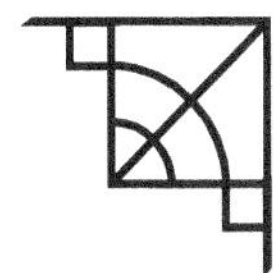

CHAPTER NINE

Excerpt from the *Times Union,* Albany, New York, Thursday, August 16, 1923.

SECOND MYSTERIOUS DEATH OF BEVERAGE COMPANY EMPLOYEE

ALBANY – A celebration to promote a new beverage produced by the Empire State Beverage Company turned tragic late yesterday afternoon. Mrs. Prudence Nichols, the daughter of the owners, Mr. and Mrs. Nathan Turner and the executive secretary to her father, collapsed after drinking Champagne Twist, the sparkling new imitation champagne product. While attempts to resuscitate Mrs. Nichols proved futile, an ambulance brought her to St. Peter's Hospital where she was pronounced dead. Mr. Walter Lennon, the brother-in-law of Mr. Turner who also was employed at the facility, was murdered in June while at the Port of Albany. Police are investigating and ask anyone who may have information on the death of Mrs. Nichols and the murder of Mr. Lennon to please contact them at police headquarters.

A somber atmosphere prevailed at Empire Advertising on Thursday. Caleb noticed Mr. Stevenson's usual firm countenance was sullener and more morose. Mrs. Stevenson remained in the main office, tending to small matters to keep her mind from thinking of the tragedy she witnessed yesterday.

Both Caleb and Mr. Stevenson called Mr. Turner and expressed their most sincere condolences on the death of his daughter. Understandably, he and Mrs. Turner were still quite shaken and while Mrs. Turner remained at home, Mr. Turner mentioned he planned to spend part of the day at the facility. He needed to keep the business going and it would alleviate the grief permeating his mind.

Caleb was about to begin work on a new contract when his telephone rang. It was Gabrielle, informing him that Mr. Stevenson had called a meeting. He figured he would address everyone this morning. He made his way down the hallway to Mr. Stevenson's executive office. He entered and sat next to Mrs. Stevenson, who apparently had been crying. She dabbed at her eyes with a handkerchief and tried to maintain a semblance of stability.

Polly, Peter, Roy, Jeff and Gabrielle entered, almost like robots, and sat quietly at the conference table. Minerva and Wilbur came in afterward, Minerva ready with a pad and pen. Caleb turned his attention to hear what Mr. Stevenson wanted to tell them.

"I am too saddened to begin to speak," he began. "But I feel I must address my staff about the incident from yesterday. Mrs. Nichols died in front of us, a most dreadful occurrence. I called the Turners at their home last night. I spoke with Mrs. Turner who was too distraught to say much. They spent most of the night at the hospital. I spoke with Mr. Turner a little ago. The doctors recommended an autopsy to clarify the circumstances surrounding her death."

"An autopsy?" Roy asked incredulously. "We all drank *Champagne Twist* and none of us became ill. Maybe there was something wrong with the bottle from which it was poured."

"Possibly," Mr. Stevenson said. "We don't know from which bottle Mrs. Nichols had a sample tasting." He sighed in great frustration. "I was not happy with the notice in this morning's paper. The article makes it appear as though the actual drink caused her death."

"Which may mean it may lose its projected market value," Minerva added.

Mr. Stevenson agreed. "Can anyone remember what happened at the taste testing before Mr. Turner asked everyone to raise their glasses in a toast to the new drink?"

Nobody spoke at first, until Polly cleared her throat. She looked around and then at Mr. Stevenson, meeting his eyes coolly, as though she enjoyed speaking before the others.

"There was a thunderstorm and the lights went out. It was rather frightening, actually. Then the lights came back on and we were about to raise our glasses in a toast, as Mr. Turner told us. It was quite pleasant up until that time."

Gabrielle agreed. "I didn't see which glass Mrs. Nichols drank from, but as Roy said, it couldn't have contained anything toxic. We would have all gotten sick if that was the case."

"Everyone seemed to enjoy the drink," Wilbur observed.

"I didn't hear anyone complain," Minerva put in.

"I thought I heard a door close after the lights went out," Peter said.

"That may have been when Mrs. Turner asked someone to get candles and flashlights," Roy told him. "I heard it, too."

"No, I thought it was before," Peter insisted.

"My father-in-law seemed flustered by something as he addressed the visitors," Jeff said. His face held incredulity. "I thought he was either losing his balance or overcome by the brilliance of the event." He hesitated. "If anyone is wondering about my feelings on the death of my wife, I am shocked as much as the rest. My wife and I did not get along but I certainly did not wish any calamity on her." His tone held conviction and no one at the table seemed to doubt his honesty.

"I remember he leaned on the podium for support," Gabrielle reflected.

"Maybe something upset him," Polly suggested.

"He did look rather faint," Wilbur commented.

"What about the funeral arrangements, Jeff?" Roy asked Jeff.

Jeff had a cigarette in his hand, which he extinguished in a nearby ashtray. "Well, I don't really know, Roy. I will speak to my in-laws. In the meantime, I don't really wish to discuss my wife's death. So if you will all excuse me." He got up and walked rather briskly out of the room.

Caleb could tell Jeff was stunned by the sudden demise of his wife. He heard them quarrel and didn't he threaten her, too? Of course, that was just talk. Unless he really meant it and his demeanor with them at the moment was a façade. He blinked as he realized Mr. Stevenson continued to address them.

"We have suffered much loss recently. First, the murder of Mr. Lennon, also from the beverage company. Then the unexpected death of President Harding, which the nation is still grieving. Now the premature death of Mrs. Nichols. I suggest we continue with our operations but refrain from answering questions from the press. I expect telephone calls and even visitors from local newspapers, but we will not comment in respect to the Turners."

"I read in the paper the police plan to investigate," Roy said. "Does that mean they think it may be murder? Another murder involving the beverage company?"

Caleb looked at him from across the table. Roy had an irritating habit of asking the most sensitive questions, without thinking of the ramifications or the effects on anyone else.

"I do not know what to think at this point," Mr. Stevenson said, frowning in consternation. "But I do not believe it was murder, simply an unfortunate accident. I will let you know more details as I keep in touch with the Turners. My wife and I plan to visit them later today."

Minerva agreed. "Wilbur and I will send our condolences to the Turners, too."

"If the drink was poisonous, maybe she drank from the wrong glass," Polly suggested.

Everyone looked at her, expecting an explanation. Caleb wondered how she came up with such a ludicrous idea. Even Mrs. Stevenson shook her head vehemently. He looked around the table and thought everyone seemed to accept his viewpoint. Anyone could have drunk from the bottle that contained the sour drink. It was bad luck for Mrs. Nichols. Caleb felt uncomfortable as ideas began forming in his mind, which he pushed aside as he continued listening to Mr. Stevenson.

"The Turners and my wife and I believe this was an unfortunate accident. I do not want you to contemplate anything else." He reiterated his dissention in talking to the press.

"We don't know which bottle," Roy added. "After we filled the glasses, the bottles were thrown out. The facility workers removed the garbage."

"I suppose there's no way to have the bottles tested," Minerva said.

"Mr. Turner told me they had taste-tested previously," Caleb added. "He didn't find anything wrong and nobody became sick."

"Mr. Turner mentioned he would halt production until further notice," Mr. Stevenson continued. "He would have current bottles tested. I think it was bad luck Mrs. Nichols sampled the drink from a bottle that was not fermented, sour and most likely full of residue."

"But to cause death like that?" Roy questioned. "A sick stomach, maybe, but death?"

Mr. Stevenson added nothing more, too disturbed over yesterday's event. He dismissed them and only Mrs. Stevenson stayed to assist her husband. The rest filed out, still reeling from the shock. They headed for their own sanctuary, feeling the need for solitude and contemplation.

Caleb found consolation at his desk. His thoughts raced to the taste testing event and to what occurred before the sudden demise of Mrs. Prudence Nichols.

Jeff leaned back in the swivel chair in his office, lit a cigarette and threw the match rather carelessly into the ashtray on his desk. The others had retreated to their own workspace but as he had so often felt, he was grateful he had his own office. He was not in the mood for even seeing his associates much less talking with them. He had had enough of Minerva, Wilbur, Roy, Peter and Polly for now. Even Caleb got on his nerves. His mind flew to yesterday and the taste testing.

After the ambulance had taken Prudence to St. Peter's Hospital, he declined to go. His in-laws went in the ambulance, but he claimed he could not bear the thought of seeing his wife in the emergency room. He had to come up with some excuse. Admittedly, he was surprised at what happened, but at the same time, he felt relieved.

No divorce proceedings, he thought smugly, drawing heavily on his cigarette. He would not have to bother facing the judge for the divorce to be finalized. He had to live down his tempestuous attitude toward Prudence who he had grown to despise with every passing day.

Few people knew her, he thought bitterly. Even her parents were blind to her. Their marriage was a mistake and he deeply regretted it. He blamed himself for not seeing what she was like from the beginning. He would never get involved with a flapper again. He shook his head disgustedly, wondering what he ever saw in her to begin with

With Prudence out of the way, he just might land a percentage in the Empire State Beverage Company. He maintained civil and friendly relations with his mother-in-law and father-in-law, both of whom thought well of him, to his advantage. So too bad for you, Prudence dear, we'll see who gets the last laugh. And court won't be an issue, he thought gladly. One less expense to worry about. Of course, he had a good lawyer, so he was never worried to begin with.

On the other hand, what exactly did happen yesterday that caused Prudence to peel over and become so violently sick? As far as he knew, she did not have an ulcer or any stomach issues. For her to become so ill after drinking *Champagne Twist* was quite a surprise. Unless, as the Stevensons mentioned and the others acknowledged, there was a bottle that was unfermented, sour, bitter and maybe contaminated, causing gastric upset, leading to death. But then Jeff thought it rather unlikely, as Prudence had always been healthy as a horse.

He leaned forward and put his arms on the desk, rather angrily and yet feeling liberated. He had wanted free of his wife, but this was not the course he wanted to take. He assumed the police would investigate and he assumed suspicion would center on him, especially with the brief argument that ensued before the toast.

He admitted he was not impressed with *Champagne Twist*. While he drank it out of politeness, as the Turners were standing nearby, and Caleb and the Stevensons, too, he did not particularly enjoy it. He thought it had a rather gritty aftertaste. He was surprised the Turners did not realize it. Caleb mentioned they performed taste testing before the product was marketed.

Well, that is hardly my concern now, Jeff thought. He finished his cigarette and lit another. He noticed he almost depleted his pack of Lucky Strikes. He knew Caleb smoked Lucky Strikes too but he would not ask him for any. His relationship with Caleb was cordial but he was not about to approach him or anyone else in this godforsaken advertising agency. His thoughts returned to his wife, violently ill on the floor at the taste testing event, everyone aghast, shocked, horrified and not knowing what to do. He shook his head scornfully.

Let's see how money-hungry Stevenson handles this one, he thought contemptuously.

It was later in the afternoon. Peter was busy at his desk, answering inquiries from prospective businesses and established clients. He looked up and saw Polly stroll in, carrying her steno pad and pen. She looked at him quizzically.

"Hard at work, Peter? I'd have thought you would be finishing up by now."

Peter put down his cigarette. "There is still work to be completed. Our commitment to the Turners met an unexpected end."

Polly sat in the chair before him. "I know what you mean. It may hurt sales of *Champagne Twist* as well as their other products." She paused. "I still can picture what happened. Poor girl, she gasped for breath and that was the end."

Peter looked up from a letter he was writing. "I'd appreciate if you don't mention it any further. For now, we can only hope our agency is not hurt by the negative publicity in the newspapers and on the radio."

"They've been playing it up, haven't they? I read another article in the *Albany Evening Press* just now. Of course, the papers are always eager for a scandalous story." She looked around the office. "Where's Roy? Did he leave already?"

Peter crushed his cigarette. "No, he's in with Mr. Stevenson. Apparently, the police will be here to speak to us and most of the people who were at the taste testing."

Polly suppressed a laugh. "There had to be close to a hundred people there! They cannot possibly speak to everyone. Including Mayor Hackett? That's rather insulting."

Peter agreed. "They may limit it to people who were near Mrs. Nichols at the time. Certainly, we were all standing near that table when Mr. Turner proposed a toast."

"You mean, when we raised those silly plastic glasses to murder?"

He looked at her coldly. "You better watch what you say, Polly. It hasn't been determined what happened."

"Jeff could have had enough of his wife. Didn't we hear them argue just before the toast?"

"Are you implying he poisoned his wife?"

Polly shrugged. "They didn't get along and were in the process of divorcing. Maybe he found an easier way to eliminate her from his life."

"I doubt he'd resort to something like that." He handed her a folder containing letters that needed typing. He explained the nature of the proposals and to whom they were being sent. "We may increase our business in Amsterdam, Gloversville, even Utica. We cannot afford to lose potential contacts, even if they're not in the immediate area."

Polly eyed him carefully, choosing her words. "Peter, you seem rather aloof, just not yourself. We haven't gone out in some time. You've always enjoyed the social scene in Albany. The gang at the speakeasy on Lodge Street misses you."

Peter looked up, surprised. "How do you know that? Were you there by yourself?"

Polly nodded. "Of course, dear. I'm not the sit at home type. I love the nightlife, you know." Peter didn't say anything and was busy with folders on his desk. Polly opened the folder he handed her and glanced through the letters. She commented they looked like worthwhile recommendations. She asked Peter if he had seen Gabrielle.

"She's working with Caleb in his office, taking dictation and sorting through the mail."

Polly mentioned Mrs. Stevenson had been so preoccupied since the event yesterday that she hardly spoke to her. Not that she missed chatting with the boss's wife, she added.

"Keep a civil tongue with Mrs. Stevenson, Polly," Peter suggested. "We have to watch our backs now, you know. What happened yesterday may affect our jobs here. We could all be fired for the outcome yesterday."

"How could we be fired? Manufacturers at the beverage company would be fired, not us."

Peter shook his head. "We promoted them, remember. We got the ball rolling."

"This is terrible, Peter. Suppose someone else got sick and died from that drink?"

"That's what Mr. Stevenson is worried about. But I don't think it will happen. It was the one bottle, which unfortunately was thrown in the garbage."

"None of us became sick," Polly added. She hesitated. "Do you remember Mr. Newcomb?"

"Who?" Peter asked. He moved the candlestick phone to a corner of the desk.

"Mr. Cyrus Newcomb who owned the Clinton Street Hotel. It was like twenty years ago. I wasn't working in Albany then. You might remember him."

Peter put his head down and did not look up at her. His tone became irritable and rather harsh. He told her he had more projects to complete and she could leave now, as she was no longer needed. He thanked her for her assistance.

Never easily rebuffed, Polly hesitated in the doorway. She knew he used her when he wanted, for more than one reason. She could easily ruin him, but the game playing was part of her and she enjoyed her conquests. She smiled slyly, as he kept his head down, ignoring her. Suddenly, she felt a surge of expectancy as though she harbored knowledge of something hidden, that she would ultimately use to her advantage.

"Let's not be so cocksure, Peter," she told him firmly. "We all have secrets to hide."

Mr. Nathan Turner sat at his desk in his office on the upper floor of the Empire State Beverage Company. It was well after nine o'clock and he had spent most of the afternoon and the evening at the facility. He found reassurance in his office, although just outside his door, stood the empty office where his daughter worked. He had seen to business operations as usual, hoping to dispel the anxiety of his daughter's death from his mind.

He called his wife to tell her he would be home shortly. He worked with her on the wake and funeral arrangements. It was decided to have an autopsy performed, as they wanted to know for sure what caused their daughter's sudden death.

Mr. Turner was a distinguished man, who looked much younger than his seventy years. An active lifestyle and positive outlook contributed to his fine appeal. He was grateful to his loving wife Louise for her contributions and his supportive daughter, Prudence. They would give her a proper burial, as soon as the autopsy report was completed.

The facility staff had gone home for the day. From below, he heard the sound of cleaning and he knew the maintenance staff was still working. It was foolish to be here so late, he supposed.

His mind turned to the taste testing and the crowd, staring up at him as he told them to raise their glasses to the new *Champagne Twist*. His thoughts were reeling, still in shock. Of the most unlikely places, it was something out of a nightmare. He thought his vision had seen double or he was losing his mind. But he knew what he saw. He would say nothing to his wife. She was still distraught over their daughter. But perhaps she saw the same thing, too.

He remembered his brother-in-law's friendship with Mr. Cyrus Newcomb. A good soul, Mr. Newcomb. Walter mentioned the fight that erupted at the hotel when he was there that night but he helped break it up. Brave man, Walter, he thought reassuringly. It had to be 1915, eight years ago, he thought. He remembered Mr. Newcomb died in 1920. Mr. Turner and his wife had enjoyed dinner at the hotel and always found Mr. Newcomb pleasant. He died in another part of the state after his retirement. He wondered if his brother-in-law knew something he did not share with him and his wife. Perhaps he saw what he saw yesterday. The thought sent a chill down his spine.

Mr. Turner was still reeling from the shock. An improbable chance, here in Albany, again! He shook his head. He must think of his daughter's burial first. He then decided he had spent long enough at his office. He put away a few folders, his fountain pen and tidied his desk. The cleaning crew had already left and the building was extremely quiet. He did not hear the footsteps on the stairs leading to the upper floor.

It was not until five o'clock the next morning that Mrs. Turner noticed her husband had not arrived home. She had fallen asleep on the living room sofa and realizing her husband was not at home, immediately called his office. Upon receiving no answer, she called the police.

As the workday had not begun, it was quiet as the police officers arrived at the facility. Finding the front doors locked, they saw the back door ajar and entered. Staff had yet to report, but they detected a light from the upstairs offices. Approaching the stairs, they called out to Mr. Turner and receiving no answer, entered his office.

At first, they did not see Mr. Turner. Proceeding to the desk, they found him slumped on the floor, his shirt and vest saturated in blood. He had been stabbed repeatedly in the chest and left for dead.

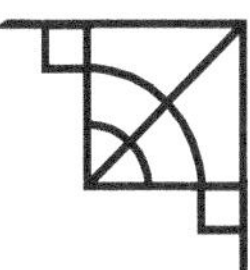

CHAPTER TEN

Within a half hour, the Empire State Beverage Company was bombarded with police, who closed the area surrounding the building with rope. A police photographer had finished taking pictures, while officers searched through Mr. Turner's office looking for clues. Inspector Harris and Lieutenant Taylor were first on the scene, after receiving the news from the responding officers. Inspector Harris looked at the mutilated body of Mr. Turner. He had seen many horrific crime scenes in his line of work, but none so brutal. He turned his attention to Lieutenant Taylor, who had been writing in a pad, while also combing through the office, hoping to find something the killer left behind. Inspector Harris went up to him, shaking his head.

"Whoever killed him was full of rage. You can almost feel the anger by the wounds."

"Mr. Lennon was killed in June and now this," Lieutenant Taylor said, contemplating another murder of a beverage employee. He dated his notes for Friday morning, August 17, 1923.

"Mr. Turner's daughter died from drinking the champagne drink," the Inspector added. "We don't know what happened with Mrs. Nichols until we receive the autopsy. I understand the family ordered one, so we should know the results pretty soon. Headquarters told me Mrs. Turner has already been contacted, but she refuses to come here. She is overcome by the death of her daughter and the death of President Harding. We'll have the body taken to the hospital morgue. I don't know if Mrs. Turner would want an autopsy performed on her husband. She is already waiting for one to be performed on her daughter."

"We will go to see her later this morning," Lieutenant Taylor said. "For now, I want to speak to workers here who may know something from yesterday."

Inspector Harris, Lieutenant Taylor and the other police officers questioned the entire staff of the Empire State Beverage Company with little results. They commented they had not seen Mr. Turner yesterday morning, as he was with his wife at home, making funeral arrangements for his daughter, Prudence. He arrived later in the afternoon, just as many were leaving for the day. He seemed in as good spirits as possible, given the circumstances, and retreated upstairs to his executive office. He had little contact with the staff for the remainder of the workday.

Miss Medford was questioned extensively, but she also could add little to assist the police regarding Mr. Turner or Mrs. Nichols. She had been present at the taste testing but noticed nothing out of the ordinary. She commented Mr. Turner seemed to stagger at the podium, then the lights went out during a thunderstorm, but he appeared his usual self when he proposed a toast afterward. She did not know what happened to Mrs. Nichols and did not see her drink the new beverage. She did not speak to the Turners during the taste testing event. She also did not have the opportunity to speak to Mr. Turner when he arrived yesterday. Admittedly, she was surprised he would show up, given the tragedy of his daughter's death. She left work yesterday at five o'clock, her usual time. She planned to attend a memorial service for President

Harding at her church and did not wish to arrive late. She noticed Mr. Turner was busy in his office, so she left without saying goodbye.

Police officers also contacted the cleaning staff by telephone, informing them of the calamity of their boss. They expressed shock and outrage but could not provide any additional information on what occurred. Mrs. Mildred Kilpatrick had spoken briefly with Mr. Turner last evening, upon emptying the garbage in his office, but he seemed laconic, morose, and not inclined to talk. Mr. Gerard Hollis and Mr. Jason Summers, long time employees, had not noticed anything remiss with Mr. Turner, except for his rather quiet demeanor. They had not noticed anyone else in the building. Regarding Mrs. Nichols's sudden violent illness, Mrs. Kilpatrick added they emptied the trash from that afternoon and bottles and the plastic glasses used were discarded. They were informed the taste testing had broken up after Mrs. Nichols became ill, although the cleaning crew was not in the room when that occurred. Mrs. Kilpatrick, Mr. Hollis and Mr. Summers left upon completion of their shift at ten o'clock. As far as they knew, Mr. Turner was still in his office. They encountered no one near the building upon exiting.

Inspector Harris looked around the offices of the upper floor, including that of Prudence Nichols. He did not see anything to provide clues to the brutal murder of Mr. Turner. The other offices were incredibly clean and void of anything incriminating. He met Lieutenant Taylor in the hallway outside Mr. Turner's office.

"The best course of action is to speak to Mrs. Turner," he told him. "There is nothing here to provide information. No witnesses, no clues, no weapon, nothing."

"We'll have the place dusted for fingerprints," the Lieutenant said.

"Let's return to headquarters. I'd like to call Mrs. Turner to see if she'll speak to us. First, her brother was murdered, now her husband.

And her daughter died on Wednesday."

They walked down the stairs, giving instructions to the police crew, informing them of the removal of the body to the hospital morgue. They then left the building on the way to headquarters.

The news of the murder of Mr. Nathan Turner spread swiftly throughout Albany. While the headlines continued on President Harding's sudden demise, much attention was given to the murder of Mr. Nathan Turner. Radio stations in Albany and Schenectady reported on the vicious slaying. The *Times Union*, *Knickerbocker Press* and the *Albany Evening News* carried articles about the murder of a local executive, linking it to the murder of Mr. Walter Lennon in June.

Word reached Caleb by telephone from Sister Catherine who called him from Mrs. Turner's house on Englewood Place. Mrs. Turner insisted she call Caleb, to inform him of the calamity. She mentioned she was staying with Mrs. Turner, as she was too overwrought to be alone.

Caleb hoped there would be a semblance of some normalcy on Friday morning, although with President Harding's death and the death of Mrs. Nichols on Wednesday, he knew that would be rather difficult. Upon hearing the news from Sister Catherine, he was too shocked to formulate words. With the murder of Mr. Lennon, the strange death of Mrs. Nichols, the sudden demise of President Harding and now the murder of Mr. Turner, he wondered what else could possibly happen. It was as though dark clouds settled over them, he thought, replacing the handset. He placed his head in his hands wearily and then looked up and saw Gabrielle in the doorway.

She was tense, even frightened. Her voice rose in extreme agitation. "Mr. Turner was murdered in his office last night! Everyone's talking about it. It's in this morning's paper and Mrs. Stevenson heard about it on the radio in the main office just now." She paused. "Mr. Stevenson put in a call to Mrs. Turner and spoke to Sister Catherine. She mentioned she had just spoken to you."

Caleb nodded and added he had not seen this morning's newspaper yet. He also had not listened to the radio prior to arriving at work. He could hear talking from in the hallway. It was obvious the agency was in turmoil.

"Gabrielle, Caleb," Minerva said, appearing in the doorway, rather flushed and out of breath. "Mr. Stevenson wants to meet with us right now."

Another meeting, Caleb thought wearily, of a different matter.. He followed Gabrielle and Minerva down the hallway to Mr. Stevenson's executive suite. Roy, Peter, Polly, Wilbur and Jeff were already there. Mrs. Stevenson was crying rather steadily, almost inconsolable. Caleb and Minerva sat with the others while Gabrielle sat next to Mrs. Stevenson and tried to comfort her. Mr. Stevenson got everyone's attention.

"I spoke with Sister Catherine and I understand she called you, Caleb. I have received the most devastating news. It is in this morning's newspapers as well as on the radio report. Mr. Turner was murdered in his office, apparently last night."

He held up a hand to ward off any comments. He then took a breath and continued.

"I called my contact at the Albany Police. He told me it was an extremely brutal crime."

Within a moment, nearly everyone asked questions, causing much confusion. Minerva commented Mr. Turner seemed fine at the taste testing. Polly agreed Mr. Turner was in good spirits at the beginning of the event, but then looked like he would faint as he started to speak. Wilbur and Roy commented they had the same opinion before the lights flickered and went out during the storm. Gabrielle mentioned the excitement of the event most likely affected him and everyone seemed to agree. Peter told them he did not see anything unusual before or after the taste testing, regarding the death of Prudence or the death of Mr. Turner. Wilbur expressed concern for Mrs. Turner and Minerva commented she was glad Sister Catherine was with her at this most grievous time. Mrs. Stevenson continued crying softly, crossing herself and silently saying the Hail Mary.

Nobody knew Mr. Turner personally, except Jeff who spoke highly of his father-in-law. He commented they had a good relationship and he never saw a bad side to him. He rather enjoyed his company and the same for his mother-in-law. He had no idea who would want to harm Mr. Turner unless it was a botched robbery attempt.

Mr. Stevenson shook his head. “My contact at the police department told me nothing was taken. Like his brother-in-law, his wallet was still on him. A thief would have taken something, especially a wallet containing money.”

“Maybe something is happening we don’t know about,” Roy prophesied.

“What do you mean?” Wilbur asked.

Roy shrugged. “Well, Mr. Lennon was murdered, then Mrs. Nichols drank the new beverage and died and now Mr. Turner. There must be a pattern we’re not seeing.”

“Roy, I think that is for the police to determine,” Caleb told him.

“Maybe not,” Polly said thoughtfully. “Never hurts to learn things, you know.”

“I wouldn’t pry into something that doesn’t concern you,” Jeff warned her.

"I plan to visit Mrs. Turner this afternoon," Mrs. Stevenson said tearfully. "I already spoke to Sister Catherine, who mentioned a brief visit would be appreciated by Mrs. Turner. She told me the police are on their way now to see her, so this afternoon would be a good time."

Mr. Stevenson agreed. "Why don't you leave in the afternoon? I will finish business here and join everyone later." He paused. "I would like to personally offer condolences to Mrs. Turner."

"What about your wife's autopsy?" Roy asked. Jeff.

"An autopsy?" Wilbur said, surprised. "Is it even necessary?"

"I haven't heard anything about it yet," Jeff said, smoking incessantly. "I called the hospital and gave them my name and number, so they will contact me once it is completed. Of course, an official report will be issued, stating the cause of death." He paused. "I am concerned about the death of my father-in-law. He was murdered and I would like to know what happened."

Caleb observed Jeff as he nonchalantly continued smoking. He was too casual about his wife's death but appeared genuinely preoccupied about his father-in-law.

A heavy silence hung between them. Swirling through their minds were the murders of Mr. Lennon and now Mr. Turner, the strange death of Prudence Nichols and the unrelated but still extremely devastating death of President Warren Harding. Peter mentioned he was still dealing with the president's unexpected death and everyone agreed it was overwhelming and unsettling.

It was then agreed they would visit Mrs. Turner at her home that afternoon.

The evening editions of the local newspapers continued to feature articles on the murder of Mr. Nathan Turner. Radio news also reported on the heinous crime, commenting on the possible link with the murder of Mr. Walter Lennon in June. City residents learned the details of both murders, along with the unexpected death of Mrs. Prudence Nichols.

Much to Mrs. Turner's chagrin, several employees of the beverage company submitted their resignations. They cited an unsafe environment and would not work there if Mr. Turner were not present. Staff had dwindled, but the facility was still in operation. Mr. Turner's death only added to their increased fear and worry. Reporters showed up unannounced at the Turner's home on Englewood Place, until Sister Catherine opened the front door and threatened to call authorities. They also arrived in droves at the facility until a police officer briskly told them to depart.

Mrs. Stevenson had already arrived at the Turner house by the time Caleb, Gabrielle and Roy rang the doorbell. It was late afternoon, close to four o'clock. Caleb had hoped to leave earlier, but with current contracts and letters to be typed, the hours flew by. They took the trolley up Central Avenue and got off at the corner with Northern Boulevard. Walking in near silence, they proceeded along Northern Boulevard, turning right on State. Brownstone houses lined the street, overlooking Washington Park. The park lay to their left, serene and peaceful in the sunshine, with children on swings, boys playing baseball and girls jumping rope. Mothers and nannies were on hand to restore order as needed.

Caleb glanced at them, but his mind was too preoccupied about the recent murder. Crossing State, they turned into Englewood Place and reached the imposing mansion. Caleb walked up the sidewalk, rang the doorbell and waited. Roy mumbled a few words but neither Caleb nor Gabrielle felt much like talking. It was shortly answered by Sister Catherine, who smiled upon seeing them and moved aside for them to enter.

Caleb was favorably impressed with the interior and although not there for a social call, he could not help but admire the comfortable furnishings, the large dining room off to the left and the modern kitchen in the back. They followed Sister Catherine to the right, where Mrs. Turner was sitting on a sofa. She appeared dazed and confused, staring straight ahead of her, blankly, not speaking or moving. That she had been crying was obvious by the handkerchief she clung to. Mrs. Stevenson sat next to her, attempting to comfort her and encouraged her to pray and ask God for direction in this calamitous time.

"Mrs. Turner, you have a few visitors here," Sister Catherine said pleasantly.

Mrs. Turner looked up and saw Caleb, Gabrielle and Roy. At first, it was as though she did not know them, but then recognition settled in and she forced a weak smile, beckoning them to sit.

An awkward silence prevailed, while Sister Catherine sat in an armchair near the sofa.

Caleb continued to admire the rich furnishings, the chintz covered sofa, armchairs, the navy blue draperies and the ornate antique lamps on the end tables. Quality furnishings that spoke of money, he thought, not enviously but admirably. He glanced at Gabrielle and Roy, wondering what they were thinking and hoping they did not make any slips, especially Roy. He decided to clear the air and addressed Mrs. Turner.

"Please accept our condolences, Mrs. Turner. I wish I could say something to alleviate your pain and sorrow."

Mrs. Turner looked at Caleb and thanked him. "You are an intelligent young man, Caleb. I only wish I had a son like you. My only child died Wednesday and now my husband was murdered last night. My brother was murdered in June, so now I have nobody. I am alone."

Caleb nodded understandably. He too knew aloneness. His only diversions were his work and the grueling exercises to keep his muscles in shape. His experiences at West Point prepared him for arduous risks and great physical endurance, but adjusting to an empty life was not part of the curriculum and certainly, murder was out of his realm. Mrs. Turner was still speaking to him.

"...you are a special young man, Caleb," she went on and he wondered when she would stop reaping so much praise on him. "My husband and I appreciated the time and effort you gave us for the publicity of the new drink. Sadly, that is behind us now."

"We're here for you, dear," Sister Catherine said soothingly.

"Anything you need, please let us know," Mrs. Stevenson reiterated. "My husband and I will be here as soon as you need us. Polly, Peter, Wilbur and Minerva wish you the best. They were unable to come here today but may call at another time."

"I am terribly sorry, Mrs. Turner," Gabrielle said, looking toward the older woman feeling much remorse. "I didn't know Mr. Turner, but I enjoyed the taste testing event Wednesday."

Roy agreed. "I spoke briefly to him. He seemed in good spirits."

Mrs. Turner nodded. "Yes, I felt the same. I have no idea what happened to my husband. He was overcome as he started to propose the toast."

Sister Catherine spoke up, quite firmly. "Mrs. Turner, it is best not to review what we already know. The police questioned you extensively."

"The police were here already?" Caleb asked.

Sister Catherine nodded. "They informed Mrs. Turner what happened earlier. I was here when they came this morning." She paused. "They questioned us about the taste testing and Mrs. Nichols's death. We could not provide them with any further information. We mentioned Mr. Turner seemed overwhelmed at first, then regained himself and started to speak."

"We saw that too," Roy commented. "It seemed like he was overcome by something."

"Or maybe by someone," Gabrielle suggested.

"What do you mean, Gabrielle?" Mrs. Stevenson asked.

Gabrielle shook her head. "I don't really know. But I noticed he stared out onto the crowd, ready to propose the toast and then it seemed like he would faint."

Caleb agreed. "Something appeared to disturb him."

No one could recall anything untoward at the taste testing or before the event. Mrs. Turner mentioned she told the police her husband was on amicable terms with the staff at the beverage company, his brother-in-law, his daughter and even his son-in-law, Jeff Nichols. Roy spoke up at that moment.

"Jeff and Mrs. Nichols had some words that afternoon. It was before Mr. Turner asked the crowd to raise their glasses."

Caleb wished Roy had kept his mouth shut. There was no need to mention that unpleasantness and he only hoped Mrs. Turner was not distressed by it.

"I don't think it's the best time to discuss that," Caleb said firmly, looking at Roy. "Mrs. Turner needs our support. The police will investigate and learn whatever they can."

Sister Catherine smiled. "Thank you, dear Caleb. You are an angel from God."

"Will the police speak with you again, Mrs. Turner?" Caleb asked.

Mrs. Turner shrugged. "I don't really know, dear. I imagine they will come again. I am waiting on the autopsy report on my daughter."

Sister Catherine disappeared into the kitchen and returned with a tray, bearing cups, a coffee pot and a jug of cream. She placed it on the coffee table and then retreated to the kitchen and returned with another tray, containing a plate of sweet bread and grapes.

Caleb, Gabrielle and Roy helped themselves, while Mrs. Stevenson poured coffee for herself and Mrs. Turner. Sister Catherine poured a cup for herself and for a few moments, there was relative silence, as though there was not much more to say. Caleb was pleased Mrs. Turner was sipping coffee, which seemed to restore some color to her pretty face.

"You are all so wonderful at the advertising agency," she said, looking especially at Caleb. "I am so dreadfully sorry it did not turn out the way we would have liked."

Caleb put down his cup. "Mrs. Turner, it isn't your fault that the taste testing ended on a sour note. The police will investigate and learn the truth."

"For my daughter's death to be attributed to murder would be too much for me. I do not believe I could bare it."

Caleb felt anxious and inwardly dreaded the days ahead. "Do the police think your husband's death was a random killing, or possibly a robbery gone wrong?"

Mrs. Turner shook her head. "My husband was killed savagely as though whoever did it held a vendetta against him. I cannot imagine who as my husband did not have enemies that I knew of. The same with my brother. There was no robbery in either case."

Roy and Gabrielle were too stunned to speak. Caleb looked at Mrs. Turner with extreme pity and remorse. Mrs. Stevenson continued sitting next to her, sipping her coffee and silently praying. Sister Catherine managed to keep a stern face, although she too appeared aggrieved. At that moment, the doorbell rang again.

"That must be my husband," Mrs. Stevenson said.

Sister Catherine went to the hallway and returned with Mr.

Stevenson. He looked quite aggrieved himself, having some difficulty walking. He acknowledged his wife, Caleb, Gabrielle and Roy and felt sorrow for Mrs. Turner, who looked at him with much anticipation, even dread.

"Hello, Mrs. Turner," Mr. Stevenson said, with much pain on his face. He continued standing. "I came here as soon as I could from the office."

Caleb looked at Mr. Stevenson carefully. He could tell something troublesome would be told to them. He knew by the expression on his worried face.

"Please accept my heartfelt condolences on the loss of your husband." He paused awkwardly, as though stalling. "This afternoon, I spoke to my contact at the Albany Police. The police officer mentioned they saw you earlier. He assured me they will come here to see you again this evening with the autopsy results." His face wrinkled into tight lines. "I already conferred with the remaining staff at my office. I thought it would be better if I brought the news to you first, instead of the police." He took a deep breath.

An apprehensive silence permeated the room, as though they knew something unfortunate was forthcoming. Caleb noticed Mrs. Stevenson was extremely pale, while Gabrielle and Roy were too preoccupied and dismayed to speak. Mrs. Turner appeared too bereaved to comprehend anything else. Caleb hoped it would not be what he dreaded. Looking again at Mr. Stevenson, he thought the older man would collapse.

He cleared his throat and spoke rather hoarsely. "Mrs. Turner, I am sorry to tell you your daughter died of arsenic poisoning."

Upon hearing this unexpected and devastating proclamation, Mrs. Turner stood as though to address Mr. Stevenson and then slumped forward in a dead faint. Sister Catherine moved sharply forward and with assistance from Caleb and Roy, settled her on the sofa, a pillow behind her head. Roy produced a flask from his pocket containing whisky, but Sister Catherine told him the Turners did not allow liquor in the house. She ordered Mrs. Stevenson to call the Turner's personal physician, Dr. MacBride, who arrived shortly and administered to Mrs. Turner.

Caleb looked at the woman on the sofa, feeling extreme sadness. With the death of her daughter, it would now be considered murder, unless it was proven there was arsenic in the soda itself, which he knew was foolish as nobody else became sick.

The doorbell rang again, startling the people in the living room. Gabrielle volunteered to answer the door and returned with Inspector Harris and Lieutenant Taylor of the Albany Police.

Sister Catherine asked for the doctor's assistance, as she noticed Mrs. Turner regaining consciousness. She started to carry on, crying inconsolably and uttering incoherent phrases. Dr. MacBride administered a shot of morphine and she soon began to relax, stabilizing her position on the sofa. Rather glassy-eyed but more in control, Mrs. Turner looked at the people in her living room, wondering what had happened and why they were all there. Dr. MacBride told her not to talk, but to listen as the police were there and it was important they speak to her.

Caleb thought it was an inappropriate time, but the bad news had already been conveyed so he imagined the initial shock would diminish. Mr. Stevenson introduced himself and his wife, along with the others to the police officers and mentioned he had already broken the news about the true cause of her daughter's death. His contact at the Albany Police informed him, as he had dealt with the police department numerous times over the years.

Inspector Harris mentioned in cases of undetermined and suspicious deaths, autopsy results are always released to the police. Mr. Stevenson then introduced the police officers to Mr. Caleb Dean, a chief account executive, Mr. Roy Carter, an account executive and Miss Gabrielle Woods, a secretary and file clerk from his agency. Sister Catherine introduced herself to the police officers, and then motioned them to sit on the armchairs, to enable them to speak to Mrs. Turner. She went to the dining room and with Roy's assistance brought in extra chairs for the rest. Inspector Harris cleared his throat while Lieutenant Taylor took out his small notepad and prepared to write.

"We are extremely sorry, Mrs. Turner, for the devastation you have experienced recently. We are still investigating the murder of your brother from June. You husband's death will be given every priority."

"Please, Inspector," Dr. MacBride cautioned. He was a heavyset man in his fifties, with a fatherly appearance, compassionate but not too patient with law enforcement. "I do not wish for Mrs. Turner to become agitated again."

"It is quite all right, doctor," Mrs. Turner spoke weakly from the sofa.

"Can you tell us what happened at the taste testing, Mrs. Turner?"

"I wish I could," she said, trying to regain her strength. "I have suspicions, of course, but honestly, I don't remember anything that could help you." She paused. "Now, my daughter's death is murder, too."

Sister Catherine encouraged her to be still and not dwell on the unpleasantness. She turned to the police officers as though she resented their presence and only wished they would leave.

Lieutenant Taylor asked the others what they remembered about the taste testing. Caleb offered what information he could; Mr. Turner was about to propose a toast and asked the crowd to raise their glasses, when he clutched at his chest and leaned against the podium for support. Gabrielle and Roy reiterated what Caleb told them. Mrs. Stevenson mentioned she did not see anything to disturb Mr. Turner unless he saw something no one else knew about. When asked what that could possibly be, she told them she had no idea.

"This is a serious calamity," Mr. Stevenson said, trying to maintain his dignity. "The news of the murder of Mr. Turner has devastated us."

"Can you tell us more about the taste testing event, Mrs. Turner?" Inspector Harris asked.

Mrs. Turner looked at Caleb. "This handsome young man from the advertising agency arranged it. Perhaps you should ask him."

Caleb flushed somewhat as the police officers turned their gaze upon him. He explained about the publicity campaign, how it was open to the public without registration and that the purpose was to promote the new beverage *Champagne Twist*. There was light fare and Mr. Turner had a phonograph playing 78 records. Some attendees danced too, he added. It was a rather festive and light atmosphere and people were enjoying themselves.

Lieutenant Taylor had been scribbling in his notepad. "Is there anything else you can tell us about the event, Mr. Dean?"

"It went smoothly until there was a thunderstorm and the lights went out," Caleb said, reliving the moment vividly. "Mrs. Turner searched for candles and flashlights and at about the same time the lights came back on. Mr. Turner requested people to raise their glasses in a toast to the new beverage. That is when Mrs. Nichols became ill and collapsed onto the floor."

Mrs. Turner then spoke with newfound strength. "Perhaps it was due to bad water, stale fruits and sugars used during production. I remember my husband spoke of small levels of toxics found in other beverages in the past, but they were never extreme. There was a cupboard containing arsenic as a cleanser, too."

"We have already spoken to the cleaning staff," Lieutenant Taylor said.

"What do you remember about the taste testing, Mrs. Stevenson?" the Inspector asked.

Mrs. Stevenson shook her head. "I saw what the others saw, although I do remember Mr. Nichols arguing with his wife. It wasn't very pleasant, but it did not escalate." She hesitated and Mr. Stevenson picked up where she left off.

"Jeff Nichols and his wife are in the process of divorcing. Apparently, they were not on speaking terms. Jeff is the accountant at my firm and an excellent one. He made it clear he did not look forward to the event at the beverage company, as he did not want to see his wife. They had words, as my wife mentioned, but fortunately it did not last long."

"I remember Jeff threatened his wife," Roy offered.

Caleb again wondered why Roy was so insensitive to reveal comments at such an inopportune time. Inspector Harris turned to him and asked him to explain.

"Well, Jeff grabbed her by the arm and mentioned something about you would really do that or something to that effect. I think it had to do with his wanting part of the company and how Mrs. Nichols had already spoken to her father. We all heard it since we were standing the closest to Mrs. Nichols and Jeff."

"My staff was present at the event," Mr. Stevenson said. He mentioned the names of the rest of his employees and their duties, as they coordinated the taste testing event with Caleb.

An awkward silence fell upon them in the exquisite living room. Mrs. Turner was too overcome to comprehend more and just looked at Roy as though not even hearing him. Sister Catherine was rather dismayed at what he told them, although the rest already knew about it. Lieutenant Taylor had been scribbling in his notebook and thanked Roy for the information.

"Tomorrow my team will interview people in the neighborhood of the beverage company," the Inspector said. "On Monday, we plan to speak with the production crew. They should shed some light on the ingredients used in the drink."

"There was a thunderstorm and the lights went out," Gabrielle offered. "We really didn't see anything, it was so dark in the room."

"About how many people were at the taste testing event?"

Mrs. Turner shrugged. "Close to a hundred, I'd say. It was quite an event, more people came than my husband and I expected. Mayor Hackett was there and reporters from the local papers and radio. It was running smoothly until my husband began the toast. He told the crowd to raise their glasses to the new *Champagne Twist*. Then my daughter became ill."

"Was that before or after the lights went out?"

"Afterward. My husband's demeanor and the lights going out delayed the toast. I don't know what caused my husband to stumble. He reached for the sides of the podium for support. I thought he would faint." She added that her husband enjoyed excellent health and did not have a heart condition.

"The plastic glasses and the bottles used that afternoon were thrown out," Gabrielle told the police officers. "After Mrs. Nichols became ill and was taken away by ambulance, the taste testing broke up. I saw the cleaning crew throw out the empty bottles and discard the used glasses."

"Will this be released to the press?" Dr. MacBride asked. "I do not think it is a good idea since there have been reporters turning up here, pestering the Turners."

Sister Catherine agreed. "I've had to chase them away."

"The murder of Mr. Turner has already been in the news," the Inspector reported stoically. "The police release information to the press. The autopsy and the death certificate listed possible homicide as the cause of your daughter's death. Possible means it is undetermined yet. That can change, of course."

"My brother, husband and daughter have been murdered," Mrs. Turner cried from the sofa.

Mrs. Stevenson tried to calm her. Dr. MacBride and Sister Catherine suggested she rest upstairs and for the police to speak to her again later. Sister Catherine and Dr. MacBride led her out of the living room and up the grandiose staircase. The police officers then turned to Caleb and the others.

"We will be in touch with you again as well," Inspector Harris told them. "We would like official statements from everyone, since you were nearest to Mrs. Nichols."

"You are welcome at my agency, Inspector," Mr. Stevenson said. He gave him the address on State Street, saw them to the door and then returned and looked at his wife, Caleb, Gabrielle and Roy. The strain was apparent in his face, even his posture. He cleared his throat and in his authoritative manner spoke to them. His wife remained at his side on the sofa.

"Something is happening we are not aware of," he said. Before Roy could interrupt him, he continued. "I suggest you let me know if you come upon anything you believe may be relevant to these deaths. We do not want any further disturbances."

Caleb noticed as Roy and Gabrielle chatted quietly while Mr. Stevenson put his arm around his aggrieved wife. It was obvious they were all disturbed over the recent murders and now the devastating news of the demise of Mrs. Nichols, a possible homicide as the police officer called it, according to the coroner. Certainly, the unexpected death of President Harding still weighed heavily on their minds, too.

His thoughts were chaotic. Maybe it was just an accident, after all. Soft drink production may contain some arsenic. It was her bad luck that she drank from the contaminated bottle.

He felt powerless, as though the whole world was falling apart. He experienced an overwhelming sense of doom.

In a comfortable brownstone house on Myrtle Avenue, Peter sat at the kitchen table, finishing the dinner Polly prepared. It was early evening and although the sun still shone brightly, the days were getting shorter and the air was not as thick with humidity as in previous weeks.

After leaving the agency, Peter and Polly shopped at the market on Lark Street and then headed over to his brownstone on Myrtle Avenue. With his substantial income, Peter purchased the house almost twenty years ago. He admitted it was rather large, with four bedrooms and two baths, but as he was married at the time, he expected to start a family with his then wife. As that marriage crumbled after only a few years, he decided to keep the house as he enjoyed living in it and the convenience to downtown Albany. It also was close to Polly's apartment on lower State Street. With only a short trolley ride, she would arrive at Myrtle Avenue.

Polly sat across from him, too preoccupied to have much of an appetite. Upon seeing Peter completing the delicious meal of roasted chicken, salad and warm bread, she got up and started to prepare coffee. A chocolate cake was in the icebox ready. Peter lit an after dinner cigarette, feeling quite satisfied. He watched as she fussed with the coffee, setting the pot on the stove and turning on the gas burner. Her usual cheerful countenance was subdued, even her face was downcast and the makeup she wore did not alleviate her depressed state. He asked her what was bothering her.

"Are you serious, Peter?" she said, almost harshly. "Prudence Nichols was murdered! Are you not aware of that? And now Mr. Turner was murdered in his own office last night!"

After Mr. Stevenson spoke to his contact at the police station, and before leaving for the Turner's house, he told the others about Mrs. Nichols dying from arsenic poisoning. They expressed incredulity, even outrage that another premature death occurred to a member of the Turner family. Mr. Stevenson did not state that Prudence was murdered, although with poison in the drink, it left nothing to the imagination. And Peter knew Polly had a vivid imagination. Mr. Stevenson left later in the afternoon for Mrs. Turner's house, while Minerva and Wilbur left soon afterward. Only Polly and Peter remained. They tidied their desks and departed within an hour.

Peter looked at her, understandably upset. But there was something else bothering her. Peter knew Polly quite well. He sighed as she filled his coffee cup and took the chocolate cake out of the icebox. She set two plates on the table and cut the cake, handing him a plate.

Polly returned to her seat. "I found out something about Mr. Cyrus Newcomb."

Peter sipped the hot liquid. "Who in the world is he? Should I know him?"

Polly nibbled at her cake. "He did business with Mr. Stevenson over twenty years ago."

Peter blew smoke toward the ceiling. "And?"

"He knew Mr. Lennon. I looked at the file in the spare room on Mr. Newcomb's publicity. I think it was in 1915. There was a fight at the hotel and Mr. Lennon was there."

"I still don't see what you're getting at."

She changed the subject. "Who do you think killed Mr. Turner?"

"I have no idea. He was pleasant on Wednesday, during the taste testing." He paused. "Now Mrs. Nichols was poisoned. I wonder if it was deliberate." He paused. "Too bad the taste testing didn't turn out well for us. Or I should say for Caleb. It was his stupid idea to begin with."

Polly agreed. "I had reservations. I should've known something bad would happen."

Peter continued puffing at his cigarette. "Do you think Mr. Turner had a heart attack? He did clutch his chest, you know."

Polly shook her head. "No, something else upset him."

"You found something out, I assume."

Polly shrugged. "Perhaps," she said, casually.

"Rather puts Jeff in a bad spot," Peter remarked. "I've heard the spouse is always under suspicion in cases like this. Now he won't need to get a divorce."

Polly laughed. "That's true. Jeff must have a secret closet. Nearly everyone hides something. Perhaps even you."

"Perhaps even Caleb," he said. "You know, the West Point graduate?" He took a mouthful of chocolate cake. "You shouldn't go snooping around the office, Polly. Remember when we were sorting through the old files before the publicity for the Turners began? After you left, I swore someone had been standing outside in the hallway listening."

"Well, I didn't see anyone in the hallway," she said simply. "I'm not the only person who snoops, as you call it. Gabrielle has access to all of the agency's files. She can look through them whenever she wants."

His mind flew to the taste testing event and Mr. Turner clutching his hand to his chest, looking out onto the faces assembled, all with a glass in their hands, ready to raise them in a toast for *Champagne Twist*. Of course, there were so many people present. He looked at Polly across the table, as she sipped her coffee. She was talking about the death of President Harding and how upsetting it still was, and now the new president, Calvin Coolidge in office. She rattled on and on, for what Peter believed was a cover up for more devious and unsettling thoughts.

He tried to remember exactly what transpired at that ridiculous taste testing. He would not discuss it with Polly or anyone else, for that matter. She always kept everything to herself anyway. She harbored certain knowledge and even suspicions—but so did he.

Minerva stirred her coffee and looked over at Wilbur, who sat in an armchair reading the *Albany Evening Press*. They had arrived at their brownstone house on upper Madison Avenue, across from Washington Park and had already eaten dinner. Minerva prepared coffee and served it in the living room. She turned on the radio to listen to popular tunes and the pleasing voice of Bessie Smith helped to while away the evening. Wilbur looked at her over the top of the newspaper.

"Delicious meal, dear. You're the best cook, Minerva."

"Did you want to go out this evening, Wilbur? We could see a movie at the Ritz. Mary Pickford's new film is showing. I think Charlie Chaplin's movie is still at the Albany Theater. Or we can go shopping on North Pearl Street."

Wilbur lowered the paper. "Not tonight. I think I'd like to just stay in for now."

Minerva sipped her coffee. "Lots of commotion recently, wouldn't you say?"

Wilbur buried his face behind the newspaper. "I don't want to hear anything more about the Turners or President Harding. Personally, I did not care for Mr. Harding and as far as the Turners are concerned, they were never any of my business to begin with."

Minerva listened as the rhythms of Duke Ellington began and the soothing sounds of jazz filled the living room. She looked around the comfortable furnishings of the brownstone they bought only a few years ago, when the market for homes was fortuitous after the Great War. They were lucky to find this gem of a house, in a pristine neighborhood. It was richly furnished, with the most modern décor and an elaborate radio counsel against the far wall that cost quite a penny. Wilbur purchased it at Whitney's last year and Minerva admitted she did not care about the price. She enjoyed listening to it while home. They were silent for some time, until Minerva put down her coffee cup on an end table, rather forcibly causing Wilbur to look at her questioningly.

"Wilbur, there has been too much going on recently. I am still disturbed over President Harding's untimely death. I didn't know too much about him, but it is still quite upsetting."

Wilbur continued reading the newspaper. "It is rather unsettling."

Minerva agreed. "I am afraid, Wilbur. Terribly afraid."

"Of course, Mr. Stevenson was foolish enough to listen to Caleb and his harebrained ideas. I knew it would not be a success. After what happened to Mrs. Nichols, I cannot imagine anyone stupid enough to buy that horrible drink."

"Jeff will be under suspicion. He doesn't have to bother with a divorce proceeding."

Wilbur moved the paper to look at her. "That's one way to look at it."

"Just the other day, in the office, I heard Polly mention Mr. Newcomb from Albany. She's always snooping around the office."

Wilbur did not look up from the newspaper. "I saw Roy snooping around Mr. Stevenson's office once. Honestly, I wouldn't listen to Polly. She's nothing but gossip." He paused, then lowered the paper, meeting her eyes. "Let's hope old man Stevenson doesn't decide to close the agency because of the recent events. Bad press for us since we sponsored the ridiculous taste testing in the first place. He could do that, you know."

Minerva sighed, toying with her string of pearls. "What will happen to us, Wilbur?"

He spoke firmly and to the point. "I'm sure you know everyone is looking out for himself or herself. Nobody gives a damn about you or me. It's dog devour dog, Minerva. We have to watch our backs at all times."

Wilbur returned to the newspaper and Minerva stared blankly at the radio console, listening to the pleasant voice of Ethel Waters. She wondered about the Turners. Perhaps they were not as stellar as every one assumed. They held secrets, of course. But precisely what those secrets were remained to be seen.

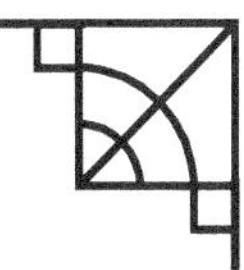

CHAPTER ELEVEN

On Saturday, the eighteenth, police conducted thorough door-to-door inquiries throughout the vicinity of the beverage company, including nearby homes, businesses and factories. In addition, the police launched media appeals in the local newspapers and on the radio for information to assist in their investigation. Numerous people were questioned over the weekend, but few could provide valuable clues or information on the brutal murder.

The murder of Mr. Nathan Turner caused extensive public indignation. City residents read in horror of the brutality of the killing. Radio reports stated Mr. Turner and his brother-in-law, Mr. Lennon were highly regarded in the Albany business community. Their murders were an atrocity to the city. As a newspaper reporter surmised, it was a clear indication of the rise in crime and violence in the capital city.

The newspapers and radio reports also carried stories pertaining to the mysterious death of Mrs. Prudence Nichols. Details on the taste testing event centered on the possibility of murder, that Mrs. Nichols had been the victim of foul play. Several noted Mayor Hackett attended and that the poisonous drink could have been for him. Much speculation followed and the newspapers and radio announcers had little facts on which to base their announcements. Nevertheless, the stories continued, mentioning the third death of an employee of the Empire State Beverage Company; the murder of Mr. Walter Lennon in June at the Port of Albany, the brutal slaying of his brother-in-law, Mr. Nathan Turner, the owner of the company and the strange death of his daughter, Mrs. Prudence Nichols. Several articles noted Empire Advertising, who conducted the publicity for the new champagne style beverage, hosted the event.

Inspector Harris and Lieutenant Taylor were at the beverage company that Saturday morning, interviewing employees who worked the weekend shifts and who were familiar with Mr. Turner and Mr. Lennon. While most commented on their friendly disposition, no one could offer evidence on their sudden deaths. They were not acquainted with them outside of the facility. The production crew also had little contact with them.

Regarding Mrs. Nichols, employees reiterated what was told earlier. She kept to herself in her office next to her father's executive suite and rarely entered the production areas. She was more in line with the business end of the company and employees had little if any contact with her. A few had helped arrange the taste testing, but no one remembered the bottles that were placed on the tables for display or from which case the contaminated battle came from.

Arsenic was mentioned as a cleanser and disinfectant, which was stored in the cabinets in the production area. It also was mentioned that slight traces of arsenic, while harmless, would at times be used to dilute the bitterness and harsh tasting fruit residue in the beverages they produced.

After concluding the staff interviews, Lieutenant Taylor sat at a table in the production area reviewing his notes. Inspector Harris joined him and shook his head, having interviewed everyone present in the building. He commented they were at a loss for the three deaths, without any witnesses or leads.

"Mr. Turner's office was thoroughly investigated," he explained. "We thought there might've been something he left behind. Unfortunately, we found nothing to help in the investigation. And the same for Mrs. Nichols's office. She kept everything in her desk, but there was nothing incriminating to point to someone who may have wanted to kill her."

The Lieutenant met his eyes across the table. "It may be that she happened to drink from a bottle that had higher traces of arsenic. Perhaps too much got into a particular bottle."

"Seems unlikely," Inspector Harris said impatiently. "Right now we're dealing with three deaths from the same family. There must be a pattern we aren't seeing."

The Lieutenant agreed. "I think the same person who killed Mr. Lennon also killed Mr. Turner. From the brutality of his murder, it seemed like the murderer was angry. Most robberies do not contain such overt violence."

"Nothing was taken, including his wallet, which contained thirty dollars in cash. Same with Mr. Lennon. So, if robbery was not a motive in both killings, why were they killed? And especially Mr. Turner, so brutally. His murder appears a crime of passion."

"I wonder if that poisoned drink was meant for Mr. Turner. From what I understand, the lights went out during a thunderstorm. That would have given someone enough time to put arsenic in the drink and leave it on the table where Mr. Tuner was standing."

"But there were others there, too. Besides, who carries arsenic around on their person?"

"Unless someone knew where it was kept. It could be an inside job, although from our interviews, no one seemed to hold a grudge against Mrs. Nichols or Mr. Turner."

"I don't think it was an inside job. I believe someone or something at the taste testing event was a threat to Mr. Turner. Something disturbed him greatly. Didn't they tell us how he clutched at his chest and leaned against the podium as though he would faint?"

"Perhaps he was overcome by the event, the publicly and all the people there. Mrs. Turner told us there had to be at least a hundred people in attendance that day."

"I'd like to speak to the advertising firm that initiated the publicity," Lieutenant Taylor said decisively. "We already spoke to Mr. Dean, Mr. Carter, Miss Woods and Mr. and Mrs. Stevenson. Of course, Mrs. Turner was understandably beside herself. We will go to see her again, perhaps either later today or tomorrow."

"Perhaps the advertising people could tell us more," Inspector Harris said.

"I'll contact the mayor's office, too," the Lieutenant said thoughtfully. "Mayor Hackett is an observant man. Perhaps he saw something no one else saw."

"We know the Nichols exchanged words, right before the toast. It was before the lights went out during the thunderstorm. Seems odd they would quarrel and then Mrs. Nichols drank the new beverage and had convulsions and later died."

"When we go to the advertising agency, we'll speak to Mr. Nichols as well as the others."

"Perhaps the glasses were mixed up during the thunderstorm when the lights went out."

Lieutenant Taylor tapped his pencil on the table in extreme annoyance. At this point he did not know for sure what to think.

"We'll continue speaking to people here and in this neighborhood," he said.

"Do you think another homicide could be forthcoming?"

Lieutenant Taylor stopped writing. He knew a killer rarely stopped with one victim. In this case, there were three victims, from the same family and the same place of business.

Inspector Harris cleared his throat. "The autopsy report stated death by poison, which was the arsenic in the drink. We should contact the coroner and see what more he can tell us." He paused. "We've seen when the coroner has not been able to make a firm decision on the cause of death. While the arsenic no doubt killed her, he did reach a conclusion of undetermined, possible homicide. Perhaps he was not sure at that point."

Lieutenant Taylor nodded, but he was thinking profoundly of the recent deaths. Mr. Lennon, Mrs. Nichols and then Mr. Turner. Mr. Turner was attacked in a rage of anger to cause such a horrific crime scene. Mr. Lennon was stabbed, but not as viciously. Mrs. Nichols drank the poisoned *Champagne Twist,* but was it murder or an accident? He was inclined to think the former. Unless the drink was meant for someone else, possibly Mr. Turner, and she drank it by mistake.

They continued their questioning of residents and businesses in the neighborhood near the beverage company. Residents commented they did not know the Turners or anyone employed there. Upon returning to headquarters, Inspector Harris contacted Mayor Hackett, but he could not recall anything relevant about the taste testing event. He commented he did not know the Turners well, but on the few occasions when he spoke with them, he found them personable and pleasant. The Inspector also called other people they knew had attended from information provided by Mr. Stevenson, Mrs. Turner and Sister Catherine, but nobody could provide any worthwhile information as to what occurred or if anything was amiss. So far, the investigation into the murders of Mr. Lennon, Mr. Turner and the death of Mrs. Nichols had stalled, with no leads or suspects. The police investigation continued, resolutely. Police feared more violence would be forthcoming.

Monday, the twentieth of August was a cloudy and humid day, with intermittent peeks of sunshine behind thickening clouds that hinted at the possibility of showers later in the day.

At Empire Advertising, the atmosphere was quiet and subdued, with the workday carrying on as usual but with little conversation. The telephone rang, the mail arrived promptly, the morning newspaper was delivered but the continued tension and anxiety inherent was very much present.

Caleb arrived at nine o'clock, had no sooner settled at his desk when Gabrielle appeared in the doorway. She told him Mr. Stevenson wished to see him. Caleb asked her, rather anxiously, what it was regarding.

"He didn't say," she told him honestly. "He seemed pretty serious."

Gabrielle returned to the main office while Caleb got up and glanced at himself in the wall mirror. His blond hair was neat, but he ran both hands over it, rather uncertainly. He straightened his tie, pulled his vest into place over his narrow hips and then turned back to his desk, to retrieve a pad and pen in case notes were needed. He walked down the long hallway to the end and turned right into Mr. Stevenson's formidable if not comfortable executive suite. He saw him behind his massive desk, looking large and intimidating. He nodded to Caleb and then motioned him to sit in a chair before his desk.

"Good morning, Mr. Stevenson," Caleb said, not sure what to expect.

"Good morning, Caleb. Or as good a morning as it can possibly be given the recent events." He cleared his throat. "Caleb, as you know, I take great pride in my work. My life has revolved around this agency. Empire Advertising was founded many years ago. We have always delivered the best to our clients. I am greatly disturbed by the brutality of the murder of Mr. Turner. Mr. Lennon's murder was also upsetting. The death of Mrs. Nichols has caused my wife and I much pain, not only because she was the daughter of a fine couple like the Turners, but because it occurred during our of our sponsored events."

Caleb sat still, not sure where this was headed. He watched as Mr. Stevenson continued speaking, obviously much distressed and overcome. He assumed he did not call him to his office to grieve the recent deaths.

"Caleb, there is someone I want you to see," he told him. He moved a paper aside and looked at it carefully. "There is a highly respected private investigator here in Albany we have worked with before. You may not know him, as you were not working here at the time. His name is Mr. Sheppard. Mr. Sloan Sheppard. His office is located at 100 State Street, about a five minute walk from here."

Mr. Stevenson looked forward, thoughtfully. "I remember Mr. Sheppard from his previous employment, as a junior investigator in a detective agency. It was while employed there that he assisted us with a fraudulent company. He opened his own office just three years ago. He is also incredibly young, not much older than yourself, Caleb. I have not conferred with Mrs. Turner, as I am sure she is still too upset at this time, but I do not believe she would protest Mr. Sheppard investigating. For her sake and the name of this agency, I plan to hire Mr. Sheppard."

Caleb started to speak but Mr. Stevenson held up a hand, signaling him to silence. Caleb knew when his boss wanted his full attention. Obviously, he had not yet finished speaking.

"The police in this city tend to let weeks and even months go by without solving crimes. While I am sure they are competent, I am not one to allow the grass to grow beneath my feet. Especially since our reputation may be at stake."

"What do you mean, Mr. Stevenson?" Caleb asked him.

"As I mentioned, the death of Mrs. Nichols occurred at one of our events. Potential clients and established ones may not want to work with us after such a devastating event. I do not want that to happen. The press has already mentioned Empire Advertising sponsored the event. No blame can be placed on this agency. Negativity could turn clients away from utilizing our services."

Caleb did not think that would happen. The Empire Advertising Agency had a solid reputation and a firm client base, but he kept his opinion to himself. He agreed Mrs. Turner was too overwrought to inquire into a private investigator, especially with planning the funerals for her husband and daughter. Mr. Stevenson had his own reasons for wanting to hire this Mr. Sheppard. He was rather taken aback by his firm and rather forceful demeanor.

"I already spoke with Mr. Sheppard this morning. He mentioned he received an invitation to the taste testing but regretted he was unable to attend. He is busy with family court, divorce proceedings, catching bootleggers and other legal issues but he is willing to assist us." He stopped suddenly and looked at Caleb.

Rather flustered, Caleb fumbled for words at first. "You want me to speak to this Mr. Sheppard, a private investigator?" He never had reason to contact a detective.

"Mr. Sheppard expects you at his office after lunchtime today," Mr. Stevenson mentioned. "His office is located on the fifth floor of 100 State Street."

"What do you want me to tell him?" Caleb asked, rather meekly.

Mr. Stevenson frowned. "Mr. Sheppard mentioned he read the newspaper articles and heard the news on the radio. I told him about the taste testing and the work leading up to it. He cannot promise anything, but he told me he would look into it. That is why I am sending you to meet him. I trust you above everyone in this agency. I know I can count on you to relay the correct information." He paused. "Mr. Sheppard is a fine man, quite distinguished in his profession. He is a diligent and resourceful investigator. He will learn the truth and bring this matter to rest." He crushed his cigarette irritably and reiterated his stance. "I am doing this not only for Mrs. Turner's sake but for our reputation. If we lose clients, we will have to close our doors."

Caleb knew money was always at the forefront. Practically everyone in the agency was consumed with it. The root of all evil, he thought as he returned to his office.

The Albany City Savings Bank Building, proudly known as Albany's first skyscraper, opened in 1902. Its convenient location within the city's commercial district enabled it to serve a broad range of businesses, including law firms, stockbrokers, insurance offices and private investigations. At ten stories with an ornate clock tower and a large cupola, it was the tallest edifice in the city.

At around one o'clock, Caleb left the agency, walked the short distance to 100 State Street, and stared up at the imposing office building, He had walked past it many times but never had occasion to venture inside. He ran his finger around the collar of his shirt. It was still humid and the sun made a strong afternoon appearance. His cap helped block the intense rays from his face.

He stood on the sidewalk a moment, irresolute. While he appreciated Mr. Stevenson's confidence in him, he did not understand why he had to speak to this private investigator. Certainly, Mr. Stevenson, since he was already acquainted with him, could have spoken in person with him himself or Mrs. Stevenson, for that matter.

Dodging the sidewalk crowds, he bravely decided to enter. He looked quickly at the wall directory to verify the floor he wanted, and then entered an elevator. The attendant closed the gates and along with a few others, it slowly began its ascent toward the upper floors. Caleb told him he wanted floor five and upon arriving, the gates were opened and he and an executive got off. The man scurried off in one direction and Caleb thought of asking him if he knew where Mr. Sheppard was located. For a moment, he felt like a lost child seeking direction. He noticed a wall directory. Glancing at it and finding the correct office, he made his way down a rather dimly lit hallway until he saw a placard reading *Sloan Sheppard, Private Investigator* to the right of the door.

He knocked and waited. As there was no answer, he was unsure if he should knock again. He then heard someone approach the door and soon he stood face to face with Mr. Sheppard. He smiled upon seeing Caleb.

"Mr. Dean from Mr. Stevenson's office? Please come in."

Sloan moved aside, allowing Caleb to enter. Sloan closed the door and returned to his desk, settling comfortably on the swivel chair and reaching for a cigarette he had in an ashtray. Caleb sat in a chair in front of him, taking off his cap and looking around quickly. It was a small office, yet reasonably furnished with a rather large desk where Mr. Sheppard had several piles of folders and paperwork, a candlestick telephone, a penholder, a dish containing paper clips and next to the telephone stood a paper fastener.

Caleb looked at the man behind the desk. Certainly, well dressed in a pristine shirt, tie and vest, rather rugged looking, too, as though he had endured much perhaps in his professional life. His jet-black hair was unconventional, wavy and worn back from a prominent forehead. Caleb guessed his age, as Mr. Stevenson mentioned, not much older than his own thirty, maybe thirty-three or four. He wondered if he had served in the military, too.

Caleb was favorably impressed with Mr. Sheppard. He listened as he spoke intelligently and knowledgeably about private investigations, his start as a junior investigator before opening his own agency three years ago. Caleb thought any young woman would find his height and muscular frame appealing. He could imagine Polly swooning over him. He certainly looked the part of a private investigator. As Sloan continued speaking, Caleb could tell his exceptional intellect gave precedence to his formidable abilities to resolve issues and seek justice for his clients. He watched as Sloan puffed at his cigarette.

"As I mentioned, I spoke at length this morning with Mr. Stevenson," Sloan said, knocking ash into an ashtray. "Actually, I received an invitation to the taste testing at the beverage facility but was unable to attend. I read about the murders of Mr. Lennon and Mr. Turner in the newspapers."

"There is also the issue of Mrs. Nichols," Caleb said.

Sloan nodded, at the same time taking up a fountain pen. He turned back a page in a notepad and began to write. After a moment, he looked up at Caleb.

"May I call you Caleb? Feel free to call me Sloan. Or Mr. Sheppard if you prefer."

Caleb smiled, feeling more at ease. He listened as Sloane continued speaking.

"I conducted business for Mr. Stevenson when I was a partner in an investigation agency several years ago. I kept notes of all my cases. It was about a fraudulent company. I remember a Mr. Cyrus Newcomb, who owned and operated the Clinton Street Hotel. He hired me through the agency to investigate some of his customers. Turned out many were gangsters who used the hotel for illegal business dealings."

Caleb frowned. "Why is that important, Mr. Sheppard?"

Sloan puffed at his cigarette. "Mr. Stevenson ran a campaign to promote Mr. Newcomb's hotel. I completed my work for Mr. Newcomb around the same time."

He held up two piles of papers, fastened by clips. The first was the assignment he completed for Mr. Stevenson regarding the fraudulent company and the second pertained to Mr. Newcomb, of the Clinton Street Hotel. Sloan glanced through these notes and commented that before the Great War, there were some rough characters who frequented the Clinton Street Hotel. He mentioned Mr. Newcomb was acquainted with Mr. Walter Lennon, who was murdered at the Port of Albany in June. He concluded he was glad he assisted Mr. Newcomb in halting such deviousness from occurring on his premises.

Caleb remembered he came across the file on Mr. Newcomb in the spare office. He listened as Sloan continued speaking.

"Before committing myself, I want to be sure I can resolve this case. I spoke with Inspector Harris, who also gave me background information on the murders." He paused, looking at Caleb carefully. "Why don't you start at the beginning and tell me what you know?"

Sloan judged his visitor as quite professional in his demeanor and appearance, rather serious, thoughtful but troubled and anxious, most likely because of the recent unsettling events. Sloan figured he was a young man unused to such turmoil and was reticent to speak about it. As he detected hesitancy from Caleb, he resorted to a tactic he used when addressing reluctant clients. He invited him to speak about himself and his background.

Finding that easier, Caleb told Sloan about his work at the Empire Advertising Agency, his graduation from West Point nine years ago in 1914, his work at an army base in western New York and his decision to return to Albany, his hometown, for employment while still in the reserves.

He spoke about his associates at the agency, and their daily routine in working with clients. He then mentioned the letter he received from Mr. Turner, requesting his assistance in promoting their new champagne style imitation drink, *Champagne Twist.* He spoke about the taste testing event, how the lights went out during a thunderstorm and how Mrs. Prudence Nichols became quite sick upon drinking the beverage. He told Sloan she died at the emergency room at Albany Hospital, while the next evening Mr. Turner was brutally murdered in his office. Lastly, he mentioned how an agency employee, Jeff Nichols was the husband of Mrs. Nichols and how they were in the midst of a divorce. He heaved a rather heavy and exhausted sighed as though rehashing the details of the recent events was too much for him. He looked expectantly at Sloan.

Sloan had been writing in his notepad. He paused and looked up at Caleb.

"These events have disturbed you, Caleb," he said soothingly. "It is only natural. The recent death of President Harding has made it difficult to concentrate on my work."

Caleb agreed. "The president's death disturbed me a great deal, too."

Sloan nodded and encouraged him to continue.

"I don't know what happened at the taste testing," Caleb said uneasily. "It was my idea and the Turners were happy with the suggestion. Mayor Hackett was there. Nobody saw anything regarding Mrs. Nichols."

"Was her husband there?" Sloan asked.

Caleb nodded. "Before Mr. Turner asked everyone to raise glasses in a toast, they had a disagreement of sorts. I was standing near the table and heard it. He grabbed her by the arm and threatened her, then he let go and she sought out her parents. The lights went out and it was pitch darkness for a while. The lights came back on soon enough."

"Do you think the arsenic was put in Mrs. Nichols's drink by her husband?"

Caleb was appalled at the thought. "That didn't occur to me. I don't think Jeff would do something like that." His voice held uncertainty.

"What else can you remember about the taste testing?" Sloan prompted him, continuing to write on the notepad.

"I heard a door close in the darkness," Caleb said, remembering the event in hindsight. "I don't know if that is relevant. Mrs. Turner told someone to search for candles and flashlights, which were used but within a little while, the lights came back on."

"And where was Mr. Turner during this time?"

"When the time the lights were out, I really don't know. The flashlights were turned on and I remember he was standing near the table in front of the podium, next to his wife and daughter. We also stood near that same table, with our glasses, ready to propose a toast."

"Mr. Walter Lennon was employed at the beverage company," Sloan commented. "He was murdered at the Port of Albany in June. Mr. Stevenson mentioned he was the brother-in-law of the owner. Mr. Stevenson did not know him. Do you know anything about him?"

Caleb told Sloan he did not know Mr. Lennon and had only met the Turners when he went to the beverage company to discuss the publicity campaign. While he knew of the Turners from his associate, Jeff Nichols, he had never had the opportunity to meet them previously.

Sloan stopped writing and finished his cigarette, extinguishing it in an already overflowing ashtray. He was silent for a few moments then addressed Caleb again, with much fervor and determination.

"I wonder if the drink containing the arsenic may have been meant for Mr. Turner. During the blackout, Mrs. Nichols may have picked up the glass that was intended for him."

"Whoever wanted to kill him did it the next evening," Caleb said, shivering slightly.

Sloan nodded. "That may be a possibility. Did Mr. Turner have any enemies? Was there someone present who held a grudge against him? I cannot conclude with any satisfaction that the same person who killed Mr. Lennon also killed Mr. Turner or that Mrs. Nichols died from a glass that was purposefully laced with arsenic." He paused. "Mr. Stevenson mentioned that the death certificate and the autopsy report for Mrs. Nichols listed her death as undetermined, possible homicide. Inspector Harris told me he intends to speak with the coroner."

"I wish I knew more, Mr. Sheppard," Caleb said. "Other than the quarrel between Jeff and his wife, I don't remember anything else that happened before the lights went out that would have caught my attention."

Sloan looked at his calendar for August. It was a busy month, with appointments scheduled, dealing with fraudulent claims, family court, custody cases and divorce proceedings. He told Caleb he would like to speak to his associates who were present at the taste testing, including the Stevensons. He asked if tomorrow afternoon were possible. He would speak to Inspector Harris and schedule a visit with Mrs. Turner. He anticipated visiting the beverage company as well.

"I'll let Mr. Stevenson know that you plan to stop by tomorrow afternoon," Caleb told him.

He rose and Sloan saw him to the door. "This weekend I will be stationed at Watervliet Arsenal as part of my commitment to the reserves. But I am available for the rest of this week."

Sloan shook hands with Caleb. "No worries, Caleb. I respect the men who defend our country. I will not impede on your weekend." He opened the door for him. "I look forward to my visit tomorrow afternoon."

Caleb thanked him and watched as the door closed. Making his way thoughtfully along the hallway, he knew he had taken the first step. As he pressed the button for the elevator, he wondered what the next steps would involve and if more unsettling events would occur.

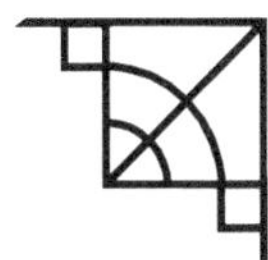

CHAPTER TWELVE

Sloan found the proximity of the Empire Advertising Agency convenient. He finished his morning appointments on Tuesday and after a rather hastened lunch at a nearby deli, he walked up State Street until he came to the corner, directly across from the State Capitol. He entered the office building and noticed the wall directory, with *Empire Advertising Agency* listed on the fifth floor. Glancing toward the elevators, and realizing there was a sizeable crowd waiting, he saw the open staircase and bounded up the stairs, arriving at the fifth floor in no time.

Upon entering the agency, he was greeted pleasantly by Mrs. Stevenson, who was seated behind her desk in the main office. She was in the middle of typing but stopped and welcomed Sloan to the agency. She introduced herself, remembering him from the work he completed for them years ago and then presented Sloan to Gabrielle and Polly. Gabrielle and Polly smiled at Sloan, admiring his chiseled face, height and commanding appearance.

Sloan mentioned he was there to see Mr. Stevenson as arranged yesterday by Caleb. He was impressed with Mrs. Stevenson, rather matronly but distinguished. He noted Gabrielle and Polly, young and eager, the inquisitive type, dressed in the flapper style, wearing excessive makeup and lipstick, especially Polly. He glanced around the main office and saw three desks with quite a bit of paperwork, along with typewriters. Mrs. Stevenson led him down the long hallway to her husband's office, where she mentioned he was awaiting his arrival.

Mr. Stevenson got rather heavily to his feet, as though in considerable pain and shook hands with Sloan. He invited him to a chair and asked if he wanted tea or coffee, which he declined. Mrs. Stevenson then left the office, leaving the men to their business.

"Thank you, Mr. Sheppard, for coming here today," Mr. Stevenson said, his face wrinkled in consternation. "It is a pleasure to see you again. I remember fondly the work you accomplished for us." He paused. "You will excuse my wearisome appearance. My wife and I have suffered much loss recently. The deaths of Mr. Turner, his daughter and Mr. Lennon have disturbed us a great deal. We also have been much affected by the passing of President Harding, my wife perhaps more than myself. Nevertheless, the president's sudden death and Calvin Coolidge as our new leader have been most unsettling." He sighed. "Caleb told me yesterday of his visit. I am pleased you will assist to resolve the issues surrounding the recent deaths."

Sloan could tell he spoke with much dignity. He remembered Mr. Leonard Stevenson as a man of great honor and prestige, who took pride in his accomplishments. Obviously, he was unused to unexpected deaths, certainly not murder. He listened as Mr. Stevenson continued to address him.

He explained in detail what Sloan already heard from Caleb; the taste testing event at the beverage company, the heavily promoted *Champagne Twist* drink, the publicity campaign and the fanfare that greeted the drink's debut. Mayor Hackett was in attendance and members of the press. It was quite festive and the atmosphere was light and diverting, with music and dancing, until Mr. Turner began to speak from the podium.

"He clutched at his chest as though in pain," Mr. Stevenson recalled. "There was a thunderstorm and the lights dimmed, and then went out completely. We were in the dark for a while until flashlights and candles were lit. By that time, the lights returned and Mr. Turner proceeded to propose the toast he started before the lights went out."

Sloan had his notepad with him but found his notes already conveyed this information. He asked Mr. Stevenson if he remembered anything else that could shed light on what happened to Mr. Turner, his daughter or his brother-in-law.

"I was not acquainted with Mr. Lennon. I have met the Turners previously and they are fine people. I did not know Mrs. Nichols, although her husband is employed here as my accountant. Currently, they are in the process of divorcing. Mrs. Turner is extremely distraught at this time. I believe she is still at home. She is being cared for by Sister Catherine, a nurse from St. Peter's Hospital who is also a friend of my wife."

Sloan decided to change course. "Mr. Stevenson, do you remember Mr. Cyrus Newcomb?"

Mr. Stevenson's face wrinkled tightly. "Mr. Newcomb? Well, yes, I believe I do remember him. Quite a humble fellow. He ran the Clinton Street Hotel and we did a publicity campaign for him once." He paused. "Why do you ask?"

Sloan looked up from his notepad. "I remember the work I completed for you while I was employed at the other agency. I also assisted Mr. Newcomb in checking out several patrons of his hotel who, upon my investigation, were gangsters, conducting illegal business. I looked through the notes I kept on his case and I noticed he mentioned you worked for him in promoting his hotel. He also was acquainted with Mr. Lennon. That was 1915."

"Yes, I do remember it was in 1915. What's the point?"

"There may not be one. I am attempting to discover any relevancies between your agency and people who have known you, your staff and the Turners. There were multiple arrests at that time. From what Mr. Newcomb mentioned, Mr. Lennon was not involved in the illegal activity." He paused. "How long has your staff been employed here?"

"Mr. Nichols, my accountant, has been here many years. As I mentioned, he is Mr. Turner's son-in-law. Mr. Cunningham, an account executive, over ten years. Except for my wife and I, everyone is relatively new to the agency. They would not remember Mr. Newcomb."

Sloan nodded. "May I speak to the rest of your staff, Mr. Stevenson?"

"I will call Gabrielle whom you already met to request the staff to come here. We'll meet at the conference table and you can speak to them together."

He reached over, picked up the handset of the phone and barked rather firmly to Gabrielle to round up the staff for a meeting in his office immediately. Replacing the handset, he looked at Sloan rather arrogantly, pleased he could summon his staff at the drop of a hat.

Within minutes, several people entered the executive suite and sat methodically at the long table, as though by routine. From their expressions, Sloan deduced they expected the worst and were used to it. He joined Mr. Stevenson at the table, sitting across from Caleb and Mrs. Stevenson.

Mr. Stevenson introduced them to Mr. Sloan Sheppard, the private investigator he hired to look into the recent deaths of Mr. Turner, Mrs. Nichols and Mr. Lennon.

Caleb looked at Sloan as his gaze traveled around the long table, taking in his associates and summing them up. He noticed his eyes rested on Minerva, who looked the efficient secretary, although her face appeared downcast and sullen. Next to her sat Wilbur, looking stonily, a cigarette in his hand. Caleb noticed as Sloan appraised Roy and Peter with a quick sweep and a brief nod of acknowledgement. He likewise nodded to Mrs. Stevenson, Polly and Gabrielle.

Sloan learned Wilbur Hill was a chief account executive, like Caleb. Mr. Stevenson explained Roy Carter and Peter Cunningham were assistant account executives. Polly Ormerod served as the office clerk and typist, along with Gabrielle Woods. Minerva Hill was a secretary who assisted Mr. Stevenson. Mrs. Celeste Stevenson was the main office manager, who oversaw the daily routine of the agency. Mr. Stevenson heaved a sigh of relief, as though glad introductions were over. He then continued speaking, quiet seriously, requesting everyone's attention.

Caleb noticed Jeff was not among them. He wondered if Mr. Stevenson realized it. After a few minutes, Jeff sauntered in, rather carelessly and sat next to Minerva. He explained he was in the middle of an expense report and wanted to complete it before tackling other financial records. Mr. Stevenson nodded, as though excusing him for his delay. He cleared his throat and addressed the people seated around the table.

"Mr. Sheppard is here to speak to us about the taste testing, the murders of Mr. Turner and his brother-in-law, Mr. Lennon and the death of Mrs. Nichols. I am most concerned with the death of Mrs. Nichols. She died during an event that we sponsored. While we are in no way responsible for what happened to her, the public may think otherwise. That is why I have hired Mr. Sheppard, to find a common link if there is one and to discover why these deaths occurred."

"You think someone killed Mrs. Nichols?" Roy asked Sloan.

"I have just started my investigation," Sloan said reasonably. "I cannot make a judgement just yet. It is too early to tell."

"Shouldn't Mrs. Turner have hired you?" Polly said awkwardly to Sloan.

"Mrs. Turner is not strong enough at the moment," Mrs. Stevenson said quietly. "She is under a doctor's care. She has to plan two funerals quite soon as well."

"Maybe that glass was meant for someone else," Gabrielle suggested.

"And my wife drank it by mistake?" Jeff said, rather testily.

"Then who was it meant for?" Minerva asked.

"We don't know if these deaths are related," Peter said.

"Personally, I think it's rather thrilling," Polly said foolishly. "I've never been involved in a real murder mystery before! You're a real detective, Mr. Sheppard?"

"I think it's up to the police to discover who killed Mr. Turner and Mr. Lennon," Jeff said irritably. "As for my wife, she drank some of that *Champagne Twist* drink that was rotten."

"You think it's that simple, Mr. Nichols?" Sloan turned to him.

"I don't want to think otherwise," he answered blandly.

"Two employees of the same company murdered," Mrs. Stevenson said rather sadly. "And we are not sure about poor Mrs. Nichols. She collapsed right at our feet! It was dreadful!"

"Someone may have laced the drink with arsenic on purpose," Roy said. "Maybe it was not meant for Mrs. Nichols, but someone else. Maybe Mr. Turner."

Polly agreed. "After the lights came back on, perhaps Mrs. Nichols picked up the wrong glass. There was confusion in the darkness, after all."

"People were kind of panicky," Peter commented. "I admit I didn't like the darkness, either. When the lights came back on, maybe she did pick up the wrong glass."

Everyone started to speak at once before Mr. Stevenson, almost losing his patience, urged them to silence. He cautioned them not to make irrational judgements when there did not exist any proof.

Sloan asked where they all were at the taste testing and what they remembered about the event. Unfortunately, no one could provide any specific answers. Minerva and Wilbur commented they were near the table where Mrs. Turner and her daughter stood, but they were chatting with a few people and did not notice anything out of the ordinary. Gabrielle told Sloan she was next to Caleb and saw nothing unusual. Caleb, Roy and Peter commented they thought they heard a door close in the distance after the lights went out but nothing beforehand. Polly also commented she remembered hearing a door close somewhere.

"We raised our glasses in a toast to the new drink," Caleb said, looking at everyone around the table. "That's when Mrs. Nichols became so ill and fell to the floor."

Sloan asked if they were acquainted with Mr. Lennon. Nobody knew him, except Jeff, who commented he had met him at his in-law's house once or twice.

"Do the police really think Prudence's death was murder?" Mrs. Stevenson asked Sloan. Her tone held the conviction that it could not be possible, but she knew deep down that it was certainly likely. She looked at Sloan almost pleadingly.

"I will speak to them later today," he told her. "The verdict on the autopsy and the death certificate was unknown for cause of death, possible murder. My contacts at the police department will inform me on the progress of the investigation."

"The police in this city drag their feet," Peter said, puffing at a cigarette. "With all of the speakeasies around town, I imagine they have their hands full."

Roy agreed. "Mr. Lennon was murdered in June. That's over two months ago!"

"Investigations take time, Roy," Peter said firmly. "Solutions do not happen overnight."

Sloan looked at the faces assembled around the table. He mentioned he would appreciate the opportunity to speak to them separately later, which was met with obvious reluctance, even dread. Polly commented rather fearfully that she knew nothing and Gabrielle and Minerva added the same. Mr. Stevenson ignored the nearly hysterical outcries and addressed them again.

"While Mr. Sheppard is investigating, I expect everyone's cooperation. We cannot have any bad publicity for this agency. As I mentioned to Caleb, in the event former and potential clients turn away from us, we may have to close our doors." He paused, as he realized he held their attention to his proclamation. "Thank you for interrupting your work to meet Mr. Sheppard. This meeting is over for now."

Chairs were pushed back and footsteps shuffled to the door, out into the hallway. Mrs. Stevenson thanked Sloan for his visit and assured him she would speak to Mrs. Turner, to inquire if she were strong enough to speak to him. Mr. Stevenson shook hands with Sloan and thanked him again for his assistance.

"I'll see you to the door, Mr. Sheppard," Caleb offered.

Sloan joined Caleb to the hallway and out to the main office where Polly and Gabrielle were busy at their desks. Sloan reiterated he would be in touch again soon and left the agency.

Someone was lying, Caleb thought, bypassing Gabrielle and Polly on the way to his office, ignoring whatever they said to him. Mr. Sheppard must have realized that, too. But who amongst his associates had ties to the Turners, Mr. Lennon or even the beverage company? There were at least a hundred people at the taste testing. If it was determined Jeff's wife was murdered, who would poison her and why? Was Jeff capable of such brutality? Unless that poisoned glass was meant for someone else, most likely Mr. Turner. As he surmised, the murderer returned and finished him off the next night.

He glanced along the quiet hallway, rather uneasily, then entered his office, momentarily forgetting about the recent catastrophic events.

At Albany Police Headquarters, Inspector Harris sat at a long table in a conference room, reviewing his notes on the murders of Mr. Lennon and Mr. Turner. Lieutenant Taylor sat across from him. They were silent for some time until the Inspector cleared his throat, while puffing at a cigarette. He knocked ash into an ashtray and addressed the lieutenant.

"The medical examiner mentioned Mrs. Nichols's death may have been deliberate, but there was no way he could tell for certain."

"Except that there was arsenic in the glass," the Lieutenant added. "No one else had a motive for doing her in. It must rest with the husband."

Inspector Harris studied his notes. "Who at the event would hold a grudge to poison that glass? Surely, it could not have been intended for Mrs. Nichols. After the lights went out, there was confusion. When the lights came back on, she picked up the wrong glass."

"It could've been meant for either of the Turners. Perhaps someone had an axe to grind with either Mr. Turner or his wife and decided to lace that glass with the arsenic."

"The facility staff mentioned arsenic was used there. Someone knew where it was located."

At that moment, a police officer, a youngish man of no more than twenty-five, stuck his head in the door to tell the Inspector there was a phone call for him, a Mr. Sheppard. He wished to speak to him about the Turners.

Inspector Harris looked up and nodded. "Thank you, Officer," he said, dismissing him.

"What is Sheppard up to now?" Lieutenant Taylor asked. "Is he investigating these cases?"

"We'll soon find out," Inspector Harris said, grabbing the candlestick phone off his desk. Upon lifting the handset, he heard the familiar voice of Sloan Sheppard on the other end. He greeted him pleasantly and asked what he could do for him.

"Hello, Inspector," Sloan said. He was in his office at the Albany City Savings Bank Building, having returned there from his appointment at Empire Advertising. "I met today with the staff of Mr. Leonard Stevenson of the Empire Advertising Agency. I am working for him to uncover the truth behind the recent murders and the death of Mrs. Prudence Nichols."

"How is Mr. Stevenson involved?" Inspector Harris asked, finding it rather odd he would hire a private investigator to look into the recent murders.

Sloan explained Mr. Stevenson wanted him to investigate the murders of Mr. Turner and Mr. Lennon, stating that Mrs. Turner was not capable of such actions at this time.

Inspector Harris nodded, not quite comprehendingly. "We are investigating the murders of the two gentlemen as well as the death of Mrs. Nichols." He explained what the medical examiner told them about Prudence's death; that the arsenic laced glass could have been meant for someone else and Mrs. Nichols picked it up by mistake, given the blackout during the thunderstorm.

Sloan agreed. "What do you know about Mr. Cyrus Newcomb, Inspector?"

Inspector Harris looked at Lieutenant Taylor. "Well, not too much, Mr. Sheppard. That was quite some time ago. Why do you ask?"

Sloan explained how he worked for Mr. Newcomb in 1915, investigating gangster activity at his hotel while at the same time Empire Advertising was running publicity for the Clinton Street Hotel. In his notes, he mentioned the arrest of several area hoodlums, who frequented the hotel owned by Mr. Newcomb. Inspector Harris asked if he considered a possible connection.

Sloan puffed at a cigarette. "From my recollections, he was a personable man, who ran a decent establishment."

"I don't see what that has to do with the Turners," Inspector Harris said.

"It is ironic that Empire Advertising and I worked for Mr. Newcomb at roughly the same time in 1915. Gangster activity was rampant before the war. Mr. Newcomb was concerned his premises were being utilized for illegal activity and he was proven correct."

"I do remember several arrests," Inspector Harris said. Several gangsters had died since then. He remembered Mr. Steven Lubbock, Mr. David Winslow and Mr. James Prouty were arrested for bootlegging, had served time and were released. Their names were not on any current arrest records or most wanted lists. He did not know their current whereabouts.

Sloan jotted down the names. "I will further investigate Mr. Newcomb. I know he is deceased, but I want to learn more about him. I'll also try to track down these men."

"They haven't been arrested since," the Inspector pointed out. "At least not in Albany."

"Gangsters have a notorious reputation to seek out trouble," Sloan remarked.

"I think it's a long shot, Mr. Sheppard," Inspector Harris told him.

"Let's plan on going to Empire Advertising tomorrow morning," Sloan said. He ended the conversation and Inspector Harris replaced the handset on the candlestick telephone. He put it back on his desk and returned to his chair with a forlorn expression, as though there was much more in the works he was unprepared for.

"What else did he tell you?" Lieutenant Taylor asked, seeing his colleague's face.

"He thinks there may be an angle with Mr. Newcomb. Remember him from years ago? Officer Davis brought it to our attention. There were gangsters using his hotel for illegal activity. Mr. Sheppard was hired by Mr. Newcomb to investigate."

"I remember that now," the Lieutenant said. "Mr. Sheppard brought down a rather nasty bunch of gangsters here in Albany."

"I had forgotten he worked for Mr. Newcomb to investigate possible gangster activity."

The police officers were silent a few moments, conflicting thoughts swirling in their minds.

Inspector Harris picked up the cigarette he left in the ashtray. "What connection could there possibly be with Mr. Newcomb? Was he acquainted with the Turners?"

"Officer Davis told us Mr. Lennon knew him," the Lieutenant said.

"We'll speak to Mr. Stevenson's staff. No one there was involved with the beverage company. Except Mr. Nichols, the son-in-law."

"We'll go tomorrow morning," Lieutenant Taylor said determinedly.

At the Albany City Savings Bank Building, Sloan replaced the handset on his telephone after speaking with Inspector Harris. He had a lot to think about, his mind in deep contemplation.

What he thought might turn out a murder investigation he now realized had roots buried deep in the past. While he could not yet draw specific conclusions about Mr. Newcomb, he found it ironic his name should turn up in the investigation of Mr. Lennon. There may be nothing in that, of course. However, Mr. Lennon worked at the beverage company. And he was present when there was an altercation at the hotel owned by Mr. Newcomb. Sloan remembered his investigation for Mr. Newcomb yielded several arrests of gangsters and their molls who used the hotel for illegal activity. The Inspector mentioned a Mr. Steven Lubbock, a Mr. David Winslow and a Mr. James Prouty. The names sounded familiar but he would need to look through his old files again. The police would have complete records of the men and women arrested in 1915 who frequented the Clinton Street Hotel. There might be a link somewhere, but what it was he could not yet determine.

He scratched his head, causing a few strands of black hair to fall over his forehead. From what he deduced this morning, the employees of the advertising agency seemed like an odd bunch, more than likely they knew more than they were willing to admit. Sloan knew secrets abounded in a murder investigation and this case was purporting to be no different. The only normal ones were Caleb and Mrs. Stevenson. Even Mr. Stevenson seemed larger than life, as though he too knew something he did not wish to discuss.

Impulsively, he picked up his telephone and asked the operator to connect him with the Empire Advertising Agency. He was pleased to hear Mrs. Stevenson at the other end. He informed her he planned to visit again tomorrow morning and at that time wished to speak to the staff in more detail. Mrs. Stevenson assured Sloan she would relay that message to her husband and the call ended. He then glanced at the wall clock and saw it was close to five o'clock.

Usually, Sloan enjoyed working late, as the building was practically devoid of people and it was extremely quiet. Feeling somewhat restless, he found he was not prepared to stay after his usual hours. He decided he would catch the trolley back to his apartment. He enjoyed exercising at the local YMCA but he was too preoccupied to think of weight lifting. He locked his office door and instead of waiting for the elevator, entered the stairway,

Sloan knew he had to act quickly. His intuition told him the case was far from over. It was the beginning of a tangled web of murder, lies and deceit. There were connections to the past, but exactly what they were and how they affected the current situation was still uncertain. Possibly, Mrs. Nichols was not the intended victim but Mr. Turner. But why would someone kill Mr. Turner and Mr. Lennon? Robbery was eliminated as a motive. The Newcomb angle may be a dead end. On the other hand, it may be the missing link to the entire case.

Motivated by a strong desire to see justice prevail, he entered the lobby with a firm step. He exited the building and crossed busy State Street to await the trolley.

CHAPTER THIRTEEN

Wednesday morning saw three men of the law arrive at Empire Advertising. As Sloan walked briskly up State Street, he nearly collided with Inspector Harris and Lieutenant Taylor as they exited their patrol car. He greeted them cordially and was pleased they were headed for the agency, too. He wondered how the staff would embellish three men questioning them at once. Certainly, someone would entertain them with far-reaching and even ludicrous accounts of what occurred, although based on fact. Information would be distorted, even exaggerated. From his vast experiences in investigations, Sloan knew many people had something to hide; the presence of the law would unsettle even the dispassionate suspect.

Sloan led the way into the office building and to the elevators. Arriving at the office doors, Mrs. Stevenson looked up and was pleased to see Sloan but rather disenchanted upon seeing the police officers. She got up and shook hands with them.

"Good morning, Mr. Sheppard," she said pleasantly. "I spoke with my husband who knows of your visit." She paused, looking at the police officers. "I did not know the police intended to come here today, too."

Sloan nodded. “They are investigating the recent murders, too.”

“Well, it’s better to have all the fish in the same pond,” Polly said, looking up from her typewriter, wiping her forehead. It was extremely hot. “Kills two birds with one stone, doesn’t it?”

Mrs. Stevenson, rather embarrassed by Polly’s preposterousness, introduced the police officers to Polly and Gabrielle and then led them down the hallway to her husband’s executive suite. Mr. Stevenson, busy at his desk as always, looked up and showed surprised at the men in the doorway. He anticipated Sloan’s visit but not the police officers. His wife explained what Sloan had told her, which he reluctantly accepted. She soon departed as Mr. Stevenson waived the men to chairs at the conference table. He got up and limped toward them, settling at the head of the table, looking tired but stoic.

Mr. Stevenson acknowledged Sloan. “Mr. Sheppard is a fine investigator who will resolve this issue to my satisfaction.” His tone implied it was up to Sloan and not the police department who had yet to discover who murdered Mr. Lennon over two months ago. “You are welcome to speak to the staff as you please, gentlemen. They already know of your visit, Mr. Sheppard. But we did not know of your visit, Inspector Harris.”

Sloan sensed a certain friction and asked if he could see Caleb first, while the police officers decided to speak to the ladies in the main office. Mr. Stevenson got up rather testily and pointed down the hallway to Caleb’s office. Inspector Harris mentioned they would find their way to the main office. Sloan watched as he grudgingly retreated to his desk while he walked off to see Caleb. Caleb looked up as Sloan stood in the doorway.

“Mr. Sheppard, it’s great to see you again,” Caleb said, welcoming him. “Mr. Stevenson told us you’d be here this morning. I heard the police are here, too.”

Sloan entered the office. “Inspector Harris and Lieutenant Taylor from the Albany Police are here to speak to everyone, including you.” He paused. “Is there more you can tell me from that day, Caleb? Something you forgot that came back to you?”

Caleb returned to his desk and picked up the cigarette he left in an ashtray. “When the lights went out, it was rather unsettling because it was so dark. I heard a door close in the distance but didn’t think anything of it. Then the lights came back on and everything was normal.” He hesitated. “Would you like to speak to the other members of the staff?”

“That is my intent,” Sloan said decisively. He carried his notepad and was prepared to write information down as he saw fit.

Caleb directed Sloan to the office shared by Roy and Peter. They looked up, somewhat startled. Roy asked Sloane what he could help him with.

“I’d like to know what you remember about the taste testing, Mr. Carter and you as well, Mr. Cunnigham. And perhaps a little about yourselves, too.”

Roy stiffened slightly, unused to dealing with any kind of law enforcement. He glanced over at Peter, who spoke up before he had the chance. He told Sloan he was from Albany and that he had been talking with several people in attendance, enjoying the festivities, the music and the dancing. Roy mentioned he was from Dunkirk, New York and graduated from the State Teachers College in Albany. He told Sloan that Mr. Turner clutched at his chest and reached for the podium, but he seemed fine afterward. Mrs. Nichols became ill after drinking *Champagne Twist* and collapsed onto the floor.

Sloan looked at Roy Carter, a young man who appeared right out of college or close to it. Perhaps intimidated by the older workers, sullen, insecure but ambitious enough to wreak havoc for others in his ruthless climb to the top. While appearing diffident, Sloan knew from experience his type usually masked an entirely different persona, one that was calculating and clever. Peter Cunningham, on the other hand, was rather outspoken, even abrasive in his tone, as though he had had enough of this murder investigation and wanted nothing more to do with it. Sloan detected a certain deviousness masked by forthrightness. His face contorted into tight lines and his mouth drooped, a sign of discontent and anxiety.

Sloan asked if they knew Mr. Cyrus Newcomb of the Clinton Street Hotel. Neither Roy nor Jeff knew him or were acquainted with the publicity campaign Mr. Stevenson conducted. He also asked if they knew how arsenic could have been placed in the glass from which Mrs. Nichols drank. Again, Roy and Jeff shook their heads, unable to help.

"There is nothing more we can tell you, Mr. Sheppard," Peter reiterated.

"Jeff might know more," Roy volunteered as though to take the emphasis off of himself.

Inspector Harris entered the office just then, wishing to speak with them. Caleb excused himself and returned to his office while Sloan ventured to his next meeting. He entered the hallway and noticed Mrs. Stevenson conversing with Mr. Wilbur Hill.

"Mr. Sheppard, this is Mr. Wilbur Hill, a chief account executive. His office is at the other end of the hallway, with Minerva. Why don't you speak with Mr. Sheppard, Wilbur?"

Sloan looked carefully at Wilbur Hill and thought there was nothing he wanted less than to converse with a private investigator. Reluctantly, he led Sloan down the hallway to his office that he shared with Minerva, who was busy typing a report. She was so engrossed in her work that she did not notice they had entered.

"Minerva, this is Mr. Sheppard," Wilbur said, sitting behind his desk. "He is here to speak to us about the taste testing event."

Minerva stopped typing and looked up at Sloan. "Of course, I remember you. It's nice to see you again, Mr. Sheppard. Please, take a seat."

Certainly cordial enough, Sloan wondered what they were hiding. Like Roy Carter and Peter Cunningham, they appeared unused to questioning. At a quick glance Sloan thought Wilbur was in his late fifties, rather hard-faced and determined, an executive with a no nonsense approach. Sloan judged Minerva around fifty and while pretty in a conventional sense, her mascara and bright lipstick most likely covered up more than her features. They seemed an unlikely couple. He listened as they spoke of the advertising agency, what their worked involved and how much they enjoyed the industry. Sloan asked what they remember about the taste testing. Minerva spoke up first, rather excitedly.

"The lights went out and it was so dark in that room! Mr. Turner proposed we raise our glasses to the new beverage. He looked ill as though he would faint. Then the lights came back on and Mrs. Nichols peeled right over and collapsed onto the floor."

Wilbur agreed, puffing at a cigarette. "It did happen rather fast and was totally unexpected."

Sloan nodded, taking a few notes. "Where do you come from, Mr. Hill?"

Wilbur told Sloan he and Minerva were from Binghamton and that he had worked in advertising there and in Norwich before moving to Albany three years ago. They commented how much they enjoyed the capital city, the many fine restaurants, department stores and dance halls. He mentioned they purchased a brownstone on upper Madison Avenue, near Washington Park. Sloan told them he also lived in that area. They concurred it was a wonderful part of the city, with access to the trolley to take them downtown.

"Employees of the beverage company have been spoken to as well as the cleaning staff," Sloan explained. "Arsenic was found in the glass from which Mrs. Nichols drank. It is unclear how the arsenic got into the glass, unless it was some of the beverage that was spoiled."

"I admit I did not like the beverage too much," Wilbur said. "I thought it had a rather bitter taste. I only sipped it while we raised our glasses to the toast."

"I wasn't too fond of it, either," Minerva agreed, looking at Sloan steadily. "Perhaps there was the answer, Mr. Sheppard. Some of the drink may have been poisonous by accident, of course."

"No one else became ill," Sloan pointed out.

There followed an awkward silence. Sloan asked them if they knew Mr. Turner, Mr. Lennon and Mrs. Nichols. They denied ever having met them and only saw Mr. Turner and Mrs. Nichols the day of the event. They did not know Mrs. Turner had a brother, never having met her either. He inquired further if they knew Mr. Newcomb of the Clinton Street Hotel. Wilbur mentioned he knew of the hotel when he lived in Albany years ago but did not know Mr. Newcomb. Minerva did not know of him or the hotel.

"Jeff Nichols is the accountant here," Wilbur offered. "He was married to Mrs. Nichols and was on good terms with his in-laws. He and his wife argued the day of the event. I found it rather embarrassing. I thought they would go at it tooth and nail."

Minerva agreed. "They were in the process of divorcing."

Sloan was writing in his notepad, not convinced they were telling the truth. Inspector Harris appeared in the doorway and like musical chairs, Sloan got up and offered his seat to the police officer, thanking Minerva and Wilbur for their time.

As Sloan entered the hallway, he saw Jeff Nichols speaking with Lieutenant Taylor. From his expression, he seemed defensive and not pleased to be questioned. He felt further animosity which Sloan noticed as he approached and requested to speak to him. The Lieutenant nodded toward Sloan, as though he needed all his strength to deal with such ambivalence. He excused himself, as he wished to join the Inspector with Wilbur and Minerva. Jeff led Sloan to his office, where he sat at his desk and lit a cigarette. Sloan watched as he puffed rather anxiously, fidgeting with items on his desk, before asking him what he could do for him. Sloan waited until he made eye contact and then asked what he remembered about the taste testing.

"I've already spoken to the police officer. The lights went out and it was total darkness until someone found candles and flashlights. Then the lights came back on and my father-in-law began to make a toast. I didn't realize we raised our glasses to murder." His tone implied it was simple and straightforward. He looked at Sloan, dreading more inquiries and wishing he would leave him alone.

"Your associates mentioned your father-in-law clutched at his chest and reached for the podium for support," Sloan said. "Do you remember that?"

Jeff nodded. "He was just excited about the event, Mr. Sheppard. My father-in-law tended to be high strung, that's all." Again, he implied there was nothing to worry about.

"How long have you worked here, Mr. Nichols?"

Jeff told Sloan he graduated from college with a degree in accounting and began his career in Albany, for several accounting firms, before landing his current position with Empire Advertising over ten years ago. He was the only accountant on staff, which enabled him to prioritize important financial records. He worked closely with Mr. Stevenson, who had great faith in his abilities.

Sloan detected a slight sarcasm to that remark. While the older man may have faith in his attributes, most likely Mr. Nichols had little regard for him and could care less if he dropped dead at his desk. He asked Jeff if his divorce was finalized. Jeff shook his head.

"No, we had not yet gotten to that stage. But now that Prudence is dead, it won't matter."

Sloan felt animosity combined with nonchalance, as though his worries were over and he no longer had to deal with his troublesome wife. He had dealt with many divorce cases but could not remember such insensitivity and lack of empathy from one partner to another. He thanked Jeff for his time and headed for the main office, where he encountered Polly at her desk. She too was busy typing but stopped upon seeing Sloan.

"Hello, Mr. Sheppard," she said pleasantly. "There is so much work to be done in an advertising agency! Look at these reports that need typing!"

She pointed to a modest pile of handwritten drafts, waiting for official documentation in typed form. He listened as she spoke about her work at the agency. He could not help notice Polly Ormerod was rather attractive, about forty, wearing the latest stylish summer dress with a fine string of pearls. She continued speaking to Sloan as though he were the one person she wanted most to see, as though he were her best friend. Gabrielle joined them and inquired about the murder investigation. She lamented she could not tell him anything he did not already know.

"Mr. Turner seemed flabbergasted about something," Gabrielle pointed out, as she stood alongside Polly's desk, looking at Sloan. "I thought he would faint! It was really bizarre."

Sloan nodded. He asked Polly about herself. She told him she was from Albany, divorced, did not have children and was dating Peter. Gabrielle was also from Albany and graduated from a secretarial school. He asked if they were acquainted with Mr. Cyrus Newcomb of the Clinton Street Hotel. Polly continued typing, as though she did not want to answer him. Gabrielle mentioned she did not know him or the publicity the agency carried out and Polly also stated the same. Sloan wondered which of them was not being honest.

Polly then turned to him, puffing at her cigarette. "Mr. Turner looked at the crowd and we were about to raise our glasses to the new beverage but then he clutched at his chest." She put down her red tipped cigarette to answer an incoming call.

Gabrielle turned to Sloan. "When the lights went out, I heard a door close in the distance. When the lights came back on, Mr. Turner seemed fine. Mrs. Turner and Mrs. Nichols were there, too. I wish I could help you more, Mr. Sheppard, but that's all I know."

He thanked the women for their time. He noticed Mr. Stevenson had entered the main office and was speaking with Inspector Harris, Lieutenant Taylor and his wife.

"Thank you, Mr. Stevenson," Sloan said, coming up to him and shaking his hand again. "I will be in touch with you shortly."

The police officers also thanked the Stevensons and then joined Sloan in walking out of the main office and into the lobby to await the elevator. Inspector Harris looked at Sloan curiously.

"Fine bunch of characters, wouldn't you say, Mr. Sheppard?"

Sloan nodded. His mind returned to Mr. Cyrus Newcomb and the possible connection with the Turners. Mr. Lennon was acquainted with Mr. Newcomb. Of course, that did not mean anything. It was indeed a long shot, as the Inspector mentioned. Nobody at the agency knew Mr. Newcomb, but someone may have been lying. Mr. Stevenson mentioned he was unaware of gangster activity at the hotel.

"Mr. Sheppard? The elevator is here," Lieutenant Taylor said, rather loudly.

Sloan shook his head, coming out of his reverie. He joined the police officers in an already crowded elevator on its way down to the lobby.

Later that same day, after arriving at her apartment, Polly sat at her vanity table and looked at herself in the mirror, applying fresh lipstick. She planned to dine with Peter this evening and wanted to look her best. She applied rogue and powder, brushing her fine hair back from her forehead. She wore a sleek black dress, which fitted her shapely figure appealingly. A radiant string of pearls highlighted her pretty face. She glanced at the clock on her nightstand. It was almost six o'clock and Peter should arrive soon.

Polly lived in a pleasant one-bedroom apartment on lower State Street, not far from the capitol and within walking distance of Empire Advertising. It also was convenient to the trolley, enabling her to easily reach Peter's house on Myrtle Avenue. During the summer, she would walk to his house, passing the Cathedral of the Immaculate Conception and the Governor's Mansion. Tonight, Peter was coming to her place and they planned to dine at Keeler's downtown.

Rather bitterly, her mind drifted to the advertising agency. No one at that claptrap gave a damn about her, maybe not even Peter. Her income paid the bills but that was it. She knew Mrs. Stevenson did not approve of the flapper lifestyle. She was surprised she was in favor of the vote three years ago. She cast her ballot for Mr. James Cox, the Democratic contender in 1920, who lost to Mr. Harding. Honestly, she never pictured Mrs. Stevenson a suffragist.

She did not know Roy too well, which was for the best, as he looked just as foolish and lost as Gabrielle. She tolerated Gabrielle, who she knew was smitten with Caleb, the military man who seemed more concerned with his muscles than with females. She could imagine him in a bodybuilding contest. She admitted his physique certainly caught her eye.

Jeff was divorcing his wife from the beverage company, the owner's daughter. How foolish, she thought crudely. The Turners were loaded with money and he actually wanted a divorce? Of course, he had been with Empire Advertising forever, it seemed, so he must not be hurting financially. At least he would not have to worry about a divorce proceeding. She rather envied him. Her own divorce five years ago had been costly and painful.

She had a steady relationship with Peter, whom she had grown to admire. He used her when he wanted, which annoyed her at times and at other times, she played right along. Of course, Peter did not know she used him too, but for a different purpose.

She considered Minerva and Wilbur two money-hungry fortune hunters out for all they could get. Indeed, they had amassed quite a bit of money, cleverly reaping the benefits of the lucrative stock market and working in another part of the state before moving back to Albany. And foolish Mr. Stevenson hired them. She doubted he even checked references, like he did with her and Peter, too. She didn't know about the others. Minerva and Wilbur were competent enough and the older man was pleased. Good help was hard to find, as Mrs. Stevenson once commented.

She got up and went to the bureau. She lit a cigarette, drawing on it heavily, while looking out the window onto State Street and the back of the capitol building. There were plenty of people enjoying the late summer early evening, strolling with their dogs and others pushing baby carriages. She opened a drawer and looked at a folder. She ruffled through the pages until she found some copious notes she had scribbled, rather hastily. She nodded in satisfaction.

She approached the window, anticipating Peter on the front steps. Impatiently, she walked to the kitchen, where a bottle of bourbon Peter bought from a bootlegger was on the counter. She poured a glass, feeling the liquor burn in her throat. It was a wonderful and splendid life. She smiled maliciously. The future looked bright indeed.

Roy sat in the living room of his comfortable apartment on Dove Street. In his right hand, he held a cigarette and in his left a glass containing whisky, mixed with ginger ale, as he preferred it. He swirled it around before taking another gulp, almost finishing it in one swallow. Not to worry, he thought, as he eyed the whisky bottle on his kitchen table.

Roy lived alone in a modest one-bedroom, a simple walkup apartment, not far from Myrtle Avenue where Peter lived. Of course, Peter was lucky enough to afford a brownstone but Roy could not yet indulge in such a luxury. He did not have the large financial earnings as Jeff or Wilbur and Minerva.

Roy rather missed Dunkirk and contemplated returning to his hometown. He hated the long train ride out to the western part of the state. Albany held more opportunity and the capitol was where the action was located. But he decided a visit home would not hurt.

At times, he felt somewhat intimidated by his male counterparts at the agency. He was of medium height, unlike the others who stood at least six feet or more. Especially Caleb who was six foot three and must weigh two hundred pounds with his bulging biceps and muscular frame. However, Roy had more on his mind than such trivial matters. His goal was to earn more money in as easy a way as possible.

His income was supplemented by his wise investments in the stock market. And like Peter, he aspired to purchase a brownstone house on fashionable Myrtle Avenue. He had an excellent broker who kept him well informed of the current market situation. He heard on the radio that 1923 was another stellar year for investments and 1924 was projected to be just as advantageous. He thought the death of President Harding would affect his investments and the market in general but fortunately, that did not happen.

That ridiculous taste testing event. Well, Caleb, it didn't quite turn out the way you expected, did it? To Roy it appeared as if Mr. Turner was stunned or taken by surprise. Maybe the size of the crowd. After all, there were quite a few people looking up at him.

How terrible for the lights to go out during the taste testing! It was pitch dark in that room and rather unsettling, scary even. And that loud clap of thunder! Shook the whole building, too. Mrs. Turner turned on a few flashlights and lit candles. By that time, the lights came back on. Roy remembered the stunned faces on everyone. Mrs. Stevenson was aghast, horrified. That nun, too, was shocked. Mr. Stevenson seemed to appear out of nowhere. And where were Jeff and Peter? They showed up afterward, too. Only Jeff could hold such antipathy toward his wife. Only Jeff could resort to such a dastardly deed.

He got up and fitfully turned on the radio. He found a station playing popular tunes and soon relished hearing the soothing voices of Rudy Vallee, Bessie Smith, Ma Rainey and Ruth Etting. He worried when the Big Boss told them the agency could close if there was negative publicity surrounding the death at the taste testing. The public was finicky with whom they conducted business and any negative press could hurt Empire Advertising, despite its longevity. He read in the papers that Empire Advertising, much to Mr. Stevenson's chagrin, sponsored the taste testing. He grimaced at the thought of looking for another job, although Albany was certainly prospering now.

He finished the whisky, refilling his glass from the bottle on the kitchen table. Roy had connections with a local bootlegger, who kept him supplied with liquor as needed. It was rather expensive and certainly illegal but he knew he was not the only person in Albany who dealt with bootleggers. Once when he visited Peter at his Myrtle Avenue brownstone, he noticed several empty whisky bottles in his garbage. He wondered what Peter and Polly were scheming, as they appeared secretive, even devious, as though they were hiding something.

Roy stared at his radio, listening to Rudy Vallee. His mind was not so much on the music but on something else. He returned to the sofa and picked up the *Albany Evening Press*. He thumbed through the pages but he could not concentrate on the news. He gulped more of the whisky. He would look out for himself, of course. He just might take a trip to Dunkirk after all.

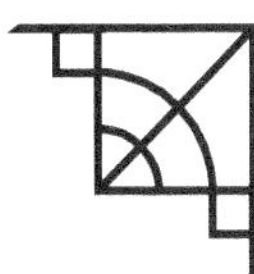

CHAPTER FOURTEEN

Caleb spent a hectic week at Empire Advertising. Inspector Harris and Lieutenant Taylor returned, questioning everyone at length, trying to determine exactly what happened to Mr. Turner and his daughter at the taste testing.

From all accounts, the police determined Mrs. Nichols was murdered; that the poisoned glass was meant for her father and that Mrs. Nichols, in the melee after the blackout, picked up the glass intended for him. The police did not elaborate but Caleb accepted it, as he previously believed that as the truth. He commented that since Mr. Turner was murdered the next evening, it seemed like whoever killed him, realized the mistake and wanted to finish him off.

The police officers then solicited further assistance into the murder of Mr. Lennon, but that also was a dead end. As they learned previously, no one at the agency knew Mr. Lennon, except Jeff, who again mentioned that while he had met his wife's uncle, he spoke to him only briefly. They mentioned Mr. Cyrus Newcomb but no one knew him or had even heard of him. While still uncertain of a possible angle regarding Mr. Newcomb, Inspector Harris wondered who was lying and what information was being concealed. Mr. Sheppard seemed convinced there was a connection although at the moment, he failed to find one.

Grudgingly, the police officers knew inquires at Empire Advertising reached a conclusion, although not a satisfactory one. They again spoke extensively to the Stevensons but could not gain any further information. When questioned about Mr. Cyrus Newcomb, Mr. Stevenson repeated he had conducted publicity for Mr. Newcomb in 1915, but that was eight years ago. He had no contact with Mr. Newcomb since that time.

By Friday, Caleb was glad the weekend was ahead of him. He looked forward to his reserve duty at the Watervliet Arsenal. He was out the main office doors before five o'clock and upon returning to his apartment, where his duffel bag was already packed, he hopped on another trolley on Hamilton Street to take him downtown, where he switched for a northbound trolley for Watervliet.

The Watervliet Arsenal was convenient for Caleb, as he did not have to travel too far from his apartment. He looked at the large facility and upon entering, he was assigned numerous weekend duties. As a West Point graduate, he was already a Second Lieutenant which meant he skipped the more mundane duties assigned to other reservists. Soon he was involved with maintaining records of the cannons in the military's inventory as well as ensuring weapons were within compliance.

A long weekend but satisfying as Caleb was extremely dedicated to serving his country. On Sunday, his duty over, he returned to his apartment, rather worn out but exhilarated, nonetheless. By late afternoon, he decided he was ready for a long and strenuous exercise routine. He could think of nothing better to alleviate the stress of the murder inquiry than a rigorous physical endurance regimen; what he was accustomed to while at West Point and the army base.

In gym shorts and a tank top, he headed over to the jungle gym in Washington Park, where he masterly used the monkey bars, counting well over a hundred pull-ups. He performed leg extensions, tricep extensions, sit-ups, pushups and stomach crunches. He saw a football lying on the ground and he practiced kicking it in the air in the open grass, running to retrieve it and then kicking it again. He performed this activity several times until he noticed a young woman approaching him from the corner of Willett Street and Hudson Avenue. He watched as she crossed into the park and came directly toward him. He recognized Gabrielle. She looked forlorn and morose, as though she had been sad, even crying.

Caleb wiped sweat from his forehead and face with his tank top. He held onto the football and greeted Gabrielle, wondering what she wanted and how she knew he was even there.

"Hi, Caleb. I knew you were at the Watervliet Arsenal this weekend for your reserve duty." She paused, looking at him intently. "I called your apartment but there was no answer, so I figured you would be here. I know how much you like to exercise."

He looked at her, almost pitifully, wondering what she was thinking. He felt rather foolish in his exercise clothes, his face and blond hair soaked in sweat, knowing she was observing him. While at West Point and on active duty at the military base, he lifted weights and exercised with his platoon. For Caleb it was unnatural to see a young woman when he exercised.

"I just got back a little while ago," he explained, uncomfortably. "I wanted to exercise before supper. Back to work tomorrow." He paused. "Something wrong, Gabrielle?"

She appeared downtrodden, even exasperated. She approached him and reached out to him. Before he knew it, she buried her face in his muscular chest, oblivious to the sweaty tee shirt, and sobbed softly, clinging to him almost desperately. Caleb kept his arms at his side, not sure what she wanted of him.

"Let's go over here," he told her. He pointed to a set of wooden benches near the jungle gym. There was no one else around, so it was rather quiet. A few people were walking through the park, as it was still light and pleasantly warm. Caleb put the football down on the ground and turned to Gabrielle. At first, she did not speak, and then she collected herself, dried her eyes and looked at him.

"Caleb, there is a murderer loose and we don't know what could happen next. I admit I'm scared! Suppose someone from the agency that we don't know had an axe to grind with the Turners! That means we've come face to face with a killer and we're not even aware of it!"

Caleb stretched his long legs. He too had similar thoughts but he did not voice them aloud. He did not know what to say except to comfort her as best he could.

"The police are still investigating. So is Mr. Sheppard. They will figure out what's going on. Mr. Sheppard is an experienced private investigator with a proven record. He'll get to the bottom of it, Gabrielle."

She looked at him, rather irritably. "Suppose this killer strikes repeatedly? Mrs. Turner could be the next victim. They've already killed Mr. Lennon, Mr. Turner and their daughter."

"What makes you think Mrs. Turner may be killed?"

"I don't know. I couldn't sleep last night. Roy asked me to a dance hall but I couldn't go." She paused. "There may be something hidden we don't know about."

"What do you mean?" he asked her cautiously.

"The police haven't found who killed Mr. Lennon. Now they have Mr. Turner's murder to deal with and Mrs. Nichols, too. She may have taken the glass with the arsenic that was mean for her father! If someone at the beverage company didn't kill Mr. Turner, then who did?

And Mr. Lennon, too. They bring up that Mr. Newcomb, whoever he was as though we knew about him."

Caleb nodded. "There's a file on the publicity for his hotel in the spare office. Tomorrow I'll take another look at it. Maybe we can find out more about him."

Gabrielle appeared relieved. "That's a good idea, Caleb."

They walked off toward Willett Street, turning left onto Madison Avenue. They arrived at the intersection with Dove Street and crossed, heading for Elm Street. Gabrielle apologized for crying so much, then abruptly turned and walked down Elm Street to her apartment.

Caleb stared after her, the afternoon sun beating down on him relentlessly. The memories of Mrs. Nichols lying dead at his feet came back to him. Finally reaching Irving Street, he climbed the steps to the brownstone house, his mind deep in conflicting thoughts.

At six o'clock that evening, Sloan rang the doorbell of the mansion belonging to the Turners. As he stood on the doorstep, he looked around and marveled at its beauty. A large two-story house, containing windows that looked out onto the wide lawn. Just across Englewood Place was Washington Park and to the left was State Street, lined magnificently with brownstone houses. Certainly not a neighborhood he had occasion to visit often. He turned toward the door as he realized it was opened. He saw an older woman, looking at him rather suspiciously.

"Hello, I am Mr. Sloan Sheppard, private investigator. I spoke with Mrs. Turner on Friday and she invited me here this evening to see her."

"Yes, I know," the elderly woman said abruptly. "Please come in."

Sloan assumed this was not Mrs. Turner, from her voice over the wire. He looked at her rather questioningly. Reluctantly she introduced herself as Sister Catherine, a nurse at St. Peter's Hospital and a friend of Mrs. Stevenson and Mrs. Turner. She led Sloan into the living room, where Mrs. Turner was sitting on the sofa, rather dazed and confused, thumbing through the latest issue of *The Saturday Evening Post*, while sipping a cup of tea. She looked up as they entered. Sister Catherine introduced Sloan and invited him to sit in an armchair.

A comfortable room, he thought glancing around at the rich furnishings. Certainly, spoke of much money. An adequate place for an executive like Mr. Turner and his family to live. He looked carefully at the elderly woman on the sofa before him.

She looked tired and drawn, whatever energy she had was used up by the recent deaths. She appeared lifeless, as though every breath was an effort. While she maintained a certain dignity to her poise and coiffure, Sloan knew she had weathered the recent storms badly. He was surprised she held up as well as she did. He smiled and thanked her for seeing him this evening.

"I understand you are investigating for Mr. Stevenson," she said weakly, putting the magazine on the coffee table in front of her. "That is commendable of him to appoint you, Mr. Sheppard. You are quite well known here in Albany."

Sloan thanked her for the gracious compliment. He talked briefly about his career in investigations and as a librarian, his appointment as a junior investigator with a firm before opening his own practice in 1920. Since then, his duties had multiplied prodigiously and he worked diligently to resolve cases for his clients.

"I have buried my brother, my husband and my daughter, my only child," Mrs. Turner said, again speaking very weakly. "This has been dreadful, Mr. Sheppard, absolutely dreadful."

"Mrs. Turner, please, you must not get upset," Sister Catherine begged her.

She glanced at her, nodding. "Yes, dear, I know, but I find if I talk about it, it is better than keeping it bottled up inside." She turned to Sloan. "What can you do for me, Mr. Sheppard?"

"I'd like as much information as possible about your husband, brother and daughter," Sloan said, to start. "The police believe your daughter drank the glass that was intended for your husband. Would you tell me what you think may have happened?"

Mrs. Turner sighed, and then began a rather lengthy discourse on the taste testing event. The planning, the execution, the toast in which her husband encouraged glasses raised for the new beverage and his apparent weakness just before the lights went out during the thunderstorm.

"I was there also, Mr. Sheppard," Sister Catherine added. She looked at Mrs. Turner. "If you don't mind, Mrs. Turner, I remember everything so well."

Mrs. Turner told her to speak for her, as she sipped the tea. She leaned her head back on the sofa and listened as Sister Catherine told Sloan what she knew of the events of that afternoon.

"Mr. Turner clutched at his chest," she explained. "He had been about to propose the toast, as Mrs. Turner explained, but he was so flabbergasted at something that it rendered him speechless."

"What was it that caused him to act like that?" Sloan asked her.

Sister Catherine shrugged. "We don't know. Then the lights went out and it was pitch dark in that room, rather unsettling. People were brushing past us, stepping on each other's shoes, apologizing and complaining about the darkness."

"I told one of our workers to find flashlights and candles," Mrs. Turner offered. "He returned with several but by then the lights returned."

"Where was your husband at that time?"

"He was next to my daughter and I, in front of the podium. I think he came to make sure I was safe. Poor Mr. Turner. He went back to the podium, with a glass, and proposed the toast."

"And Mrs. Nichols picked up a glass, too?" Sloan asked.

Mrs. Turner nodded tearfully. "Yes, then she became terribly ill. I really don't want to discuss it any further, Mr. Sheppard."

Sister Catherine agreed. "What else can we help you with, Mr. Sheppard?" Her tone held firmness as though he had already extended his stay and she wished for him to leave. Her expression was stern as if she guarded Mrs. Turner from anything unpleasant.

However, Sloan was not easily put off. He changed course and asked Mrs. Turner about her brother. Mrs. Turner seemed to perk up a bit as she spoke.

She told Sloan about her brother Walter Lennon who became a widower at a rather young age. He worked as an executive with her husband at the beverage company. After his wife's death, she and Mr. Turner invited him to live with them in the Englewood Place mansion. She commented it was large enough and he had practically half of the house to himself. He and Prudence got along well and he was her godfather and rather doted on her, as he and his wife did not have children.

"The police have already searched his bedroom," she added. "There was nothing to find. My brother lived a blameless life. I encouraged him over the years to find another suitor, but he was not really interested."

"Can you tell me about the evening when you last saw him?"

"We were at the Valencia downtown, having dinner. He mentioned he wanted to shop at Whitney's and left us about eight forty. He promised he would take the trolley back. That was the last time we saw him, until the police called to tell us they found him at the Port of Albany."

"Do you know why he would go to the Port of Albany that evening?"

"I wish I could help you, Mr. Sheppard. I have no idea what he was doing there. It was a pleasant evening but that area is known for bootleggers and gangsters, so why he went there is unknown to me."

Sloan had been writing in his notepad. He asked Mrs. Turner if she was familiar with Mr. Newcomb and the Clinton Street Hotel. She nodded in recognition.

"Yes, I remember Mr. Newcomb. A friendly man. Mr. Turner and I enjoyed dinner at the hotel and the food was fabulous."

Sloan nodded. He listened as she continued to elaborate on the Clinton Street Hotel, where they had spent time with her brother at the restaurant and for other events, such as charity auctions and programs for disabled people.

"My brother was most influential in helping others," she explained. "He took great pride in his civic duties." She paused. "Mr. Turner and I admired his volunteer work."

Sloan appreciated the obvious respect Mrs. Turner had not only for her brother but also for her husband, whom she referred to as Mr. Turner. From his experience, it was common in marriages among the older generation. He thought rather highly of such a term of endearment.

He explained about his work for Mr. Newcomb in 1915, where he assisted law enforcement in arresting several area gangsters. The hotel was used for bootlegging, drug smuggling and prostitution. He was hired by Mr. Newcomb to end the illegal activity that occurred at that time.

"Do you know what became of Mr. Newcomb?" he asked her.

Mrs. Turner paused. "Well, I know he retired and sold the hotel. That was either 1918 or 1919. Poor man died in 1920. I remember reading in the *Albany Evening Press* about his death. I believe he died somewhere else in the state." She frowned. "Oh yes, I remember now.

He was from Corning, New York. He told us he wanted to return to his hometown."

"I remember the hotel burned two years ago," Sister Catherine mentioned.

Mrs. Turner nodded. "Clinton Street has become rather an undesirable part of the city. Years ago, around 1910 or so, Mr. Turner and I would take walks around that neighborhood."

"We see many patients from that part of the city in the emergency room," Sister Catherine commented. "The police are called to that neighborhood quite often, too."

"Mr. Stevenson told me his agency did publicity for Mr. Newcomb in 1915," Sloan said. "That was around the same time he hired me to bring down the illegal activity at his hotel."

"My husband and I met the Stevensons around that time," Mrs. Turner said. "They were having dinner there, too. Some of the local businesses around the hotel were busy. There was a florist shop. Mrs. Marion Harper was the owner. I think she is still in business."

"Do you remember anything about gangsters at the hotel?" Sloan asked.

Mrs. Turner nodded sadly "Yes, I remember my brother mentioning it to us. I read about it the papers, too. He was there when a brawl broke out. Fortunately, he was not involved but he witnessed it. He told us some of the gangsters had ties to Al Capone in Chicago."

"How dreadful," Sister Catherine exclaimed.

"It was not the fine establishment as Mr. Turner and I remembered it."

"Then why would your brother go there, Mrs. Turner?"

Mrs. Turner shrugged. "He was an acquaintance of Mr. Newcomb and Walter was lonely at times. He enjoyed chatting with him and others at the hotel. My husband and I did not monitor my brother. He was old enough to choose what he wanted in life."

"The gangsters who frequented the hotel were arrested," Sloan told them. "They served time and were released, although it's anybody's guess where they are today."

Sister Catherine shuddered slightly. "That is most disturbing, Mr. Sheppard. Do you think the gangsters could still be here in Albany?"

"I imagine they could be just about anywhere," Sloan said grimly.

Monday morning Sloan attended to several clients with whom he had scheduled appointments. Two were for custody proceedings and the other a divorce settlement. By late morning, he closed his office and headed outside to catch the trolley.

He walked to the corner of State Street and South Pearl Street and caught a southbound trolley that brought him to the corner of South Pearl and Morton Avenue. He got off and walked north on Morton until he came to Clinton Street.

It was some time since he had visited that part of the city. Walking steadily, he realized how decrepit it had become. Looking northward, he knew he was not far from the Schuyler Mansion, a historic site. He walked along Clinton Street, noticed vacant storefronts, and boarded up establishments. Most likely speakeasies flourished here, although he did not know of any. He then spotted the florist shop Mrs. Turner mentioned. Without anything to lose, he decided to enter and see if he could speak to the woman behind the counter. She was arranging flowers in a vase and asked what she could do for him.

Sloan introduced himself and explained that he was investigating the murders of Mr. Lennon and Mr. Turner. He wanted information on Mr. Cyrus Newcomb and the Clinton Street Hotel. He asked if she remembered anything that could help with his investigation.

Her name was Mrs. Marion Harper and she had owned the florist shop on Clinton Street for over twenty-five years. She was a robust middle-aged woman with a fine head of black hair and pleasant brown eyes, rather talkative, much to Sloan's surprise. He was accustomed to reluctant shop owners but Mrs. Harper was happy to supply any information he needed. She explained how she and her late husband started from the bottom up and worked hard to have their business a success. She mentioned the decaying neighborhood, but she maintained a steady stream of customers and new clients found their way into her store by word of mouth. She mentioned she did not know anything about the recent murders and was not acquainted with the Turners, although she remembered Mrs. Turner came in to buy a floral arrangement once or twice. She mentioned she and her husband were acquainted with Mr. Newcomb.

"Did you ever have occasion to go inside the hotel?" Sloane asked her.

Mrs. Harper looked at Sloan in some surprise. "Of course, Mr. Sheppard. Mr. Newcomb and my husband and I were like family! We watched each other's backs! He ran the hotel for over thirty years! His business was just dandy until the hoodlums ruined it."

Sloan gently prodded her for more information. Mrs. Harper was willing to cooperate.

"Mr. Newcomb was worried about gangsters using his hotel for illegal activity. Unfortunately, he was proven correct. They were there for bootlegging, drug smuggling, even prostitution! He told me he saw call girls using his place for their business!"

"Did you have the chance to meet Mr. Walter Lennon at the hotel?"

Mrs. Harper shook her head, putting aside the vase in which she placed a bushel of flowers. "No, but I remember Mr. Newcomb told my husband and I about him. He worked at the beverage company in North Albany, didn't he?"

"Yes, along with his sister and brother-in-law." Sloan paused, as a customer came in to pick up a floral arrangement. He waited for the woman to leave before continuing. "Do the names Steven Lubbock. David Winslow and James Prouty sound familiar, Mrs. Harper?"

She thought for a moment. "No, I can't say I recognize them."

Sloan explained they were part of the gang who frequented the hotel. He told her he had worked for Mr. Newcomb in 1915 to end the gangster activity, resulting in numerous arrests. She nodded in remembrance.

"Mr. Newcomb told us he hired a private investigator. I knew your name rang a bell! It's nice to meet you after all this time." She paused. "We would head over there for dinner once or twice a week. The neighborhood started to go downhill, so we just went home after we closed."

She seemed lost in thought until Sloan asked if she remembered anything else about the gangster activity or Mr. Newcomb. She smiled wryly, as she conjured up memories of her acquaintance with obvious fondness.

"He was from Corning, New York originally. I don't believe he or his wife had relatives."

"Do you know the names of people in Corning he knew?"

Mrs. Harper told Sloan she would look through her address book. She disappeared behind a curtain to the back room and returned shortly with a rather long date book, containing telephone numbers and addresses. She flipped through several pages, placing it on the counter. She looked at several names, until one came back to her in recognition.

"Here is the name of someone I met once. He was a good friend of Mr. Newcomb." She grabbed a pad and printed a name, address and telephone number. "Mr. Thomas Walton of Corning, New York. Maybe he can tell you more."

"Was this Mr. Walton a friend of yours, too?"

"No, not really. My husband and I got to chatting with him at the hotel. He gave us his address and number in case we ever were in Corning."

"Do you know if he was at the hotel the evening of the brawl that resulted in the gangsters being arrested by police?

Mrs. Harper shook her head. "I couldn't tell you. I remember he told us he enjoyed visiting Albany and always stayed at the hotel when in town, so maybe he was there then."

"Do you know his age, by any chance?"

Mrs. Harper frowned. "Hard to say. He was a widower, like Mr. Newcomb. By now, he must be in his late seventies. Mr. Newcomb would be about that age if he were still alive."

"Do you know if this Mr. Walton was acquainted with the Turners and Mr. Lennon?"

"Quite possibly. Since he frequented the hotel as a guest, he may have chatted with Mr. Lennon. I don't know about the Turners. But I can't say for sure, of course."

Sloan took the slip of paper from her. He asked her if she remembered the evening when there was a brawl in the hotel and several gangsters were arrested. Mrs. Harper shook her head.

"We were already closed by the early evening. Mr. Newcomb told us about it the next day."

Sloan told her it was in 1915, the year he worked for Mr. Newcomb. Mrs. Harper mentioned since then the neighborhood steadily declined. She stayed away in the evenings, as she was afraid for her life. After work, she and her husband would lock the front door and go directly home.

"Whereabouts was the hotel on Clinton Street?" Sloan asked her.

Mrs. Harper came around from the counter and led him to the front windows overlooking the street. She pointed to the right and north, toward Delaware Street. She commented it was now vacant, used primarily as a parking lot.

"Do you remember when the hotel burned, Mrs. Harper?"

She nodded, rather sadly. "Yes, it was a kitchen fire that caused it, not long after Mr. Newcomb died. He sold the hotel in 1918 and moved back to Corning. He passed away in 1920."

She paused as a woman and a small child entered and approached the counter. She asked Sloan if he needed any further assistance.

Sloan held the slip of paper gratefully. "Thank you, Mrs. Harper. You have been most helpful with this information."

She smiled and then turned her attention to her new customer. Sloan left the florist shop, exiting onto Clinton Street. Walking to South Pearl Street to catch the trolley back to his office, he knew Mrs. Harper had given him a great deal to think about.

After lunch at a nearby diner, Sloan returned to his office. He retrieved the mail from under the door and stepped inside. As he expected, it was warm as he had closed the window before heading to Clinton Street. He opened it and allowed fresh air to ventilate the room.

Settling at his desk, he loosened his tie and unbuttoned the top of his vest. He felt extremely warm, despite the refreshing breeze. He put aside the mail and looked at the information Mrs. Harper had supplied him. Mr. Thomas Walton of Corning, New York. He debated whether to call or to plan a trip to Corning. Of course, Mrs. Harper did not know if he was still alive.

Today was only Monday and a quick glance at his calendar told him he had a full week of appointments. It would be difficult to travel to the western part of the state, as he knew it would involve a long train ride. Most likely, he would need to change trains in either Syracuse or Binghamton, which would increase his travel time, before heading on to Corning. It would be nearly impossible to make it in one day. He discounted a personal visit to Mr. Walton and instead decided to contact him by telegram. Mrs. Harper guessed his age in the late seventies, so there was a chance he was still alive.

Before placing a call to Corning, he decided to speak to Inspector Harris at Albany Police Headquarters. Upon picking up the handset, he asked the operator to connect him and in no time, he was speaking directly with the Inspector. He asked Sloan what progress he made in his investigation of the Turner and Lennon murders, as well as the death of Mrs. Nichols.

Sloan explained his visit yesterday evening with Mrs. Turner and Sister Catherine and the information they imparted. He relayed his visit to Mrs. Harper at the florist shop on Clinton Street and the name she gave him of a Mr. Thomas Walton of Corning, New York, who was acquainted with Mr. Cyrus Newcomb. He planned to send him a telegram, provided he was still at the address Mrs. Harper provided. Upon hearing from Mr. Walton, he would place a long distance call to Corning to speak with him directly.

"What do you think he can tell you?" Inspector Harris said dubiously.

Sloan lit a cigarette and blew a cloud of smoke in some frustration. "Mr. Newcomb was acquainted with Mr. Lennon and Mr. Walton visited the hotel often. He may know something pertinent to the case. I believe there is a connection and I intend to find it."

"I have some information to give you," the Inspector said. He ruffled through a few papers. "My team looked into the whereabouts of Steven Lubbock, David Winslow and James Prouty. We can eliminate them as possible suspects. They are all accounted for."

Sloan knocked ash into an ashtray. "In what way? They were arrested, too."

"They served their time and were released," the Inspector told him. "Mr. Lubbock lives in Canada and has no local address or relatives. Mr. Winslow died in a shootout during an armed robbery committed in Brooklyn in 1919. Mr. Prouty is married and lives in California. He also does not have a local address or any ties to this area. Mr. Lubbock and Mr. Prouty are clean and have no convictions other than the arrests in 1915. The other gangsters arrested at the hotel in 1915 have also passed away and a few were released. I checked our files for the last fifteen years but have not found any police reports containing names of the gangsters arrested in connection with the Clinton Street Hotel. Looks like that lead is a dead end." He paused and then changed course, reiterating his previous conviction. "Lieutenant Taylor and I believe the poisoned drink was meant for Mr. Turner. Mrs. Nichols drank it by mistake."

Sloan puffed at his cigarette irritably. "I agree the poisoned drink most likely was meant for Mr. Turner. Mr. Thomas Walton of Corning may know more about Mr. Newcomb and Mr. Lennon. I believe there is a link between these men. Mrs. Turner is still recovering from this horrendous ordeal. For her sake as well as for Mr. Stevenson, since he retained me to resolve this case, I need to find that link."

"So what is your next course of action?" the Inspector asked.

Sloan spoke determinedly. "To bring the guilty party to justice."

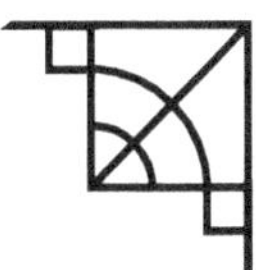

CHAPTER FIFTEEN

Tuesday morning, August twenty-eighth, was a cloudy, rainy day in downtown Albany. An unexpected warming trend blanketed the city and residents knew the dog days of summer were by no means over. People scurried along State Street and North Pearl Street, dodging raindrops as a deluge came down in torments, then stopped as soon as it started.

Caleb was settled at his desk, reviewing the morning edition of the *Times Union*. He had forgotten his umbrella and as he glanced out the window, he realized he just missed the rain. His looked at the political headlines, most notably an article about the first hundred days of the new leader, President Calvin Coolidge. He did not know much about him but he believed he was a worthy successor to President Harding. The country was reeling from the shock of Mr. Harding's death and Caleb admitted he too was still stunned by it.

Turning the page, he glanced over advertisements for *Palmolive Soap, Hershey Chocolate, Borden Ice Cream* and *Camel Cigarettes*. He noticed the Mary Pickford film *Tess of the Storm Country* currently at the Ritz Theater as well as the Charlie Chaplin movie *The Pilgrim* playing at the Strand Theater. He read that Charlie Chaplin was considered the biggest star of 1923.

On the next page, several articles highlighted the projected remunerative analysis for the remainder of 1923 and the optimistic outlook for 1924. Caleb read how everyone from the Rockefellers, the Marx Brothers, secretaries end even housewives invested in the lucrative stock market. The dividends were so enormous that analysts predicted continued prosperity and encouraged everyone to put money into the market, to reap the benefits of investing and enjoy newfound wealth and security.

Caleb folded the paper and put it aside. He did not notice any new articles on the murders of Mr. Turner or Mr. Lennon or even any mention of Mrs. Nichols. He was surprised he had not heard from Mr. Sheppard. The police must have concluded their inquiries and reached a stalemate, with no arrests or leads. He shook his head, wondering how long before the culprit was apprehended. He had confidence in Mr. Sheppard although he wondered if he was still investigating or had given up. Possibly a lost cause, Caleb thought drearily. He assumed he would have heard from Mr. Sheppard if that were the case. He looked up and saw Mrs. Stevenson in the doorway. She mentioned her husband wished to speak to him.

"Of course, Mrs. Stevenson," Caleb said. She looked worn and rather tired, as though the recent events had taken a toll. And how could they not, he thought grimly. The murders affected everyone in the agency. Negative publicity from the taste testing in the newspaper could negatively affect the agency, as Mr. Stevenson predicted. He hoped that was not the case

Despite his status and the three years of his employment at the agency, Caleb always dreaded going to Mr. Stevenson's office. He never knew what exactly to expect. His boss was rather moody at times and given to bouts of anger. Rarely was his wrath directed at Caleb, although he had experienced it a few times in the past. He got up, straightened his tie and vest and proceeded down the hallway to the executive suite of Mr. Stevenson. He knocked on the door and Mr. Stevenson waved him in, not greeting him and barely taking his eyes off a report.

Caleb sat in front of his massive desk, expecting the worst. He waited for the older man to speak. He shuffled the report and put it aside, then looked up and addressed Caleb.

"Caleb, I have some good news, for once." He paused uncertainly, choosing his words carefully. "I spoke with Mrs. Stevenson last night and we have decided that we want you to serve as the interim president of the agency, while I am resting at home."

It was that simple, taking Caleb by surprise. It was the last thing he would have expected. He did not know that Mr. Stevenson was not in good health. He thought he looked the picture of vitality for a man of his advanced age. Certainly, his wife appeared pristine. Then he knew the recent events and the death of President Harding affected them and he must have felt he needed a break from the agency. He did not think the Stevensons ever took vacations. He blinked as he realized Mr. Stevenson was speaking to him.

"I am still disturbed over the recent murders and find I cannot concentrate on my work as before. Therefore, I am entrusting you to handle our business affairs, including inquiries, current contracts and future promotions. I leave that up to you to tell the staff of my decision."

Caleb found his voice, although still in shock. "Are you leaving the agency, sir?"

He shook his head. "No, I will be here a few days, although I plan to stay home often. If you were to need me for any reason, you can always call me. And if you needed to speak to me in person when I am not here, you know where we live on Dudley Row."

Caleb nodded. He knew very well the opulent brownstone house the Stevensons lived in on fashionable Dudley Row, not far from the State Capitol. He looked at the man behind the desk and imagined in his over thirty years of advertising and public relations work, he had never encountered murder.

"I have not heard from Mr. Sheppard," he said with tight lips. "We have been interrogated extensively by the police and I hope not to be subjected to that again. However, I would ask you to contact Mr. Sheppard or perhaps go to his office, as it is within walking distance."

"I will contact him. Is there anything else?"

Mr. Stevenson nodded. He explained he wanted Caleb to collaborate with Peter, Jeff and Wilbur on a new contract for the Hampton Hotel. Roy was busy finishing other contracts. Upon completion, he expected Roy would also assist Caleb. He emphasized to Caleb he was now in charge. He expected operations to run smoothly. It was an enormous responsibility, but he was assured of his initiative and intelligence.

"My wife is disturbed over the president's passing," he said quietly. "Mrs. Stevenson and I discussed the assassination of President McKinley, just twenty-two years ago." He sighed, in obvious trepidation. "We remember it quite well. A very upsetting event, happening in our state. A Republican and a fine man. You were a mere child then, Caleb."

Caleb nodded, although he had never seen Mr. Stevenson in a reminiscent mood before. He then supplied Caleb with details on the Hampton Hotel and the projected publicity campaign. He mentioned he wanted the preliminaries completed before Labor Day.

Nothing more was said about the murders of Mr. Lennon, Mr. Turner and the unexplained death of Mrs. Nichols. Not even Mr. Sheppard was mentioned further. It was as though all was back to normal and there was money to be made and contracts to be signed.

But Caleb knew Mr. Stevenson was preoccupied. The recent murders hung over their heads like an enormous thundercloud, with a brewing storm about to erupt at any moment.

After speaking with Mr. Stevenson, Caleb returned to his office and put in a call to Mr. Sheppard but after six rings, he hung up. Most likely, he was working on a case. He sighed rather irritably, assuming Mr. Sheppard would get back to him shortly. He then rounded up Wilbur, Peter and Jeff, telling them he needed to speak to them in his office.

He sat at his desk with them before him, dreading what he was about to tell them. A cigarette and a slurp of coffee were all he had before he made his pronouncement.

"Mr. Stevenson will be stepping down as the president," he told them. "I will be the interim president, until he is well enough to return. I will handle matters of finance, promotions, and publicity campaigns."

He looked at them and not one moved a muscle. Only Jeff man aged to speak, although he was clearly surprised.

"So what does that mean, Caleb? More money in your pocket?"

Caleb swallowed hard. "I really don't know. I didn't ask Mr. Stevenson about that."

"Oh come on, Caleb," Wilbur snickered. "You'll have more dough in your pocket if you're the acting president. Pretty soon you'll be the president for sure."

"And how you resent it," Jeff said, looking at Wilbur as he sat next to him.

Wilbur shook his head, rather casually. "If that is what Mr. Stevenson wants, then so be it."

Peter looked at him carefully. "You've had your eye on the presidency for a while, Wilbur. This may impede that, of course."

Wilbur had a cigarette between his lips. He puffed almost angrily, while looking at Caleb.

"Is that what you called us here for?" Jeff asked. "I do have ledgers to work on, so if you don't mind, Caleb, I'd like to return to my desk."

His safe haven, Caleb thought. Rarely mixing with the others and most likely harboring secrets. He noticed Jeff's demeanor was impatient, even bothersome as though he wanted to take care of his own business and not be bothered by anything else. He watched as Jeff rose and walked out of his office, despite his request to remain. He looked at Wilbur and Peter.

"Any news on the murder investigation?" Peter asked.

Caleb shook his head. "Not so far. I haven't heard from Mr. Sheppard." He paused. "Mr. Stevenson wants us to get going on the new contract for the Hampton Hotel."

Caleb explained to them the circumstances surrounding the publicity for the Hampton Hotel, one of downtown Albany's premier hotels. He planned to contact the manager to determine his needs for the campaign. He mentioned it needed to be completed by Labor Day.

"Mr. Stevenson wants it finished before Labor Day?" Peter asked incredulously.

Caleb nodded, reluctantly. "Next Monday is a holiday, so we need to act fast to get as much done as possible before then. Just the preliminaries for the campaign."

Peter asked if Roy would join them and Caleb told him after he finished his current projects. He then divided tasks between Peter and Wilbur and including Jeff as well, setting a priority for organizing the publicity campaign. While he talked, Caleb noticed neither Wilbur nor Peter paid him much attention, their minds seemingly focused on other matters.

"Caleb, when is that private investigator going to call it quits?" Peter asked, his face twisted into tight lines. "I assume Mr. Stevenson is paying for his services or is he using agency money?"

Caleb crushed his cigarette in the ashtray, losing his patience. "I don't really know, Peter. Why don't you ask him yourself since you're so concerned?"

"Jeff would know if he's using agency money," Peter said.

"Not to worry, Peter," Wilbur said, turning to him. "Mr. Stevenson has plenty of dough, he can afford the cost, for sure. Besides, he is concerned with the agency's good name."

Peter's tone was sarcastic. "Well, you're most likely right. And who knows, maybe there'll be more action surrounding this whole damn mess that Caleb got us involved with."

"That I got you involved with?" Caleb said. "What does that mean?"

He shrugged, puffing at his cigarette. "Your harebrained idea of the taste testing. None of this would have happened if we hadn't gone there. I thought it was a waste and look how it turned out. Certainly, not good for us and the agency."

Caleb was silent. He knew Peter had a right to express anger. He realized two lives might have been spared if the taste testing did not occur. But he could hardly be blamed for it. He thumbed through a few papers on his desk, not looking at them.

Wilbur and Peter exchanged a few words, before getting up to leave. Peter turned in the doorway and looked back at Caleb at his desk.

"Maybe it'll never be solved, Caleb," he told him, rather seriously. "Maybe whoever killed the Turners will go free."

Roy sat at the table in the spare room, going through old files of previous clients. Across from him sat Polly, who was busy taking notes in a notepad. She intended to type up the report later in the day. She looked up at Roy.

"How many more files do we need to review?" she asked.

Roy had a cigarette between his lips. He puffed incessantly, his mind too preoccupied to even hear what Polly said to him. She repeated her question, looking at him curiously.

Roy extinguished the cigarette in an ashtray and blew smoke irritably. "Sorry, Polly. I've got too much on my mind. I have a contract to finish and need to review these old files, too." He paused. "And I keep thinking of the murders, of poor Mrs. Turner and how she must be suffering."

Polly nodded, although her manner was insolent. "I wouldn't worry, Roy. It all comes out in the wash. Perhaps the guilty person will never be caught."

Roy loosened his tie. It was still quite warm even for late August. "You really think so?"

She shrugged indifferently. "Murderers do not brag about their deeds. On the other hand, once someone has killed, most likely there will be more murders to follow."

Roy grimaced. "There have already been three, Polly. Poor Mrs. Turner had to bury her entire family! Poor lady, she must be overcome with grief. I'm glad Mrs. Stevenson goes to see her often. Sister Catherine was helpful, too."

"You mean that nun that was at the taste testing? She seemed like a matron to me. Bossy, domineering, know-it-all. Just the type I despise."

Peter stopped by to tell them the news about Caleb. Polly and Roy looked at him in surprise, and then returned silently to their work. They watched as he left the spare room, leaving them to ponder what was just told them.

"Caleb will perform well," Roy said optimistically. "He's intelligent and knows the business." He cringed slightly, wondering about his own future at the agency.

Polly almost laughed. "Let's not be naïve, Roy. Caleb has had his eye on the presidency for a long time. I'm sure Wilbur is infuriated by this news."

"Caleb always worked closely with Mr. Stevenson," Roy commented. "He must trust him enough to make him the interim president."

"Perhaps," Polly said indifferently, not looking at him.

Roy closed a folder and looked at Polly. His tone was uncertain, cautious. He asked her what she thought of the recent murders. He commented that the police think the poisoned drink wasn't meant for Mrs. Nichols. Polly lifted her head and spoke in her usual flippant way.

"So they've determined Mrs. Nichols was murdered? I thought just as much. Probably drank the glass meant for her father." She continued writing. "I have a particularly good idea who was responsible. And if you think long and hard enough, you will, too."

In the main office, Gabrielle and Minerva helped Mrs. Stevenson sort folders into numerous file cabinets. It was a long and tedious process but they knew it needed to be completed as they were acquiring new clients.

Minerva wiped sweat from her forehead. It was still hot and the office as usual was not well ventilated. Her hair in its usual bob drooped a bit due to the humidity. Gabrielle also felt the heat but managed to retain a certain calmness, despite the arduous conditions. Her curly red hair was fixed neatly, her small face outwardly tranquil, but the strain of the unsolved murders began to take effect. She listened as Mrs. Stevenson started to talk.

"My husband and I decided to have Caleb as the interim president while Mr. Stevenson is home resting." She paused, as she noticed the startled faces before her. "We thought of this for some time but with the recent devastating news, my husband's health has been of concern. Therefore, Caleb will now be in charge. My husband will still come to the office, of course, but not every day as he used to."

Minerva cleared her throat. "I'm sure Caleb will do a fine job."

Gabrielle agreed. "Will Caleb work with Jeff in handling the financial matters of the agency? Mr. Stevenson always left that up to Jeff. He is our only accountant."

Mrs. Stevenson smiled. She looked pristine and composed as usual, but an unspoken strain lined her face, unmistakably. "Of course, dear. Business will proceed as usual, with Caleb the first point of contact. We trust he will perform exceptionally well."

"Will this change in leadership begin soon or after Labor Day?" Minerva asked.

Mrs. Stevenson commented it would start soon. "Mr. Stevenson and I plan to relax over the long holiday weekend. He is getting Caleb ready to take over this week."

Gabrielle and Minerva murmured appropriate comments and continued with their work. Gabrielle returned to her desk and began to type. Minerva finished with the file cabinets and went to the office she shared with Wilbur.

Mrs. Stevenson decided she would call Mrs. Turner soon. Poor dear, how she had been suffering. She was so strong and resilient, even graceful to endure such hardship. Mrs. Stevenson was appreciative of Sister Catherine and the help she gave to Mrs. Turner.

She sighed and returned to her desk. She looked over at Gabrielle, as she was busy typing. She then glanced over her shoulder, toward the hallway that led to the other offices. She shuddered slightly as she realized an uneasy and rather unsettling silence had settled over the agency.

Mrs. Louise Turner sat on the sofa in the living room of her elegant home on Englewood Place. She had been reading the latest issues of *True Story*, *Reader's Digest*, *Redbook* and *McCall's*. She glanced at the *1923 World Almanac* on the coffee table. Mr. Turner always enjoyed reading the almanac but Mrs. Turner preferred her magazines. A cup of tea was on an end table but upon sipping it, she realized it had gone cold. She put the magazines on the coffee table, fingered the string of pearls around her neck and smoothed down her dress. She was nervous, rather afraid and for good reason.

It was early evening and Sister Catherine had left a little while ago. She prepared a fine meal of chicken, rice and vegetables for Mrs. Turner but she only nibbled at the food. Sister Catherine regretted she could not stay, as she was on duty at the hospital. She was alone tonight, which did not bother her, as it gave her time to think. She and her husband had never bothered with servants, although they certainly could have afforded such a luxury. Mrs. Turner preferred to cook and clean herself, especially while her daughter was growing up. From in the hallway, she heard the grandfathers' clock strike seven. Mrs. Stevenson called earlier. A good friend and such a devoted lady, so steadfast in her religious beliefs.

I have buried my brother, my husband and my daughter, she thought painfully. She sighed, got up fitfully and put on the radio, turning the dial until she found a station playing symphonic music. She hoped the melodies would calm her nerves. She walked around impatiently, her mind going over and over what occurred at the taste testing event.

Her husband saw something that made him clutch his chest and lean against the podium. Then that clap of thunder, the lights went out and Prudence drank poisoned *Champagne Twist*. Who would want to poison Prudence? My son-in-law, of course. Then Mrs. Turner realized frighteningly the drink must have been meant for her husband. The next night poor Mr. Turner was murdered in his office. She could not go into much detail to the police or Mr. Sheppard. She was not sure herself. However, there was something bothering her and she had her suspicions.

She paced the floor, reliving the moment, seeing the startled face of her husband. Her vision turned to the crowd and back to Mr. Turner. She followed his eyes and wondered who or what he saw. She and her husband had lengthy talks about past events at the beverage facility. She had a hunch and although not one to normally take risks, Mrs. Turner decided to make some inquiries of her own. Certainly, the police would not know anything.

Earlier she had looked in the Albany City Directory for a telephone number. She went to the telephone in the hallway and gave the operator the number. She was taking a chance, calling at a residence, but she had to bring closure for herself. The police took forever to resolve issues in this city if they ever did at all. She waited for the call to go through, the endless ringing, until the voice she wanted answered. She spoke, rather nervously, but steadily and got straight to the point.

"I think I know what my husband saw at the taste testing. Should we discuss it or just let it go? I could talk to the police, of course. Or that nice Mr. Sheppard. I have not mentioned anything, but I just might. I've been doing a lot of thinking and remembering."

She listened to the voice on the telephone and then hung up the handset. She looked at the telephone irritably. She would take matters into her own hands. Enough time had been wasted. When the police officers and Mr. Sheppard were last here, she was too distraught to come to terms with what she knew. But now she would tell them her suspicions. She looked at herself in a hallway mirror, fluffing up her gray hair. Her face held few wrinkles and despite the devastating recent events, she did manage to sleep at night. At almost seventy, Mrs. Turner thought she aged well and kept her youthful vitality.

Feeling stronger and more in control, she decided she would go to Washington Park after all. She had nothing to lose and besides, the fresh air would do her good. It was a little after seven o'clock and still light out. She gathered her keys and locked the front door. It was warm and pleasant, the sun slanting lazily with a light breeze, invigorating for an evening stroll.

It was early the next morning when a woman walking her dog in Washington Park discovered the body of Mrs. Louise Turner. Her lifeless form lay undisturbed in a ditch, her skull crushed by a cement block.

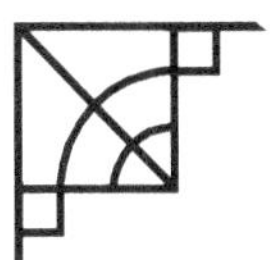
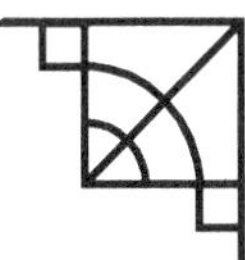

CHAPTER SIXTEEN

Wednesday morning, Sloan arrived earlier than usual to his office. The trolley downtown from upper Madison Avenue was not as busy as it would be within an hour and he practically traveled by himself. Upon reaching the corner of State and South Pearl Streets, he jumped off and strode up State until he reached the Albany City Savings Bank Building.

He entered the lobby and greeted the elevator attendant, who showed surprise upon seeing him at that early hour. He opened the gates and brought Sloan to the fifth floor. The hallway lights were off, as the cleaning crew finished their overnight duty, so Sloan reached for the wall switch and the hallway was illuminated with a rather dim but sufficient overhead light.

Finally settled in his office, he reached for the folder on the Turner case. He sighed in some trepidation. He left the office late yesterday afternoon and headed straight for Western Union on State Street to send a telegram to Mr. Thomas Walton in Corning, New York. He explained the information he was seeking and asked if Mr. Walton could assist in some way. He gave his office address and phone number, hoping he would answer him, as Sloan stated it was urgent.

From his apartment last night, he decided to place a long distance call to Mr. Walton in Corning, but there was no answer. The operator confirmed it was a working number, so either he was not at home or was away. He could only wait and see what may happen.

The morning wore on and Sloan attended to several clients who had appointments concerning child welfare, divorce, inheritance issues and fraudulent checks. He had no sooner finished with the last client, ushering a husband and wife out the door, when a Western Union messenger arrived. He greeted Sloan pleasantly and handed him a telegram. Sloan fished in his pocket for a dime to give the amiable youth in the doorway, then taking the telegram he returned to his desk, ripped it open and spread it out flat on his desk. He looked at it carefully.

WESTERN UNION TELEGRAM

Received at Albany, NY via main wire, Wednesday, August 29, 1923.

Mr. Sheppard:

Visited Mr. Newcomb often. Have pictures of gangsters.

Will send by airmail. Call if you wish.

All best,

Mr. Thomas Walton

Corning, New York

Sloan read the telegram several times, before placing it aside. He lit a cigarette and leaned back on his chair. Finally, he felt progress was made. He had an inkling he was on to a vital lead. He decided he would call Mr. Walton again this evening, even before receiving anything from him. Airmail from the western part of the state to Albany should be no more than a day or two. He wondered how he had pictures of the gangsters unless he had taken them himself. He settled down to continue work for other clients when his telephone rang. Upon answering, he heard the stern voice of Inspector Harris. He knew instantly something was wrong.

"Mr. Sheppard, there has been another murder."

Sloan knew murder was not unheard of in Albany, with its elevated crime rate, especially as prohibition and gangsters proliferated. He waited to hear more.

"It's Mrs. Turner," the Inspector said gravely. "Mrs. Louise Turner. Her body was found this morning in Washington Park."

Sloan heard the Inspector clear his throat before speaking again. "I will call you later. Looks like we are back to square one."

He replaced the handset and clenched his fists tightly. His mind raced to Mrs. Turner and their meeting on Sunday. She must have surmised something that pertained to her husband but did not communicate those suspicions to anyone. It did not seem that she alluded to having knowledge. She might have figured out what caused her husband to become so disturbed at the taste testing. Sloan wondered if she made demands, such as hush money, but would a woman of her wealth and status resort to blackmail? He wondered the same for her brother. He was rather angry with himself for not realizing Mrs. Turner harbored knowledge but was reticent to share it. He would never know for certain what information she withheld and why.

Time was of the essence now. He had to resolve this case quickly, for he knew a murderer did not stop once threatened and if desperate would undoubtedly strike again.

The alarm clock woke Caleb from a deep sleep. Stretching lazily, he threw the sheet aside, padded to the blinds and opened them, allowing the sun to stream in, causing him to squint. He took fresh underclothes from the bureau and left them on top of the bed. He then entered the bathroom, turned the bath water on, waiting several minutes for it to become warm. He removed his boxers and stepped into the shower.

He thought he heard the telephone ringing but the warm water was so invigorating; he was reluctant to end it. He pushed back the shower curtain, listening, then turned off the faucet and reached for a towel. He stepped into his bedroom and had no sooner put on fresh boxer shorts when the telephone rang. He was reminded of the morning he learned about President Harding. Certainly, it could not be more bad news. He glanced at his alarm clock and seeing the early hour, wondered who would call him at this time.

He heard a high-pitched female voice on the other end. He recognized Gabrielle, who was in near hysterics. She was practically incoherent and Caleb had all he could do to calm her down. He asked her to explain what was wrong.

"Caleb, something terrible has happened!"

That much was obvious and he waited for her to continue. He wished he had his cigarettes nearby, but realized he left them on his nightstand. He sat down on the sofa and told her to tell him what was wrong.

"I tried reaching you but there was no answer! Caleb, this is just so terrible! Roy called and told me. It's on the radio, where he heard about it. I am so frightened!"

"Heard what on the radio? Gabrielle, please tell me what is wrong."

He heard her take a long breath. "It's Mrs. Turner. She was murdered last night in Washington Park! Her body was found there this morning."

Caleb sat up straight. "Are you sure, Gabrielle?"

"Put the radio on. It's on the news and I'm sure it'll be in the evening paper."

"Do the Stevensons know about it?"

"I wasn't sure if I should break the news to them. Roy mentioned he would call the others. I don't think he felt comfortable in calling Mr. Stevenson."

Caleb was stunned and for a moment was speechless. He wondered how Jeff would react to the murder of his mother-in-law. He realized the entire Turner family had been murdered; first Mr. Lennon, then Mrs. Nichols, Mr. Turner and now Mrs. Turner. He held the handset tightly, as Gabrielle continued speaking to him.

"The Stevensons must be told, if they don't know already."

Caleb had the distinct impression she wished him to tell them the unfortunate news. He told her he would contact them and then ended the call. He entered his bedroom, picked up his cigarettes and returned to the living room. He ignored the radio, as he had heard the devastating news from Gabrielle and that was enough for now.

He sank onto the sofa, his feet up on the coffee table, lighting a cigarette and forgetting about breakfast. Anxiety and apprehension went through him. Like Gabrielle, he felt afraid.

On the corner of South Hawk Street and Lancaster Avenue, the area known as Dudley Row was an address of much prestige. A beautiful and refined neighborhood, it obviously was for those who could afford such opulence and enjoy the magnificent stately brownstone houses and the proximity to the State Capitol and downtown.

From her kitchen window, Mrs. Stevenson could see the capitol building and the trollies traversing State Street. She never tired of the view and she loved living in the heart of Albany.

At the moment, she was busy fixing breakfast for her husband, who had just entered the kitchen. She turned from the stove and served a plate with scrambled eggs and bacon. She filled his cup of coffee and then joined him at the table.

"I don't plan to go to the office today," Mr. Stevenson said as he stirred sugar in his coffee. "I trust Caleb will handle anything that comes up."

Mrs. Stevenson agreed. "He is such a wonderful young man. I do hope he and Gabrielle will see more of each other. I know she is rather fond of him."

Mr. Stevenson scowled. "Celeste, you know I do not approve of office romance. I never encouraged it and prefer that you stay out of it."

Mrs. Stevenson demurred. "Of course, dear. Why don't we listen to the morning news? I'll put the radio on in the living room." She left the kitchen, entered the living room and turned the radio to WGY where the morning news report was underway. She turned up the volume and then returned to the kitchen, where she began to cut a corn muffin and pour another cup of coffee. They continued eating in relative silence as the news reporter gave the most recent city headlines.

...The body of Mrs. Louise Turner was discovered early this morning in Washington Park. Mrs. Victoria Whiting of Albany was walking her dog and found Mrs. Turner's lifeless body around five o'clock. Police were contacted and confirmed the victim was Mrs. Louise Turner of Albany as identified by Mrs. Whiting, who was an acquaintance of Mrs. Turner. Mrs. Turner suffered severe head wounds and died from blunt force

trauma. Mrs. Turner was the widow of Mr. Nathan Turner, the president of the Empire State Beverage Company, who was murdered in July, the sister of Mr. Walter Lennon, also a victim of homicide and the mother to Mrs. Prudence Nichols, both of whom were employed at the beverage company. Police request anyone with information to contact them at police headquarters...

Mrs. Stevenson half rose from her chair and then sank back down, too aghast to comprehend what she just heard. Mr. Stevenson stopped eating and looked at his wife across the table in shock.

"Who would kill Mrs. Turner?" Mrs. Stevenson said tearfully. "Such a lovely woman."

"The same person who killed the others," her husband told her, trying to maintain a semblance of normalcy. His expression conveyed his distress upon hearing about the murder.

"I should call Sister Catherine," Mrs. Stevenson said. "She must know what happened."

She was about to get up to enter the hallway when the doorbell rang. Unaccustomed to morning visitors, Mrs. Stevenson, quite flustered, went to the front door and soon returned with Caleb. He greeted them and sat at the table, where Mrs. Stevenson offered him coffee. He politely refused and then began to speak.

"Gabrielle called me earlier with some devastating news. She told me Roy called her and that he planned to call the others to let them know what happened."

"We already heard," Mr. Stevenson said stonily. "Terrible what's happening to this city."

"Poor Mrs. Turner," Mrs. Stevenson cried, visibly upset. "Such a good soul and how she suffered recently. I will have a Mass said in her honor."

Caleb cleared his throat. "I was going to call to tell you about Mrs. Turner but I thought it was better to come here in person."

Mr. Stevenson nodded. "That is most kind of you, Caleb. My wife and I appreciate your concern." He paused. "I imagine this recent murder will appear in this evening's newspapers."

An awkward silence ensued, until Mr. Stevenson addressed Caleb again, rather forcibly.

"Even if Roy informed everyone, I would like you to speak to the staff about this recent event. They may have heard about it on the radio, too. In any event, it is up to you to hold the agency together. Something is happening that my wife and I are unaware of." He paused. "Have you heard from Mr. Sheppard?"

Caleb shook his head. "I called yesterday but there was no answer. I will try him again today."

Caleb looked at Mrs. Stevenson. It was obvious she was having a difficult time, as she continued crying softly. A quick glance at the man at his side told Caleb his boss was just as equally disturbed, although he refrained from exhibiting any outbursts. He could tell his feelings were smoldering as though at a breaking point.

"This is just terrible," Mrs. Stevenson exclaimed. "Another murder of someone we knew, so close to home. And the death of President Harding, too. Too much bad news. It's too much to comprehend! I am scared to even leave the house!"

Mr. Stevenson managed to control his nearly hysterical wife. He commented the police would investigate and find the culprit. He reminded her Mr. Sheppard worked for them to draw a conclusion to this case. He reiterated his confidence in the private investigator and his stellar reputation in the city.

There was an uneasy silence before Caleb announced he would leave for the office. Mrs. Stevenson thanked him for dropping by, but neither she nor her husband offered to accompany him to the front door. It was apparent the Stevensons were still stunned over the news, so Caleb told them he would see himself out.

Once outside, a warm sun and a light breeze greeted Caleb as he came to the corner of South Hawk and Lancaster Street. He headed toward State Street, deep in thought.

Who would kill Mrs. Turner and why? Possibly, she knew something but did not say anything to the police or Mr. Sheppard. Maybe she knew what disturbed her husband at the taste testing. He remembered seeing Mr. Turner as he clutched his chest and reached for the podium. He was clearly startled, even alarmed. There must have been a reason for Mr. Turner to react as he did. What exactly was it?

Caleb arrived at Empire Advertising and saw Gabrielle and Polly in the main office at their desks, immersed in their work. They barely noticed as he entered. He greeted them but received only a perfunctory response in return. He was about to enter the hallway to go to his office when Polly turned and spoke to him, rather abruptly.

"Caleb, shouldn't we talk about Mrs. Turner? You are the head of the agency now. Another death in the Turner family. Do you think it's connected somehow to the taste testing?"

Caleb loosened his tie, already he was sweating and the day had not even begun. It was still warm and humid and the air in the office was uncomfortable as usual, but Polly's remark was insolent, even mocking. Observing her carefully, he figured she knew more than she told, most likely wondering why he had not reached a conclusion to the unfathomable situation yet. He kept his patience while speaking to her.

"Yes, Polly, I intend to speak to the staff as soon as everyone is here." He added nothing more and noticed Gabrielle looking at him, almost pleadingly, as though she were about to cry. He turned back to Polly. "Will you let me know when the others have arrived? I'd like to call a meeting as soon as possible." She seemed taken aback much to Caleb's satisfaction.

Settling at his desk, he picked up the telephone and asked the operator to connect him with Mr. Sloan Sheppard in Albany. As usual for the morning hours, he had to wait as many calls were being placed at the same time. Finally, the operator connected him and he was soon speaking with Sloan, who also had recently arrived at his office.

"Good morning, Caleb," Sloan said. "I was going to call you later today. You haven't heard from me yet because I have been following up on leads regarding the Turners." He explained the possible lead from Corning, New York, but did not divulge too much detail. He expected to speak to someone soon who may have information, including photographs relevant to the investigation.

Caleb was unsure what he referred to but decided not to ask for more details. "Have you heard about Mrs. Turner?" he asked Sloan.

Sloan explained he received a call from the police earlier, telling him about the most recent homicide. He expected questions from Caleb, as he knew his anticipation for the resolution was paramount but he reminded him it had not yet been concluded. He heard the disappointment on the other end of the line.

"Most likely Mrs. Turner knew or suspected something," Sloan mentioned. "Only a man strong enough to use a cement block would kill someone like that."

"It could've been a woman," Caleb said, still in shock.

Sloan puffed at a cigarette. "I need to confer with the police again and wait for the pictures from the gentleman in Corning. Once I draw definite conclusions, I will get back to you."

Caleb hung up on a less than satisfactory call, but Mr. Sheppard's firm and resolute voice was full of assurance. He did not understand the Corning angle, although he knew it dealt with Mr. Newcomb who ran the Clinton Street Hotel.

He looked up and to his surprise saw Polly in the doorway. Her eyes sparkled and her expression was cunning and rather devious.

"Everyone's here, Caleb," she announced. "Should I tell them to come to your office or Mr. Stevenson's table?"

Caleb wondered what was passing in her mind. Her demeanor alone irritated him. "Tell them to meet me at Mr. Stevenson's table. I'll be there in a minute."

She walked off, Caleb collected his notepad, and a fountain pen, fixing his tie and vest, prepared to answer questions from his associates. Upon entering Mr. Stevenson's suite, he saw them seated at the long table, smoking, chatting and waiting for him to start. Only Gabrielle acknowledged his presence.

Caleb sat at the head of the table, placed the notepad in front of him and began to speak.

"Roy contacted us about the murder of Mrs. Turner. Mr. Stevenson wanted me to speak to everyone today. This is another travesty that will be investigated. I anticipate a resolution to the case is near."

"You know who is responsible?" Roy asked, flabbergasted.

Caleb looked his way. "I spoke with Mr. Sheppard. He did not divulge much information yet. Mr. Stevenson and I have trust in his abilities as an investigator."

This remark was met with skepticism and murmurings of dissent. Minerva asked for the details of Mrs. Turner's death. Roy spoke up and explained that she was found in a ditch in Washington Park early this morning.

"A shame for the Turner family," Wilbur commented.

"Just bad luck," Jeff commented, puffing at a cigarette. "What else could it be? Maybe she slipped and fell in a ditch and hit her head. Do the police even know for sure what happened?"

"According to the report on the radio, she died from blunt force trauma," Roy said.

"That means she was hit on the head," Polly put in awkwardly.

"It's more than just bad luck," Peter spoke up, rather irritably. "Certainly, her husband's murder was not bad luck. Whoever killed him must have had a vendetta against him or the company since it was so brutal."

"What does Mr. Sheppard think, Caleb?" Minerva asked.

"He will be in touch once he has followed up more leads," Caleb explained, not wishing to provide too much detail. "Does anyone have information about Mrs. Turner?"

"What kind of information?" Jeff asked, clearly perturbed. "I knew her better than anyone here. Maybe someone was drunk and did her in. She shouldn't have walked through Washington Park alone, especially in the evening."

"That's beside the point," Roy said. "Englewood Place borders the park so she must have been used to walking around that area."

Caleb felt the hostility while looking at the faces around the table. No one could add anything to the murder of Mrs. Louise Turner. He told them the Stevensons were clearly shaken and that they expected to remain at home today, as they were too upset to come to the office. He anticipated Sister Catherine would visit them soon.

There were many further comments; more violence in the city, Washington Park no longer a safe place, the future of Empire

Advertising in jeopardy with negative publicity connected to the taste testing and the Turners, a concern of the agency closing and everyone losing jobs. Caleb tried to reassure them although he too held the same apprehensions. He thanked them and dismissed the meeting. Only Gabrielle lingered while the others walked out.

"That was quite an effort for you," she said. "You are an exceptional leader, Caleb."

Caleb looked at the pretty red haired woman in front of him as he collected his notepad and pen. "We need to continue with current projects, just as the Stevensons want."

She joined him to the hallway and returned to the main office, while Caleb retreated to his desk. He picked up a folder containing the campaign for the Hampton Hotel and attempted to immerse himself in current projects, but his mind kept returning to the recent events; the taste testing and the Turners. He thought of Mr. Lennon. And what about Mr. Newcomb? Mr. Sheppard seemed to think that was a vital link to the whole ordeal.

Caleb decided to look at the folder on Mr. Newcomb. Entering the spare room, he turned on the ceiling light. Nothing had been touched or out of place. He knew Roy and Polly had worked on files here yesterday. He went to the file cabinet where he found the folder on Mr. Newcomb. He looked through the drawer and not finding it, opened the drawer underneath it and thumbed through all of the folders.

With no luck, he opened the remaining two drawers and still not locating it, he decided to look through the other five file cabinets, spending nearly half an hour searching for a folder that had been there recently. There was no reason for anyone to have need of it.

He straightened up from the last drawer, closed it with his foot and looked at the file cabinets irritably. His search had been in vain. The file on Mr. Cyrus Newcomb was missing.

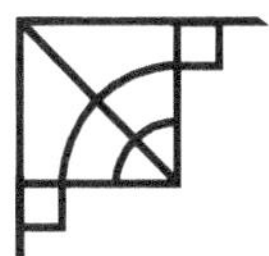 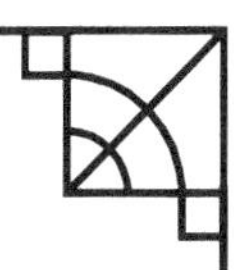

CHAPTER SEVENTEEN

Sloan ensconced himself comfortably on the sofa in the living room of his apartment. The candlestick telephone was on the coffee table, a pack of cigarettes and a cup of tea were on an end table next to him. He held the piece of paper from Mrs. Harper concerning Mr. Thomas Walton in Corning as well as the telegram he received from him this morning.

It was almost seven o'clock on Wednesday and the heat had dissipated leaving in its wake a pleasant and comfortable late summer evening. He had read the article on the murder of Mrs. Turner in the *Albany Evening Press* as well as the *Knickerbocker Press*. He heard about it in detail on the news broadcast on WGY. He sighed and reached for the telephone.

He asked the operator to place a call to Corning, New York and gave her the number. After a minute, it started to ring, at least five times. Sloan contemplated hanging up when finally a young woman answered. Sloan asked for Mr. Walton and upon identifying himself, she told him she was his niece who cared for him. She put the handset down and Sloan could hear talking in the background before the handset was picked up and an elderly gentleman spoke, rather gruffly, but congenial enough.

"Hello, Mr. Sheppard. I figured you would contact me. I haven't been to Albany in a few years. Did you receive the pictures I mailed you yet?"

Sloane thought his manner rather blunt, which was advantageous in seeking information. He told him he had not gotten them but assumed tomorrow at the latest. He thanked him for sending them and asked if he could speak to him if he didn't mind.

"Of course, Mr. Sheppard," the elderly voice said. "What can I do for you?"

Sloan explained how he was hired by Mr. Stevenson of Empire Advertising to inquire into the recent murders of Mr. Lennon and the Turners. He told him Mrs. Turner had recently been murdered while in Washington Park. He spoke to Mrs. Marion Harper, who owned a florist shop not far from where the Clinton Street Hotel stood. He asked if he could provide him with any information.

"I remember Mrs. Harper and her husband," Mr. Walton said. "Nice people. I gave her my contact information in case she and her husband ever traveled to Corning. But I didn't know the Turners. I remember Mr. Lennon, a regular at the hotel and a friend of Mr. Newcomb. Quite a rowdy place over the years." He chuckled slightly and Sloan pressed him for more information.

"From what I remember, gangsters and their molls made a habit of using the hotel for their business. I had a camera with me one night and snapped a few pictures of them without them knowing it. Then once a dispute broke out. Next thing, there was a brawl and the police were called. They discovered the gangsters had been using the Clinton Street Hotel for illegal business."

"Didn't Mr. Newcomb know this beforehand?"

"He didn't turn them away because they were frequent customers and always ran up a large bill. They drank, smoked, dined and stayed frequently, too. With such business, who would say anything to the police? Mr. Newcomb wasn't involved in anything of that kind himself, of course. He was suspicious of them as time went on, but he allowed them to stay. Mr. Lennon also had suspicions and spoke to Mr. Newcomb about it."

"Do you know what Mr. Lennon might have said to Mr. Newcomb?"

Mr. Walton told Sloan he had no idea. "I think he might have recognized one of the gangsters, maybe even a few of them. There are several gangsters still operating in Albany, from what I read in the Corning and Elmira newspapers."

Sloan acknowledged that gangster activity had increased in the city since the advent of prohibition. He asked Mr. Walton if he remembered any gang members in particular and if the names Steven Lubbock, David Winslow and James Prouty were familiar to him.

"No, I didn't know them," he told Sloan. "I never spoke to the gangsters as they pretty much kept to themselves. One of the gangsters was rather boisterous. I think he was a leader. I remember his name was Conrad Finnegan."

Sloan lit a cigarette and blew smoke, while printing the name. "Can you describe this Mr. Finnegan to me please?"

Mr. Walton paused, then remembering his days at the Clinton Street Hotel, described the gang members, in particular Mr. Conrad Finnegan. He mentioned that was eight years ago, in 1915, so he was afraid his memory was not the best. Sloan realized the importance of what he just heard. He listened intently while Mr. Walton continued speaking.

"I know he had an arrest record in Albany. He was one of the most notorious gang members. There was a rumor those gangsters swindled Mr. Newcomb out of money, too."

"Was Mr. Finnegan a friend of Mr. Newcomb?"

"I doubt it. Mr. Newcomb didn't associate with gangsters. He kept a respectable establishment. You'll see Mr. Finnegan in the photos and the others, too." He paused. "I'm awfully sorry to hear about these murders. I didn't know Mr. Lennon well but he seemed pleasant enough. His wife died and he had no children, so he often spent time at the hotel."

He thanked Mr. Walton for his time. Mr. Walton appreciated the chance to speak to him and wished him well. Sloan then returned the handset and placed the telephone back on the coffee table. He picked up the cigarette from the ashtray meditatively. He was close to solving this case. He had an accurate description and an arrest was imminent. The photographs Mr. Walton sent him should clinch it. He puffed at his cigarette, satisfied that a resolution was forthcoming.

Caleb and Gabrielle had gone to a cafe on South Pearl Street after work. They ordered sandwiches and French fries, with ice cream for dessert. A satisfying meal, to which Gabrielle admitted she did not realize she was so hungry. They lingered over their coffee and ice cream. Within a short time, more people entered and soon most of the tables were full.

Caleb it a cigarette for her and one for himself, then sipped his coffee. It was a pleasant early evening, the sun going down slowly and the after work crowd dissipating from downtown. He asked Gabrielle if she had plans for Labor Day. She shook her head, knocking ash from her cigarette into an ashtray.

"No, I just plan to stay around Albany. I may go shopping at Whitney's. I need new clothes for the fall season. A new sweater and a hat would go with my fur coat."

Caleb nodded. He mentioned he would use the jungle gym at Washington Park as usual.

"You keep yourself in such fine shape," she commented admirably. "I suppose that was part of your military training. I've always admired West Point graduates."

Gabrielle smiled, causing him some embarrassment. He was unused to compliments on his exercise routines or his physique. He did not know what Gabrielle expected of him, but at the moment, he preferred to maintain his distance. He remembered Mr. Stevenson frowned on office relationships. She asked him what he thought of the murder of Mrs. Turner.

"She must have known something," he said, blowing smoke toward the ceiling. "Maybe she wanted to take matters into her own hands. I think the same person who killed Mr. Lennon and Mr. Turner killed Mrs. Turner." He paused. "And caused the death of Mrs. Nichols. too."

"I wish I could remember what happened at the taste testing," Gabrielle said. "It all happened so fast, especially after the lights went out. That was rather scary."

"Mrs. Nichols drank from the wrong glass," he told her. "Mr. Sheppard thinks it was meant for Mr. Turner. Then the killer returned to finish him off the next night."

Gabrielle shuddered. "How terrible! And now Mrs. Turner!"

He mentioned the missing file on Mr. Newcomb from the spare room. He told her he had searched for it in the afternoon and could not find it anywhere. Gabrielle nodded.

"Polly has it. I saw her looking through the old files again. She mentioned she kept it at her desk. She didn't say what she wanted with it."

"Why would Polly want that file?" Caleb wondered. "Mr. Newcomb's campaign was completed in 1915. She didn't work for Mr. Stevenson then. She wouldn't know about it."

Gabrielle agreed. "Who knows with Polly," she commented casually, sipping her coffee.

Caleb then looked up and saw Peter and Wilbur enter the café. As it was nearing the dinner hour, the cafe was filling up. Much to his chagrin, the only available table was one closest to them. Wilbur and Peter sat at the empty table and greeted Caleb and Gabrielle pleasantly. Wilbur commented the food was excellent at the café and Peter and Polly always ordered the turkey club sandwich. A waitress appeared and took their orders. An uncomfortable silence ensued, until Gabrielle rather awkwardly asked them what they thought of Mrs. Turner.

"Poor lady," Peter said, accepting a cup of coffee from the waitress. "Who in the world would do something so horrid?"

Wilbur concurred. "She seemed nice and gracious, too."

"Maybe Jeff knows more than he's telling," Peter said. "She was his mother-in-law, after all. He's the only one of us who knew her, which he readily admitted."

"I'm sure Mrs. Stevenson is upset," Wilbur said, putting sugar in his coffee. "Sister Catherine should help her. She seemed very friendly and supportive, too."

"Funny seeing both of you here," Peter said, lighting a cigarette and changing the subject.

Caleb commented they decided at the last minute to get something to eat before catching the trolley. Gabrielle asked about Minerva and Polly.

"Polly is at her apartment listening to an Eddie Cantor special on the radio," Peter said as the waitress appeared with their orders. "She loves Eddie Cantor."

"Minerva went shopping at Whitney's," Wilbur explained. "She wanted to get a head start on buying new clothes for the fall. Afterward, she planned to stop at Union Station to get a timetable for trains to Utica. It is Labor Day weekend, after all."

And still no resolution to the unsolved murders, Caleb thought irritably. While he did not mind chatting with Gabrielle as she sat prettily across the table, he was in no mood for making small talk with Wilbur and Peter. He found their manner insolent and insulting. Their attitude about the Turners was loathsome. He had always found Wilbur impertinent but Peter also acquired much of the same abhorrent characteristics. He wondered if he and Polly had relationship problems, causing him to change his disposition. He knew Peter played the field. He was surprised he would settle for someone like Polly unless he just used her as he wished. He glanced at Gabrielle whose look told him she was ready to depart.

"Great seeing you guys," Wilbur said, his mouth full of a roast beef sandwich.

Caleb and Gabrielle made desultory comments, mentioned they would see them tomorrow and after settling the bill with the waitress at the cash register, left the café. On the sidewalk, they crossed at South Pearl Street and State Street. Neither spoke until Gabrielle turned to him, rather anxiously, just as a trolley approached.

"There's something happening I don't know about. Like I'm not privy to it."

Caleb joined her on the trolley, keeping his thoughts to himself.

Polly put on the radio and eagerly turned the knob until she found the station she wanted. The soothing voice of Eddie Cantor resonated throughout the apartment. She loved Eddie Cantor and his *No, No Nora* was one of the biggest hit songs of 1923. She heard the announcer proclaim Eddie Cantor the rising star for 1924. She planned to shop at Whitney's for the 78 of *No, No Nora* so she would not have to wait to hear it on the radio. The phonograph player Peter bought her was sitting dormant in the corner as she had few 78s to play. She sighed in frustration. She needed more cash and knew how to get it.

She lit a cigarette, kicked off her high heels and retreated to the kitchen, where a half empty bottle of bourbon was on the counter. She enjoyed the taste of the liquor, feeling refreshed and even rejuvenated. She contacted a bootlegger she and Peter knew well. She was expecting him to arrive soon, so she went to the door and unlocked it. The downstairs door was always unlocked, much to the irritation of many tenants, but it did not bother Polly. She lived in a safe neighborhood and never worried about crime. She left the money on the hallway table for him, along with a tip. After all, she considered her dealings with the bootleggers important as they kept her replenished as needed.

She puffed at her cigarette, swallowed more of the liquor and sat at the sofa, listening to Eddie Cantor crooning his songs. The world looked different now. People would think she had been lucky with the stock market. Peter and Wilbur played the market and enjoyed reaping the benefits. Of course, she also had a broker who kept her informed of the current trends, but she had other ideas. She never thought of resorting to blackmail, but she would make demands. She looked after herself because nobody else gave a damn about her. Including Peter.

She went to a corner table, where she kept a folder. Taking a pencil from her handbag, she wrote boldly MR. NEWCOMB on the cover and laughed slightly. Mine to keep, she thought jeeringly.

After thumbing through it, she tossed it on the coffee table. She was surprised Mr. West Point did not find it out for himself. Poor foolish, naïve Caleb, with his bulging muscles and military attitude. She relaxed on the sofa, sipping the bourbon, feeling optimistic and rather carefree. She puffed at her cigarette, thinking a great many devious thoughts.

Soon, someone knocked on the apartment door. She called to her visitor that the door was open and to leave the liquor on the hallway table, the money was there for him. Her back was to the door, as the sofa faced the windows overlooking State Street and the capitol.

She continued smoking, sipping the bourbon and was unaware of danger. But it came silently behind her. She felt an overpowering blow, swift and powerful, on the side of her head that rendered her to a dark and painful oblivion. The file on Mr. Newcomb was snatched from the coffee table before the intruder left the apartment.

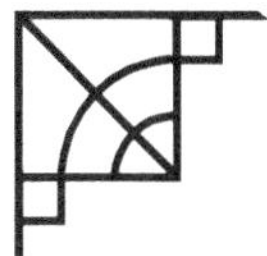
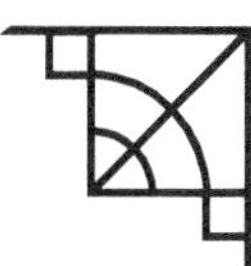

CHAPTER EIGHTEEN

Upon arriving back to his apartment, Caleb entered his bedroom and changed into his exercise wear. He considered heading over to Washington Park and the jungle gym. He slipped a tee shirt over his head and grabbed a pair of white socks from his bureau, prepared for his exercise regimen, when the telephone rang.

Entering the living room, he looked at the telephone somewhat irritably, as he was not in the mood for idle talk. He knew it could not be Gabrielle as he just saw her to her apartment. While barefoot and almost stubbing his toe on the coffee table, he snatched up the handset. He was surprised to hear Peter on the other end.

"Caleb, there is something you should know."

Caleb sat on the couch, prepared for anything. He waited to hear what he would tell him.

"Polly is in the hospital," he explained gravely. "Someone attacked her in her apartment. I called the police and they know about it already."

"What?" Caleb said, rising from the sofa. He was too shocked to formulate more words.

Peter explained that after he and Wilbur finished eating at the café, they went their separate ways. He walked to Polly's apartment on State

Street, as it was not far from the café. He mentioned Wilbur caught the trolley to Madison Avenue. When he entered Polly's apartment, he saw her lying on the floor in front of her coffee table, the left side of her head bleeding profusely. He called the police and an ambulance and she was taken to St. Peter's Hospital, where she was listed in critical but stable condition with a severe concussion.

"I'm still here at the hospital," he told Caleb. "I called Roy and he's here, too. I tried Wilbur and Minerva but they must not be home yet."

"How do you know someone attacked her?" Caleb asked.

"An injury like that doesn't come from falling," he said curtly. "Right now I want to speak to the doctor, so I will try to call you again later." He hung up and Caleb replaced the handset, feeling rather confused.

He leaned back on the sofa, reached for his cigarettes and lit one, exhaling a large cloud of smoke irritably. So much had been happening with no resolution in sight. He sat on the sofa at least a half hour, expecting Peter to call him back. He had just turned on the radio when the telephone rang once again. Thinking it was Peter with more news on Polly's condition, he was surprised to hear Mrs. Stevenson.

"Hello, Caleb, dear. I hope I have not caught you at a bad time." She paused. "My husband and I have been resting and thinking about Labor Day weekend fast approaching. We would like to invite you on Saturday for lunch. I've called the others, too, although I could not reach Peter or Polly. It has been a long summer and we want to show our appreciation for your hard work."

He told Mrs. Stevenson he would be pleased to accept her invitation for lunch on Saturday. He commented it was kind of her to think of everyone during this difficult time. Mrs. Stevenson sensed a slight anticipation in his voice. She asked him if something was wrong, other than the unsolved murders and President Harding's sudden death.

Caleb took a deep breath and told her about Polly. He could hear her sigh and utter sounds of shock and disbelief.

"Who got into her apartment?" she asked, horrified. "This is a safe neighborhood. Polly's apartment isn't far from Dudley Row. Do the police know what happened?"

Caleb told her he did not know the details yet. He had just spoken to Peter from the hospital.

"Please call us when you learn more about Polly," Mrs. Stevenson told him. "Sister Catherine must be at the hospital. She might know more about her condition." She hung up rather quickly, leaving Caleb more confused than ever.

He decided to call Gabrielle and Jeff, as he believed they should be informed, too. While not especially close to Polly, they did see her every day and he felt it only appropriate they be aware of what occurred. He reached Gabrielle and told her the news. She mentioned she had just spoken to Roy at the hospital.

"He told me the doctors aren't sure if she'll survive," Gabrielle said, fearfully. "Someone broke into Polly's apartment and attacked her!" She was afraid, living alone. She told him she would put a chair against her door before sleeping. Caleb told her to call him if she needed him.

He replaced the handset on the telephone and sat back again on the sofa. He decided to call Jeff at his apartment on Dove Street. He gave the operator the number and waited for the call to connect. It rang at least six times before he decided to hang up. He blew smoke in great frustration. There was no telling where Jeff Nichols was this evening.

On Thursday morning, Sloan was at his desk early as usual, anticipating the arrival of the pictures from Mr. Walton. In the meantime, he called police headquarters and spoke with Inspector Harris. He told him about the conversation with Mr. Walton from Corning and that he was expecting photographs from him in the mail. He mentioned the gangster named Mr. Conrad Finnegan, who frequented the Clinton Street Hotel.

Inspector Harris whistled. "Conrad Finnegan, did you say? He was rather well known in this city, with quite an arrest record; bootlegging, robbery and drug smuggling. I believe he served time around 1905 or 1910 but was released. I know he had accomplices, too." The Inspector then told him about the attack last evening on Polly Ormerod in her apartment on State Street. He mentioned she was at St. Peter's Hospital where doctors were treating her for a concussion.

Sloan drummed his fingers on the desk. He voiced his opinion that the murderer was desperate now. He contemplated the possibility that Polly. Ormerod was blackmailing the murderer. He mentioned he wanted to look at a mugshot of Mr. Conrad Finnegan to see if it matched the pictures of gangsters from Mr. Walton. The Inspector said he would search through files to locate the mugshots of gangsters involved with criminal activity at the Clinton Street Hotel.

Sloan hung up, realizing just how cunning, devious and manipulative gangsters operated to suit their purposes. Before long, he was soon occupied with the rest of the morning casework. A new client arrived, disputing a custody case and another pertaining to a divorce decree. By late morning, the mailman arrived with a special delivery envelope.

Sloan thanked him and grabbed his letter opener. He slit the long envelope, extracting the contents. He read a note from Mr. Walton, explaining that the man in the center of the first photograph was Mr. Conrad Finnegan. He looked at them carefully, noting the gangsters, in particular Mr. Finnegan. He reviewed them all and recognized someone else.

He sat at his desk, contemplatively. He then reached for the telephone rather urgently to call Inspector Harris again before someone else got hurt.

Sloan arrived at police headquarters later in the afternoon. While speaking with Inspector Harris, he reiterated the urgency of the mugshot of Mr. Conrad Finnegan, along with the other criminals arrested in connection to the Clinton Street Hotel.

Sloan closed his office, hopped on a trolley on State Street heading northbound for Central Avenue. He carried the envelope he received earlier from Mr. Walton. Upon arriving, he was greeted by Lieutenant Taylor, who ushered him into a receiving room, sparsely furnished with a table and two chairs. Sloan recognized the room, as it was utilized for interviewing witnesses and executing warrants. On the table was a rather large folder, full of papers. The Lieutenant explained Inspector Harris was interrogating a witness to a burglary in another room and would be with him shortly. He left him in the room, as he had to answer a call on Western Avenue of an armed robbery attempt. Sloan sat at the table and turned his attention to the folder before him.

A crime file was usually full of useful and some useless information but Sloan eagerly opened it and looked carefully at the documents. He came upon records of the gangsters arrested while at the Clinton Street Hotel. He read pertinent information on Mr. Steven Lubbock, Mr. David Winslow and Mr. James Prouty and several others in relation to the arrests. He already knew about these three men. Notes stated the others were either no longer in Albany, were deceased or still serving time for other charges. He came across documentation related to Mr. Conrad Finnegan. He looked at this information with interest.

He was born in Elmira, New York in 1865. He had a long list of convictions for grand larceny, passing bad checks and bootlegging in Buffalo, Rochester, Seneca Falls, Waterloo, Geneva and other places around the state, including Albany. Apparently, he was part of a gang, quite active in Albany, perhaps because the capital was a hotbed of crime and where bootlegging and the underworld proliferated. Further notes detailed arrests were harsh, as Mr. Finnegan was known as a violent criminal. He then looked square into the mugshot of the criminal. He shook out the photographs from the envelope he received from Mr. Walton. There was no question of who he was looking at. Sloan sighed, then continued reviewing the documents.

He read about Mr. Finnegan's accomplice. Previous interrogations included suspicion of petty larceny and bootlegging, fraud and falsification of documents. Evidently, there was no arrest, just suspicions. His accomplice's name was Sidney Bernard, also of Elmira.

Reviewing the arrest record, he noticed Mr. Finnegan served time in Albany and had been released. Too lenient, he thought grimly. Mr. Lennon, the Turners and Polly Ormerod were a threat to the murderer. The link between Mr. Lennon and the hotel was obvious. Mr. Lennon must have recognized the gangster here in Albany and confronted him, demanding hush money to avoid revealing his real identity. Sloan still found it hard to believe a man of Mr. Lennon's decorum would resort to blackmail, but more than likely, that was the case.

Sloan desperately thumbed the multitude of pages, looking for information he needed to provide the missing link. Almost at the very end, he came upon a document listing previous employment held by the gangsters, including Mr. Conrad Finnegan. Surprisingly, some were of reputable businesses, in different parts of the state.

He read how Mr. Finnegan was employed at the Empire State Beverage Company in 1892 but was fired for stealing, threatening an employee and his previous arrests. A note mentioned Mr. Nathan Turner, who explicitly stated he did not want a criminal at his facility and adamantly mentioned the inappropriate conduct of this employee. It further mentioned Mr. Turner did not know of his previous criminal record. If he had known this information, the report stated, Mr. Finnegan would have never been hired to work at his facility. However, his past returned to haunt him, which if revealed would ruin his name and reputation in Albany, but murder and assault now entered the picture. Sloan found it odd Mr. Finnegan would return to Albany. Under a new name and after so long a period, obviously he did not expect recognition. To his surprise, that was not the case.

He heard Inspector Harris in the hallway about to enter. He would share with him what he discovered. Sloan then closed the folder, his thoughts reeling from the conclusions inexorably forming in his mind.

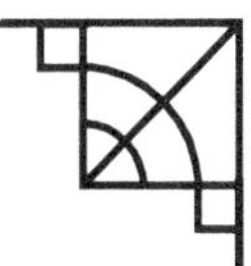

CHAPTER NINETEEN

Friday, the thirty-first was not as hectic in downtown Albany during the morning rush. Trollies were nearly empty and the sidewalks, while busy were not as congested. Many residents were lured to begin the weekend earlier than usual. With the start of Labor Day, the weather was magnificent; clear, sunny skies, light breezes and no rainfall. In an article in the *Times Union*, Mayor Hackett proclaimed the last official summer weekend was glorious and encouraged residents to partake of the Labor Day festivities in Washington Park.

Seated at his desk, Caleb wished he had taken the day off, like so many others. He sipped his coffee, eager to begin the day. Gabrielle asked him to see the movie *Safety Last!* starring the comedic actor Harold Lloyd at the Ritz Theater tonight. It was held over and she wanted to see it. Caleb read a review in the *Albany Evening Press* that mentioned the hilarious scene when Harold Lloyd dangled from a big clock over a city street! He told Gabrielle he would be glad to see the film with her.

Much to his surprise, everyone was in the office. With the exception of the Stevensons, who were still working from home, no one was absent on the Friday before Labor Day. He remembered Wilbur mentioned he and Minerva planned to travel to Utica. He heard Jeff say something about visiting family in Auburn. Roy told them he might take the train to see his parents in Dunkirk. He assumed Union Station would be jammed with holiday travelers. Before five o'clock rolled around, he contemplated calling a meeting but decided against it. There were too many unanswered questions, especially pertaining to Polly. He also noticed that everyone was rather on edge and tense after learning about her attack.

When he spoke to Peter earlier, he told him she was making progress but was still not completely healed. She suffered a bad concussion but the doctors were hopeful she would pull through. She was still at the hospital and Peter told Caleb he planned to leave early today to go to see her. He also mentioned police spoke to him at length about her assault. Upon their search of her apartment and speaking to other residents in the building, they concluded nothing had been taken so robbery was eliminated as a motive. An unopened bottle of bourbon was noted on the hallway table, but that was hardly considered a reason to attack her. As usual, the police were still investigating the incident.

At around mid-morning, Minerva appeared in the doorway, looking depleted, nevertheless holding herself together. She told him Mr. Sheppard was on the line and wished to speak to him.

Caleb picked up the handset from his telephone. He was eager to hear what Mr. Sheppard had to tell him.

"Good morning, Caleb," Sloan said, from his office. "I spoke with Albany Police and have spent time at headquarters, reviewing files of previous criminals. I believe I know who was responsible for the murders of Mr. Lennon and the Turners. I shared my viewpoint with the police and they agreed. We feel an arrest is imminent."

Sloan told him he did not want to provide the information yet. He wanted to confer with Inspector Harris again and then the police would make the arrest. He mentioned he received a call from Mrs. Stevenson, inviting him to their house on Dudley Row for lunch on Saturday. He told Inspector Harris to go to the Stevenson's house later in the day. He mentioned Mrs. Stevenson told him everyone from the agency planned to attend, too. She and her husband wanted to show their appreciation for his help in investigating the murders.

"Have you told the Stevensons the conclusion you reached?" Caleb could not help but ask. "And why would you ask the police to go to the Stevenson's house during the luncheon?"

Sloan knew he was anxious for the conclusion of the case. He reiterated he did not want to divulge anything at this time. "Mrs. Stevenson told me her husband has not been well. The enormous stress of the last two months had taken a toll on his health. I understand they left you in charge of the agency."

Caleb acknowledged his new role, albeit a temporary one. He mentioned a file on Mr. Cyrus Newcomb, which had been in storage, had been taken by Polly Ormerod. He did not know why she took the folder, as she had no need for it. He then told him about the attack in her apartment and that Polly was still at St Peter's Hospital, being treated for a serious concussion.

"The Inspector told me about the attack," he told Caleb. "But he didn't mention a folder anywhere. Most likely whoever attacked her saw it and took it."

"Must have contained incriminating information," Caleb added.

Sloan agreed and thanked Caleb for his patience and perseverance during the course of the investigation. "I'll see you tomorrow at the Stevenson's house."

Caleb was about to ask Sloan more questions, but the connection ended. Feeling rebuffed, he replaced the handset reluctantly. He wondered what Mr. Sheppard learned and who would be arrested. A dark premonition took hold of him, a foreboding of something extremely unpleasant and unexpected.

Roy sat in Wilbur's office, conferring on the new contract for the Hampton Hotel. It was a major campaign and would earn the agency a lot of money. He wrote extensively on the hotel and already spoke with the manager, describing what the publicity campaign would entail. His notepad in front of him, he meticulously wrote down further suggestions Wilbur offered.

The Hampton Hotel was an Albany landmark and within walking distance of Union Station, on the corner of State Street and Broadway. While in competition with the Ten Eyck Hotel and the Kenmore Hotel, a recent renovation saw unprecedented growth and the publicity would ensure continued popularity with residents and visitors alike.

Roy glanced up from his notes, crushed his cigarette in an ashtray and looked at Wilbur, who was busy signing his name to several contracts. He watched as Wilbur finished signing his name, smiling broadly, as though seeing dollars signs already.

Roy did not work often with Wilbur, but with Mr. Stevenson out of the office, Caleb assigned him to assist with the Hampton Hotel campaign. He was not too comfortable with the older man as he knew he was not patient with the younger staff. He was about to leave when Wilbur asked him if he planned to attend the Stevenson's luncheon tomorrow.

"I told Mrs. Stevenson I will attend," Roy said. "I thought you were going to Utica?"

"And I thought you were going to Dunkirk," Wilbur said curtly.

"I might take time off this fall," he answered, keeping annoyance from his voice. "It's too long a train ride for just the weekend."

Wilbur commented that he and Minerva might take the trip on Sunday, returning Monday. Earlier in the year, he bought a brand new Duesenberg Model J, promoted as one of the most popular cars of 1923. He mentioned they looked forward to driving it to Utica. They considered taking the train to Utica, but Union Station would be busy during the holiday rush. He added nothing more until Roy bluntly mentioned the attack on Polly. Wilbur lit a cigarette and tossed the match in the ashtray on his desk. He looked at the younger man carefully.

"Do you think the person who killed the Turners was responsible for the attack on Polly?" Roy asked him.

Wilbur blew smoke, obviously perturbed. "That's up to the police to find out."

Roy bent down to his notes again.

Jeff listened as Peter spoke about Polly's stay in the hospital, her prognosis and how doctors anticipated her release. Minerva was there conferring on the new Hampton Hotel contract. She was grateful Polly survived and Jeff made appropriate remarks. He thought Jeff would not stop talking about it and he had all he could do to tell him to end it.

Personally, he loathed Polly Ormerod. He found her nosy and meddlesome. He never liked her and he did not think she was too popular in the office. He was surprised Peter would remain with her unless he was desperate for female companionship. He was surprised too that Minerva expressed such remorse unless she was just being kind.

Minerva told Peter she might visit Polly at the hospital this weekend if she and Wilbur do not travel to Utica. They planned to attend the luncheon at the Stevensons tomorrow and Peter commented he would attend, too. Jeff mumbled he also was invited and would attend.

He mentioned he needed to finish the current budget. They left his office, leaving Jeff to his work. He leaned back on his chair brooding, a cigarette between his lips. He would attend the luncheon at the Stevensons tomorrow. It would look bad if he did not attend. He would go to Auburn another time. He then thought of Polly Ormerod, attacked in her apartment. He did not give a damn about her or any of the other rotten bastards in this godforsaken agency. He hated them all as much as he hated his wife and his in laws. They could all go to hell, he thought bitterly, dead or alive.

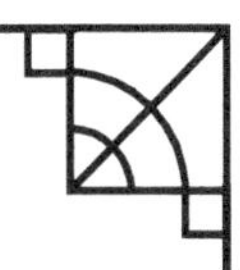

CHAPTER TWENTY

The next day, Saturday September first, was just as magnificent as Friday; warm, golden sunshine, a light breeze and clear skies. Washington Park was filling up with crowds, enjoying the warm weather and the festivities to mark the end of the summer.

In his apartment on upper Madison Avenue, Sloan sat at his kitchen table, reading the morning edition of the *Times Union*. He had gotten up after eight o'clock and now, an hour later, he was still in his boxers, a tee shirt and barefoot; a leisurely Saturday morning. He had opened the living room windows, letting in the refreshing air, before it got too hot. The radio was on, and the soothing sounds of Ethel Waters, Ruth Etting and Rudy Vallee filled the apartment agreeably. He finished breakfast, was drinking his second cup of coffee and was about to light a cigarette. He ran his fingers through his thick black hair. He had a lot to think about pertaining to the Turners.

He had already placed two telephone calls. The first was to Inspector Harris, to inquire about the arrest. He mentioned he planned to attend a luncheon at the home of the Stevensons, along with the rest of the agency staff. Sloan stressed the importance of the Inspector's presence as well. An arrest should be made this afternoon, without fail.

Sloan ruffled the pages of the newspaper, and then noticed an article stating the difficult time currently for the Empire State Beverage Company. With the loss of its president, a Mr. Stanley Martin, an interim president, was managing the company until another leader could be finalized. The beverage *Champagne Twist* had stopped production, as its sales plummeted after the murders and advertisements were pulled soon after.

Sloan puffed at his cigarette and sipped his coffee. His mind drifted to his conversations with Mrs. Harper and Mr. Walton, which were paramount to the solution of this gruesome case. The second call he placed was to St. Peter's Hospital to inquire about Polly Ormerod. He was fortunate to speak with Sister Catherine, who told him Polly was making progress and would be released soon. In time, she may be able to remember what happened but for now, it was too soon. Sloan thanked Sister Catherine and ended the call.

He finished his coffee and contemplated making another pot. He wondered what Polly Ormerod knew and if she actually saw her attacker. The police mentioned Peter Cunningham found her sideways on the floor, so she was most likely attacked from behind. But why would she be a target of violence? Blackmail, of course, he knew from long experience and probably the same for Mr. Lennon and possibly Mrs. Turner, despite their wealth and social status. These people knew information or at the least, surmised the truth and confronted the guilty party.

He got up, turned off the stove and entered the bathroom, filling the sink with water to shave. Suddenly, he thought of Caleb, who just might derive a conclusion like the others. He realized the compelling need for the arrest before more lives were in danger.

In his apartment on Irving Street, Caleb was also preparing for the day. He had showered and selected his clothes for the luncheon. He looked forward to spending the afternoon with the Stevensons and Gabrielle. It was close to noon and he did not want to be late. He did not know if the others would attend, although he assumed they would. After all, it was nice of the Stevensons to host a luncheon after a difficult summer. Before venturing to Dudley Row, he planned to stop at the office, to retrieve items he left there yesterday.

He applied shaving cream to his face and began using the razor when the telephone rang. The sound startled him, resulting in a fine cut on his neck. Feeling the sting, he rinsed his face and quickly went to answer it. He was surprised to hear Gabrielle.

"Caleb, are you still going to the luncheon at the Stevensons?"

"Of course, Gabrielle, but after work yesterday, I realized I left my cap and sunglasses in my desk. So I thought I would head over to the office first and then walk to the Stevenson's house."

Gabrielle sounded disappointed. "I was hoping we could go together."

Caleb assured her he would not be long. He enjoyed the movie last night and afterward they stopped at a coffee shop for tea and pastries, a real treat. He liked her company and he could tell she was rather enamored of him. He mentioned he was in the process of shaving and would see her this afternoon at the Stevensons. He hung up and returned to the bathroom.

He applied fresh shaving cream and carefully used the razor. After rinsing his face, he combed his hair, and then dressed in stylish slacks, a shirt and tie. He donned a vest, as he felt his appearance was not complete without it. He grabbed his keys and headed for the door.

It was a beautiful late summer day, perfect for Labor Day weekend. He considered waiting for the trolley, but it was so pleasant in the sun, he decided to walk. He headed down Dove Street until he came to the corner of State Street. He turned right and continued past marvelous brownstone houses and the capitol building until he came to the top of State Street hill. He crossed at the light and entered the office building, finding it quiet on Saturday. A few people were present, but not nearly as many as on a typical weekday. He greeted a custodian on the ground floor, then decided to bypass the elevator and bounded up the stairs. Arriving at the fifth floor, he took out his keys and was about to unlock the office door when he realized it was already open. Finding that odd for a weekend, he turned the knob and walked in.

The main office lights were off, so he reached over to the wall and turned on the switch. He proceeded to his office and his desk. He opened the top drawer and extracted his cap and sunglasses, feeling foolish for leaving them yesterday. Of course, he had been so preoccupied recently, he was not surprised on his forgetfulness. He put his sunglasses in his front pocket and folded the cap in his pants pocket. Satisfied he accomplished his goal, he was about to head out when he noticed the spare room door open and the light on. The hallway was dark and quiet, with only an illumination from the ceiling light in the spare room. He walked over and stood in the doorway. At first, he did not recognize whom he saw. He then realized it was Minerva at the file cabinets, her back to him, looking through the files hastily and rather angrily, as though she was searching for something and not finding it.

"Hello Minerva," he said. "I'm going to the luncheon at the Stevenson's house. Aren't you and Wilbur going, too?"

Minerva turned, clearly startled. She tried to formulate words but uttered only incoherent mumbles. She continued looking at him, aghast and obviously alarmed, speechless, her eyes bulging with fear and anxiety. A momentary silence occurred and then all at once Caleb knew. He knew what she was doing; she was searching for information on Mr. Cyrus Newcomb. A cold wave of fear, apprehension and then understanding hit him as he stood in the doorway.

"You killed them," he spoke hoarsely, seeing the picture clearly. "You're responsible for the murders. You're looking for more files on Mr. Newcomb that could incriminate you. You knew Polly found the other folder and figured it out. The Turners and Mr. Lennon must have known something about you, too." He paused, noting her fearsome expression. "On Saturday you didn't think anyone would come here." He continued looking at her, as he realized he had stumbled upon the truth. "Now I had better call the police."

He was about to return to his office to use the telephone when suddenly he was struck from behind, a searing blow on the side of his head. He fell forward onto the floor, darkness and pain descending over him.

"Mr. Sheppard, how nice to see you again," Mrs. Stevenson said pleasantly. She smiled warmly, welcomed him into the hallway and looked up at his tall, handsome figure approvingly, noting his fine features and clothes. "Peter mentioned Polly might be released soon, praise be to God. My prayers for her healing were answered. Please come in and say hello to my husband."

Sloan arrived close to twelve thirty to the pristine brownstone on Dudley Row. He followed her along an immaculate hallway until they entered a well-furnished and comfortable living room. He found Sister Catherine, Roy Carter and Peter Cunningham already there, drinking coffee and chatting with Mr. Stevenson. Mr. Stevenson greeted Sloan and beckoned him to join them.

Sloan sat in a plush armchair near an ornate fireplace and gave the room a quick look. It was richly furnished, with chintz-covered armchairs, bookcases in the wall, a handsome fireplace and a long and fashionable sofa. He knew Dudley Row was an impressive neighborhood in Albany. Obviously, the Stevensons lived well and the rich furnishings proved it.

He nodded to Roy and Peter, who likewise acknowledged him by making desultory remarks of little significance. Sloan mentioned he was glad Polly's condition had improved. Peter told him she was faring much better. Sister Catherine greeted him cordially and commented on the lovely weather, perfect for the long weekend. Mrs. Stevenson appeared carrying a tray, on which reposed bacon and cheese on crackers. Sloan helped himself as did Sister Catherine, Roy and Peter.

More small talk ensued; agency business, the current Hampton Hotel campaign and future clients. Roy asked Sloan about his investigations, how long he had been in business and if he were an Albany native. Mr. Stevenson mentioned the rise in crime in Albany and how deplorable the city had become. Peter commented how he did not find the police in this city too competent as crimes went unsolved for months, even years. He kept a cigarette to his lips, his disdain for law enforcement apparent.

Just then, the doorbell rang again and Mrs. Stevenson soon returned with Gabrielle. She smiled, looking pretty and feminine in a floral summer dress. Her curly red hair and small face were enchanting and Sloan noticed how Roy and Peter looked at her more than once. She sat next to them on the sofa and expressed her gratitude to the Stevensons for inviting her.

"Of course, Gabrielle," Mr. Stevenson said, ever the patriarch, sitting like a giant in his armchair near the fireplace, across from Sloan. "You are an invaluable asset to us and we appreciate your diligence at the agency."

Gabrielle blushed slightly. She turned to Peter and asked him about Polly.

"She may be discharged from the hospital this weekend," he said, blowing smoke. "The doctors have been pleased with her progress. I plan to go there after leaving here today."

Gabrielle looked around, greeting Sloan and noticed Caleb was not present. She asked about him. Mrs. Stevenson had just returned from the kitchen and set a plate of deviled eggs on the coffee table, along with a bottle of ginger ale. She retrieved glasses from a sideboard and placed them next to the bottle.

"Caleb isn't here yet, dear," she commented. "Neither is Jeff. I'm sure they'll arrive soon."

Gabrielle accepted a glass of ginger ale. "He called and told me he was going first to the office to retrieve his cap and sunglasses he left in his desk, and then he planned to walk here." She glanced at the windows overlooking Dudley Row. "It's so warm and pleasant today."

Mrs. Stevenson straightened up from placing the tray on the coffee table. She glanced at her husband. "Minerva called earlier and mentioned she and Wilbur would be late. She didn't say if anything was wrong." She shrugged. "Perhaps they have errands to run. After all, it is Saturday when most people have chores."

Her rationale seemed to satisfy everyone, except Sloan. A dark forewarning and uneasiness went through him. He listened as they continued talking, his mind racing. He then placed his glass of ginger ale on a nearby end table.

"If you will excuse me, Mr. Stevenson and Mrs. Stevenson, but I will return shortly." He stood and looked at the startled, uncomprehending faces around him. "I need to go to your office."

Mr. Stevenson looked at Sloan curiously, although rather perturbed. "For what purpose, Mr. Sheppard? Gabrielle told us Caleb will be here soon. I do not imagine he would need your assistance at the moment."

Sloan mentioned Inspector Harris, who should arrive soon, inciting further curiosity from the startled faces before him. "Tell him I am at your agency and for him to go there at once."

"What's happening, Mr. Sheppard?" Gabrielle inquired.

"Police at the agency, Mr. Sheppard?" Mr. Stevenson said, appalled.

"Mr. Sheppard, is something wrong?" Sister Catherine asked concern in her voice.

Sloan asked Mr. Stevenson for the keys to his agency. Reluctantly, Mr. Stevenson told his wife to retrieve them from his desk in the corner. She handed them to Sloan, questioningly. Sloan thanked her and proceeded to the hallway. He was making for the front door before Mrs. Stevenson practically stopped him in his tracks. She looked at him irritably and spoke with a trace of annoyance in her tone. She reiterated that Caleb would arrive soon.

"You may be wrong, Mrs. Stevenson," Sloan said as he stepped out the front door onto the steps. He looked back at her, rather urgently. "Caleb may need my assistance and the police, too, before it's too late."

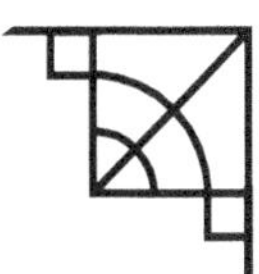

CHAPTER TWENTY ONE

A cacophony of noise awakened Caleb from unconsciousness; footsteps, file cabinets opening and closing, angry voices. He blinked several times, while still on the floor of the spare room. He attempted to rise and without sufficient strength, leaned against a wall for support. His vision was rather clouded at first, until he focused and saw Wilbur almost in front of him, pointing a gleaming knife directly at him. He noticed another knife on the table. He then saw Minerva still going through file cabinets and Wilbur ordering her to hurry up and to search the old man's file cabinets in his office. Minerva skirted out of the spare room, leaving Wilbur holding Caleb at knifepoint.

"Should've minded your own business, Caleb," Wilbur said maliciously. "You're dead meat now. I can't have you blabbering to the police or that Sheppard. You'll come with us and you'll never be found. You're an interfering bastard."

The gleaming knife pointed straight at him rendered Caleb speechless. His head throbbed painfully and to speak was an effort. He focused more clearly and knew the man in front of him would use the weapon he held. He had already killed before so he would not waste time in killing again. He realized the predicament he was in and knew there was no chance of anyone finding him here unless Gabrielle mentioned it to the Stevensons. But even then, they would not see any risk, as nobody knew Wilbur and Minerva were here or even suspected them of murder. He was trapped, with notorious and violent gangsters who would not hesitate to kill again. He looked at Wilbur and saw the madness in the older man's eyes.

Minerva returned, telling him she searched extensively through Mr. Stevenson's file cabinets and could not locate any more information on Mr. Newcomb. Wilbur seemed to accept this, while ordering her to grab the other knife. Caleb watched as she picked up the long blade and pointed it menacingly at him. He then found his voice, weak but firm and addressed Wilbur.

"Why are you doing this? You're bound to be discovered."

Wilbur laughed harshly. "Too late, Mr. West Point. We'll be long gone by the time the police catch on. You're too smart for your own good. I didn't plan on killing you, but we can't have witnesses left over."

"Like you killed the Turners and Mr. Lennon?" Caleb found the strength to say.

Wilbur moved sharply forward and struck him across the face. "You don't know half of what's happening. You should've stayed out of it."

"Why did you kill them? Were they a threat to you?"

Wilbur laughed again harshly. "I wouldn't wonder about the reason, Mr. Soldier Boy. By the time they find your body in a ditch along the Hudson River, we'll be long gone."

"We should've gotten rid of him earlier," Minerva said. "I knew he was bound to catch on."

"Is that why you killed the Turners? And attacked Polly, too?"

Minerva laughed, a distorted, heartless chuckle. "I took care of that interfering bitch. I destroyed the file she found on Newcomb.

She doesn't know I attacked her, anyway. Her back was to me and she never saw it coming."

At that moment, they heard the main office door open. Wilbur looked at Minerva, surprised and unclear what to do next. Sloan entered the hallway, followed by Inspector Harris, Lieutenant Taylor and two police officers. Wilbur then grabbed Caleb roughly by the arm, stood him up, and put the knife against his throat, while Minerva kept the other blade pointed directly at him.

"Drop the knives," Sloan ordered them. "You'll never get away with it. There are police here and downstairs. Drop the knives, now!"

"Never, Sheppard," Wilbur said. "We're taking him hostage and you'll never find his body." He laughed harshly, keeping the knife at Caleb's throat.

"How did you know we were here?" Minerva asked irritably.

"Miss Woods mentioned Caleb came here," Sloan told them. "I have the keys from Mr. Stevenson but turned out I didn't need them. Sloppy job, Mr. Finnegan, leaving the door unlocked. Gangsters are usually cleverer than that."

"I'll kill him in a heartbeat," Wilbur threatened, keeping the knife at Calcb's throat.

"You're a smart man, Mr. Finnegan," Sloan said, as he continued standing in the doorway to the spare room, the police directly behind him. "Allow me to introduce Mr. Conrad Finnegan and his accomplice, Miss Sidney Bernard, two of the most wanted gangsters in the state." He stood aside allowing Inspector Harris, Lieutenant Taylor and the officers to get a better look at them.

"So you've figured out our identities," Minerva mocked, while keeping the knife directed at Caleb. "It'll be easy to cut up this idiot. I won't hesitate to do it."

"You're a clever woman, Miss Bernard," Sloan said, carefully evaluating the situation. "But not smart enough to fool the law."

"And who'll stop us from putting an end to Mr. Military here," she mocked again.

Even warnings from the police officers did not deter Wilbur and Minerva. Still Wilbur held onto Caleb from behind, keeping the knife dangerously close to his neck, while Minerva stood next to him, her knife pointed precariously at his chest. Wilbur ordered them to move, enabling them to leave the agency, with Caleb as hostage. Sloan and the police stepped aside as Conrad Finnegan, alias Wilbur Hill and Sidney Bernard, alias Minerva Hill walked past them, with Caleb in tow. Wilbur kept the knife at his throat, while walking to his right, Minerva behind him, her knife pointed directly at his back.

They were just about to enter the main office, when Caleb, gathering his strength, kicked Minerva with his right foot, disrupting her equilibrium, and the knife clattered to the floor. Looking back at Minerva and caught off guard, Wilbur also stumbled enabling Caleb to tackle him and wrestle the knife from his grip. An intense struggle ensued, but the older man was no match for Caleb's strength. He pinned Wilbur to the floor as the police officers reacted quickly, assisting Caleb to overpower him. Sloan, Inspector Harris and Lieutenant Taylor moved sharply forward and subdued Minerva. They fought furiously while the officers placed them in handcuffs, amidst an extremely loud outburst of invective. The police officers led them out of the agency and outside to the awaiting patrol cars.

Sloan went up to Caleb, rather shaken, and settled him into Gabrielle's desk chair. He looked up at Sloan, not fully comprehending what just occurred. Inspector Harris commented they would take the gangsters to headquarters for booking then left the agency.

Sloan looked at Caleb and tried to comfort him. "Do you want to go to the Stevenson's luncheon? Mrs. Stevenson prepared a nice meal. But I'm sure they'll understand if you don't want to go." He looked at the younger man, still dazed from his ordeal.

Caleb had forgotten about the luncheon. He nodded and told Sloan he would go to the Stevensons. Sloan helped him to his feet, the climactic scene momentarily forgotten.

Labor Day brought continued pleasant weather conditions to Albany. It was perfect for picnics and outdoor activities in Washington Park. However, little of these diversions affected the associates of Empire Advertising.

Upon their arrest on Saturday, Wilbur and Minerva spoke candidly, almost proudly, of their criminal endeavors. Minerva admitted the attack on Polly and how she took the folder on Mr. Newcomb from her apartment. Wilbur knew Mr. Turner recognized him and killed him, along with his wife and brother-in-law. Mr. Lennon saw him in Albany, confronted him and agreed to meet at the Port of Albany, demanding hush money. He received a telephone call from Mrs. Turner, who claimed she arrived at a conclusion. He agreed to meet her in Washington Park, where he killed her with a cement block. The glass containing the arsenic was meant for Mr. Turner. When the lights went out, Wilbur put the arsenic in his own glass, and left it on the table, where Mr. Turner and his wife stood, without their realizing it. Even in the dark, he knew his way around the facility and where chemicals, cleansers and poisons were kept. He commented that the windows provided enough light for him to get to the cupboard containing the arsenic in the production area. Nobody from that part of the facility saw or heard him, except for the closing door, which was heard by many in the taste testing area. He admitted he did not expect Mrs. Nichols to pick up the glass intended for her father.

He told the Inspector that he and Minerva were not introduced to Mr. Turner at the taste testing event as he was busy with the caterers, just to Mrs. Turner. He mentioned Mr. Turner recognized him when looking out at the crowd to propose the toast and glasses were raised. He returned to the facility the next night and stabbed Mr. Turner to death. Wilbur did not anticipate being recognized after thirty years but apparently Mr. Turner did recognize him, causing him to stumble in complete shock at the podium. He admitted he and Minerva, alias Sidney Bernard were never legally married, but used the alias Hill. Inspector Harris planned to contact Sloan by telephone to relay this information.

After the tumultuous events at the agency, Sloan and Caleb walked to Dudley Row and upon entering the Stevenson's brownstone, Mrs. Stevenson could tell something was wrong. Even Roy and Peter were taken aback at seeing him. Sloan explained what just occurred at the agency, to everyone's shock and horror.

Mr. Stevenson suggested he rest upstairs but Sister Catherine took decisive action. She insisted he go to St. Peter's Hospital for evaluation. A taxi was called and she and Caleb went together, although he protested he was feeling much better. Sister Catherine assured them Caleb would receive the best care and would see him home afterward. Mrs. Stevenson decided to postpone the luncheon. She apologized for the inconvenience but was too disturbed over what occurred to Caleb and the revelation of Wilbur and Minerva. Mr. Stevenson continued sitting in his armchair by the fireplace, too numb to speak.

On Monday, Labor Day, the brownstone on Dudley Row was filled again, with a much brighter atmosphere. Roy and Jeff arrived, along with Peter and Polly. Mrs. Stevenson exclaimed surprise at seeing her, but Polly smiled and told her she was feeling fine. Soon after, Caleb, Gabrielle and Sister Catherine appeared, rather morose but glad for the company. Sloan arrived last and thanked Mrs. Stevenson again for inviting him.

Seated at the table in the opulent dining room, they enjoyed a delicious lunch of ham, turkey and potato salad. Afterward, they settled in the living room where Mrs. Stevenson entered, bearing a tray with coffee cups and a jug of cream. Gabrielle helped bring in the coffee pot and sugar bowl and together they passed around cups.

Gabrielle joined Caleb and Roy on the sofa, while Peter and Polly sat in armchairs near Sloan. Jeff sat in an armchair near the fireplace, next to Mr. Stevenson.

"How did you figure it all out, Mr. Sheppard?" Jeff asked. "My in-laws have been wiped out, including my wife. I had no idea of the real identity of Wilbur and Minerva."

"None of us knew," Peter said, regrettably.

Sloan put his cup on an end table, his cigarette in an ashtray and looked at the faces before him. "Mr. Lennon was the first victim, a seemingly innocent man who recognized someone."

"You must mean Wilbur," Roy said.

Sloan nodded. He explained that Wilbur Hill, whose real name was Conrad Finnegan was a notorious gangster who operated primarily in western New York State. His moll, Miss Sidney Bernard, who they knew as Minerva Hill, was his accomplice. They were active in bootlegging, drug smuggling and prostitution.

"Then why were they here in Albany?" Gabrielle asked.

"To make more money," Sloan said simply. "Inspector Harris

explained it to me. Conrad Finnegan had an arrest record in Albany, but with his new name and after so many years, he assumed his identity was safe. That is, until the afternoon of the taste testing and he was recognized by Mr. Nathan Turner."

"My father-in-law never mentioned him," Jeff spoke up.

"It was over thirty years ago," Sloan continued. "From his own admission and what I saw in the police file on the Clinton Street Hotel arrests, Wilbur was once employed at the facility and was familiar with the layout of the building. He knew Mr. Turner recognized him when he looked out onto the crowd of people as he was about to propose a toast. During the storm when the lights went out, he knew where arsenic and other chemicals were kept. He rushed to a cupboard in another room, when you heard the door close after the lights were out. He put the arsenic in his own drink and before the lights came back on, he left that glass on the table, near Mr. Turner. Unfortunately, Mrs. Nichols drank from that glass, so it did not go as planned."

"He went back to the facility the next night and stabbed him to death," Roy said.

"Mr. Lennon recognized Wilbur Hill as one of the gangsters who frequented the Clinton Street Hotel," Sloan continued. "He demanded hush money and decided to meet him at the Port of Albany. That sealed his fate."

"How terrible," Sister Catherine said, clearly shaken.

"Why was Mrs. Turner killed?" Peter asked.

"She must have realized her husband recognized someone. She looked out at the crowd and, upon seeing her husband's expression, thought it could have been Wilbur although she did not know him by that name."

"Did she plan to blackmail him?" Mrs. Stevenson asked.

Sloan puffed at his cigarette. "Most likely she realized the knowledge she had could destroy him, so she contacted him and agreed to meet him. Mr. Finnegan was quite strong, killing her with a cement block. It was getting risky then, but he did not want to take any chances. He needed to protect his identity and murder came easy to him."

"If his arrest record in Albany was over thirty years ago, why would he care if he was recognized?" Caleb asked.

"Because Mr. Conrad Finnegan and Miss Sidney Bernard were extremely dangerous criminals with a violent past," Sloan explained. "Mr. Finnegan did not expect to be recognized, not thinking someone at the beverage company would remember him, including Mr. Turner since it had been so long ago. He had aged in over thirty years."

"I'm surprised he even went to the taste testing," Peter said.

"He thought his identity was secure as Wilbur Hill," Sloan continued. "From Mr. Finnegan's own words to Inspector Harris, they were not introduced to Mr. Turner upon arrival at the facility for the taste testing, only to Mrs. Turner. He mentioned Mr. Turner was busy with the caterers when they arrived. He had already been recognized by Mr. Lennon and would not tolerate anyone else standing in his way of his illegal activities." He paused, drawing on his cigarette. "As Conrad Finnegan, he had quite an arrest record here and around the state. He was still active in bootlegging, where the gangsters he associated with here in Albany did not know him. It was a perfect cover, while the money rolled in. They were associates at Empire Advertising, appearing to live a blameless life. It worked well for them, until they were recognized."

"Did you recognize him from photographs, Mr. Sheppard?" Mrs. Stevenson asked.

Sloan nodded. "Mr. Walton from Corning, who knew Mr. Newcomb and Mr. Lennon, had taken photographs of the gangsters once while at the hotel. He sent them to me and I recognized Mr. Finnegan, alias Wilbur Hill and Miss Bernard, alias Minerva

Hill. I then looked at the police file and saw the match from their mugshots."

"Polly, what did you know about them?" Caleb turned to her.

She smiled weakly. "I didn't know much, although I had suspicions. I looked at the file in the spare room on Mr. Newcomb, where it mentioned names of gangsters. I recognized Wilbur and Minerva in a photo. I don't know why it was in that folder unless Mr. Stevenson put it there."

The older man looked up upon hearing his name. "I worked for Mr. Newcomb in 1915 on a publicity campaign. He told me about gangsters using his hotel for illegal business. A friend of his took pictures and gave a few of them to Mr. Newcomb. He put them in the publicity folder but honestly, I thought nothing of it. I had no reason to look at that folder, as his publicity campaign was concluded at that time."

Polly nodded weakly. "I asked Minerva about the picture and her background, but she brushed it off and told me I was mistaken. I could've blackmailed her but decided it was too dangerous and I didn't trust Minerva. From her attitude, I could tell she was lying."

"So she attacked you to keep you quiet," Peter said, looking at Polly.

"I feel somehow responsible," Mr. Stevenson said, from his armchair near the fireplace. "I should've never hired Wilbur and Minerva. They seemed like genuine people, with experience in public relations and advertising. I needed competent people and they fit the bill fine."

"You didn't know about them beforehand," Caleb told him.

"Why was Minerva at the agency on Saturday?" Roy asked Sloan.

"They wanted to locate information on Mr. Newcomb before it fell in someone else's hands. They worried there was more on him that could incriminate them."

"Did they intend to kill Polly?" Gabrielle asked, horrified.

Sloan nodded. "Minerva realized Polly was on to her and felt threatened. She attacked Polly, and luckily for her, she noticed the file on Mr. Newcomb and took it."

"I left it on the coffee table in the living room," Polly told them. "After attacking me, she must have looked for it. Convenient for her it was right in the open."

"What will happen to Wilbur and Minerva now?" Jeff asked.

"Wilbur admitted to killing Mr. Lennon, Mrs. Nichols, Mr. Turner and Mrs. Turner," Sloan explained. "Most likely he will receive the death penalty. Minerva attacked Polly and conspired with Wilbur in planning the attacks. I imagine she will receive an extended sentence."

"I never thought of gangsters in Albany," Sister Catherine said uneasily.

"Gangsters operate just about anywhere," Sloan said gravely. He explained how gangsters worked in areas where money could easily be made. Despite the thirty years and their new names, Wilbur and Minerva feared being caught. After Wilbur was recognized by Mr. Lennon, they knew they had to safeguard their identities. Wilbur and Minerva were never legally married, so their identities were not as husband and wife.

"Did they believe they could continue their criminal life?" Peter asked incredulously.

Sloan puffed at his cigarette. "They wanted to blend in, while still involved with gangster activity here in Albany. From what Minerva told police, they were worth quite a lot of money and lived well. Albany is a key spot for bootlegging and rumrunning, with easy access to the Hudson River. Their bootlegging involvements were quite lucrative." Sloan concluded that most likely they intended to continue their illegal and clandestine activities, under perfect cover while employed at Empire Advertising.

"I knew nothing about their real identities," Mr. Stevenson mumbled regrettably.

"We must thank Mr. Sheppard for his intuitiveness," Caleb said, smiling at Sloan.

"And that you are still alive," Gabrielle said, looking at Caleb.

"You've been a tremendous help, Mr. Sheppard," said Mr. Stevenson gratefully. "My wife and I appreciate all that you have done to remediate this situation."

"I also offer my sincere appreciation to see justice done," Sister Catherine said.

Peter, Polly, Roy and Jeff concurred and thanked Sloan for his assistance. An empty silence followed until Mrs. Stevenson spoke, smiling, obviously much more relaxed.

"Why don't we enjoy my chocolate cake," she said pleasantly. "I'll make another pot of coffee. Gabrielle, dear, would you help me to serve?"

They got up and entered the hallway. Mr. Stevenson ushered them to the dining room, where more coffee and a delicious confection awaited them.

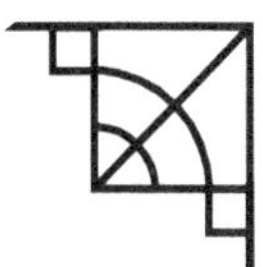

CHAPTER TWENTY TWO

Caleb looked at himself in the mirror of his bureau. It was late Saturday morning, September fifteenth, and he was about to depart Albany for Watertown, for a two week duty at Fort Drum. He was dressed in his army combat uniform and army boots. He combed his blond hair and secured his military cap on his head.

It was two weeks since the revelations of the recent murders. The news made headlines in the local newspapers and on the radio. The Stevensons returned to the agency, only three days out of five. Mrs. Stevenson told Caleb they preferred he handle executive duties while Mr. Stevenson recovered from the shock of the recent events. At Empire Advertising, the atmosphere was rather subdued although assignments and publicity campaigns continued as usual. The revelations of the true identities of Wilbur and Minerva, the murders and the attacks on Polly and Caleb were still fresh in their minds. Polly worked half days until she felt strong enough to return for the regular full week. Gabrielle assisted her in completing assignments as needed.

Just after Labor Day, Caleb received instructions in the mail to report to Fort Drum on the fifteenth. He informed Mr. Stevenson, who expressed admiration for his commitment to his country while admitting he would be sorely missed. He mentioned they looked forward to his safe return. Caleb mentioned he appointed Peter in charge in his absence to which Mr. Stevenson heartily concurred.

The warm late summer weather continued, with sunny skies and light breezes. Caleb took a last look around his apartment, then grabbed his duffel bag, containing the necessities of travel and headed for the door. He decided to take the trolley downtown from Hamilton Street. Upon arriving at Union Station, he noticed it was not too busy, perhaps because Labor Day was over, kids were back in school and summer vacations had ended. He received his train tickets in the mail from his commander, who would meet him at the station in Watertown. He looked forward to seeing his platoon, where as a leader he oversaw and participated in drills, fighting maneuvers and combat formations. He also intended to dedicate more time to tactical exercises and weight lifting as part of his military routine.

He sat in the waiting room, looking up as a diligent young man wrote train departures and arrivals in chalk on a blackboard posted to the wall. He noticed his train was running ten minutes late due to a signal failure near Schenectady. After what seemed an eternity, the train, on route to Watertown and Alexandria Bay, with a final destination for Ogdensburg, was posted. Caleb grabbed his duffel bag and slinging it over his shoulder, joined a small crowd on the platform. The train gently pulled into the station and the conductor jumped off, announcing its arrival.

Before boarding, he glanced toward the station and noticed a young red haired woman looking around, as though searching for someone or something. She then spotted Caleb and he realized it was Gabrielle. Hurriedly, she made her way across various tracks and went over to him, rather breathlessly. She looked up at him admirably.

"I wanted to say goodbye," she explained, smiling. "I was afraid I would miss not seeing you." She paused. "You certainly are handsome in your uniform, Caleb."

Caleb smiled, and then met her eyes. She went forward and he held her, rather tightly. The turmoil they endured over the summer melted away and she felt secure in his strong arms. He released her, mentioned he would write and looked forward to seeing her upon his return. He heard an announcement that his train was soon departing. He looked back at her, and then entered and found an empty window seat, where he tossed his duffel bag on the overhead rack.

He turned to the conductor who checked his ticket, then settled back as the train slowly started to pull out of the station. The usual aloneness he felt dissipated as he realized Gabrielle meant so much to him. He looked out the window again and saw her still on the platform. As the journey began, a satisfied feeling came over him, knowing his devotion to his country and a special young woman were in his heart.

THE END

The 1920s Mystery Series by Michael Sinclair
featuring Sloan Sheppard, private investigator

An Unfortunate Coincidence
The Consequences of Murder
Murder in Cucumber Alley
Darker than the Night
Raise Your Glass To Murder

www.ingramcontent.com/pod-product-compliance
Lightning Source LLC
Chambersburg PA
CBHW071106250626
47159CB00002B/627

* 9 7 8 1 7 8 3 2 4 3 1 6 7 *